'Allan Gurganus is our verbal magician. He turns factorial rabbits into poetic doves. Every sentence contains a surprise, but the brilliant surface doesn't dazzle us from peering into the tender human depths.'

Edmund White

'In these layered, often funny narratives, close reading is rewarded as Gurganus exposes humanity as a strange species.'

Publishers Weekly (Pick of the Week)

'*Local Souls* leaves the reader surfeited with gifts. This is a book to be read for the minutely tuned music of Gurganus's language, its lithe and wicked wit, its luminosity of vision – shining all the brighter for the heat of its compassion. No living writer knows more about how humans matter to each other. These are tales to make us whole.'

Wells Tower

'A Mark Twain for our age, hilariously clear-eyed, blessed with perfect pitch.'

La Monde

'In these three novellas, Allan Gurganus breathes so much life into the town of Falls, North Carolina, the reader is able to walk down its streets and mingle with the local souls. This book underscores what we have long known – Allan Gurganus stands among the best writers of our time.'

Ann Patchett

Also by Allan Gurganus

The Practical Heart
Plays Well with Others
White People
Oldest Living Confederate Widow Tells All

Local Souls

Allan Gurganus

corsair

Constable & Robinson Ltd.
55–56 Russell Square
London WC1B 4HP
www.constablerobinson.com

First published in the US by Liveright Publishing Corporation,
a division of W. W. Norton & Company, Inc., 2013

First published in the UK by Corsair,
an imprint of Constable & Robinson Ltd., 2014

ISBN: 978-1-47211-244-6 (paperback)
ISBN: 978-1-47211-324-5 (ebook)

Printed and bound in the UK

1 3 5 7 9 10 8 6 4 2

First,
last,
always
for
Jane Holding

'French provincial towns are about like what your hometown was when your father was a boy, before movies, the radio and the family car changed all that. Your father wasn't bored. Neither are the provincial French.'

– Instructions for American servicemen in France, World War II, issued by the U.S. Army

'I did the best I could with what I had.'

– Joe Louis

CONTENTS

FEAR NOT

*For Diana Evans Ricketts
and Tom Lightwater*

OVERTURE

E VERYBODY LOOKS BETTER singing. Especially fifteen-year-olds.
The same dutiful adults turn up at all these high school
musicals. I'm early tonight. Claiming two front-row seats, I spread
my sogged overcoat. This toasty auditorium smells of industrial
floor wax. Student adolescence keeps walls infused with a sebaceous
sweetness akin to curry.

Tonight's three-hour *Sweeney Todd* will star my teenage godson.
Well, no. He'll actually play Pie Customer #1. But the boy is
premed. We don't *want* a future actor. We want one mighty well-
rounded college application.

This freezing November evening, the rain-ponchos crinkling
indoors look doused, not attractive. Kids onstage grow annually
more slim and gifted. In their fringe and songs, how lithe each one.
Why does such zest make us, their adult sponsorship, look ever
more bushed? Just once I'd like some glamour out here among the
grownups smelling tonight of wet wool.

Teen ushers seat older arrivals. I have time to consider random
irks, stray hopes. Twelve days and nine hours back, I FedExed
north my Civil War novel. Spent seven years writing it; the War
took only four. While my New York agent is either reading it or
continues her partying, I've finally fertilized my houseplants. I

sent a candy-gram to my favorite ailing aunt before recalling her diabetes.

So I feel grateful doing godfatherly duty here. I never miss his science presentations, soccer games. Pie Customer's divorced father lives six states away. I get to be the stand-in. Afterward I feel more civic, butch, opaque. Look, I've brought our boy these nice red tulips, just a wee bit frostbitten.

Umbrellas collapse. Theatre-lovers shuffle in bragging of all they've done to get here. Our supposedly high-end River Road, it always floods first. Damp cars outside will mostly show you faded Democratic election-stickers two administrations old. In here we'll prove liberal in toe-tapping through this season's "People Who Need People." Come intermission, we will grin, nod, chat. Condemning worsening local traffic and George W. Bush's latest pointless foreign war. Mostly we'll stand around praising each other's kids. *Truly.* Has there ever been a bunch more gifted?

Good crowd tonight, considering predicted sleet. Old folks keep teetering in. They need walkers just since last year's *Carousel.* They've been coming to these musicals since their own kids, now retired to Florida, belted out 1961's "Steam Heat."

I keep scanning for my dear friend Jemma, mother to my brilliant godson. Keep checking the time, awaiting my agent's verdict, half-thinking it'll be announced onstage. Took me years to just research the war epic. My house still resembles general headquarters: wall-sized battle maps, victims' daguerreotypes, one dented bugle. What future subject will ever stir me so? I've gladly fetched up here instead of waiting near my landline. Anyway, it's after NY office-hours. Thank God for friends and their dazzling kids, the sweet stir others make. Still, I need another project.

Here's Jemma, childhood pal, first-reader of my prose. Pie

Customer's mom holds a brand-new yellow legal pad. She has agreed to review this show for our *Falls Herald-Traveler*. Her likely rave will surely list the complete cast-crew-ushers. Already she sits jotting notes. Wish I'd brought my laptop, even without a new subject . . .

I'm just about to ask her why adults look so much dowdier at musicals starring adolescents, when in walks a couple glamorous enough to prove me dead-wrong. Hello. My exhausted narrative capacity, if not yet stirred, twitches.

Smiling, they ask if seats beside ours might be free. "Please, all yours." Both are tall athletic blondes with dark eyebrows; their shearling ski jackets match. Windblown, he looks ruddy; she glows nicely-rosy. This storm seems engineered to show off their complexions. I swear they belong onstage and not out here among grandparents' Greenpeace backpacks, sandals worn over hideous Peruvian socks.

They're the lion-kingly young parents all high school drama students must want. Instead of, well, *us*—my lovely friend and me, earnest, informed, fiftyish and counting.

Jemma nods at newcomers, gives them a real grin but then, for my eyes only, hand-letters a message across her pad. Nodding others' way, she shields from them these words:

NOTICE PAIR. SAVE HUNCHES. STORY AFTER. GOOD.

I, finding myself becalmed and itchy between novels, I, seated between my dearest friend and two hot strangers new to me, welcome a sudden challenge. I've just been sitting here, bracing for another Suzuki-Method-teens' atonal stab at Sondheim. Any competing tale-making task excites me. Even without a stubby pencil or an Apple product in hand, aren't all real writers always writing?

I—shy, intent—beam geniality toward our new lank ones. They've settled, easy with each other and soon me. They introduce themselves. I accept each warm hand offered. They give first names only, plus their daughter's last singing role here—Julie in *Showboat*.

"Sure. Carried it, really. Yale Drama candidate. But would we *want* that for her, is the thing?" I soon quip about tonight's Sondheim: "Even for kids smart as ours, pretty thorny score, eh?"

She smiles: "And such a wholesome moral! One straight-razor trimming London of all that's sick, I mean . . ." We demonstrate chuckling. We're proving ourselves committed to our teens. We're also showing we can—when briefly left alone—outdo our kids at caustic eye-rolling.

The child orchestra starts tuning up. However cute, that bassoonist sounds tubercular. Kids' conductor, rumored to also be a composer hugely-gifted if as-yet-undiscovered, needs a shave. We can tell tonight's score is going to be tough. Poor guy's already sweated through his shirt-back.

As the couple shucks outerwear (yellow ski-lift tags dangling) I swear I smell cedar. These two might be anywhere under forty. She is saying, "Haven't seen you-all since your boy really helped put over 'Nothing Like a Dame.' Fantastic number, right?"

She explains: their girl will play tonight's mad bag-lady. (Who'll turn out to be the Demon Barber's long-lost wife.) "Uh-oh," the young husband adds. "Hope we're not blowing the play's family secret for you. Had to really smudge up our girl fairly well, just to keep Cara from looking perfect and young. Keeps shining through. Still, she seemed super-into-it, didn't she, babe?"

His left hand falls open across on her jeans' right thigh. Around us, older married couples sit chewing over town politics. But husbands address just husbands; gray-haired wives side-by-side converse. How brave are these young lovers? They keep staring *at* each other!

The strapping young man hurries off for refreshments. He soon brings his lady tonic-water with precisely three lime slices pre-squeezed. I'm sensing concord. Her hair is pale and, as we chat, his hand slides right up under it; he now sits massaging her, ridding her nodes of last workday tension. And she? So used to being touched by this young pro, she chats right through it. Her neck half-crooks, catlike, settling pivoting back against the expert corners of his usual pleasuring. (*How am I doing?*)

LIGHTS DIM AS, last thing, our pair joins hands. They smile as if about to witness Broadway history! Being such a unit, they seem cut off from us. And yet, watching the two tilt nearer footlights, it's lonely not being one of them.

Intermission lets us truly talk. We do get jostled by a mother seeking better seats. This handsome woman of a certain size accompanies twin boys, ten, blond, amazing-looking. I say, "Sorry, taken." She leaves miffed. During the last acts' songs (except those featuring Pie Customer #1) I sit describing for myself the two beside me: Maybe he's fresh-back from long business-travel to China? Seems a postponed reunion is in progress. Something blocked their first-run at romance.

Bet he quarterbacked for some good county school. Guy still gives off a jivey kind of student-government-leadership buzz; that still seems to half-surprise her. His eager-beagle energy softens her actress-caliber looks. The woman's face comes close to being beautiful but turns back last-thing. Seems some loving sacrifice she's made for him.

Finally curtain-call. If fatigued, we do manage our mandatory voluntary standing-ovation. (Parenthood is already a standing-order standing-ovation.) By now, our humid auditorium smells of warmed rubber boots, cold brownie crumbs. My tulips, inverted, appear asleep. Cast-and-crew's kid-siblings doze along every aisle, nested into whispery nylon coats.

Jemma and I say 'bye to the lovebirds, and we all vow to sit together next time. Maybe even catch a bite somewhere after? The young husband pats my upper back. "Was great. Hey, man, you guys still know what *fun* is."

Surely a compliment to live by!

PIE CUSTOMER #1 is bound for his cast party. And, as soon as his mom and I are on our own, Jemma laughs. Swears she half-expected those two to start tickling one another like kindergartners.

"But I really *like* being near people that affectionate." I'm already defending them. "Maybe bachelorhood makes me notice it more, but isn't that rare among married straights? They're almost hand-some enough to turn up in ads, even movies. Cannot miss the erotic energy. Microwave popcorn going. What're the odds of holding on to that, and with a teenage kid?"

"There's something I should tell you." Eyes lowered, she goes somber, almost scaring me.

SCHOOL PARKING-LOTS, UNDERLIT past-sundown, look bleak as prison yards. Summer heat must've distorted white-painted lines into going this fudge-rippled. November makes everything worse. As do musicals concerning cannibalism.

Driving off school land, Pie Customer's mom shows me her most sphinxlike grin. "Well?" she asks. "I wrote 'Notice Couple.' I did not write, 'Come *On To* Couple'! Knew you needed a project. Next time, while waiting for the judgment on your book? maybe take a magazine assignment. You do get edgy, dear. —But, what'd you *make* of them?"

"Okay. I do have a leet-tle something worked up for you. —But first, *why?*"

Smiling, shaking her head no, not yet—there's some big secret I must earn.

That's fine. We've just been told that, even if over fifty, we still know what fun is.

"Well here goes nothin', Sherlock Junior. Mmmm—I'd say: Real family-unit-feel. Something prevented their getting together to start with. Maybe bad first marriages? Some barricade I'm feeling. Like they only connected after a trauma. Maybe even some resort-tsunami-rescue-type thing? Something dramatic, yeah. They act so continually relaxed about finally being *with* each other. Gratitude's always attractive. (But, you notice they were not on terms with other parents? Not a greeting, no seats saved. And even after catching every musical for, what? years. They must usually sit in back or I'd have noticed them.) The honeymoon's not over by a mile. Both in great shape. See how the whites of their eyes stay so clear? How do some people 'get' that? I'd guess it's *her* family has the money but who cares about all that? In closing, to rest my case: pretty much made for each other. That's what little I've got right now. —But *why?*"

Then my friend tells me.

DRIVING THROUGH THE worsening sleet—traffic signals swinging like the severed heads of French aristocrats, our view blasted under hurled bushels of maple leaves—my best friend explains the history of this couple's meeting. She states their tie, their consequent loyalty, their destined trouble. She hints why others tonight looked else-where, ignoring the pair's sweet superior warmth.

My intelligent Jemma lays out for me their love's backstory. The romance sounds so inevitable it's immediately too complex. And, soon as I hear their history's pivot, I know. Know I'll soon be telling it. If just to myself. WHY? (Well, I've *shot my bolt on the Civil War. You can truly holler "Appomattox" only once.*) Besides, caught atypically off-guard tonight, I need to understand this better. I write for myself and strangers.

To be learned then heard, it must be told. Gladly I accept the job. But, first? where I'm taking you—with your full adult permission, of course—is not toward make-believe. Believe me.

That school-play, that wet night, the most handsome couple not in New York, it all happened precisely as I've told you here. What I'll next reveal cuts as close to Documentary as any trained liar ever dares go.

How scarce is "a truly happy couple"?

How rare is "the cure for cancer"?

LAST THING, I ask Jemma for whatever name this couple shares. I say as soon as I get home I might start maybe researching them. You could call this my invasion of their privacy but I truly had no choice. A storyteller's first task is knowing the tale when he sees it. Easy when one's this human.

Within a week I'd Googled them silly. Beyond their stolid credit-ratings I soon gathered JPEGs from separate high school annuals. Their "activity photos," so precious to me now!

The best info often found me by accident, fateful doublings-back. Birth-certificates? right online for all to see. Out there in cyberblue? so much about us each just floats, resting latent. Any stranger's keystroke-resurrection can uncloud us, send us crashing back to earth in sleet-crystals and shards. How to protect ourselves? We really can't.

But I swear that I, a bachelor-stranger-godfather, now intend to offer mostly kindness. No, better, fairness.

Tracing such a union has produced this joint biography far richer than my own. Speculation is a compliment. Curiosity becomes voyeurism that, once quantumed, can go dignified again. This pair soon filled for me a ragged trench left behind by all my breastwork tunneling into the American Civil War.

I never labored so hard. I soon found myself cross-eyed while bent before 1970s microfilm. After hours-long car trips, I descended into mildewed summer basements. (Know how many southeastern county courthouses still lack central-air?) Their few friends proved too shy to go on record. I nosed around a Coast Guard rescue station off Maine's black rock shore. I flirted with the ancient lady archivist of a now-defunct charity in Newport News. I needed fuller access than she dared yield me. So I took her out to lunch and, with no expense account but my own on-spec, bought her one huge Cobb salad (with cowboy-worthy sirloin strips) and two Bloody Marys. Then a third "to maybe just sip." By 4 p.m. she said okay she'd let me see the file, though she'd first need to go home and nap.

I, respectful, understood the couple could not be poked with certain questions. I had to do the work. I needed it. And now it is my fault, responsibility and pride. I have taken in hand this pair's true documented history. Naturally I've tried breathing real life into these local souls—apart and finally together.

I'm still straining to see them, see them through.

During one overambitious high school *Sweeney Todd*, my simply getting to sit beside them, it was so much fun.

LOCAL SOULS

I'd not known why.
Now I do. As you will soon.
I swear to God at least 81% of the following is true.

CURTAINS UP

SQUINTING IN THIS beach glare feels as good for you as exercise. Beside our giant lake, so many pretty people wear new bathing suits. Odd, the girls that look best act the most ashamed.

We're entering Independence Day, at Moonlight Lake, three miles from Falls, NC. It's 81 degrees and something terrible is about to happen yards offshore.

For now, from jade-green depths, leafy bits of foam keep slopping over bathers pink, white, brown. Children squeal. Water's pleasure's so acute it seems a test. One biplane drags across sky's lower fourth the trembling legend: HUNGRY YET? SANITARY SEAFOOD.

Souvenir towels pave this mobbed beach. Paths are voluntary. Transistor radios play the summer's three big hits. Youngest kids, big-eyed if still willing, let themselves be buried under sand by gleeful older brothers.

And, visible from this pastel beach, a weekend captain of one twenty-two-foot Chris-Craft loses sight of the water-skier he's pulling two hundred yards out into the lake. (One red nylon towline just got tangled on a log twelve feet underwater.) The towed guy leaves his yellow skis to float, plunges under waves to free his line. The fourteen-year-old daughter of the man about to die, she

13

sunbathes face-up. In a row of girlfriends, she rests on heated sand detergent-white.

Sometimes she gets these premonitions. They register as starter -migraines. Across her eyesight, a prismatic see-through honeycomb will drop. She wonders if one's coming on. Or are these paisley shapes, printed back of eyelids, stamped there only by noon sun?

It's now, just as yonder boat captain—worried at his best pal's disappearance—turns the craft shoreward; now, just as—one gin-and-tonic cooling his free hand—he guns that fuel-injected outboard—it's now the missing swimmer, holding his untangled towrope aloft, re-achieves air to gasp while laughing. It's now a 350-horsepower Pleasure-Craft outboard—revved to top speed—intersects the precise point of said skier's bobbing up now. How clean and effective: one stainless-steel propeller decapitates the smiling water-skier.

Birds overhead give cries of curiosity before diving toward possible nutrition. Few humans on the beach have noticed yet. One toy poodle stands urinating, with an air of patience, onto the picnic hamper of swimming strangers. A college boy, selling sno-cones, glows multicolored under his umbrella dyed the three major tints of ice cream.

The daughter has been resting in a covey—seven other freckled girls almost-as-pretty, hoping to bronze. The nanosecond her father's mind stops working, something jerks her clear to sitting. She turns off friends' radio. She tears away her sunglasses. She stares down her own brown body's length and out into our lake's ten thousand blue acres. Bobbing there is one familiar boat, now idled.

She sees its driver wave his arms, then signal toward something. Turning that way, his single passenger, her mom. The squinting girl, rising, now cups hand over eyes. She notes how the two adults keep peering into Moonlight Lake at one spot growing brilliant wine-colored.

Her sleepy friend's face is hidden under an opened *Seventeen* magazine, worn today as sun-shade hat. Even this friend senses some shift in beach action and asks, "What? *Which* boy's back?"

OWING TO THE death, our girl's mother will go haywire sort of permanently.

But not yet. That woman out there, in a white one-piece, simply standing in the pleasure craft, continues smoking. Having just witnessed a terrible severing, this trim woman finds she can still act poised. With trauma's merciful delay, she has registered little past three words: "Another Boating Accident."

Such numbness leaves her effective at least these next few minutes. Soon she's grappling with one long-handled fishing net. She takes it from the distraught captain—family doctor and life-long buddy of the floater. In darkened water, it's hard to tell where the victim mainly is. "Here," she calls, "you pull that, that's biggest. I'll try fishing out this, the . . ."

What she scoops aloft appears to be the, yes, her husband's head. Its face still bears an expression. The lateral seam shows where a grin just vexed to grimace.

She keeps biting her cigarette, eyes shying from her own smoke. The widow has entrapped this roundness in a net designed to just snag bass. Two other persons on the beach start noticing. One is a child newly-buried by his brothers. Now represented aboveground only by one crew-cut head that yells, "Gross-out. Lookit!"

Drifted closer to shore, the boaters are seen hauling onboard legs and the torso. Three more witnesses now point. "Hey, that shouldn't . . . Is that a man's?" They whistle to friends. "Hey. Want to *see* something?!"

At last today's shellac-dark lifeguard blows his silver whistle.

AND ONLY WHEN stepping from the boat, only upon finding her daughter in a crowd, only then did the widow's screaming start. It simply failed to quit. Even when they wheelchaired her into the hospital, even when her cries upset the ER then the small Psych Ward whose other patients she was said to have "set off." Finally, her dead husband's boss, the Planters' Savings and Loan president, having heard the improbable news by phone, volunteered his coastal hunting lodge as her retreat. This meant that she—should steady hollering continue—would be audible to nothing more inclined toward psychological panic than migratory coastal birds and water moccasins.

THE GIRL'S MOTHER could not undertake her duties as a surviving-spouse. Fact is, she would skip her husband's funeral. "Too much for me. We all have limits." Falls' leading white mortician would call the young banker's burial both the best-attended and the very saddest one in memory; but then that undertaker got caught saying this every six years or so.

The boat captain and his skier had been so close so long they physically resembled one other. They each had an unusual dented chin. They'd stood godfather for one another's children. That one of them should kill the other meant—to the town of Falls—some brotherly law of nature's symmetry had been broken. Best buds for life! Far better to be shot by some arbitrary out-of-towner. In high school there had even been rumors of one beach weekend's mischief: The two had seemingly got caught in a latticed outdoor shower.

16

They'd been doing something that their teen friends judged entirely too frisky to catch happening and then leave unreported. It was something boys their age most often do alone. Since both proved competitive, maybe were they racing toward their finish lines? Excess beer was blamed. That and a teasing coldness displayed the previous midnight by two heartless Raleigh debs. Somehow this shower-stall grappling had been forgiven. It got compared to the too-cruel horseplay known only between brothers.

His widow announced she would never ever speak again to Dr. Dennis S——. He was the man whose boat had guillotined her spouse. She despised herself for even being onboard. And what had she been doing when it happened? Had she been monitoring her beloved water-skier and reporting towline trouble to their skipper? No. Simply seated, smoking (a "Lucky Strike"!), simply watching shoreline bathers. Water sports had always bored her but "the boys" talked her into this boat-ride. They lied, saying she'd tan faster at noontime on the actual surface of Moonlight Lake.

Having helped get severed body parts onboard made her, in her own mind, forever complicit. She announced herself an accessory after the fact. Suspended in that fishnet, one familiar face awaited her. Its peculiar expression looked less tortured than perplexed. Her banker husband, being on holiday, had failed to shave for once. Stubble blued the jaw without a neck. She would re-greet this sight in her next decade's hollering dreams.

THE DAUGHTER OF the man killed had always been being very lovely. Exemptions offered such prettiness stayed invisible to her, of course. But privilege's easements were clear to anyone homelier. Being an only child, she'd forever considered her prospering parents her own best friends. They never quite spoiled her but certainly came close. They secretly referred to how she'd saved their lives. The banker, with his handsome wife, had been driving their girl and two friends to a dressage and sailing camp on the North Carolina coast. Traffic was dense. They kept passing (then being passed by) an electric blue Ford hot rod and one big silver Chrysler with Jersey plates. These drivers took chances, failed to signal and generally behaved like vacationing Yankees in an urban hurry.

One of their daughter's friends now patted the banker on his shoulder and suggested that his child was presently having a fit. He signaled, pulled right over, found his daughter dead-white, stiff. She could only explain that something new was filming up before her eyes. "Caking up" was the odd term this child used. Shapes like honeycomb but filled to overflowing with kaleidoscope colors. And through this scrim, she saw something horrible waiting. She whispered as her father bent nearer, "Something so bad has to happen next." It scared him and he soon walked her around outside the car. He took care to keep her little friends from hearing but they already had. Ever after, the car's passengers regarded the girl with such gratitude they all tried keeping her gift a secret. She at last got her breath. Slowly her dad pulled back into beach traffic and it was only while rounding the next curve they saw the worst accident ever. That hot rod and the silver car had somehow jackknifed under a yellow moving van and all were ablaze, raw passengers strewn across the road and one young one, red, hurled into a tree.

The father and mom kept quiet about their daughter's foresight. But they revered her more for this sign of strange talent.

She herself attributed Falls' favoritism less to her personal looks than to an intelligence self-evident. Plus Luck of course. At four-teen, she half-sensed that some guardian-aura forever attended and even half-clothed her. (Her mother owned a crystal "cake caddy,"

18

one clear domed pedestal that both protected and displayed whorls of white frosting otherwise too easily squashed.)

Even her "hardest" teachers at school tended to give way before this naturally-platinum-haired daughter of our bank's rising vice president. —Some people's futures look so smooth, only sadists would bother delivering even temporary setbacks.

SIX MONTHS BEFORE her father's death, the daughter received an inconvenient nickname. As a child without siblings, she'd forever envied girls whose big brothers dubbed them Little Bit or Sandy. But she found you cannot choose for yourself a flattering reference to just your peppiness or coloring. The name they laid on her was only meant to tease. It found her; she immediately despised it.

You see, she made a mistake. She always hated when that happened. During her middle school's Christmas pageant, teachers needed a loud narrator. Most girls ducked it, hoping for the "Mary" role. (Even though smiling Mary never had one line.)

As for announcing, boys' voices, at fourteen, kept cracking. Some auditioning kid, sliding toward soprano, would giggle himself. He had that little control. She couldn't help joining in. Her laugh emerged a hee-haw bray that, being "low," always sounded ventriloquized, out of character.

So—born a blonde, destined to look good in white—especially while standing bookended between today's duck-feather wings—she found herself the announcer. She became "Angel #1."

That was not her nickname. That one she might have endured. Teachers placed her high on a ladder disguised as one giant cardboard rock. From up there, bathed in yellow light, she would tell cowering bathrobed shepherds, "Fear not . . . for unto you is born this day . . ."

But snowstorms Christmas week meant the performance never got a proper run-through. Pageant-standards were pretty low hereabouts. Some folks believed: Why even bother with "tech-rehearsals" when we live this far from our state capital? Who really finally cares? Nobody mistakes our dressed-up kids for real angels or the actual Baby Jesus. Besides, in a town so small as Falls, whatever might go wrong likely will, right? And with a maximum number of witnesses! Best just smile and hope the Easter one rises to higher performance-standards.

Sound equipment, borrowed from a local college, was only being activated as the Christmas Eve audience shuffled in. So, when her music cue finally came, in front of three hundred merrymakers, announcer Angel #1 found she didn't trust the mike pinned deep within her right wing's down.

Being a straight-A perfectionist, she leaned nearer her Peking duck feathers and—to assure she was really truly audible—roared: "*Fear not!* (Wait; is this doggone thing even *on*? I swear to God . . . poor planning). *Fear not?* (you guys getting *any* this? See, but I keep, but it's not . . .). ('S working? great), Feeeear NOT!"

She provoked a huge laugh. All the tensions and pressures of the Christmas season got jostled loose by just such silliness. Laughter arrived in chapters. Such mirth had not been meant as harsh.

If some plainer girl—whose father were not a trim bank officer—had got hooted at like this, laughter's edge might have proved more raw. Three hundred cacklers might've driven the poor girl to some nunnery, stunting her for life. Instead, tonight's slip just showed our Announcing Angel to be a brave and forceful charmer. Even if over-miked and under-sure, hadn't she stood high up on that cardboard boulder, gilded in light while looking, throughout, as pretty as hell?

No one chuckled louder than her parents. (They told her later,

"Stars always turn mistakes to their advantage, dear. That's how people *know* a star. You were the high point of tonight's otherwise kind of so-so show. It's our only funny Nativity, ever. And people will remember. Don't we all want people to remember us? Relax, you're always darling.")

But the *Fear Not* "took." Her folks and everybody else in Falls soon advised each other, during polio vaccinations or upcoming tax seasons, "Oh, well, when in doubt *Feeeear NOT!*" and snorted again. Nobody could say why it had been hilarious, her standing up there, so solemn a perfectionist pissed-off, not knowing she was audible, then busted even by the littlest kids. Why that much laughing? *Her* guess ran: pure meanness.

Small towns, being untraveled literalists, do tease a lot. Falls stays famous for its battles and grudge-matches. What big cities might call *Sadism* little towns name *Fun*. And because Fear Not so hated the nickname, her parents saved it mostly for those times they praised her while alone together upstairs.

If she overheard some cute town-boy call her that, she simply turned her back on him, snubbing even her school's good-looking quarterback; thus proving herself more fearless.

THAT JULY FOURTH her father got killed, Fear Not stood recalling the nickname she'd been nailed with last December. Waiting knee-deep in warm water, she was soon pacing Moonlight Lake. Girlfriends tried to ready her for the boat's coming ashore. In it, her father's divided body. Strangers had their cameras out. The sno-cone boy had even rolled his bright stand nearer surf, the crowd.

Our girl could not have felt more fearful and unmoored. Why? She'd understood at once: *Till now, nothing had actually been protecting her, had it? Early belief in her own exemptions? merest pride and superstition. The only other time she'd come near death, some caking spell or sign had made her sick. That spared her parents and friends.*

But not today. Fear Not's ruined faith in her own safety (and the world's) frightened this wading child nearly as much as her dad's dismemberment. If such a thing can happen today during recreation-hours twenty minutes from home, what cataclysm might befall some older homely untanned person on some rainy day more inland? Her heart went out to this invented stranger.

It'd been easy till now, acting kind toward those all treating you with deference. But manners weren't laws. Courtesy was a privilege; it also sprang from stupid Luck. Well, here Luck quit! She'd enjoyed fourteen years of it, then came this bladed moment. Thirty strangers waded toward the landing boat to look in at a body. One camerawoman asked her wading husband, "Think I need the flash, Ed?"

Fear Not saw even her best girlfriends pull instinctively away from this and her. Their very worry for her made her suddenly repulsive. After being considered an ice-princess, she'd tipped into some "uh-oh" category scarcely noticed till now.

Her father's best pal, everybody's handsome doctor, had stood drinking gin in direct sunlight. He'd likely got tipsy unexpectedly. Then, veering his teak craft into wider panicked circles, seeking his dear friend, he'd overcorrected his course. At that moment he pushed "Fear Not" here from Luck to Fate. Her two-part nickname, a phrase from the second chapter of Luke, today became one unit: "Fearnot." Rammed from two words about resisting fear to a life-long reason for it.

Fellow sunbathers, her closest girlfriends (two saved by her station-wagon premonition), saw blood, announced, "We'll be back at the cottage. We're only in the way here." Then four of six, shaking sand from towels, stumbled off from her at a half-run.

22

FEAR NOT

The banker's daughter, arms crossed, remained thigh-deep in mild lake. She looked concentrated as someone whose college entrance exam gets administered as a sudden pop-quiz:

Q: Why do most adults live in fear of storms, traffic
   deaths, their babies' failure to thrive?
A: Experience.

Her mother disembarked and saw her. Then the screaming started.

A HEARING WAS held with lots of awful publicity. The *Falls Herald-Traveler* published boating charts. One white X indicated "death site." Another edition showed the diagram of an ordinary adult male's outline with dotted lines hand-sketched across his neck.

A legal team for the doctor responsible brought so many positive character-witnesses, no actual charges were filed. Doc Dennis had been one popular general practitioner. Not even a charge of "manslaughter" was lodged.

Doc Dennis's father had owned the cotton mill. But, to the rich boy's credit, instead of simply taking that over, he—though always known as a lazy student—tried everything to get himself into the state med school; he somehow became his hometown's doctor, helping others at stupidly reasonable rates. He lacked the selfless talent of Falls' beloved family practitioner, Marion Roper. But people swore Doc Dennis meant well, despite a growing drinking problem. Everybody drank then. If not while pulling water-skiers on Moonlight Lake at high noon, with the actual glass in your hand.

So Falls' newspaper had to editorialize, praising Fearnot's dad, the "fallen" banker who'd been two-time Kiwanis Young Man of the Year. And our opinion page did state that the doctor's fuel-injected 350 h.p. "Pleasure Craft" outboard had just been "way too much motor for a that-sized boat."

The young physician felt so eaten up with regrets, he retired from practice for two months. Other, older doctors (Roper included) filled in for him. Young Dennis seemed obsessed with replotting his failed nautical strategy. He lived lost in a generalized acid-bath of self-disgust. Doc Dennis S— soon showed his own signs of mental instability.

Ignoring his wife and kids, he deeded most of his inherited textile stock to the young woman newly-widowed and her only child. People said it would, in the end, have been a mercy if Doc had really served some hard-time. He'd begged the judge for a penance fierce and public enough.

The banker's grieving wife would not come downstairs to see the culprit. She refused his costly orchids and Sunday phone-calls. People told Dennis to be patient, not to press her now. Trust time. Friends urged him to return to practice: he needed work, he was making himself sick. Everyone knew how much he'd loved his friend. Unable to address the widow, Doc spent whatever hours allowed with the dead man's fourteen-year-old daughter.

The doctor, aged forty, could not find a coffee shop in Falls where the sight of him with Fearnot did not cause staring then a stir. A rushed chattering first ran along the lunch-counter; then hushed politeness fell, making for better eavesdropping.

Doc soon drove over to pick the girl up after school. The two would head out into the countryside. They'd tool along some rural mail-route not known for its beauty. He would restage aloud the whole ordeal. It had been, he cried, all his fault his fault his fault.

Doc Dennis must have convinced himself that such talk also helped the girl to grieve. Fearnot was his goddaughter after all. But most often it was she comforting him: "Could have happened to anybody." "No one but you really blames you." "Everybody knows you loved my dad past you-all's even being brothers." "You'd give your soul to get him back." —Such phrases the child repeated as if by rote to a middle-age doctor who needed to hear each and daily. Doc Dennis himself had often used these very lines first on patients then their survivors.

Three ready-made sentences contain so much of human consolation: "I love you," "I'm real proud of you," "I am so sorry for your pain." It seemed odd that a dead man's daughter should be offering such sentiments to her father's executioner, but she did. Meanwhile, she sometimes sat in his car imagining the doctor's own wife and grammar-grade kids waiting for him at their dining-room table back in town.

Fearnot herself felt comforted by Dennis, his being so like her dad in face and gestures. Men's chin-dents seemed carved by a single surgeon bent on giving both a similar Viking-edge. The physician had long ago, in the way of lifelong friendships, taken to sounding like the man he would later kill. Some people swore such imitation came from simple hero-worship. They said such boyhood admiration had lately helped make Dennis a better person, less a brat.

Both born Scotch-Irish, both grew tall and athletic. The future doctor proved more nervous and fast-moving, tending to blink. By the time these two turned thirty-five even their blond hair started silvering alike, from the outer edges inward. They'd lately been mistaken not just as brothers but twins.

To sell newspapers post-accident, the *Falls Herald-Traveler* emphasized such similarities. Boys' near-identical high-school-annual portraits became a front-page staple. The boating mishap, a gory story, had everything. "If it bleeds, it leads," journalists say, and this one hemorrhaged for months. Both gents were highly-placed, good-looking, family guys. Their joint fate was more widely reported thanks to a certain tasty Cain-Abel angle. "Inseparable friends" led to thoughts of one's head. Quiet rumors about their high school showering reemerged.

After a funeral attended by six hundred, the doctor fell silent around others, including his own confused wife and kids. Doc Dennis finally started seeing patients again. But, by now, he felt most safe with Fearnot.

Her dad, during high school, had been elected student body president. The future-banker worked after school in his well-liked father's seed-and-feed store. They lived in a narrow if tidy house on Villa Street. Young Dennis, far richer, never nominated for office, mainly built pep-rally bonfires and played a witty harmonica in school talent shows. Since his father owned and managed the mill, Dennis needed no weekend- or summer-jobs. He was considered fun and pretty, notable for owning the best red luxury-roadster to ever gather dust in our school lot. As citizen and student, Dennis never quite caught up with the easy loping dignity of his quiet pal. Seeing his poorer buddy wear a mended tweed jacket, Dennis had his father's seamstress patch a brand-new blazer of his own. The rich boy saw and accepted his friend's superior standing in Falls, but others guessed it had always peeved him.

After the decapitation, our local paper kept publishing Doc Dennis's own high school yearbook portrait. At eighteen he looked almost disabled by handsomeness. Beneath the grinning image ran cryptic lines written by one "Anony-mouse":

FEAR NOT

Dimpled, adored, everywhere visible.
If facile and slight and just slightly risible.
What some would call Promise, others term Moisture.
And yet the whole world will still be your oyster,
Dennis the Menace.

Some said he chose med school to offset lingering doubts about his basic smarts, his gravity. He'd had to work hard to even get through basic course-work, he always admitted that. Finally, as Falls' youngest family physician, he'd made himself welcome then indispensable. Like his competitor, Doc Roper, he was good in the office, weak at getting out patient bills. Dennis was elected to the vestry at All Saints Episcopal. He'd be present at eleven o'clock service, sometimes wearing tinted glasses, however bad Saturday-night's hangover. Till the boating mistake, he seemed to have finally outrun and outranked his old rival and best friend.

DOC DENNIS AND Fearnot were soon observed sitting by the side of one-lane rural roads. They would be seen talking there while using hand-gestures, shaking their heads, plainly acting out some event still emotional for both. His car was parked out beyond Moonlight Lake in a farming community where doctors still made house-calls; any physician's vehicle was therefore widely-known from being often-awaited. Locals guessed why Dennis would venture so far from town and with whom. Folks needed their attractive doctor to be sane and back at work. So, in an act of unusual mercy (or self-interest) Falls' town gossips held back their usual worst. "Haven't those two been through enough already? Who *else* can get them past this? Not her mother. They say she's off the deep-end forever. Catching that in her bass-net, who can blame her?"

Parking unchaperoned with a dead friend's teenage daughter would only be allowed a doctor so beloved, only one lovely girl half-orphaned in this interesting a public way. Maybe such ditch-bank heart-to-hearts would help both mourners. Each had lost weight. Each looked shaken. And when you offered either one condolences downtown, they acted like people just admitting to themselves that they are going deaf while not quite ready to consult a professional. Meaning: They stared at your lips not your eyes. Tilting too far forward, they nodded a lot.

FEARNOT'S MOTHER RARELY left her bed. She now smoked as if enlisted by some government-project that required her, as a patriot, not to eat, only to inhale her nourishment, unfiltered. After the boating accident, a new fear found her: flood. Everyone pointed out how our Lithium River, though it varied in depth, was lately just a goodly little brook. But she felt secure only on her home's second floor. The banker's wife could not admit to having witnessed his sudden death, its sounds and sight. She could not bring herself to even look upon the boat-owning culprit. She pointed out how he had drunk the boat's every drop of gin while she, busy smoking, had tasted none.

People swore Doc Dennis, so apologetic he appeared bent, had aged a decade in six months.

THE NEXT STEP is mysterious yet understandable if you think about it long. The doctor, despising himself, endlessly admitting that his power-craft navigation had varied from the standard practices of anybody safety-minded, this same doctor once nicknamed Dennis the Menace now sought forgiveness before a very pretty (if raw-eyed) girl of fourteen called Fearnot. Her

28

mother rarely knew where the poor child was. The mother had given up school carpooling, saying that the steering wheels of cars and boats looked too weirdly alike.

Doc Dennis, being Fearnot's godfather, was the person her family had handpicked to provide her moral education. For hours on end, this guardian and his charge talked alone in his big brown Chrysler sedan. It had become the autumn after the summer's outboard beheading. It proved the wettest fall on record. You know how two people in a stopped car—during some comically-hard country-downpour—fog up their windows and soon feel even more a quiet unit? Now we must move to rank speculation.

Say her housebound mother is of no use to Fearnot. Say the poor fellow keeps crying in that coughing choppy way grown men finally do. Say this particular day she has been especially missing her dad. Say that, from her passenger-seat, she shifts left to console her stricken godfather. Say she kisses his tears. Say he, newly 41, is the exact age her able missing poppa would also be now. Say she sees a man still slender, hair starting to go valuably silver. Say the fellow present, like the one gone, acts as earnest-harmless yet guarding as any family's good collie. Say the doctor would do anything to comfort his godchild.

He returns her gentle kiss. From their crying, both their shirt-fronts are dampened to a patchy translucency as he hugs her. In adjusting his grip upon her, imagine he accidentally touches her left breast. Its sweet votive-candle warmth feels steadying, buoyant, a new source of latency, of contact, consolation. Surely the feel of her beginning yielding life there stirs him. Only a dead man would not be stirred.

Say she herself longs to escape into comforting him fully. Say she has noted all his gestures that're like her father's, certain exact phrases, even a solemn twinkling way of refusing pity that most guarantees a nice fellow's getting it. Somehow, by distracting him, Fearnot seeks to finally calm herself. Say these two have often remarked how—during such long drives nowhere—they sense their dead favorite's spirit-residue alert here in the car with them, in the backseat, even closer. Say that, as any two dry sticks—pressed testing-shifting one against the other—can create a friction sufficient to heat toward flame, some new element springs alive between them. It's their own first try at providing warmth for a man who lost his head in the tepid green waters. Today it forces them beyond usual caution, past church-worthy control. There is no decision, simply action suddenly. If a blouse has six buttons, you start with the one at the top and open the lowest last.

Imagine how, in her grief, she feels she's some way consoling her fun-loving father regarding his own death (just as he resurfaced holding aloft the red towrope, gasping while laughing, as he gulps that first fresh air).

Imagine the doctor, her godfather who, at her christening, publicly vowed to help direct her lifelong spiritual-ethical instruction. He is today counting on *her* to say, "No." Just as Fearnot depends upon his maturity and worldliness, his Episcopal office-holding, his medical degree, his understanding of village decency.

Say both of them are quite literally crazed with grief. Say only lust can overtake grief's cold force with its counterclaim nearly as heavy. Say lust can fill a void with no more qualm than water fills a blasted mine. It is difficult to tell then where one force ceases and a new surge has commenced. Say that these two mourners love each other like father and daughter, but are grief-blasted free of any old taboos blocking their way.

Imagine late this afternoon that he forgets his wife has dinner

30

waiting, forgets his kids at table staring at the sunburst wall clock. He never imagines their little stomachs might be making funny hunger sounds. Just say, by evening, Dr. Dennis S— has a whole new thing for which to blame himself. Say Fearnot pretends it never happened, this her only time. It did not occur except as some final emphasis to what began with her father's cleverly untangling his towrope under clouded lake water. Till, triumphant, lifting red line overhead into clarity, he found air then Doc's whirring blade atop him.

KNOW THAT SOME several months past that rainy afternoon in a car, this same lean girl is trying to climb a nylon rope in gym class. Fearnot is usually the first one up. Her lady-teacher, always appreciative of every lovely lass in motion, notices something. She summons the girl into her office. Coach Stimson, closing her door, says she just wonders. The girl freely admits to confusion, a lack of having any sort of real period for a group of months. Even while using her own fingers, she cannot quite count right. Nor does the child, still fourteen, seem to understand all that such idle tallying might imply. The lady-coach goes, "Were you absent from one of my Health Class lectures, young lady? A fairly important one?"

The girl's mother, who's been too fearful to even venture downstairs below what she now terms "the waterline," is called to school immediately for a discussion with both gym teacher and school nurse. Their tone scares Fearnot's mother into venturing down toward her home's first floor, then driving her own boat-sized white Cadillac. The nurse and one female guidance counselor stand by. The girl has, in simplest terms of innocence, just told them who the father is. She says it was no one's fault. Just as any random water-skiing accident might be blamed on, well, weather conditions, sight lines, geometry, and no one person.

Fearnot's mother, arrived for the conference and at once informed, screams to such an extent the nurse must lurch to motion. A tranquilizer-hypo has been readied for the girl but the mom gets stuck first. Drugged, the mother in her flowered hat, an appropriate purse over one arm, swings out of the coach's office and yells Dr. Dennis S—'s name and deed to a whole gym full of girls' intramural basketball, and to fifty-odd parents gathered to watch. Fear-not, following, sees only open mouths in rows. Any hope of courtly secrecy is ended.

Then the girl's mom becomes very vengeful. She feels understandably upset about what a doctorly best friend has done, first to her husband, then to their one child. There is a sad incident where the mother, turned vigilante in her grief, sets the doctor's brown family sedan ablaze. That car is the admitted site of insemination and it's suddenly visibly on fire during eleven o'clock service at All Saints. The mother uses this smoky disturbance outside church to run right down the aisle toward him. Pointing, she openly accuses him (witnessed by his wife and three young children) of impregnating his own trusting goddaughter, not quite fifteen. "Justify yourself, dog. Before God, your family and me. Justify yourself, you complete and total red-dicked hound."

Then, thanks to volunteers from the choir, Fearnot's mother is physically restrained, dragged for immediate counseling into the rector's office. It is quite a mess.

ON THE FIRST anniversary of the boating mishap, having driven his own family to a coastal resort in Maine where they'd go unrecognized, this same young doctor waits till midnight. Then, diving off a moonlit beach, he Australian-crawls on out toward New Brunswick, Canada. Back at the rented cottage, Doc Dennis's wife, aware of the ominous anniversary, insomniac and restless, finds his note on the kitchen table. She phones 911. A Coast Guard cutter intercepts the doctor against his will; he has swum four miles straight out. He appears to be naked. He plainly intends to swim till he cannot. Dr. Dennis is institutionalized for three months, then released. The news of this attempt on his own life, joined with the boating mishap prior to fathering a child on his own innocent goddaughter, requires his family's moving to a new town.

They choose one in Maine. And, as of last year (Google tells us) this semi-retired medico was still practicing part-time. He is much revered locally, and it is easy to find online a "Dr. Dennis S— medical school scholarship, established by the countless Cobscook Bay residents that 'Doc' first befriended then cured. This man, as quiet as he is self-disciplined, has proved capable and essential here. May his tradition of healing be passed along to . . ." Etc.

DURING THOSE TIMES a girl in Fearnot's condition got sent away to Newport News, Virginia, to "visit Auntie," actually an institution. The place, once a tobacco-magnate's mansion, has been retrofitted for young women with brief if unhappy sexual histories. Not one framed picture of a mother or a baby is seen in any of its thirty walnut-paneled rooms.

Fearnot lives there during her pregnancy's remaining months. All is normal. The baby will be put up for adoption. Its papers guarantee the biologic parents' names will never prove traceable. Just as Doc Dennis tried to disappear into the North Atlantic, he must have intended that the history of his outside child never be found on public record. He knows a childless God-fearing couple in rural Maryland. The man was a college suite-mate study-partner. Doc does not tell them the name of the coming child's father. Just, "A quite bright patient of mine, a teen girl from one of our leading families." Doctors can get around the usual waiting period and Fearnot's mother readily agrees. The so-called relinquishment papers will be signed right after Fearnot gives birth. The expected bastard's parentage is described as follows in a file found through a retired archivist (only after this home closed in 1979, perhaps due to improved contraception, or to more girls simply keeping their children):

> Brilliant forty-one-year-old medical doctor and newly fifteen-year-old girl placed in (his) charge and that he made her get into trouble and family way. Girl (the preg. mother) had been a popular school leader and horseback champion. Family believed to have been mod. wealthy, Father, banker, Wake Forest grad. Girl consid. very pretty and well-liked till lapse. Doctor was girl's own godfather, family friend. Used personal influence on young female for own selfish end, apparently. Neither could keep the child. Girl's mother said doctor later tried taking own life at sea but attempt was foiled (boat, Coast Guard). Every indication—pregnancy proceeds well and that child likely to be bright & presentable, judging from its fortunate if careless parentage.

In the savage kindness of such institutions, she brought her baby to term at the Burwell Home for Unwed Mothers. When found dilated to a correct number of centimeters, she was whisked to a nearby hospital, where the girl got anesthetized so that, by the time she regained full awareness, her infant was already sleeping in its new home. It had just been driven across state-lines into Maryland by qualified adoptive Caucasian parents. They'd literally been seated in a chamber marked WAITING on the far side of a room called DELIVERY. They held two folded blankets just in case: one pink, one blue. To spare her the troubling specifics that so often vex an unaccompanied mother's drugged imagination, the girl herself was never informed of her own child's sex. "*Can* tell you it was a real healthy one," is all the kindest nurse would say.

Fearnot endured usual lectures, usual crying jags. What most upset this recent mother was her uncontrollable lactation. Nurses had given her a shot to reduce her natural milk. But at night, once she rolled onto her side, Fearnot felt hot lines escape her. She had once completed a book report regarding Madame Curie. Now the heat of her own milk seemed two white lines of radium with a power to glow in darkness. Nourishment was trying to get out and go somewhere and earn its keep. The front of her blouse grew damp, recalling two transparent shirtfronts pressed together in a parked brown sedan. Other nights, as she wept, crying's hiccups released further milk till it seemed her breasts themselves were spilling blue-white tears, 98.6.

One awkwardness marred a group outing days after her baby had been "placed." In the lobby of a downtown Newport News movie palace, the old Warwick, as she entered with other girls still pregnant, Fearnot came across a stroller. The infant sleeping there looked six months old. Its parents stood at a nearby refreshment kiosk choosing candy when Fearnot ran their baby to the ladies' room. A policeman was summoned, much screaming in the tile bathroom. It was determined that Fearnot was hidden in the far toilet stall, breastfeeding an infant unknown. The child's own mother especially went crazy, yelling about disease. But the pretty girl would not return the child until confronted, counseled, finally sedated.

The policeman was Irish and the father of six and, once he learned of the poor girl's situation, he became emotional and so solicitous as to prove an inefficient law enforcer. No charges were filed.

Days later, Fearnot's own mom retrieved the new young mother, mercifully childless as before.

Fearnot's mom had been telephoned prior to the delivery. Home authorities asked her to please be present during labor. Officials stressed the difficulty faced by a fourteen-year-old giving up her firstborn without one family member present.

The widow had responded (and later regretted), "She got it *into* her, let her get it *out*."

FEELING THE WEIGHT of gossip at home, much of that brought on via the mother's public announcements and igniting of an auto, the two relocated directly to a town outside Atlanta. Since Fearnot's father had been killed in that way still discussed, nothing secured his heirs' honored place within reputable banking circles of North Carolina.

Come September this as-yet-gentle girl enrolled at a new public high school under her real name. Within one year, she'd been elected alternate cheerleader and student body secretary. Her secret(s) stayed well-kept. Two years later, she was chosen one of ten Outstanding Seniors. Under her picture—smiling while modeling a new page-boy haircut, pearls over a black sweater—this appeared:

She came from nowhere. With all our groups rushing to welcome her, she chose her own pet "clique." Her favorite would be... Everybody!

A well-rounded personality and lively mind, she had already taken several years of Russian! From the start she seemed to know

*more than us other kids. Clueless ourselves, we still felt glad. She
arrived looking perfect as a blank check. Then she slipped up and
LIKED us. Right away we felt warmer and safer and even "hipper,"
remember? If she liked us we couldn't be all that bad! Or ugly,
either. She never seemed to count on getting one thing in return. She
made certain other beauties changed their evil tunes, am I right?
"Mean" was suddenly real out of style. Girls who wouldn't look at
you before knew your name because of her. Funny, but if she transferred in during our sophomore year, why do we remember her as
being like our best friend from third grade forward? Looking back,
she basically "mothered" us, I guess. Where do certain people learn
to be so kind? Could that not be taught as a Senior Elective up
ahead? —If so, only by her. Pretty please? And thank you.*

BY AGE FOURTEEN she had lost her dad; newly fifteen she'd borne a
child then surrendered even that small stranger to several larger
ones. Up till then, Fearnot's best-known flaws had been her quiet
vanity and outsized laugh. Childhood friends swore it rushed out her
mouth wilder than any donkey's seesaw yodeling. Something would
strike her funny and the whole Sunday school class fell silent. Ladylikeness dropped behind wet leather curtains of caterwauling. "You
sound like what I heard one night when a moonshiner got caught in
his own muskrat trap!" That was what a Falls service-station owner
once told the girl guffawing. But all such giddy loudness had quit
her, age fourteen. Only now, outside Atlanta, among certain sudden
friends, did she hear first peeps of her own wit returning.

AT HER SCHOOL, there studied a shy lanky boy similarly fated to
succeed. He already stood six feet three inches tall. He did everything so well, his teachers secretly worried he wouldn't, always.

37

Soon as he glimpsed her he sensed a fellow sufferer. Excellence seemed her natural smell. The starch in her round white collar must put off the scent of a costly stationery shop the day it opens.

Though bashful, he grinned at her. The grin showed a recognition almost-pitying. Like her, he was an only child. Like her, at home, no wised-up older brother ever explained that A+'s are rarely given. He'd already mapped as his own the coming field of transplantation surgery. If some Career Day visitor had suggested "radiology" instead, he would have spared himself the energy of even answering.

In the cafeteria on her first day, other boys noted the new coed's pearls and contours. But he saw a stark X-ray of his own ambition. It half-frightened him, knowing he was not alone in wanting far too much. In Herman Talmadge High's cafeteria, as she sought somewhere to eat, he just kept smiling up at her. He determined to succeed at this, too. Tray in hand, she'd stopped beside his table.

Somehow the sight of his exposed teeth, big clean "adult" teeth, stirred her. Other Science Club kids eating with him laughed at how his goofball grin kept renewing itself. "What's up with your dufus face, Dufus Head?"

Halted there, she asked, "What?"

"You," he explained. "You here, too."

HE PLAYED GUARD on the basketball team that would become Georgia's 4A state champs. He might have longed to be less well-rounded, but did not know which evolving skill to neglect first. Unlike her, nothing had yet happened to him. If any club, team or chemistry teacher asked for something, he provided it. He was sixteen and needed very little sleep.

With silver-blond hair and hard blue eyes, he half-resembled the doctor who had killed her father then implanted her with child before failing to drown himself. The boy did not know this, of course, nor did she need to tell him or anyone. He also looked a bit like the girl's dead father and, in this, he actually resembled the lissome girl herself. These destined high school sweethearts were both elected senior exemplars then attended the University of Georgia, graduating, not quite noticing, with honors. Their appearing to be siblings first linked then calmed them. Their erotic attraction was not, as other jealous kids guessed, some form of mirror-gazing. Instead, alone together, they could leave their shirttails out. He sometimes skipped weekend shaving, though she never liked that. Both being blondes, their butterscotch resemblance became for each a kind of intermission.

The two joked about their automatic over-ease at achieving. "Up ahead," he predicted, "they'll stop handing us the pop-quizzes we saw coming and boned up on. Wonder how we'll do *then*?" He laughed. She did not.

Her cumulative record was already so full of deletions, botch-jobs. Quizzes had arrived as complete surprises. Her early success had been at pregnancy testing. Grading herself on that project, she'd long-since settled for a lifetime F. Her boyfriend knew only that her father had died in a boating accident. The rest she and her mom kept quiet.

The young couple's similarity led them into chambered silences. Tired of standing at podiums, of giving nominating speeches, they retreated into the privileged hush of only one another. Hyper-articulate around others, alone together they fell mute. This became the greatest luxury for each. They went to movies and held hands and, unlike their friends nearby, however bad the film, yelled nothing ironic. He even put up with her mother. The handsome woman talked and smoked. And talked still more, through clouding nicotine. Sometimes it seemed the smoke around her had been mass-produced elsewhere then sent to her for quality-control as she, some half-admired civic filter, continued to inhale it as if eating. Listening, he learned to sometimes nod while always sitting near a window.

He hardly needed to propose, his lovely quiet girlfriend seemed that ready.

First, though, she must tell him. Her mom had offered to do that, offering this boy a fuller family history. But the girl saw that as *her* duty. For that she knew she'd need a new factual language. All understatement. She knew her mother would narrate their joint past only through her usual tabloid words: "headless," "betrayal," "sex-crazed," "heartache," "incognito," "orphaned."

On a couch at the boy's student apartment, the girl had just been offered one fair-sized diamond ring. It'd been his maternal grandma's. His intended bride said, before he even put it on her finger, he would need to know her past a little better. First she called herself "damaged goods, basically." She did emphasize her starter-innocence. Fearnot said she had been, at fourteen, too trusting and half-lunatic with grief.

For now this young man held on to the engagement ring. Listening, he slipped it around one index fingertip of his own long blond surgeon's hand. He'd known about her father's death but lacked the technical details. She admitted she'd never properly fought off her godfather when he first touched her. She'd been mostly numb, she said. She finally confessed there'd been a child, one taken without her even discovering its sex. She said this genderless infant had been consigned to some unnamed guardian, to that limbo outer space of those born-dead.

40

Her would-be fiancé grew quieter, silent. She had told him the whole disaster in three brisk minutes. He cleared his throat. He asked if he might take a walk around their college neighborhood. "And why'd you wait to lay this on me? And what if you *hadn't?*" he asked, rising. "Seems so out of character. Can't help wonder why you'd hold this back." She shrugged. "Sparing you? Then it got so I felt disqualified from . . . everything usual. Look, I wouldn't blame you for backing out. You see me as changing your luck here? I know it's a lot."

After forty minutes he had not returned. She waited on the couch exactly where he'd left her. She felt clear: he would be wisest never to come back. That was his right. Her mother was enough of a marital disincentive! Still, she knew she would survive his exit, along with whatever followed. Odd, by now she sat feeling almost relieved. She heard a key in the lock. He stepped nearer, got down on one knee. His basketball player's length, bent into such floppy chivalry, looked fondly bow-tied. He produced the ring.

"You did nothing wrong. Hell, weren't you a baby yourself? I'd like to fly to Maine and kill that doctor. *Will* you marry me?" "Why, yes," her answer came. They wed in the college chapel a week after commencement. He enrolled that September at Johns Hopkins Med School and somehow, within three years, they had two daughters.

ONE CHILD PROVED a born actress, the other turned out to be as athletic as mathematical. The marriage seemed a good and decent fit. Her husband got extra credit for having accepted knowledge of her father's accident and her secret child. Once those setbacks had been faced, they could go unmentioned. He moved cleanly on. He always ranked either number one or two in his Med School class. His new focus became the Asian woman, also either one or two. He said his competitor's name was Amanda Chu but that class-rosters listed her as A. Chu. "Like a sneeze, right?" Some evenings he reported Amanda's small slips of second-language grammar. Competition stream lined him till his face looked like a visor. She had urged him toward surgical oncology or even his first love, the transplantation surgery stem-cell breakthroughs now allowed. But those disciplines took eight to nine years longer. She did admire his drive and envied how sanctioned it all seemed.

FOUR YEARS AND two children in, the silence between married people can sure start shifting meanings. Quietude held but now it sometimes sounded like an air conditioner's filter needed changing. They'd once kept silent in retreat from others' talk; now their own assumptions became topics to avoid. Still, she made him feel respected; he made her feel reliable then too-reliable then almost assumed.

In public, her hushed doctor-husband acted courteous toward her and, at student parties, jolly. After his radiology residency, he accepted a position near Atlanta; he said they'd both want to return, close by their aging parents. Given her mother's character (given her mother's recent Neiman Marcus shoplifting arrest), she did not remember volunteering her own such wish.

That final winter in Baltimore, during her girls' naps and play dates, she started reading Russian again. During the Cold War this language had been taught in high schools and colleges. She found she could still read Chekhov with surprising ease. She kept one Russian-English dictionary in her bathroom, another in the car. She tried to imagine her life as it might look patterned and lighted by different Russian novelists. That winter brought record snow and, despite wrestling her children into and out of zippered layers, she fought to read seven to ten paragraphs of Russian fiction daily.

Undertaken in secret it became almost a religious practice. The weather, her mood, those nineteenth century narrative geniuses trafficking in the worst which humans can endure, it seemed of one consistency, all dry and cold and white. But pure.

One heroine of Chekhov's, asked why she forever wore black, replied, "I am in mourning for my life." She had married her own aged schoolmaster who once seemed witty. She'd found herself a capital city sophisticate stranded in some garrison town as a local soul. Her explanation of her clothes showed comic self-mockery and was utterly in earnest.

Arriving in Atlanta, she watched her radiologist sit down with the realtor. Her husband would now choose their home's location. She saw him pass along the handwritten addresses of his hospital's best-known senior colleagues. She heard her partner tell the agent, "A suitable new home, maybe four thousand square feet, equidistant between these, our friends." She noted that those doctors mentioned, all in their distinguished sixties, were hardly friends. Even his new German-sounding word "equidistant" scared her, its ambition's more calibrated precision.

The gated compound was not what she'd have chosen. True, its walls were serpentine brick supporting espaliered pear trees. "But something there is that doesn't like a guard-post," she told her daughters, accepting that they'd miss the joke. Her husband now went at the politics of hospital radiology with the elbowing ardor of a high school basketball guard.

Once they moved into the house, he handed her that same list of senior mentors. He encouraged his wife to go and cultivate "the wives" (though two of the doctors listed were themselves married females). He hinted she should find those educated women who still discussed books and issues. "Some really try keeping up. And that's good for everyone, kids included." He said he'd already learned the name of the very best such local club.

She soon watched him, but as a mother might observe her own adolescent son. She kept waiting for that youngster to darken toward complexity, an adulthood. She had granted this man the right to represent her; but lately he seemed about as qualified to do that as your average "greeter" at Home Depot. For him, the doctorly pop-quizzes never stopped coming and her man proved tireless, solving these. One night after three drinks he admitted his high standing on the job. He had overheard two senior colleagues say they believed he could become "something of a radiology superstar. *Their* words." She took a long breath. He went on to say that, from here forward, he'd have his life at the hospital. He seemed to explain she would now curate their girls, her club and the house itself, okay?

HE HAD CHOSEN this outsized barn-red home, a model called "The Braxton." When she admitted to some ironic feelings about the name and its spare thousand square feet, he gave her one long minus-mark look. He soon knew to leave his wife alone in the depths of their house. He simply let her run the establishment and sometimes *mope*, as he now called it. If he stepped into a den where she sat thinking her clouded loving thoughts of persons absent, he retreated from such gloom. He only truly touched his attractive spouse if formally invited. She found herself wordlessly regulating his visits to her side of their bed. She found she'd always hated the sort of woman who rationed sex. A meter maid. But he seemed too busy or passive to complain except in sighs.

She might have preferred a grand passion. She might have preferred some strapping farm boy with dirty fingernails, a home-built motorcycle. Instead, she took inventory and found it mildly disappointing that she'd slept with just two men. Her "type"? That must be blond doctors—driven, self-critical, hand-scrubbing—mouse-quiet during sex, stone-silent after.

Given years enough of any marriage, she told herself, every efficient person surrenders to the habit of habits. Schedule soon outranks whatever's fluky and spontaneous. Till sometimes a flat tire—killing your day's first four appointments—can make you feel paroled, the weedy roadside almost glamorous.

Still, she was glad for her children, how they needed rules, regular hours. Her daughters proved articulate and nimble, born of achievers to be born achievers, without knowing there's another project option. And she knew just what to do with fellow goal-oriented towheads. She taught the girls elementary Russian without their even asking the name of this private gorgeous feathered language. The heroics of her girls' learning to walk and talk, it had made her more forgiving. Even toward her own mother, still stuck doing hours of community service. (Turned out she'd been arrested stealing three feathered Neiman hats, wearing one inside the other.)

In fairness, her doctor-husband never missed filming their girls' kinder-gymnastic meets. He tried for close-up artistic angles and, as thanks, once got trampled, fallen-on, much to the delight of spectators. Fearnot sat watching his intense recording of their daughters' minor breakthroughs. She found herself imagining her missing child, off-the-record. It had no name but "it." It belonged not even to the tribe of any one gender. Sometimes championing this little ghost made her want to wear conversation-starting black. Some nights, reviewing before sleep, she felt a jealous witness to her own rich life.

*

ONCE SHE'D GOT both daughters into first-rate local private school, despite her many other duties, she enrolled as a grad student. She'd now pursue an MA in Russian literature.

Given her unsettled girlhood, the Russians' sense of Fate had spoken to her early. She'd been assigned a decapitated father, an unsought pregnancy courtesy of her dad's killer; eventfulness in fiction did not embarrass her. Fate no longer seemed the design concept making Novels of Coincidence easier to write. Fate felt—like tidal waves or hurricanes—an inexorable, arbitrary natural force. (If she had ceased at age fourteen to believe in Luck, she now accepted Fate as Luck's adult-content replacement.)

It helped her feel less guilty for that single child-producing lapse. Fate contained a trillion human currents pooled. Blackened, it surged with uncounted marked-down lives like hers. She forever spared her husband news of how she missed the baby, *her* first. The one not his.

Being an only child herself, she always thought of her eldest as her only child, too. This, despite the evidence of two live-in daughters so visible and demanding, so adored and readily at hand. The girls, being "planned babies," seemed products of a different, drier life. The truest child was her accidental hidden one.

HER OWN AGING mother never would discuss that birth. She ignored how single mothers lately *kept* such children. These days, in enlightened circles, it was even considered chic. Newspapers claimed that over sixty percent of recent babies got born to young unwed women who simply wanted babies! The doctor's wife found it cruel that fashions in behavior changed so fast. A shift earlier might've allowed a girl to finish high school with her own out-of-wedlock child snug in its kid's room down the hall. Her irritable widowed mother might easily have claimed that baby as her own late-life slip and present joy. That way two children could've grown up siblings.

Times it felt unbearable, not even knowing which continent her baby had been carted off to. Which talents had her likely little girl developed? Whom did the child most resemble? This mother of two lively daughters sometimes found herself, while waiting at kiddie pools, studying certain older girls. Especially any talkative evident leader. If she saw a blond kid the age of her firstborn, she stared over-top whatever big Russian novel she then held.

Crying babies could somehow make her feel frantic. Odd, but six-month-olds were hardest. Hearing some stranger's infant sob made her jaw set, made her organs of reproduction inhale upward an inch and a half. Her field of vision whitened.

The few written records brought south from that "home" in Newport News had been burned by her mother.

WHEN SHE ENTERED grad school as an older student, the Internet was new, at least to her. She had secret reasons for learning what still seemed a sci-fi novelty. With all her frontal duties of Hospital Guild and social life, with so many public chores around her daughters' school, she longed for some investigative privacy. New skills would be needed to research her own lost life. She had read: what prevented folks her age from learning the computer was plain fear. She told herself she'd got over that long ago. Intuitive, she noted this technology's arriving, like Fate in a black dress, just when she felt readiest.

Over time she had become both more secretive and superstitious. Without a spouse demanding explanations and chatter, she set up her own interior lab, almost an altar. And her missing child, marked

X, stood radiant if unfocused at the center of it all. —She bought a "personal computer," guessing the gizmo might truly make her future "personal" at last.

Along the hall marked SLAVIC LANGUAGES, she took note of certain bright young grad students. A few tolerated the interest of this smiling mature lady. She endured overhearing one acned girl refer to her as "Mrs. Doris Day." That smarted; but she imagined how her daily cheer and cashmere cardigans must look to someone that scholastical and lonely and twenty-two.

One clever antisocial boy wore black leather motorcycle gear. Sometimes creaking like a hassock, he kept mostly to himself. He was among the few kids then typing class notes right into their computers. The boy's laptop wore a matching zippered leather case. Like a gunslinger, he never stepped toward to the bathroom without the thing. She watched him unfasten his in class. She saw in his hands the tender briskness of some priest unfastening his last-rites home-visit Communion kit.

She noted how fast the boy's filthy fingernails blurred over keys, eyes fixed on the professor. She determined to annex just his sexy ease at warming up technology. She cornered him after class: "Would you risk a Student Union espresso?" Though withdrawn, the boy tried carrying her briefcase across campus. "Oh, I'm still spry enough," she smiled. But found the offer touching.

Having entered her thirties, she'd worried about her loss of looks. But he paid for her coffee, using wadded ones and likely Laundromat quarters. The back of his neck looked very white. It slowly came to her—being someone nearer his mom's age—he half-liked being seen crossing campus with her, an "older blonde." She praised his evident computer talent.

"Second nature," he shrugged, jacket creaking. The boy soon

held open the library's heavy door. Sure, he'd be willing to show her certain search-function basics, why not?

She chose a corner half-hidden behind PERIODICALS IN PORTUGUESE. He sat demonstrating how to get around the Web and "launch a search." She risked observing aloud, "Don't you think the words 'Search Engine' sound like a new name for 'God'?" He let that pass without comment. His pianist's fingers brought a key phrase onscreen. She watched that pitchfork then leapfrog into crash course connections. She perched close enough beside him to know he smelled like sock-elastic and pizza dough. For all the roughness of his dirty nails and black leather, his skin showed a pallor peculiar to new babies and old men.

The simplicity of her start-up questions made him laugh, then moan. "Oooh," he shook his head, embarrassed to even look at her.

"Hey, have to start somewhere. You're the only one I've ever asked, okay?"

The kid answered in some code he considered English. He appeared to have studied, not six years' Russian, but a lifetime's speculative fiction. He soon stuttered out letter-number combinations. For starters he'd explain how programming concepts differed from Apple to Oracle to Microsoft.

"Whoa, you." She almost touched his ivory arm.

"Back up. Imagine me as someone who's been locked for life in a nineteenth century orphanage. No, say a newborn. For instance, does this thing have one plug or several? Are its signals traveling by air or through buried lines? Like that."

He turned on her a pity now becoming interest. He found it hard to back off far enough to even picture a screen so blank as hers. He soon spoke louder, as to some child about to grow restless. As he swiveled his chair, their knees bumped. He studied her tanned legs.

He told her: With every question asked then answered, she looked two years younger, did she know that?

A put-down? a come-on? both? She sensed his pleasure, teaching someone older. But that just made her feel more ancient.

She did learn very fast, fearless at acquiring what he attractively called "access." He grilled her: What was she hunting so hard? As a fellow Russian scholar, he assumed she wanted to attach the newest literary data. So much was just then coming online as the Soviet Union dissolved. His typing shot her to sites still locked within barbed-fences of Cyrillic script. For her he summoned from the steppes of cyberspace Stalin's arrest-orders for great writers he'd had executed, Babel and Bulgakov. Raw KGB files now stood unshackled to all comers. "Do you believe all this here for the taking!" He said it with a wonder finally young.

She thanked the boy, apologized for her slowness, tried praising him without seeming to flirt. But she couldn't wait for him to leave. He rose but not before restudying her brown knees. "Later," he said, adding, "Whenever." Child-lingo or some standing sexual offer. Both. Once alone, she rushed around finding an empty computer carrel. She had to be behind a door that shut. She doused overhead fluorescence and started:

Burwell Home for Unwed Mothers, Newport News, Virginia,
Records of Births, Whereabouts Babies Now?

Typing this, her hands shook. She had to poke last letters via index fingers alone.

560 related sites fired up. Lettering burned green on a black field: even that struck her as a brilliant color choice. First she got the history of one tobacco executive Burwell's Victorian home donated

to girls then called "wayward." True enough. She learned how over nineteen hundred unplanned-for children had been born to these unwed unlucky girls. But soon she hit: "Triple-encoded enforced secrecy-guarantees, precautions embedded in all adoptive documents filed since 1947, make tracing subsequent histories of 'placed' children impossible. Private detectives, hired to break the numerical-cryptography employed by Burwell, have admitted to clients 'hitting the mother of all firewalls.'"

Mother!

Despite such barricades, she saw she'd never give up. Maybe another technology would come along in five, six years? Maybe she should hire her young leather Russian scholar to help trace the missing offspring. He surely had gifts. But she feared that, after telling him her life, she'd wind up owing him too much. Still, if he somehow succeeded, she would do anything, would go back to his mildewed bath mat of a rented room. If he ever helped her find her lost lamb, she would endure his bare ribs and casual hygiene with an abased slave's gratitude. Once she viewed this as a sacrifice for her missing daughter, she allowed herself to picture all the stunts she might achieve against the concavities and seizures of his white white body.

THE YET-PRETTY STILL-YOUNGISH mother—secret parent to *three* —had long ago decided her firstborn must be a girl. She knew from high school biology: male infusion determines the sex of any child. And yet, this one time only, she claimed for herself an unscientific right to choose her baby's gender. Since she was, as a person, both unusually stubborn and highly consistent, she opted to believe herself A Girl Who Bears Just Girls. This at least made clothes-shopping for her two daughters more compelling. She kept a secret running tab of her eldest child's likely changing size. And while girls chose things, she wandered into the next-oldest section: Junior Miss.

The family was to spend two weeks of early summer on the Gulf Coast. The first day there, her missing girl would turn seventeen. The mother could not outwardly observe that birth date. But, silent, she still honored the occasion. This freckled mom happened to be wandering the beach with her husband and two legitimate children. The girls kept wanting to change into bathing suits without returning across sun-heated sand to their hotel. Agreeing, laughing, their mother stood helping them slip into their suits. They, giggling, were shielded within one large bath towel zebra-striped. The sight of them squirming, white and naked (protected) on this public beach, made the mother grin. Then she was picturing one spot of lake water, foaming burgundy.

Blinded by sun, she again found—caked before her eyes—bees' honeycomb. Its wax overflowed not amber sweetness but different-colored milks. The liquids' tints, intense as tattoo ink, were shades only a child would trust. She felt near fainting and leaned toward her tall husband for support. When she straightened she knew without understanding how: her "only child" was male.

She sat hard on sand. Her eldest daughter pulled the zebra towel over her head. She felt—at how many removes?—in the presence of a son. She could picture one cot. It was set inside a stifling green tent; on the stool, toothpaste, Coppertone, baby oil. There was a homemade birthday card signed by many children. This was some campsite, today abandoned of its kids. He must be a counselor here, his charges off on some bus trip, leaving him alone. He wore only khaki shorts. He seemed to fill the tent and had about him the air of some giant pup, atypically on his own. She could barely make out his features for the glare. Resting on the cot, looking up, he held a

52

round shaving mirror. It was his birthday and, to commemorate, he kept staring at his own reflected face. Sunlight ricocheted. She knew that, instead of admiring his features, he was consulting them. He scanned for traces of his history. Head shifting side to side, the boy kept seeking any sign of her.

Still fixed on his image caulked direct before her face, she pressed one hand across her eyes. She now claimed sunstroke. Rising with help, she asked her doctor-husband to watch their daughters' swimming. She returned half-stumbling to the hotel.

She changed into a provided white robe and settled on the balcony. The breeze there cooled her. She kept gazing out beyond her family into the swelling ocean itself. She felt lost in joy at knowing of this boy. Some firewall separation had been blasted by this proof of him. Impossible to say how . . . but she even felt ready to guess at his name. It must be that of some announcing angel. A "Gabriel." Maybe "Michael."

Ever afterward she'd be certain of her firstborn's sex. With this came an odd quickening. For one thing, her "spell" meant he still lived. Meant he'd continued hunting his own sources. He was out there, taking worthwhile risks without her. Someplace he'd become the kind of citizen that parents entrust with their little campers. She felt irrationally sure he was a decent kid and, unlike herself at fourteen, she sensed he'd held off, grown as he was, from being sexually enlisted. All this she really only guessed about him. How such information reached her, that was a detail she'd long since given up explaining.

But, the difference between even this much knowledge and nothing, oh, it seemed the difference between Luck and Fate. Yes, it was the difference between "a child they made me put up for adoption" and "my son, Gabriel Michael, just turned seventeen."

She never revealed having such a vision. Certainly not to her earnest husband. But the presence of this granted news made our wife-mother-scholar feel less parched. It made her seem more real and dear and "human," even to herself.

A LITTLE FORGIVEN, she could now act freer toward her lost son's very present baby sisters. *He* would want that, she guessed it now. So she *visited* her girls more. They were still so young they loved long pillow fights that ended in tears. Even her older daughter slept nightly with a changing crew of preferred stuffed toys. But the girls' shared hallway was already taped with ugly posters promoting the two top boy bands.

Their mom now asked for specific permission to *hang out* in the daughters' rooms, at night. Girls acted shocked; at first they even cleared clothes and toys, made actual paths across their floors. She asked if she might study the girls' fan magazines. Covers' bowl-cut guitarists looked uncomfortably juvenile. Such lads were often prettier than girls. And the daughters, being so young, innocently loved males for winning, even at prettiness! Everybody looks better singing, especially fifteen-year-olds. And maybe such doe-faced balladeers provided merciful first baby steps toward girls' facing their first hairy protrusive adult male.

Visiting daughters' bedrooms, piled between them on one four-poster, their mother now pronounced her strong hilarious opinions of their favorite boy-groups. "Now, *this* band . . ."—she pointed to a bunch with streaked hair—"should call itself *the Highlights*!"

"You are soooo weird!" her eldest squealed, a compliment.

The mom admitted that another front-boy singer was cute, true; but "being so young, he's still cursed with, look, *the beaver-teeth*." Her girls found this phrase hilarious. It seemed they'd been waiting for it. First the eldest fell off the bed, laughing. Then girls took turns falling off the bed, laughing. Next they ran around the room pointing to anything split or forked, "Eeek, everything in here's got a bad case of *The Beaver Teeth*!" Her youngest at once phoned three best-friends to repeat the term aloud, once she'd caught her breath.

That night the daughters finally heard their mother's fullest teeter-totter laugh. Being kids, their each endearment came phrased as a complaint. "Mom? you can't help it, can you? But, hee-hawing like that? you sound like one sick donkey, did you even know? Does it hurt you to? Guess what? Your laugh IS 'The Beaver Teeth'!" They all giggled separately then together. This just made their mother do far more spastic laugh-snorts, her tears all coming lovely down her face.

Both girls adored this change in her. "You're way more *fun*ner," the youngest offered. She'd allowed herself this baby-talk ungrammar. She finally felt safe from a mother who'd have recently corrected this playful loving mistake.

Absolved, as in some relay, the young mother lived assured that her son himself was somewhere else but safe. Odd, the more her daughters demonstrated their "new girlfriend" love for Mom, the more secure her distant wandering boy seemed.

She felt she'd secretly carried him for seventeen years as some papoose strapped across her upper back. Even as he'd grown to be, what?—one hundred and forty-odd pounds, she woke supporting him. But now that weight seemed, if not resolved, suddenly lessened, because shared. Her daughters' invitations into their rooms seemed unintended favors to their phantom brother. It allowed this mother of three to become more loosely herself.

She had never met him face-to-face, of course. She had never even seen him. Maybe that's why he registered as a papoose, a weight if always invisible because behind her. Then on his birthday, on that beach, they'd had their curious juncture. "A meeting," she considered it. It seemed almost a solar transmission from some worldwide web hurled loose of man-made gear. At the very moment he'd been wishing to see his mother, she—seeking *his* face—struck that very bandwidth. But this too passed into a haze. She now knew something more about him. But it only made her long to see more. She felt she'd barely glimpsed some single moment of his life, seen as if over a wall.

Maybe she'd invented it: his being male, and even a camp leader in khaki! But she told herself: if such facts proved fantasies, she'd still need to treasure and believe each one.

She relaxed into being a better mom for the little ones she could see and touch. She spent more money on her daughters' clothes and she gave them less austere advice. She now saw their giving in to fads as a sign of health, not weakness. She signed them up for subscriptions to *Tiger Beat*. When alongside her daughters in their rooms, perusing their latest issue, she let'd herself slide into being a somewhat giddy, sighing, moony girlie-girl. She kept inventing stupid terms her daughters considered classics. *The Beaver Teeth*, she even felt a little proud of that! *I missed out on so much of being a kid and foolish like this myself.* Somber, analytic, guilty, she always tried justifying whatever simply felt good.

Knowing that her other child was male, she could at least viscerally reregister the advantages all men have. Even little boys abandoned at birth.

And somehow, as she went around disguised as a person middle-aged, the missing son began to rhyme with her father gone missing when she was a child. The numbers of her son's age and her father's seemed to average out at some central spatial meeting point. She knew this must sound silly to others; so she would trouble no one. Maybe this was how religions got invented? A set of beliefs built from admiring rumors about some local martyr; eloquent adaptations to all that was missing. And yet, her son came now to seem a new guardian-figure. He now accidentally defended his half-sisters' rights and hers.

—Fridays and Saturdays she even consciously allowed herself holidays. Two days a week, she would let herself feel less upset for being tricked into giving him away.

He'd somehow survived that.

He had somehow survived even *her.*

ACT TWO

PAINT ME SOMETHING orderly once, now three steps shy of a handsome mess. A family-house can overspill its margins in mid-June. Throw two girls' bikes down willy-nilly against front porch steps. Near the garage, daub in too-blue a wading-pool. Stock it with seven Barbies floating pink, undressed. Make the home a mansion-scaled up-to-date "Colonial." Paint it the new Benjamin Moore semi-gloss called "Heritage Barn-Red."

It scarcely differs from adjacent units but—at least in this one—at noon on a weekday, the young wife-mother and co-owner kept pacing right-angles, reading fiction aloud, atypically alone.

In three hours, she'd leave 110 Pickwick Drive, Collonus Heights, Georgia, to fetch her elder daughter from summer school choral-society practice. Striding as wide as her own great room allowed, this solemn slender woman reopened a book of stories.

As tonight's moderator, she muttered test ideas aloud: "Chekhov being a doctor, his favorite phrase ran, 'No one must ever be humiliated.' Meaning what? Maybe he saw the world as symptomatic but still somewhat curable but . . . No, awful, simplistic. You are not addressing idiots, idiot. And, note to self, your talk is to-damn-*night*, girl. You've really let it drift too late this time. They'll finally all know."

She'd agreed to lead yet another book meeting. Why? So soon after getting an advanced degree in Russian lit, and this was all she'd managed? The doctor's wife felt disgusted by her own recent successes. Hadn't she become just the social leader her husband had specified? Too readily she seemed to quicken others' minds. Shouldn't that cost a person something? She already had so much darkness to answer for. But other educated women misread even that. "Always enlightening," they said. "God, but you do delve."

Can one be a carrier of light without deriving warmth from it?

Her literary insights often sounded, to their inventor at least, as surfacey as other ladies' granite countertops and improved complexions—abraded into glowing.

She recalled being the "new girl" at Georgia's Herman Talmadge High. Its student body, long bored with itself after eleven years seated facing familiars, needed sudden blondness from elsewhere, nowhere. By simply walking in, age 15, she'd become what everybody sought. General kindness seemed easy after all she had privately endured: she saw each girl-classmate as a potential mother, each boy a dangerous unintended sump-pump dad. And yet, though she appeared the very definition of Desirable, she had pleased herself so little. Was this, she wondered now, not typifying female-behavior? Or not? Why her constant terror of subtraction? Why this daily fear of being at last found out?

Mumbling concepts, the opening remarks she sensed Chekhov would not himself enjoy—it seemed she'd always settled. For which-ever of her knacks drew most praise first. As a kid, she'd been assigned, not the silent noble Virgin's role, but "Announcing Angel #1." Then she'd spoiled religious pageantry with her tech mistakes. Even those got celebrated as comedy! Her humor proved accidental as her firstborn. Times, she felt innocent of having ever made one intended joke, one true choice.

Something had befallen her when young. Everything since had leaked, dark, from one offshore mishap. Whenever she saw news footage of oil-smeared seabirds, she at once identified.

TWO LONG OATMEAL-COLORED sectional couches. Her proscribed indoor hike meant always encircling both. To mark her place within these Russian tales, she'd tucked a power-bill envelope. On it, scrawled:

> *Plain not Vanil. Yog.*
> *(Less pinching ballet slppers for C.)*
> *Admit rental disc lost, just Pay!*

The pretty woman's focus kept sliding from Literature, *To Do*, Literature, *To Do*. About Chekhov's stories so much might be said. By anyone else. She told herself again, "Simply trust abundance." Her last talk won much praise. This Atlanta commuter-community had been so recently settled, everyone felt "new here." Even closest pals accepted only the history each woman opted to present. Whole girlhood starter-marriages, dank bisexual stints in the WACS, reductions of inherited hooked noses, so much went unmentioned. Atlanta, once burned by Sherman, that day became the capital for starting over. Southerners in need of anonymity favored it. Second and fourth tries, however sooty, were encouraged here, expected.

Other women, literate and canny, felt drawn to their chair-woman's wider experience. *How* wide they could not know. Even to herself she seemed overdetermined, annealed, fused too early by some smelter's blast into being one thing only. And yet, within educated circles of exurban Atlanta, she was something of a natural star.

Why? She was intelligent, yes, pleasant-looking even on her less-good puffy days. But the others most valued a certain edgy tone of voice she lately betrayed. It kept breaking through her smoothie book-talk insights. She had just confided to club members how her own costly new house seemed designed less by an architect, more by a brochure! Others murmured, "Mmnn," nodded.

Her smartness liked to undercut itself. That made it acceptable to a club like hers. She seemed doing penance for something: A love affair with her school's headmaster? A husband in witness-protection? But, even during little aria diatribes, her mask-blank face maintained its continuing right to popularity. Others learned from that.

Last month, discussing Jane Austen again, she'd admitted aloud that—like Jane, child of the clergy and niece to admirals—she, like the membership, had been the daughter of privilege. "An only child. Born up on a pedestal. With about that much privacy and floor space!" Her mock-irritation made others laugh, just as one of her stray cackles could send her daughters into spasms of shut-eyed giggling.

Pondering January's Jane Austen novel, she'd noted how this book also ended with the usual advantageous marriage. "Perfect, isn't it? Our gifted Miss Austen, an unwed virgin, who died in her father's parsonage at age forty-one, became, naturally, the poet laureate of happy wedlock!"

This roused a bitter lasting group chuckle. Someone, nibbling almonds, actually choked. What the word "war" released in any American Legion Hall, "divorce" detonated here.

Privilege meant a lady qualified for marriage. But that implied the iron neck-brace of expecting far too much. Though Austen's last chapter "hitched" her heroine to one strapping duke with his own library and stables, the poor girl still seemed to always lack, what? "Bunny Mellon's billions, Virginia Woolf's brain, and Audrey Hepburn's cheekbones!"

(The ladies' laughter came from so deep in, it almost rang bass-baritone).

MEMBERS GUESSED: THE chairlady's girlhood must have included serious daily study. Unlike theirs. In this set where dental assistants and surgeons' receptionists had married their till-recently-married bosses, having a master's in Russian lit leant some glamour. Tonight she would speak of Chekhov, whose serf granddad had bought his own family's freedom. She would tell how young Anton C. then struggled to become a doctor and how he would use such skill to treat the poor for free.

She'd confess this was part of why she depended on him so. She would admit awaiting just such a humane calling, some worthy sacrifice. She would concede that: maybe her daughters' weekly lessons in music, dressage and ballet, maybe her husband's Sunday-dawn golf clinics, were "our form of agnostic worship." Admit it, she'd tell them, even this, their favorite book club—might be another civic way to fill dry hours. Weren't we, the luckiest of women, decorating Time instead of claiming it? Weren't we paying secret penance for those grander starter-projects we'd abandoned far too early?

Her landline, as it did eight to twelve times each bulletin-board morning, rang again as a male voice asked for someone with her maiden name then wondered if this might, in fact, be her. "Yes. 'She.' Why? Am actually in the middle of preparing something that's, as usual, overdue. I'm afraid my husband and I only take personal calls on this line." The gentled voice relented even as it kept quizzing her.

Had she not been an expert steeplechaser as a girl? Did she not lead her pep-squad at a high school in Falls, North Carolina, during one specific tournament year? "Probably," she said. "Some survey! Okay, but why?" His voice (upbeat and general as any announcer's) went on: Had she not also known a doctor around age forty, had she not known him well?

"Look, you, if this is your idea of a . . . You are so out of line. Why should I not hang up?" Pacing till now, she settled for six seconds on the third step of her home's stair landing. Then she rose and—barefoot—commenced striding again.

"But . . ." the caller hurried, had she not possibly also brought forth a child then given it up against her will (without ever seeing it or getting to touch it or being allowed to keep tabs on what sort of people got hold of her newborn)?

Leaning against the foyer wall, she finally grew quiet, motions simplified, elbows drawn nearer her torso. "Yes."

Yes, those had been the agreement's terms, right. She now admitted (to him, a perfect stranger) she had since endured tens of thousands of second-thoughts. But all adoptions were once handled that way.

"Yes," said the kindly voice. "Standard for then."

Besides, she added, at that time, she and her newly-widowed mother had lived in grief. The mother was especially strict, clear about placing the infant into a happier home than theirs could ever be. "But, true. All you said is so. About the child. I've felt terrible. My others, two daughters, don't even know. What'd be gained? Past leaving them as sad as I (and my first) must be. But why'm I telling you this? What made you go off and research me, you? How'd you even learn this? Their codes are all encrypted. *Firewalls.* Believe me, for years I've tried. Wait, but I'm, wait . . . getting confused here. What's all this sadness in reference to?"

"JUST TURNED NINETEEN," the baritone voice said. "Lucky I can scoot around the Web pretty good. Could be I've found you. God. Started to say *you have no idea.* But of course you do. You're the only one *does* know. —Look, all's I want is simple. You totally have nothing to fear. Don't even *think* of being scared. Am barely asking anything. Would never force it. Whole deal shouldn't take but about two minutes. (Having young kids, you must be super-busy.) I just want to see you, is all. Just look at you. Compare you with your picture. In my head, I mean. Then, hey, I'm gone. No strings. You'll find excellent references. Online. Everything I can prove about myself's online. Been holding down a regular 'job-job' at the Apple Store out our way. My main message to you is: you shouldn't be scared about any of this. I been over it a gazillion times. Planned out what to say. And hey, I respect the decision they made for you. Giving up the baby. I found all the clippings: your dad's dying in that bad way.

'—I just need to know what you look like. Your voice? is exactly how your voice should sound. Kind of husky, though. Hope that doesn't mean you smoke, because you really shouldn't, for a longer life. —Am I wrong to feel some interest in you, ma'am? Isn't that my right, and natural? Haven't I been picturing you every day for nineteen years?"

She leaned against the wall. "This, this is going to be . . . awkward. Of course I would *like* to make it work and somehow *will*, but . . . I'm so . . . Which state do you live in, where *are* you?"

"On your lawn on my cell looking in the window at you, Susan."

FEAR NOT

*

SHE CARRIED HER receiver to plate-glass. There she saw, sure enough, standing near her drive beside an old green Honda needing bodywork, one tall young man, good-sized. He wore a suit also green, glen-plaid. Its cloth looked shiny, a recent purchase. His black necktie might be a good choice for your first job-interview. He'd likely dabbed product into his wavy hair. He appeared well-built, the juvenile lead. But, from this distance, he could be someone forty, playing young.

THE LATE-MODEL HONDA showed one mismatched maroon door. Even that he'd waxed. The kid simply stood there. He appeared to have been waiting outdoors a good while. One fist held the cell phone to his ear. The left hand hung free. It looked manly, heavy, new. Wait. It clutched something—red foil, a heart-shaped chocolate box? Those usually get sold before Valentine's. Today was June eleventh.

He barely moved and yet his soft face looked so agitated with changing expressions, his mouth could not quite close. He seemed fearful to quite meet her gaze. Instead he focused on driveway asphalt—girls' bikes there. He seemed all too aware of a home owner studying him. Eyes lowered, his head, under her attention, bent almost prayerful.

She judged that, overlit by noon, the kid appeared roughly one-quarter too big. Professional-athlete-scale. If some male this size chose to come in here and harm her, he pretty much could. Nobody else home. He seemed fair-haired as she. Dye? She squinted. Against glass, she visored one hand. Yes, he had a squared-off reliable stance. Her own knees started losing confidence, usual spring. She felt a sharp needling stab at the center of her right breast. She sensed she might now teeter forward. She noted how his right hand clutched one red box; and hers? It held a book of short stories in Russian. Why?

The boy, dressed as for a first funeral, appeared over-alert if peaceable. Phone to ear, the heart-shaped box held close against his side, he shifted around in shoes appearing too pointy-new. She kept hearing a kind of tidal to-and-fro and, slow, understood his cell was sending her the boy's own nervous breathing. He stood awaiting a sign, formal clearance.

If young, he slouched with the patience of some hard-living older vet accustomed to service delays. He was just there beside his dented car. He had stopped it short of one wading pool full of dolls before a terraced 4,000-square-foot home.

Through her half-opened front door, she'd begun to judge and frame his features. Someone might think this stranger resembled her own missing father and a certain doctor (as he must've looked when just this age). The boy was even somewhat like her present husband. But finally her guest began to slowly appear—his dark evened brows and silver-blond hair—someone else. Of course, he was most like herself. But herself enlarged and re-plumbed male. She swallowed, keeping her own head as still as possible, matching his. That was it: this kid, he looked just like her.

A velocity of unacknowledged merit hit her now, a blade. "So *that's* why I've had this not-totally-unlucky life. That's why they keep sticking me with speaking roles, chairpersonships. My God, I've been being fairly good-looking without once believing it!" And laughed. This is how she phrased the surprise of his beauty. Seeing his visual luck gave back some of hers.

She at last spoke to the receiver, "Okay . . . you're *here*. It's *op*en."

*

SHE PADDED, SHOELESS, to her own front door. Now she felt any single step might send her off some cliff. She ducked back into foyer's shade. She considered deadbolting the entry. Phone in hand, she wondered why the powers that be had picked the digits "911" when "111" would bring help a second faster.

Somehow she didn't want neighbors seeing a young man enter her marital home midday.

The boy, having permission, fearing retraction, advanced but as a sleepwalker. Or Dr. Frankenstein's stiff-legged mistake. She could tell he breathed in shallow huffs, the very stage fright now seizing her. Against his jacket pocket he kept drying one damp palm, the other tightened on his chocolate box. At her welcome mat, he wiped soles of new shoes again, delaying. He behaved like a person never before invited into an actual human home.

Through doorframe this stranger poked in just his head. From where she stood against one wall, he made a jagged silhouette. It was not too late to send him off. She could step into the drive, meet the uninvited guest there. Shake his hand in full view of neighbors. Ask the youngster for some grace-period, time to think this over. Would he please leave her a business card? He'd have to agree. What other choice?

One actual person waited. He stood blinking half into the open door of a prospering radiologist's commodious residence. Bikes of metals pink and yellow lay scattered against steps. Once spared midday light, his eyes took time adjusting.

"*SUSAN?*" THE VOICE rang down a dark hall. Too loud.

"Yes, over here. —And, what is *your* name?"

"Michael," he stepped in, blinking. Adjusting to dimness, large hands wavering before him, the candy rattling in its box. The green suit was so new, sizing made it rustle. He edged nearer his goal. She guessed he'd purchased this outfit earlier today. Maybe, having scouted her home location, he'd driven downtown, spent freely. He had surely found the best Oxford-Cambridge glen-plaid suit available for a hundred and sixty dollars. Probably among the pawnshops and New York fashion stores of Old Town. Trying to quickly look "professional" so she'd agree to see him once. Let him see her.

It had been hard enough living without him. Susan told herself to doubt. This was a trick. She now stood four feet from her son. She felt both snow-blind and some midget-child herself. She'd never felt so short till finding she might brag about her boy this size. He handed the rattling box down, out, over to her. "It's candy. I don't know if . . . but just thought . . ."

She'd need no swab, no wait for DNA results. Her womb, his source, contracted, simplest creature recognition. His rich voice had a slight burr in it. That thrum set off a code only her marrow knew. Her *head* recognized him last.

"Hello" seemed ludicrous but she'd just said it.

THE SKIRT WAS tan-poplin, carpooling-comfortable but never meant for guests. Her blouse white Egyptian cotton, washed safe-feeling. She wore no makeup, hair just hanging loose. Barefoot, she felt unprepared for any company, especially his. Susan floated just above the scene as when she first rose to address an audience. This let her notice her own heart's pounding; she could look down and observe a collection of Chekhov stories resting open in her right hand. One red foil heart fourteen inches wide weighed her left. She managed to set both onto the foyer's yellow bench. It struck her that she had just been searching in that book for something. And here Michael was.

Nineteen years she had imagined. But never once had she made ready. How *could* a person? He walked right up to her in this cool tiled front hall. His eyes were a blue too primary. He simply stared. So near, he reacted as you might to your first ghost. No, to the first non-ghost ever encountered after a life among just those.

She could see his shivering. It struck her as pitiful but made him look less dangerous. Outdoors he'd appeared some gigantic he-cat puma. His shoulders looked bulked-up too suddenly. But, nearer, his face had kept a surface simple as a boy's. He, being ten inches taller and looking down, couldn't help hovering. But his pink mouth still hung open like some child's, fearing punishment.

So much emotion was finding then leaving them both, they each appeared half-paralyzed. At last, the young man simply smiled at her. When he did, saliva popped, white teeth showed with a single audible snap. His force registered against her front side with the crack of whiplash.

His voice steadied. He explained she was more beautiful even than he'd hoped. "I'm not beautiful," she said. "I'm not stupid but I'm not beautiful."

"Susan? This is just . . . like . . . I don't even know what . . ."

He turned aside. She wanted to hush him; she could not risk his being an idiot, however fine he looked. He now admitted sideways to the air, "I made up a speech. It won't probably be as good as in the car, but . . ." He shifted now, determined.

"I guess you were fourteen when we met. I mean when we were first together. I'm not but five years older now than you were then. I think some man forced you to. (Part of me thinks it was that doctor, the boat driver.) Some way I know he got you to, during all that confusion after your dad's getting killed. No fair. And my guess'd be, just happened the once. Bad luck, but I stayed on there, to remind everyone. Bad luck . . . for you. Then your mom took even that away. They robbed us, Susan.

"At least I get to be with you this once. Without the Internet it couldn't have happened. The people that adopted me? good folks but simple, real religious. It was a farm. They worked me pretty good. They did save up to buy me a Mac for my sixteenth. I'd been begging them, see. Said it was for school. Of course, first thing I did with it was try and leave them by hoping to find you! Not real nice of me, I know. But, since nine months before I even got myself born, seems I've spent my main time waiting to meet you."

Came a pause.

SHE LONGED TO stop him. Susan pictured him rehearsing this talk while driving the jalopy down from God knows where. Still she must let him finish. Michael had come so far through time and space to have his say.

"My plans are . . . *this*. Funny, but m'plans? all seem to end right here. Finding you has not been super-easy, ma'am. Everything was like you said, triple-coded. Firewalls back of firewalls. A few months ago I finally broke through. Then I sat there and, funny, realized there's no *fire*, not one real *wall*. Finally I'd patched together enough different jackleg skills to where I'd cracked their last subcode. Sure worth it. See, I've mostly come to try and make things up to you."

"You, *me*?" she asked.

He nodded. Michael's voice had so recently gone baritone, each sentence of it snapped into her hearing.

"Know what I think, Susan? I think we are more brother-sister than anything else, twins almost. You didn't choose to have a kid early. We're the only ones really *in* this, aren't we? Nobody will ever know what-all they cost us, will they, Susan? Splitting us up and

70

everything. —This here's about the happiest minute of my whole entire life—till NOW anyways!"

THERE MUST BE something she could say. There must be a middle-class book club Jane Austen "To Do" list for such major moments. But what volume of etiquette might ever index a reunion this weird, a gift so total?

She opened her mouth to speak, Silence seemed her only language. Not even Dr. Chekhov—possessing all compassion's force and elegance—would dare risk human speech just now. His plays are wisely built around long pauses, life's load-bearing silences.

So Susan pressed her right index finger perpendicular across her own lips. Please, no more teenage speeches, however dear. She simply moved closer, barefoot, child-high on him. She moved nearer a boy who'd somehow tracked her to this house so big it always sounded empty. Couldn't he be some confidence trickster? a decoy, some electrified angel sent to end her at first touch? If so, he'd be right to execute her. And, if justice required that, she stood ready.

Punishment made more sense than how her boy-child had been growing larger on some godforsaken acreage. This was why she'd always felt afraid. She'd been guarding him by inventing for herself certain silly local tests. The pointless early Web searches. The MA in Russian lit, another gambit meant to second-guess fate and map him. Homages, little blood payments: *What if this had never happened? What if the firewall had kept him out?*

Strangers with a farm had got to name him "Michael."

THAT WORTHY COUPLE, the husband a college suite-mate of Doc Dennis, had sat on the bench marked Waiting, holding two baby blankets, option blue: boy, option pink: girl. The second she gave life to this child he had been stolen.

Any words she risked now would emerge as smeary zoo sounds. Touch alone might and must suffice. Only human contact could prove simple and profound enough. Susan felt stupid, if most gratefully reduced. Madame Chairlady, fallen mute at last! It seemed her greatest achievement, a silence this hard-earned.

One Buckhead book group had lately tried hiring her away. They'd begged her to defect from the local club. They swore they would all read whatever novels Susan chose (or even poetry!).

—But, no! What had facile conversation ever got her? Hadn't authorities once talked her out of *him*?

ODD, BUT MICHAEL, across those years, and shut up in some farmhouse attic, seemed to have received her beamed wishes. At least he didn't appear to hate her. Her live-in daughters acted far more critical, miffed about her graduate work, peeved at her boring clothes. Michael didn't know enough to disrespect her yet. Nor did he act afraid of her.

But how could someone so luckless avoid hating others? Why did he not blame her for his lifetime's desertion? Hadn't he arrived here solely to hurt her? Susan fought back waves of elation that swerved toward nausea recalling her first morning sickness on a school bus trip. Even as she worried for her safety, for her life. Hard to trust that this was not some cruel hidden-camera show. But it was too late for asking him to please leave. To spare her just an hour to collect herself. By now that would ruin him, she knew. Then one phrase, shot full of consolation, came to rescue her. It flooded her with sanity. She spoke it aloud only for herself. Wherever had she picked this up?

72

"Fear NOT!" Susan whispered.

Her mantra-code-name joke. She'd intended it only to console and steel herself. She forgot that he, another person, was even actually here.

"Thanks," the actual son acknowledged her at once. "Wicked-good advice. —But I'm okay." Naturally Michael had taken his mother's two words as tenderly parental. Rightly *his*.

"I don't feel so scared now," he explained. "Not with you really here, right in your own house. Can't thank you enough for even seeing me. —You know? some of the parents that kids contact, won't even open the door."

THIS CLOSE, SHE lifted arms, sent them wider till each got clear around him. Given so broad a circle, she could only lace stray fingers behind the big back. Her each gesture toward him slowed itself, expecting to be batted down. She met no such rebuff. Soon it felt like these two persons hung suspended here in some clear oil. It offered slight resistance that gave license, some honeyed unaccountable slow motion.

Even lateral muscles holding up Susan's head did brief involuntary spasms: her shock at finding Michael tactile, alive. The sound she made started as pure sigh but pressed too far. And yet this pinched mousy noise didn't seem to frighten him. Instead he chuckled close against her ear, "Right! *right?*"

She rose onto bare toes. She must reach even higher to encircle whatever human-unit her infant had managed, fed by honest peasant strangers, to become. She felt again a piercing pain coring her right breast. A reminder, some task untended.

HOW TO EXPLAIN her tardiness in finding him, feeding him? How might she warn him that this house had other residents? Built too recently, the place echoed, sounding warehouse-huge. Today it felt like some stage-set B&B intended only for Republican donors. Today it looked both over-lavish and utterly impersonal. Another tasteful Atlanta furniture store. What sort of people hid within walled compounds? What sort of fearless boy could glide through such prison-like security?

Susan considered running upstairs to fetch two silver-framed photos. Her parents at their handsomest. *Here are your grandfolks*, she'd tell this strange big kid. *Here's your nose, on him. The dented chin. See? she gave you all this great skin you got.* But surely showing him his inherited jawline would just confuse things now. That could wait.

A MAN AND a woman in the foyer of the house painted "Heritage Barn-Red" finally got to actively say nothing. Any UPS man arriving would find not a thing at all odd happening here. She'd once shared smooth silences with the boy she married but those had curdled since. Some weekdays Susan's husband came home midafternoon to view his "films," this week's X-rays. It made a quiet change of scene for him. Discovering this stranger, he might mistake the kid for some door-to-door Bible salesman, an eco-crusader arrived with the usual petition in his too-green suit.

But, for this pair, what was rolling on here felt unmatched in this whole gated development or the Universe. They could now be simple. That was it. If he spoke, she was allowed finally to hear him. It seemed a miracle that every citizen gets a body apiece and that we can then direct our own toward certain others'. Talking, he'd just been a recent high school grad; silent, she could glimpse what-all waited latent. Such goodness seemed inborn.

At least he had shut up, poor kid. Stillness? unimprovable. The amount to be communicated aloud must wait. Hushed, they agreed to just go forward down the slope toward further silence. Susan thought: If only we could live the rest of our lives locked safe into this dense a quiet! There would be no blustering, no arguments. Not one syllable's apology. If only our next nineteen years might pass speechless, we'd finally be qualified to talk.

The two appeared so glad to merely hug, it became, as practiced here, almost an Olympic-level feat. Two similar strangers—if of widely differing heights—at last embraced, trying out varying international styles, metes.

She stopped making further sniffling rodenty-sounds. He simply stood, guardlike, stoic, the drum major continuing their embrace. He had to bow some from his waist in order to receive whatever upsurge affection this small slightly-older woman seemed intent on offering. Less mother, son. More a Michael finally meeting one particular Susan.

In this shaded foyer, near a front door left ajar—their embracing ran continuous. It would be smart to seek some seating place; but that might mean the briefest loss of contact. Two verticals kept savoring the safety of arms so protective and massed, arms linked within another's adult arms equally strong, also intending purely to uphold, protect.

THE PHONE RANG once deeper in the house; machine answered: "None of us is in right now, but do leave a . . ." After that, as the pair stood joined, out on porch steps, through the open door, six English sparrows, squabbling, broke into flight. A young female swerved into the dark house just above the pair's heads. Wings blurred off into the kitchen where something banged into a window. Minor glassware would be chipped or broken for the next hour, scarcely noticed.

Susan finally led him to a couch. She grabbed his right hand; its palm felt scratchy, leather. She flinched at finding his short life's calluses; inner hand felt thick as a big cat's paw-pads. She felt jealous even of the misery he'd known without her. Imagine Michael, shipped off so young to work some taskmasters' cornfields. How had Doc Dennis chosen such slavers to raise their son?

These two were entering a time when forfeited years at last filter into particulates, yielding actual minutes, usable. She knew they'd each remember every first thing presently occurring. A specific birdsong shaped like a question mark, that boy's skateboard passing repassing, these tallied as events precious, being mutual.

There was so much to ask him, there could be no starter-question good enough. Silent, she practice-phrased introductions: *Michael, meet Dwight, my husband. Husband Dwight, meet my Michael, my lost son, he found me here today.*

But stillness held—merciful, immense, complex with perfect mirroring. Some encyclopedic understatement already linked mother-son. Quiet itself seemed a rural dialect of theirs. Yes, they were one parent and her child. But interim-growth-chart steps had gone unseen. So he arrived today, like Venus, born adult.

His half-smile looked sleepy; but she understood from the inside out this lifelong symptom of her own: it just meant his contentment. Such signs, recognized in another, cannot be taught or learned, only *known*.

She had just been pacing this same great room. Jittery, preparing her talk, Susan always took sharp right angles at both couches' either ends. Somehow it calmed her, faking an almost military precision as she stalked about, overplanning. When he phoned, she'd been in just such striding form, her route's mad geometry somehow soothing. She'd just been hitting her own forehead with the paperback itself while talking usual turns.

He now pulled free of their couch and, as nervous as elated, laughing while he shook his head with sideways-marveling, Michael himself started pacing. He had never met her, never seen her house; but she watched him now patrol her very accustomed twelve-foot stretch. She watched him turn her own exact favored angles. Susan watched her boy do right-faces at the same four points she liked.

That he had long ago forgiven her seemed a wish impossible as eternal life. Now, settled on the sofa nearest, legs drawn under her, she sat studying only him. He soon joined her there. Leaning nearer, she inhaled so deeply she wheezed. Michael trailed a scent. Eyes closed, she identified: lightly-salted butter, motel shampoo, the fine lanolin of an animal still growing. She longed to cry. But could not waste that kind of time.

Something must happen next. Just the chance excited her. Susan accepted this boy's ingenuity at finding her, his plain good faith in leaping walls of fire. She already felt his gratitude rush out to meet and then quadruple hers. They even grinned alike—each's deepest dimple swagged up to the right. But such giddiness contained the terror of its ending. Having finally worked their way into one another's field of vision, how to leave this safe-zone without perishing?

This interlude already seemed some long-deferred repayment. Legs tucked beneath her, supporting his side with hers, Susan found pleasure even in hearing her own Sub-Zero ice-maker's egg-laying due diligence. Coins dropped into a sack of alms. Her father's death had stained lake water twenty feet around. But, from those dark currents, this clear child ascended. She felt time, long-divided, returning to itself in strange renewing eddies.

HE MUSTN'T LEAVE. That ugly car of his had a gear marked REVERSE. True, he kept one arm still shepherd-crooked around her shoulder here now. And yet Susan felt—even while held by this much-visiting grace—more scared than ever. Something about his height, his crafted force and Roman looks. Some quality of his half-spooked her. Hard to identify what—in such a bonus—should so unsettle her. Some Protestant filter, usually stringent in protecting from temptation, felt torn away by the simple sight of him and lost for good. Was it his arriving as a full-grown man? Was it wrong of a mother at first sight to find her own son beautiful? Shouldn't that be natural? Still, a list kept trying to form. She needed "To Do" something.

His hand moved to stroke her hair. She sensed how her hair's texture must feel—to *him*—much like his own. (She made a note to urge his leaving all such sticky preparations out of hair so fine as theirs. She'd also instruct him to say "anyway," not "anyways," and in the right use of "you and I" versus "you and me." So many silly small improving things she'd teach him first, it would be great!)

HE KEPT STARING at her face, then looking all around, then back into the eyes. Michael was thinking of leaving. She saw he feared he'd overstayed. Everything must now be taken back. He now sat—saving up this day and her. It would be a long haul back to tomorrow morning's Apple Store.

He scanned side-to-side, someone soon-departing, poor boy, checking out her home. Not with much admiration. More as he would some crime-scene he'd be quizzed about a year from now. The floor plan he would need to know to save himself in court.

"What a terrible hostess I am. Here it is, past noon. And have you even *eat*en, Michael? Jesus, the first time I get to *feed* my son, and I'm so happy I forget! What do you *want*? Anything!" At that, he curled against her shoulder, smiling. And then, as if finally convinced of finally being with her, he finally closed his eyes. More weight shifted against her ribs. Almost too much. And within seconds, she saw two neck muscles relax and Michael, slumped full along her, was asleep. "There," she barely whispered. She stared only forward, not wanting to seem greedy.

But Susan could now freely attend the lion-sized *sss*-ing of his breath. She could, slow, turn and inspect him, unembarrassed and at close range. His mouth half-open, she could see his teeth were very good, thank God. Yes, his hard life, working on a farm, begging for his own computer, had given him some junior-salesman's lapel-grabbing half-confidence. But asleep, he was only just teenaged, one raw mammoth male baby.

Proud, she inventoried the eyelashes, his massive tapered hands. The left thumbnail did show powder-blue from being slammed by something. She quaked, imagining all the strenuous labor he had done. It moved her, the picture of him working outdoors. Shirtless, being practical, shirtless if possible. Now, yes, she must also note how, between his legs, packed into and against the left side of these too-plaid trousers, there, bent clumped proof he fully qualified as one of his gender. She felt a mix of family snobbery and secular curiosity.

In the whole world, for her whole life, who else had there ever been?

SHE CALCULATED EVERY mile he'd driven to find her. She had always imagined tracing him; but all along it was *she* who'd needed rescue. She wondered what smiling lie he'd told the retired Marine Corps geezers at the gate. How had he slipped into this smart cul-de-sac driving a Honda that bad-off?

STARING OVER AT his guiltless bulk, she felt herself become a crowd come out to greet him. Her family and even the weak Doc Dennis and his other children, all gathered to admire this sleeper still half-schooled but fully formed.

Susan even glimpsed some narrow footpath toward a future. Till this today, till him, she'd never much believed in one. At age four-teen, she'd had to downgrade. She'd seen her own childish Luck, cut-short, surrender to adult-discount Fate. Did Michael's stepping in here reverse that? Might his cleverness in tracking her mean true Luck's return? It now slept tipped close against her. Luck must weigh a hundred and seventy pounds, easy.

How could there have been so little love on earth just forty minutes back and now, this suddenly, so much?

SHE MUST NOT be late to fetch her elder daughter. That part came clear. Her right breast ached again; she felt some blind command. Susan remembered—once they'd taken away her infant—she had leaked so much private milk. It felt hotter than her body-temperature; as if its own prideful chemistry kept warming it, warming it for one small lost mouth. So much had been wasted, blotting the home's overstarched sheets. She recalled nursing a baby she had borrowed at the movies. She remembered the policeman's big black shoes outside her bathroom stall. "Best to give it back, miss. You'll have your others. My wife and me got six. But, miss, that one, it's not strictly yours. Please."

How passive she had been! Shouldn't she have fought harder for this boy here? Might she not have run away while he was still kicking safe inside her? Milk was just the start of everything unclaimed. "Things To Do While You Were Out: 'Nurse Firstborn.'"

Yes. Now, feeling relieved, she reached to unbutton her white blouse. Beginning with top-button number-one, she imagined

80

breastfeeding him at last, even if the deed now offered scant food value.

Just then Michael opened his eyes. He saw her, grinned and yawned and stretched at once. He recognized at once where he was; his whole face opened like the Book of Genesis. Firewalls broke like piecrusts.

"Hungry?" She smiled toward her halted unbuttoning.

"Whoa. Maybe a sandwich, at least to start with!?" He laughed. It was how he said it.

Susan whispered down into his waking, "I've kept ex*pect*ing you." She meant she had prophesied his coming; she also heard that word admit to his awaited birth. If a young mother is forcibly etherized, deprived of recalling bringing forth the child, her bearing him never seems to end . . . Not till the child himself bounds in, then curls against her fully, one divided body closing in to finally forgive itself.

SHE'D NEED TO tell him about her present, incidentals: the all-too-decent husband, two smart daughters quick to laugh. But it seemed wrong mentioning them yet. Nor did she want those others to yet see this unlucky boy who looked like Luck itself. Even Susan had only got to stare at him these precious first, what? twenty (maybe eighty?) minutes.

The phone rang again. That Michael might leave before Choral Society-practice-pick-up already worked in her a new insanity. She knew she'd release a screech rivaling her mother's on first stepping off the boat. Susan had never felt more pity for her mom than she did right now, simply looking at this young boy well-formed. You could've almost designed such a one for yourself. And then to have sent him off to bunk with fundamentalist fascist farmers! But if, in the end, he worked hard enough to find and then return to you, didn't that make him even more yours?

"I FINALLY GET to make my boy a sandwich, bird!" she addressed the sparrow in her kitchen. It now cocked its head as if trained to. Even this wild thing seemed their pet. Susan, pulling out her very best Dijon mustard, asked young Michael's future plans, his hopes, at least. They chatted even as she pointed to his rightful counter stool while she cut bread. Kitchen walls showed the pretty glossy butter-yellow of well-being. Soon, sandwiches. The sparrow perched on a windowsill, then mantel, chandelier, valance, window again. It was getting used to having them in its room.

Susan wondered aloud about her son's schooling so far. He said, sure, he wanted to go more into computers, game theory, all that. Yeah, college would be great. But what with these unbelievable student loans you had to pay off . . .

She'd soon made him three separate sandwiches, not keeping count. She explained she'd best phone to cancel her small part in a meeting she must miss tonight; she'd explain that some pressing unexpected family matter had come up. True enough.

"But wait. Where are you *stay*ing?" she asked at last.

"Out U.S. 70 Business. Hampton Inn."

"Your eldest sister will need picking up from choir-practice in twenty minutes. I'll do that. —But, here. The house key. Now go and get your stuff, babe."

CURTAINS DOWN

"THANK YOU," I tell my friend Jemma.

We're in her car during this sleet storm. She's just explained to me the truth about the mother-son. We met them only tonight. Of course, from ancient texts and hillbilly legends I knew about such deeds. I've just never spent any time with the actual folks.

As my friend drives us home from the musical, I keep unusually silent, six whole blocks. November's storm keeps throwing gallons of rain at us, pounds of torn red foliage strike our windshield.

Jemma ends her plain version of the tale. ("So she's really his mother, see?") I already sit imagining a hundred ways one person might tell another such a saga. So many questions live hidden in it. First, you'd gather all known facts. Once grasped, those might offer you a new way of knowing. After documenting, you must imagine inward, capturing some fraction of the costs to them, the reward of it.

I turn toward my friend and say, "Thanks, really. Sad, odd. Guess it's good to know such things can happen. God, how people adapt. And it does sort of make sense, step by step, which is how we live, I guess. In days. Strange, having just met them and how much we liked them. —But, just curious, Jem, by telling me? what did you want me to *guess?*"

She smiles at my ingratitude. "Just figured it'd interest you. And they chose to sit beside us. Their story sort of found us. And because you're jumpy and exhausted from waiting to hear about your book. Your friends want you always in the *mid*-dle of your next novel. You alone will know if this sort of thing has any, what? story potential for a writer like you. Most sane ones wouldn't touch it with a borrowed pole.

"You say you're always interested in whatever brings people back to Falls. Don't you think she'd be the last person on earth to come home? Atlanta's all strangers and safe. Maybe people do return to scenes of crimes, especially crimes against them. She seems that determined not to feel ashamed. Look, would you rather I *hadn't* told you? 'Cause I can see it's already got your attention." My head shakes yes. Again I thank her: "Likely you haven't heard the end of this."

She explains how other parents at school tittle-tattle about these two. Word got out fast. In so few years since high school she hadn't changed that much. The couple ignores rough treatment. It's as if everybody sees them but no one can admit it. Might as well be ghosts here. Tonight, nobody spoke to them. No one saved seats for them.

"It scares people." Jemma keeps driving. "After he turned up in Georgia, I guess all five of them tried living in that one big house. Didn't work out. So here they are in Falls, at local pageants where she started. Her oldest daughter has real talent. I don't even know how *I* feel about it all. Only just learned about their being kin. One gossipy old teacher's aide. —Still, even before I told you the truth, I saw in your eyes you'd half-guessed, too. Now other moms here won't let their daughters sleep over at Susan's. Michael's half-sisters, they're just crazy about him. Well, you met him and see how easy

84

that is. Since he turned up with his cell phone in her drive, his mom, she's smoothed him off some. Upgraded his clothes, taught him the forks. Got him a real car. But I doubt even their older girl knows yet, really knows, not the full story.

"Susan got custody of the daughters. Has a day job, editing online. She's quit leading book groups. Likely all those trophy wives she never trusted finally felt free to cut her dead at Nordstrom's. Probably jealous all along. Simplifies things, I guess. They say she's putting him through grad school. Some math, higher math. He commutes to State. We sometimes see the four of them at movies, eating popcorn from one giant tub. They ski. People say their skiing's almost Olympic-level. Fearless, the four of them.

"Her doctor-husband, must have been a sweet enough guy, didn't make the fuss he might've in court. He's the one you have to feel sorriest for. That's one squeeze-play no husband can expect!—Still, remember what *you* said, right after meeting them? Before I even told you?"

"Uh-oh. No. Remind me."

"'Real family-unit-feel.' You guessed they likely met only after some trauma or natural disaster, 'maybe even some resort tsunami-rescue-type thing.' 'Both pretty, and pretty much made for each other.'"

"I said that? Guess I did, huh? Oh dear. Did I also mention needing to hurry your place and make us two pretty stiff drinks?!"

We laugh. Now I'm asking, do these two share a last name? I could look things up, even later tonight. What's fascinating—it's real and we just met them. Same events that overwhelm Greek dramas live on side streets paying taxes in our smallest towns. Of course, after discovering certain facts, someone careful would have to document into being the coincidences and emotions. Someone would get to. Instead of disapproving, someone could decide, where possible, to try and love all this alive.

Storm-soaked, we dodge into my friend's warm house. First-thing I build a little fire. I know where everything is. What a good use for last Sunday's *Times*. I hear Jemma in her kitchen. She's pulling out ice, our favorite glasses, half-a-bottle of Jack Daniel's.

We've settled in as firewood catches fast. We pour bourbon and find we want to make some sort of toast.

We can only think of them.

We can only choose to bless them.

So many routes to joy.
Most of them, detours.

SAINTS HAVE MOTHERS

For Elizabeth Spencer

I

My daughter often gave away my shoes. Orange rubber garden clogs, Easy Spirit flats, all migrated overnight from my bedroom to the poor. She left me standing before a closet newly-purged. She left her mother—fully-dressed, having finally found the car keys—innocent of owning footwear.

STILL, MY GIRL was born a somebody. And they can do as they like. Us others? At our luckiest we're *with* somebody.

Falls, NC, always told us she was one amazing little girl. No argument from Mom here. I never minded showing her off downtown. Very early I taught her the alphabet. Neighbors warned she'd be bored in school. But as I changed her final didies, Caitlin read aloud to me. Her efficient goodness warmed then spooked us. The first word her brother said was, "Touchdown." But Cait? she flung out both plump arms and cried up, "Love!" (Call me selfish; I would have settled for "Mommy.")

We had a cocker spaniel she named Cookie and the creature got very sick from eating part of a deer hit by some car. Pretty little golden dog but with God knows what awfulness forever going into its mouth. Caitlin was three then and her dad worked upstairs in his office; I'd stepped next door, trying to learn cooking from my one neighbor who baked. Caitie came rushing over. "Cookie's super-sick, Mom." Crying, my girl led us to our bathroom where the poor dog stood going from both ends, looking thoroughly ashamed of itself. But Caitlin, even that young, had seen all this about to happen. And, to spare my needing to clean up later, she'd hoisted a fair-sized retching dog into our tub. So I could just rinse dog-damage down the drain. Cait, sobbing, stood patting Cookie's back curls as our neighbor waved me into the hall.

"At three years old? Are you kidding? *I* would not have known to stick a streaming dog into the tub, and I'm forty. What your day-care ladies say about her is true, Jean. She's not a baby, she's the American damn Red Cross. Unsinkable. —God, Jeannie, aren't you re*lieved*?"

But I was not.

Sure, I felt proud; but also worried and—to be honest—forever slightly irked. See, I already feared for her. I resented in advance the exhaustion her very openness would likely cost her, then me. She forever left our front door open. Birds, mice, cold fronts, panhandlers, ragtag Jehovah's Witnesses, all came straight in.

—You can be so afraid *for* somebody, you grow half-scared *of* them. Is it wrong to want your child to live—safe because selfish—past age eighteen? I sensed what overmuch potential might expose Cait to.

She was intelligent as I; some would say smarter (and therefore more confident and so, kinder). Even then I guessed she'd never let that brilliance grow only self-critical; Cait would never savage herself as I've been accused of doing, as I have done.

She was born into an age when it's just great to be a girl, no questions asked. I'm from the generation where, for all our sister-talk, most women don't quite *like* women so much.

SAINTS HAVE MOTHERS

(I can tell you this . . . sons are easier.)

TODAY, IN SUN, I must look a hard sixty, not my usual forty-three. I've just survived quite the transition. Extraordinary children make outsized demands. And the parent, she meets those. Even if not a full somebody myself, I am not unbright . . . And yet, despite being first in my class at St. Cecilia's, aside from the IQ of 156 (not that IQ is everything) . . . I, despite my publishing a poem in the *Atlantic Monthly* when I was just nineteen (if one stickily titled "Spring's Gift [to Her]"), I will die famous—if at all—as this somebody's mother.

I also have the twin boys, ten. But when I hear myself described while wandering our mall, it's, "There goes Caitlin Mulray's mom. Super-smart supposeb-ly. Until you-know-*what* happened. Since then, they say she's turned semi-derango."

You know what's deranged? World events.

EVERY PARENT REHEARSES the phone-call. In my terror it always came at three a.m. . . . . I knew before I answered. It tightened my groin, one farewell birth-contraction. Shaming to be the soggy single parent mentioned on *Alive at Five*. The student described as "brilliant, missing"? Yours, your child.

I, JEAN, REMAIN basically an able person—a Democratic poll-watcher. Probably the last person alive for whom Lyndon Johnson's "Great Society" still seems great. A lapsed Episcopalian, I'm yet in love with the defrocked grandeur of the old prayer book. I continue studying my irregular French verbs (though now I only parlez with that cheerfully-pretentious gay wine-seller at Whole Foods).

Overinformed on U.S. rogue-cop anti-eco foreign policy, my

response has been to grow all our basil and tomatoes. Protesting the War for Petroleum, I've learned to change our Volvo wagon's oil filter. Like my new green rubber boots here, I'm just . . . Jean. Still clean if no longer stylish.

Most recent hard-to-memorize French verb? *Conclure: To conclude, induce, gather.*

AND NOW, AFTER our international drama so publicly endured — my own family has sent me away, as punishment. "Recuperation," my ex-husband calls it. At some Ocracoke Island B&B. Will this ferry *ever* get us there?

Caitlin's father, my ex, the civil engineer, "strongly suggested" I come here to our U.S. coastline's Outer Banks. This is the longest ferry ride I've ever taken. In my whole life, it's my first vacationing alone. I know these rubber knee-boots make me look, as my twins said . . . tsunami-ready. But I needed footgear quick after Cait's last purge. My ex and his new spouse flew east to occupy my house. They'll tend to things while I gather myself out here on my lonesome. But tell me how. No one explained that, see.

MAPPING MY DAUGHTER'S final tribute—music: choral and instrumental, eulogies by folks aged nine to eighty—was the hardest thing I've tried since pushing three babies from my body. And the most satisfying. If that sounds derango, then, hey, I stand accused.

LAST MONTH, HER grieving high school friends made our home their clubhouse. Surrounded by platters of my experimental "fusion" finger-foods, we pulled all-nighters planning our "Celebration of a Caitlin Kind of Life."

My own ignored gifts—as a poet, woman of taste, one underutilized "people person"—got somehow tapped again.

Young men Cait'd secretly swooned about for years just appeared at our house, alive-and-in-person. Actual leads from *Godspell* and *Sweeney Todd*. Two boys in Cait's class I consider handsomest are both named Matthew. I'd never really seen them offstage, not up-close. One is called BlondMatt and the other BlackMatt.

A simple knock at my front door brought me Matt the blue-eyed brunette. His right hand held purple asters with red maple leaves, a gold trumpet shone in the other. Tears streamed from sky-colored eyes.

His soft face was still a child's, the voice had dropped to baritone. "I sure see where she got her cheekbones, 'Caitie's Mom.' This thing with her disappearing into Africa has got us all so whacked. But look, one true thing is, I know the Jeremiah Clarke *Trumpet Voluntary* by heart. Could I maybe play it at Cait's Memory Mass, please? Need to. For personal clothe-ure."

BlackMatt meant "closure." (It was either a speech impediment or some essential mishearing, but did I care?) In English folk songs, there's often a pretty foolish page boy who beds the king's lady just before dying at the king's hand.

Here he stood, jet-dark hair and eyes pure crystal. So I said, "Well, well, it's BlackMatt come a-callin' at last. —Our Caitie just adored you." Such a hug I got!

MY EX, EDWARD, gave me upper-pills to bring. But I don't want my senses dulled, just now especially. Should I take beach hikes? Try "journaling"? (Hideous word, like that other clunker: "parenting.") The family sent me off to this seminar about my favorite poet, Elizabeth Bishop. There will be walking tours near nesting-sites of the many North American seabirds she described. Does this make me sound marginal? The poetry confab was just my family's excuse. Fact is they want me *gone*.

On a suburban street as much a cul-de-sac as ours, I am considered a "brainiac," a "bad left-winger." Amid neighbors' trimmed hedges and polished Lexuses, we live more *au natural*. One thing, I go all-out for Halloween. We blindfold trick-or-treaters, then make youngsters seize peeled grapes: "Cat eyeballs!" You know I've had parents phone complaints that our scenarios scare certain younger kids. Nightmares, even. "Boo!" I address such whiners. "Traditional on October thirty-first. 'Boo!' Ever hear of it?!" and hang up. No imagination.

But here on the Outer Banks, stuck alone hiking some dune, without benefit of those still depending on me, how can I recover? Without my kids, that's a challenge too abstract. I am *for* them. Literally. I need tasks. I'll willingly help short-order-grill the B&B's breakfasts. Anything. Busy is good, since it means them. Me with Leisure, that's the undertow.

THE DAY CAIT flew to Africa, she naturally cleared my closet floor of final excess footwear.

She'd admitted dreading my motherly emotions at the airport. So she invited four friends to drive her. Out back, I pretended busyness, weeding our tomato patch. Kids' red convertible honked and, with one wave, my firstborn's peace sign disappeared down Milford toward The River Road, then off into the International.

I yanked up six more dandelions, resisted sniffling, finally padded barefoot upstairs for a shower. I soon stood looking at my nude and dusty closet floor. I found myself unshod as any African village woman. Somewhere, tribal females are about to shoot up four inches

94

on various teetering wedgie-heights. High-heel divots will soon gouge many a jungle path.

And me? Stranded in the suburbs, shoeless as Eve.

HAVE YOU EVER gone mall shoe-shopping while barefoot?

—Now, *that's* loneliness. Six ladylike corns visible to all.

"You'd be about, oh, a size . . ." then they see your bare white feet pressing their cold terrazzo. A look comes across the faces of young clerks that is hilarious. —Always makes me laugh (which only spooks them more, of course).

I found these new Wellington boots—frog-green, rubber marked-to-move—on the back-page of an outdoorsy catalogue from Maine. I needed travel-wear quick. (Fact is, I'm overqualified for this public kind of trouble. I am a deeply shy person—but so unprominent to start with, no one's ever bothered wondering why.)

SOME TEEN GIRLS shoplift; our Cait, she sacrificed. (I do too but on her it looked good.) In K2, she daily handed her whole bag lunch— the requested kiwi fruit, her adored cream-cheese-olive sandwiches —to three new Mexican classmates as hungry as their dark eyes. Baby Cait saved nothing for herself, smiling. "*No problem-o, mes linda amigos, de nada.*" Finally her teacher hid, weeping, in the cloakroom. The woman wrote us, "Never in my thirty-one years as a public educator have I encountered so selfless a . . ."

In my daughter's school class are two other Caitlins. (You think you're being unique. And so did the others.) But everybody at grammar school just called the extra Caitlins by their last names. That was hard on "Johnson"; far sadder for little "Winooski." Twelve years of that. Even teachers agreed there could be only one *Caitlin*.

My daughter is less part of some gang, more the nubbin of a cult.

Her dad helped start it, praising her white-blond pigtails, the husky alto, blinky eyes swerving with a true-blue sweetness. Never any zits. The kid wakes up smiling, was literally born that way—a mewing half-grin you see on certain blind kittens stretching alive, already imagining milk.

Cait arrived able to sense any hurt animal within three hundred yards. She felt one suffering behind Falls High after a violent storm. An oak had fallen. One large crow lay stunned, slammed to the athletic track. Power lines got yanked across a newly-built field house. First Caitie rushes to the cafeteria, opens the top of her skim milk carton, makes a feeder.

As soon as this turkey-sized crow starts sipping, she scampers gymward. "Oh, super, Coach Stimsom. Awesome you're here! 'Cause power cables just fell across our field house roof. Blue sparks? smelling scorchy? good time for 911? You decide."

"Wildlife Rescuer Saves New Educational Building, Too." She was always in the papers and, of course, I felt proud, being myself pre-eminently Caitie Mulray's fan, security force, and incidental mother.

Look, when a whatever-nobody gives birth to such a somebody, does that not elevate the mom into briefly *being* one? And when her somebody disappears, is the mom not—as sort of first runner-up—expected to fill in during that missing queen's remaining reign?

STILL, I SWEAR if I left my heather cashmere cardigan hanging on the back of a ladder-back chair, if I didn't wear a pair of rundown loafers for three weeks, Caitlin summoned the Goodwill van. — Knowing her as I did, seeing how she deficit-spent her spirit all across tiny Falls, NC, I begged Cait not to overgive to immense summertime Africa, please. I had premonitions from the start. She was already essential to our Carolina animals and strangers, prettier than "pretty," rising school vice pres., our state's chief regional-quota candidate for Radcliffe, at seventeen.

But, no, Caitlin had to rush off and impress another continent, gone to teach reading to people who cannot even afford books. Don't people need spare time and bifocals to peruse a novel, even one donated? I hate sounding selfish. But did Cait listen to her literate yet unsentimental mom? Fact of Life: somebodies heed only other *some*-bodies. You're either a prime number or you're that perspiring older woman carrying everyone's heavy picnic hamper, plus the Handi Wipes and, alas, those fifteen extra pounds. —Okay, nineteen.

Just once—if only for novelty's sake—couldn't my darling have done as I asked?

No.

EVEN NOW, THAT is my question, see. That is why my ex-husband and his newest wife—a steady size 6 dress, the PhD thesis upgraded into her book on Spinoza—that's why they volunteered to move back East and mind my house, my kids. Because, Edward tells me, even after all our grief and scrutiny, he fears I would rather be told I am *right* than to hear how I am *loved*.

(That's only weird because it's usually the males' choice, correct?)

I BOUGHT THIS zip-up suitcase. Doesn't quite match the boots, see? Same catalogue, wholly different greens. Where's quality control? Wouldn't you think—with those long Maine winters to kill — employees might step outside into the snowy glare and coordinate and standardize their in-house colors?

"Gather yourself oceanside a couple-three weeks, Jean. Join other poetry types talking over your sensitive lesbian poet's bird sonnets, whatever. It'll be cheaper than ten days in some Silver Hill clinic-spa-bin. Deep breathing you need. But no more hot-flash actingsout, okay? Poetry's way easier to explain to kids and neighbors than your . . . than *you* . . ."

A middle-class form of shunning. And yet, my thoughts are oddly clear. I mean, at least it's over! The outcome is finally plain. I feel sad, of course, raw. And yet good, too. But *should* I? is the thing.

CONVENIENT HOW THEY'VE glassed-in this ferry's observation booth. Am glad we're up above the engine fumes and all those family vacationers. Look how much gear they've lashed to their cars. Ugly Styrofoam. Still, it's nice that kids get to feed Wonder Bread to so many gulls. Shouldn't the ferry provide the bread? Can't help worry if that single chain stretched back there is strong enough. —I'll keep to myself up here. And no muttering, Jean. Specially if anybody wanders much closer. Not even "single words." A person can claim that her talking out loud is "an aid to concentration." But muttering, plus too much public emoting, can get a gal demoted from red-blooded motherhood to seabird poetry.

We still have hours to that island. —Can't even see the mainland anymore.

II

Parents of other high school co-eds would corner me at malls: complaining they'd overheard daughters discuss the pain of voluntary department-store tongue-piercings. Such girls texted about which boy had the all-time best hair in grades nine OR ten. —And my Cait? busy shipping back-issue *Geographics* to three flooded schools in Nicaragua.

"But kids down there read English?" I encouraged her realism.

"What they 'read' is world imagery, Mom. You so understand this already. You, who left library art books beside our toilets all these years, you kidding? See, I believe a child can catch the habit of questioning from even one image strong enough. Art's not even needed, least not at first. Just one amazing news-photo can 'turn' a kid. The urge to read, to strive, goes on like a switch! —But, silly Mom, you know all this. You *taught* me it!"

Fellow PTA members pressed, "Jean, tell us how you 'humanized' your tween. You could charge for seminars. Your Cait seems welcome in every clique. Goths, jocks, black kids, arty fruitcakes, nobody hates her. Unlike our Millicent, sadly. Oh, and Cait's been real supportive of Millie's ceramics. Been buying the 'artichoke' teapot on-time, a dollar's lunch money per week. —Did you even know, Jean?"

I lied, nodding. "How I managed? *You* diagnose her. —I sure don't understand. She was born a very particular someone. I just held her little car coat. We still have the roadkill cemetery. By age three, Cait made me keep a tarp and shovel in the back of our wagon. If I passed some squashed raccoon, a Great Dane even, she'd scream, she'd grab the wheel till I stopped. Out of sympathy, she'd try wrecking *us*. You would not believe what I have touched and made crosses for. (Don't tell her, but I've shifted that menagerie's improved dirt into our tomato patch.) —Fact is, for me by now, boy-crazy-with-too-much-makeup sounds like fun! Be a relief compared to recycled tin cans with SAVE THE CHILDREN labels Elmer-glued to them, are you kidding?"

Other moms cleared off; they'd heard about my edge. They'd seen my too-elaborate haunted house with me wearing slenderizing black as Hostess Witch. Before the divorce, I always tried keeping my own counsel. Back then, before leaving our house, I'd ask my outfit's separate tops-and-bottoms, "Do you guys agree to even half-match?" But after Eddie moved three thousand miles due west? I quit editing. I said pretty much . . . whatever to whoever overheard.

In a town like Falls, women are so country-clubby they grocery-shop at seven a.m. wearing best jewelry and full-warpaint. Everybody auditioning. But for *what*? And if you're not in one of their three top schlock-reading book clubs, you feel banished. Even certain *Atlantic*-published writers are discounted. One thing I lack is sponsorship. Candor can leave quite the spatial moat around a person. Intelligence should bridge such gaps. But, they smell your IQ on you. Pisses them off.

IN HER SUNNY corner room that the twins envied—Cait's bed linen stayed pulled drum-tight as some novitiate nun's. I'd bring fresh laundry. I'd find my girl's weekly "Must Do" inventory-philosophy printed in three colors on her whiteboard. (I was hardly snooping, was I?):

Caitie-list, today's. 1. Do you really need it? More than others? 2. Hungry? But with a pain in any sense different from the rest's? 3. What expense basic kindness? And, considering it seems easier for you than most, how can you ever run out? Instead of toothpaste (pricey due to ad budgets), baking soda b fine. Once you save some book via memory, why keep it? Brothers Grimm took dictation from old peasant women, did not originate one tale! Popularizers as exploiters? Are novels even valid this late in human history? Can the simply Personal be separated now, teased out, from the general warp-woof of utter Globalism? Fantasy, always a distortion? Argue Escapism's morality, pro-con. Go with the Emerson again. Couldn't X-cessive current-event-junkies like Mom be called escapists too? Explore. 4. Do 12 more improving pushups per day, yes. Reread French essays. "Passé composé" still total ball-buster. Break work into smaller units? Needs breakin. 4a. Wallace Stevens.

> They said, "You have a blue guitar,
> You do not play things as they are."
> The man replied, "Things as they are
> Are changed upon the blue guitar."

5. Whether to dye eyelashes dark . . . ? Safety issues. But color would keep you fm. looking like washed-out lab rat. Being this Blond so SUX.
   —"A good song can only do well." —Woody Guthrie."

*

I STOOD HERE, replenishing her clean little midriff-baring T-shirts. Her fresh ones were resting stacked against my own midsector (fully-covered, thanks). Caitie is a list-lover like her engineer dad. They overtrust logic. She sounds, she is, soooo young. Are my girl's jottings admirable or crazed? —Why waste time on such distinctions?—her scratch-pad doodles are the workshop of a somebody.

Here hung the mind-gym of Radcliffe's next early-decision southeastern U.S. shoo-in. That's a fact; and Caitlin Mulray, originally of my own body, was already *out there*—online, com-modified—almost a geographic fact at seventeen.

I AM NOT like Caitlin, travel rattles me. Stage fright gives me near-strokes, even at PTA. I grew up on one street, married the boy from two blocks over. We then settled a literal stone's throw from our old grammar school.

Yes, I begged Cait not to spend her last high school summer off doing good in Africa. You think she listened? Am I already repeating? Probably. No, she sensed that further volunteering would look excellent on her college applications. So she went. And with her father's blessing. The rest of what occurred to her, then us, the sadness with its killer one-two shock, even got us (under Human Interest) into *USA Today*. If short and at the back and stuck below bad future gas prices. "A Model Student, a Parent's Worst Fear, and Then . . ."

—YOU KNOW HOW it is with Mothers and Daughters: Dogs and Cats.

My own mom's name was Iris. My father shortened that to Ice. "Meet my wife, Ice." A trial lawyer, good on his feet, Pop could out-argue most men but never the pale sickly girl he wedded-bedded. Ice informed my kindergarten girlfriends that she had led Raleigh's Cotillion, then played Shaw's Cleopatra at St. Mary's. Ice slept in white gloves full of white cold cream to "save my hands." Saved for *what*, Ice never said.

My childhood home's side tables were lidded with glass, glass coasters sparing even first-layer protection. Ice's being basted in unguents for life, it finally made her the best-moisturized dead lady in local mortuarial memory. Hateful person, if one singularly brilliant. Ambitious for me, of course—years of lessons at every lady-skill taught within forty miles—dressage, decoupage, floral arranging, piano. And I, offered all that prep, what did I aspire to be? Oh, picky picky, I held out for becoming *divorced mom of three*.

STILL, BEING A warmer parent than Mother, I've tried becoming super (Cait's word) at least at *this*. I've honestly given it my everything. Whatever might save or even *in*terest my girl. Whatever that costs.

—All morning on this chugging boat, I've recalled funny talks with Caitlin in my head; and in there, at least, we still share the odd giggle. I'm yet startled by her stray bilingual puns. One in three truly dazzles. Odd, I'm so unused to being on my own without the kids. I am not quite sure how I come across here. They usually interpret for me, protecting their harried, driven mom.

I did not rate a career as concert pianist, though few girl-children ever practiced harder longer. But, now at their school or ballparks you'll find me awaiting my darlings in certain choicer parking slots right up front. Yes, terror of crowds ruined my girlhood ballet recitals but now I'm fearless at beating others into the car-queue by 2:10 p.m. I'm brilliant at finding a really "good spot" one hour early so I can retrieve mine or stay late if need be—whatever my incipient geniuses need—extra-tech-rehearsal, added free-throw clinic. Once there, I am the silhouette, mine is the head stooped over her steering wheel absorbing Public Radio civics, old French tapes, replaying *Grand Opera for Dummies*. I married Ed while a rising sophomore at Sweet Briar. But even now, tucked over my car's sun visor, you'll find note-cards enabling self-improvement, even at long red lights:

Irr. French verb: Maudire: "to curse."

LIKE ICE HERSELF, I'm not a "natural" parent—too tense to be literal, not trusting enough to relax ungirdled into being Mother Earth, the turquoise-wearing bread-baker. Still, I've learned to fake a certain bovine calm. But I can ruin even that with stabs at burbling charmingness.

I've sometimes overheard my kids soothe their little friends, "She didn't mean to barge in just now and go so loud. Mom's good underneath. Only, around strangers she sometimes tries too hard is all. But you should see her when she thinks she's mainly by herself. Boy, then she can act almost happy."

Living alone with them, I am in motion by five-thirty a.m. First thing, while compiling school lunches, I read my precious lifeline the *New York Times*. (I think the headlines are messages seeking my help, smarts, untapped diplomacy.) I'll clip the odd article—anti-doping sports items for my boys, reviews of works on poetry and African economics for Cait. But I won't let them see the whole paper, the rancid world picture, till *after* dinner-hour. I am their morning filter. The world is too disturbing for those just starting out soft-boned. Let my wee ones imbibe adult-strength Chaos just a pinch at a time. Their homoeopathist, my dosages show mercy.

I'LL SKIP CAIT'S eye-popping PSAT scores, her all-state-orchestra

104

flute skills. At sixteen she won a national contest, Best Poem Concerning the Homeless. Her sestina she titled "Outside It." This meant Cait got published in a regional (if not a national like the *Atlantic*) magazine. She was soon enlisted by a local crew that distributes soup and free blankets in our Old Town's most dangerous alleys.

Her adult supervisor, this laissez-faire Quaker wearing filthy wire specs, swore he'd keep an eye on her. But when I asked how many kids worked under him on Caitie's late-night shift, he said, "Roughly nineteen, take or leave a few, why?"

Sometimes it would be 3 a.m. and she was still out wandering the street of train station bars, her backpack stuffed with pounds of power-bars for favorite junkies. The girl was seventeen and scarily pretty. She favored short tops, low jeans. Beautiful navel, if I do say so myself. Some midriffs are too ideal for even Falls' idea of a slum at 3 a.m., thanks.

One night I made Cait hysterical by loading her pajama-ed brothers into our battered wagon while patrolling the town's darkest streets. First I'd find, then guard her. I'd had a premonition. Caitlin, when busted by Mom, would roll her eyes then shoot me the finger whilst struggling even harder to blend in with the Ragged.

Once I caught her supporting a very old bum so he could pee against a wall. First I spotted her pink canvas backpack she won't ever let me wash. Helping him, she looked like a nineteenth century English nurse, newly-graduated. Cait was picturesque in the strong simple way she hoisted this scrawny bearded misfit. She did everything for him except pulling out what my sons these days—somewhat optimistically—call their *main drains*. She did appear lovely doing it.

I vowed I'd never let my daughter know I'd seen this happen.

*

—YES, A GIRL who'd give away the new novel you are reading, with just thirty gripping pages left to go. Cait passed our stuff to the Needy, meaning those even Needier than we. See, I've been clever at stretching Ed's child support. (My tricks: cheap maple syrup funneled into bottles that once held the real stuff. I only do such transfers late, the kids asleep.)

It gave my darlings a false sense of security. I clearly overdid the job on Cait. First she hated being a spun-sugar blonde; then she felt all guilty for our wealth. If she'd only known!

When I summoned her downstairs to close the front door again, she lectured me—in her most patient singsong—about how Saint Francis, when he sought virtue? had to purge himself of his aristocratic family's lavish clothes? before he could even, like, *start* being bare-boned good! Strange but in that same sainted way, I—stripped shoeless by my kid—was forced to send off for this footgear needed to begin my own jail-term holiday.

LAST SPRING, SHE runs in with a letter, tells me the homeless poem has won her a summer internship plus free transportation to said job. "Great, dear. —A ride where?"

"Africa," her smile ignites and she's immediately listing ten tropical-disease-shots she'll now need. Then I say something awful. I usually do. (Other people claim they regret making certain sharp replies, but they mean they wish they *had*. Me, I blurt, then waste my life force regretting whatever just leaked.)

"You'll cure disease in Africa over my dead body! —Young lady, you're one inch from getting into Radcliffe (and you *know* how I've always felt about that school). Now you want to jet clear to Africa, and why? To hold up old tribal-bums so they can pee against . . . straw huts?"

Horrified, she gave me such a look: first pure fear, then—far worse—the visual wash of total Caitlin pity. She settled on the floor beside my rocker. She placed her head so it must be cradled in my lap. I pressed my hand against her warm ear, her cheek.

"What hurt you so early, Mom? Your bitterness scared Dad off, okay. But I keep imagining what it's gotta daily cost *you*. Was your Ice Queen mom as frozen-solid as you say? Then I totally hate her for maiming you. For how she'd hide your lipstick, follow your dates' cars, eavesdrop on phone-calls. Harsh. I cannot imagine. Gran was truly twisted. —But, look, is it getting *worse* for you? 'Cause, lately you seem . . . Mom? let me take some of it on myself, whatever the burden. I know I'm not super-fun to live with. One grin from me at breakfast seems to work your last nerve. I see it in your face. And I'm sorry. Truly. With me trying everything out and heading to far places, it must make stuff way harder here. Even so, Mom, I can't quite see I have a choice. The divorce made you want to hold us even tighter. Probably natural, you ole sweetie. But, my growing up fast? my taking chances? that's one life path I can't refuse. Ask for anything else, Mom. —Love you. And am definitely going."

(In*cred*ible girl. —Who could not love her?)

HER FATHER JOHN-HANCOCKED Cait's every travel waiver. Anybody ask for my permission? I was not even technically a "Mrs." now. My body had just been her emergency landing chute, a chute that later got up and walked around, believing it still had rights. Edward let the Quakers off the hook in advance for whatever dire might happen abroad.

Even so, the girl was nearly eighteen. She could have left without my blessing, which—I hated myself afterward—she had not got.

*

THREE GALS FROM Cait's school are what're nowadays called "boy magnets." It's either funny or sickening how many full-grown boys and married men in cars will circle a given house containing one small-boned promiscuous girl. Or no, not even sexually-active necessarily, just beautiful (if in a far coarser way than my Caitie). But our home forever had that yellow Goodwill van swooping into our cul-de-sac.

Caitlin kept its mobile number punched among her cell's "top ten." I eventually knew the two main drivers' names. "Mrs. Indian Giver," they teased me as my station-wagon followed their truck, me honking, signaling again, *Pull over, at least give the* blender *back. No questions asked.*

LET'S SEE: CAITIE palmed off her own desk chair. She passed along to strangers my only broken-in walking shoes. Next to bite the dust, our admittedly-seldom-used backyard picnic table, then the pretty red Ann Taylor blazer I'd bought her a month before she left. "What are you, prepping me for stewardess school, Mom?" She looked darling in it too. Like a Norwegian guide at the UN.

Also missing, a solid-silver family christening cup, circa 1840 and therefore in admitted need of polish. That proved to Cait I hadn't daily earned it. (What certain of Falls' poor folks did with it, Christ knows. Melted into pawnable ingots probably.) But oh, my girl always felt wonderful afterward.

The more I yelled at Caitie, the more canonized she looked, eyes on the ceiling, lit way up. Secretly, I found her openhandedness not uncute. But I still had to instruct her, straight-faced for Character's sake.

I scowled but nobody was more a connoisseur of her beauty's many unearthly moods. It is comforting to have gorgeous kids. But you mustn't be caught gloating about your somebody's looks, especially by them.

"Radiant," the tributes all repeated. She appeared especially-so after donating major furniture. Her coloring skimmed between the silver and the pink, as platinum as I'd once been. A rosy freckled child born for causes. She is not the kind of girl who tortures you by being bad. That'd be too easy.

I once found Jehovah's Witnesses reorganizing their tracts along my granite kitchen counter with Cait feeding them my famous oatmeal cookies. Discovering six windows open in August, I'd yell, "Caitlin Mulray, we are not cooling the entire globally-warmed out-doors." "Why not, Mom?" Her comic answer undercut her own goodie-two-shoes earnestness. "Can't every citizen make a difference by lighting one little cooling ozone candle, hmm? Jeez, Mom. 'The Melting Polar Icecap That Could' might cheer up, if only each house on earth would air-cool its yard for just, like, three minutes a day . . ." then she cackled. Joking about her own solemn doomsday rhetoric. Play: a sure strategy for a person's surviving anything. Or so I told myself . . .

Caitie'd had braids since turning five. Her father claimed she looked like the teenage Ingrid Bergman. She did have the film-star skin that gives back value-added light. But, however lovely our Cait, the fact is: nobody else has ever looked like Ingrid Bergman young. (Not even her own bright if slightly off-brand daughter.)

III

SO, YES, AFRICA. My overachieving Caitlin could not stay home and simply teach wood-and-bead-craft at the state park four miles from town. Oh nooo, that'd be too typical. She had to go drill ABC's into tribal babies with flies working the wet corners of their little eyes. I feel for them, don't get me wrong. But what's the use—when one whole continent's unappeasable hunger is offered the single steamed-dumpling of my child's 99 lbs.? Or so ran my rude suburban reasoning as she stuffed the one pink backpack she'd agreed to take.

Cait asked her kid brothers what they wanted her to bring home from Africa.

"Spears? Spears!" Nicky said. Caitie made a mouth, started to do a prim explanation about the Dark Continent's actual modernity, but wisely gave that up. Look, if the place is all that up-to-date, why is she so desperately needed to come teach there at age seventeen? Her brothers' request did crack me up, though: bring us our own personal spears!

Boys are simpler creatures.

That's why we women need men so. The ultimate flattery:

Men are so simple, they think *women* are!

*

SHE LANDED IN Cape Town and promised to call me at once. I had paid in advance for a new super-duper cell phone with flash-camera attachment and all these bonus hours. I'd half convinced myself that this new appliance might *draw us closer together*. I believed the brochure! The twins and I would eat a lot of "mac and cheese" to offset this onetime telecommunication expense.

Eventually she thought to check in, explaining how her whole new country seemed a dead zone in terms of cellular reception, maybe the dry heat? One week later, from a hotel pay phone— shouting over some bad live combo's "Raindrops Keep Fallin' on My Head" (a good sign?)—she reverses charges; Cait admits her silver mobile has already been stolen. "He barely jostled me. But considering the unbelievable poverty here, who can blame one little go-to thief? He was a child. Shows initiative," she adds with a laugh.

Two weeks later, it's the day she turns eighteen, Caitlin Mulray finally lets me know she is still alive. A "somebody" always reverses charges to "whatever."

"PLEASE GO OUT and buy another phone, hon. Show some youthful initiative your*self*." There comes the pause. I know these. They always mean, What an Out-of-Shape Upper-Middle-Class Idiot You Truly Are, Pillow-Woman.

"Mother? Probably it's nerve-shredding having your first kid abroad alone. But here's a little 'Google Earth to Mother'? I am on the, uh, *veldt*. We're so far into nature, how can I phrase it? — Maybe, 'There's not even a *Target* out here, Mom'? You know I love you and want to help relax your obsessive-compulsive thing. But here's a news crawl for you—'I am in Affff-ri-ca, Mo-tther.'"

"Thank you for clearing that up, Cait. 'Across the Great Wat-er,' right?" I long to tell her that, my suburban cul-de-sac address aside,

111

I am not exactly brain-dead. I actually published a poem in the *Atlantic Monthly* when I was nineteen, barely nineteen; so she has less than one year left. Instead I literally bite my tongue.

NO, I DO not like to be sneered at as some soccer-Volvo-lump—certainly not by the person whose every jump shot, steeplechase, flute lesson I have paid for, then convincingly overpraised. But irked as I feel, with this much long-distance drying between us, I dare not defend myself, not now. That might block her next call to me, one essential to her mother's own continued breathing. So for once jolly Jean here even tries *tact*.

I ask her to describe the kids she's teaching. How many? probably cute, huh? Cait answers, Thirty hilarious and ever-so-responsive boys ages eleven to nineteen, is exactly what she says. I inquire as to what she does after lessons with her limited free time. "Oh, we eat pounds of roasted chicken feet we buy from this sweet little old man, Abas. (Mother, I guess I'd say that chicken feet are the potato chips of Africa.) Then we all jump into the pond, a swimming hole that has cypressy tannin in it so its water's black as ink but always the perfect temperature." Trying for further bonding girl-talk about clothes-and-mini-pads-and-makeup, I ask which of her two as-yet-undonated swimsuits she's brought with her. Again, the pause that chills all mothers' souls. Especially when it rolls clear back from toasty grassy Africa to milder, lawn-mown Falls, NC . . .

This silence seems a schooling flash-freeze lesson for your heart. You fear this is your starter-blast, prep for that long-dreaded night-time communiqué we parents most fear. Sleep's hush gets punctured by the three a.m. phone call from some international stranger who has just found your kid's broken form along a jungle pathway.

112

Caitlin remains silent to my wondering aloud which bikini she's favoring.

"No suit at all, hunh, Caitie mine? Brilliant. You are the only blond female in that whole jungle country. Your father, at least, thinks you look like Ingrid Bergman, young. You mean to tell me you are skinny-dipping with forty butt-naked African men 'hilarious and ever so responsive' of all ages?"

"Yeah, and?" she snaps.

"Christ, Caitlin, if I have to EXPLAIN . . ."

—I THINK IT'S that, like Cait, I have also been giving things away all my life. To others, always others. I see how profoundly gifted she is. Hard to explain how she often enters a room like delayed news of some Democratic victory. And the sec she leaves, that room feels six degrees cooler, more than ninety-nine pounds emptier.

It's organic and inevitable, my wanting her to achieve the several things I haven't. Look, I know how being really smart can jeopardize a very pretty girl. I think of my own talents, how mine sometimes seemed to cut me off from the very things those should've unlocked. Big gifts upset little people. Not to mention Beauty.

Hard admitting but, on my worst days, I wish I were as conventional and right-wing as most neighbor ladies out our way. They sense my judging. It doesn't make me a bit more popular.

"What's *she* got to be so jacked about? Hand-carving the forty pumpkins paving her yard for trick-or-treat? Her *weight*? Who her ex *was*?!" Oh, I hear them, one-aisle-over not-unloud, in discount stores. They then go on about an idolized local doctor; about who got onto the country club membership committee and how that affects their chances. People are limited. And I am not so ditzy as they claim. But name one way I might shame Falls into admitting it?

Whereas Cait sees everybody as a fellow wounded creature she alone can cure. This brings the girl so much love at once! Her prize poem was technically perfect, without ever smirking over its *finish* as mine had. My ditty was only about spring; hers faced actual hunger. At nineteen, I was still trapped in ladylikeness. (Even Plath was then, as *Mademoiselle* magazine's college guest editor.) But my Cait, she'd already cut through all that. She owned "the chops" and subject matter, both. Making shapes from the worst of the mess of the world.

My one hope? "May my child wind up with a life that is *about* her."

AFTER CAIT'S PHONE-CALL, I could not get through again. I annoyed the 1-800-Alltel support girl. Her contention was that Africa boasts excellent reception. "Oh?" I tell her. "Cells pretty prevalent? Must be hard to get booster towers set up across desert and jungle and so forth, no?" "We always support our technology. It's there for those able to access and understand it. That, madam, is why we even *use* the phrase 'World Wide.'" I hung up so fast. Imagine insulting a paying customer, and with my IQ. Still, I got the hint: Cait might've had me, if not actually blocked, then taken off her top-ten-fave list. Was our relationship changing?

TIMES I TELL myself, I'm incognito, only briefly playing Tubby Abandoned Wife. Hell, I'm so undercover I can't recall my own first, preferred identity. Though inwardly talkative, I seize up before a microphone, a crowd. This means I "dwell in shadows," as my worst girlhood poem put it. Why live disguised here in this minor town encircled by tobacco-rich farmland? Where else, with three kids? Manhattan? On *my* alimony? A single parent must do all the heavy lifting, including that most strenuous of bench presses: daily making it look effortless, even *fun*!

My folks sent me to finishing school to learn finger bowls. Teachers at St. Cecilia's urged my reading Sarah Teasdale's poems. She'd been a talented sickly St. Louis girl who wrote poems good enough to get her to Manhattan and win a Pulitzer. But she married some Missouri business-traveler. He left her at home alone till she got so sad, the poor thing killed herself. Some role model! My gender's generation was programmed to offer fullest energy to families, then boyfriends, next husbands, finally kids, grandkids. Sure it was okay for a bright girl to publish the stray poem, but only as some sidelight parsley garnish, thanks.

Whereas kids Cait's age make brutal actual choices. GIRLS CAN DO ANYTHING! her soccer team's bumper sticker announced. Youngsters've been spared their mothers' thickening ankles and slowing guilt. Today's girls scrap harder midcourt than boys often dare. Gals stand seven feet tall, fearless. Black and white Athenas passing the ball, nobody "hogging" as many of your males will. I came to half-worship her almost-championship 4A team. Once I walked into their locker room to take Cait her chamomile thermos and, naked, they all looked so muscular and long, I thought I'd blundered into the *boys'*. I felt secretly faint. A hot flash? (Great decade to turn lesbian! Bit late for gals my age to retool, alas. Me? I am a one-man woman . . . without one!)

But Caitkins wasn't just about being physically powerful; she was already promiscuous . . . with her heart. Indiscriminate. "Love!" the first word. Usually spells trouble. With some folks, Empathy itself becomes the disease.

It opened the world to her too suddenly.

AFTER AN UPSETTINGLY good school production of *Sweeney Todd*, I overheard the mom of one hefty girl-ceramicist ask Caitlin what *her* weight-loss plan was. I stepped over, answered for her, "Willful death by hunger after giving her food and mine to lepers."

"Mom is a comedian," Cait grinned both her dimples at the woman. "Only nobody has ever *not*iced."

I laughed. Some mothers might've thought, *Why, you little tramp, undercutting me publicly!* Instead I admired my daughter's thinking that up. I understood she'd said it just to cheer me. She knew I would find only a body-slam against myself truly comical.

Women's work is never done.

PEOPLE SAY I have been short with her. If only she were traveling with some trusted girlfriend whose cell service I'd provide. Some gal who might monitor Cait while sneaking me concerned sisterly bulletins, some dear little snitch.

If I were still married to Cait's dad, he might help offset my usual tensions. Eddie could once joke me past this small nightly fear or that. He'd begun our married life as one darling heat-seeking missile. Fast Eddie was I-won't-take-no-for-an-answer wearing white socks and jockeys. Cait inherited that forward-leaning drive from my pretty Boy Scout. But Ed, in lieu of helping me with her, moved to sleek Republican La Jolla. He then signed every release that'd ship her over there beyond my aid and observation. By phone, Ed insisted I relax: Cait's innocence protected her.

I shot back, "Tell that to the police. No, better, Ed, tell it to your Unitarian-Universalist God. You remind Him of her return flight's date, umkay? I'll hold you both accountable but will probably call you *first*."

Till recently, her sweet belief in others did seem to shield her. But you scan your daily papers; you read about the latest folks whose innocence just failed them yesterday utterly and all at once.

SAINTS HAVE MOTHERS

*

MY SKINNY-DIPPER ADMITTED hitchhiking, too. Across Africa. On weekends. In shorts. Probably halters. She did phone her California father; he'd later hint at little adventures never mentioned to the Warden, as she apparently calls me. What good did he think it'd do?—letting me know this? I'll leave that to you. Ed heard something about Cait's tagging along with the U.S. ambassador's son into a mine where six underpaid boy-workers had been trapped. Essay subjects found her like birds homing in on Saint Francis. She was already a shoo-in for Radcliffe. They'd written *her*.

OUR HOME PHONE—usually a-jangle with the Caitlin Waif-Advice Line—male friends in crisis over her female friends—fell silent as the tomb.

Not even *she* called us now. See, I had criticized her skinny-dipping with every boy from Tarzan Country Day. I said that. She screamed I was a racist hag-witch. I told her how, in my time, Tarzan had been white: Anglo parentage, if reared by chimps. I reminded her of a concept often lost on certain publicity-minded do-gooders, little something we call Humor.

True, Cait's swimming naked made me shrill by phone, and on her eighteenth birthday. I knew I shouldn't have. I dearly missed her. I even longed for her Edward-like lists like the last I'd found wadded in a jean pocket on laundry day: *"Turn away (her) anger. Read further Blake. Think ways to end world hunger. At least get Tori and Erick back together. (Note to self. 'No one has ever loved anyone the way everyone wants to be loved'! —So get okay with that, you!)"*

IN OUR LAST upsetting call, I'd explained receiving certain strong premonitions. She interrupted, "Little reality check here, Mom? I

117

can be in AP Calculus three blocks from home, with my desk seat belt buckled (if school desks even *had* those), and you'd still be pacing the kitchen tying up my cell during my one lunch break with your *getting more bad signs*. A miracle any of your loved ones has outlived your pessimism by a week. You, especially."

My new irregular French verb, studied at soccer games: *Moudre: To grind, pulverize.* I longed for her. It was becoming a huge nostalgia of the kind one feels for a place, for one summer at the best waterside resort ever. And yet I seemed only able to express that via warning, scolding her. Caitlin had coolly stated how skinny-dipping with one boy might be considered "invitational," whereas forty . . .

I tried not to let her hear my choking. Nine days after her birthday I'd received not one more call. No way to reach her, either. The school was so rural, drums must still be their idea of Internet. Tribe2tribe.com.

As usual, I blamed myself for her letting seven more days of stillness pass. Weeks! Torture. It was the silent treatment I'd perfected on her father, now turned full-blast against me.

Without her, for the first time since her conception, I washed our kitchen walls. I'd go to bed red-handed, bone-tired and glad to be. As if to spite me, earlier than most, menopause set seriously to work: no Halloween details, please. I even took up knitting a sweater for Cait—maroon, one abandoned three years back—only to ditch the thing again. Irritating how metal needles clicked in my own lap like some slow and spastic clock.

USUALLY FOR INTERVALS of up to three or five months, for sanity's sake, I've been strong enough to stave off one particular memory. But, during her endless silence from the veldt, it seeped back now, esp. come three a.m.

118

I'M PUSHING THE *Baby Cait, newly five, in a grocery cart. After asking her to choose her favorite cereal from among the ninety displayed, I pop one aisle over (for paper towels, smoked oysters, I remember). I come back that fast just as one short old man goes leading my blond bonbon girl away by the hand. He's carrying an unopened package of lollipops. Hasn't even paid for the things yet. And she? just smiling up at him.*

Don't they say molesters try resembling most anybody else so they'll blend in? Well, but this one was almost a midget and looked like that Three Stooges stooge with the greasy bangs, Moe? Moe, I think. Not Larry. The Shriners' Carnival was opening that same day in Falls. So here came the dreaded carny molester with a very good eye and the luck to match. When I shove him into a display of bottled grapefruit juice, much glass breaks with all the racket I'd hoped. Moe runs like holy hell just as the manager appears. "Thank God you're here," I yell. Moe has fled. Cait looks terrified of me, not Moe.

Manager says that, even if I actually did just thwart whatever alien abduction I imagined, I'd made far too much noise. I had left my fellow shoppers wading. Mr. Manager claims he'll have "the juice surcharge" ready whenever I get to the register, so take my time. But I am on my knees in a zone kicked clear of broken glass; I'm pressing Caitlin's springy shoulders in my hands and begging her why.

"Why? After all Momma Jean's lectures about following weird little men, Caitkin. Why'd you just go off with that old clown? Literally.—Why?"

"'Cause he looked so sad, Mommy. And Bongo said he needed me in more ways than you do."

"'Bongo'? Fast worker!"

As usual, on both counts, Cait was technically right. A lesser kid would've lied, claimed the old guy'd forced her. But even months afterward, I would hear my butterscotch-baby sigh. She might be playing with Cookie

119

when the point in her chin would start its killing little tremble as she asked, "Maybe he's some happier, Mom? Maybe Bong's found somebody else to play with?"

One cannot map out for a kid of five in terms too surgical what vile creeps like Bongo want her for. (That'd mean your doing violence to your girl-child preemptively; defeats the purpose, right?) I'd told and told my bonnie-blue darling, "Don't go with strangers."

But for her, you see, there are none.

IV

WITH OUR PHONE useless, I lived even more alone. I grew even more overtalkative around my adorable identicals, Patrick and Nicholas.

Teachers claim they're impossible to tell apart. But their talents differ bunches. Nicholas can draw like a young Raphael, though his chosen subject is as yet X-treme dirt bikes. He has an edgy metallic scent, whereas Patrick smells like sun-cured straw all over. Sadly, Nick got his dad's temper. But both boys also inherited Edward's big hazel eyes and ash-blond hair so thick I can only trim and thin it with a currying comb I buy in *Grooming* at PetSmart.

It's odd I speak of them so little here. But they still lived safely disguised as ordinary stay-at-home boys, unlike their Missionary Field Service of a platinum sister. With Cait gone, we three invented fun expeditions, or the boys did. I loudly seconded their every pleasure, all while fretting about her.

I championed their favorite professional teams with a spunk that first excited but soon tired them. (Like father, like sons.) I never missed one of their home-soccer games. Somehow their league put my twins on different teams playing at separate fields miles apart. Sometimes I'd be racing across Falls to cheer their alternate game quarters. IQ 161 used thusly.

*

I LATER TOLD myself I had felt it, the sec my firstborn and I lost contact. At Nicholas's semifinals soccer match, I was seated high in the stands, shouting encouragements.

The day contained a huge amount of weather. Splendid as only a golden bonus in cloudless late summer can be. You sit guessing this'll be the year's last sweaterless afternoon. Everything good rears up inside you. Almost makes your stomach ache, resenting this fare-well to warmth. And where, on the spiky veldt, had my little girl gone? Chill silence from there.

I still wore summer's zinc oxide to protect my Cait-fair skin. My sons objected, calling it "Mom's clown paint." But I use it only on my nose, forehead and certain new sunspots across the backs of either hand.

I sat surrounded by other parents' ugly Styrofoam beer coolers, listening to their cell-phone inanities: "I have an itch for green beans tonight, hon, you too?" Pul-*lease*, as my daughter often said.

But, like the parents nearby, I cheered my son for simply taking the field. Nick's just standing there in blond profile seemed so much immature perfection. Calling, "Looking *good*, Nicky," I hushed. First I pressed my midsection, then realized: a crucial sound had stopped.

Her daughterly dial-tone gone.

The new silence felt different from Caitlin's not having actively phoned these past ten days. No, this seemed forced, a kind of breaking-off. The parent simply senses things. Don't ask me how. Mothers *know*.

Despite Cait's phone strike, I'd still felt tied to her "current" in both senses. "Up-to-date" and linked by some steadying electric force binding us across oceans, language groups, continental storm

122

systems. We were also joined via her menstrual cycle just warming at its start while mine became a burnt-out case, losing interest in itself.

Atop her brother's bleacher, I tried deciding: It's simple. For the first time ever, she is just not *think*ing of you, Jean. Your girl isn't *hurt*, much less *dead*. No, it's the reverse, see? Your Cait is so original. With her, everything runs counterintuitive. She's half again *too* alive! There's your prob. She's so completely with *them* now. She could probably still *broadcast* on your frequency. But—about two minutes back—you just got checked off her psychic friends' list. Unlike Goodwill, you no longer rank among Caitlin's *frequently called*. Deal with it. As she often instructs her mom, "Get a life!"

Still, I checked my watch for later reference. I'd felt my tie to Caitlin Mulray stop at 4:51 p.m., my time. Later someday ahead, we would laugh over this. Wouldn't we?

I'd felt one womb-floor pang. Was this, in fact, the moment of her death? Or just the second Cait herself, bored of me, slashed our cord? The emotional cable hookup still seemed looped to her, joining us round the earth's curve. She hadn't even bothered coiling up her severed end. Just left it attached to me via a long-suffering lower opening; she simply hiked on across the veldt. She left the thing drying, raw, in white African dust—stretched across dirt and grass for any hungry old hyena to chance upon, choke down.

Or was I overdoing?

FINALLY I TOLD myself: You will be free and clear, Jean, only when (if) you can return her surly favor.

Tell yourself you are a woman who once had a child—a healthy somebody who, right on time, achieved her majority then opted out of thinking of you, even once per day.

Nicholas got the ball. He danced one excellent kick toward another boy admittedly more talented. I gave one great deranged Medea shriek. Too loud? It made others up here smile, then wince, then resmile wider, goggling back and forth. A fat woman beside me shifted her cushion one yard away, pulling over her ice chest's 24 Bud Lights just past my contagion.

Or wait, maybe it was just Cait's hymen! *Mais oui! zut alors.* I cackled then: Maybe I just felt *that* give way. Maybe what just stopped is not the dial tone I've known in *here* since I first conceived the little minx. Maybe it was just my daughter's virginity getting properly sacrificed to some big African chieftain's chiseled son?! Yeah, she just got flourished once. That all? I have nothing more to fear than that. She's alive but sexually active. But why did I not *know* this? See how I hurt myself?

"Come right *here*, Kiernan! Go directly to the car and lock it, son. NOW!"

Dear God, had I said all that aloud? How funny is that!

The upper bleachers were all mine now. This struck me as hilarious. What harm to laugh now, to chortle like some zinc-caked Bongo clown-witch, if she's a freak with one still-living daughter?

Jean's local fan base, it'd just dwindled further.

NO MAN HAS been in the picture since my Edward took up with his night-school ethics instructor. Now, during Cait's absence, our phone might've been unlisted. The twins lived so near pals' homes, they'd rather skateboard three blocks than bother texting, that young.

Even telemarketer fund-raisers shunned us, seeming to guess our one somebody was off-line. Gents have not exactly been besieging ole Jean here with cocktail party invitations and sexual demands, put it that way. Not even a "Bongo" type.

Here, you see, I am setting up the part where the phone actually *does* ring at three a.m. By then Caitlin had been in Africa just under two months, forty nine days. —This particular night, the twins are sound asleep, I'm feeling feverish even as I dream how my daughter is just out spreading good cheer across downtown Falls.

I'm dreaming that Cait is due back any minute, that all will be well. The phone starts so loud.

.

V

EVERY PARENT KNOWS how much it has already cost us: this sound incoming. To stop the phone's ringing we'd hack off any part of our body and feed it between the brass bell and its pig-iron hammer.

You pray this is a wrong number. But at first *brrr-ring*, the very oil in your either ear knows better. One hand cupped defensive between my legs, I sit bolt upright in bed. I answer, already panting.

STATIC GIVES THREE clicks. Sensing urgent foreignness, I hold on anyway. At last, through pulsing scratches like those of some old 78, a formal preacher's sort of voice asks, "Is this the mother? Of a girl named . . ." (And I hear what sounds like her pink backpack dumped onto a metal table, its chained name tag pulled jangling closer.) "This . . . the Caitlin Mulray mother?"

"This *she*. What? Sir, whathappenedtomychild? Please say it fast."

"Is somebody, madam, is somebody there *with* you?"

I'm thinking it odd, all this courtesy from what sounds like south of Saturn. "Yes, my sons. Many friends. Put her on. Is Cait's passport lost? Her money getting low, that it? I'm good for more. —Oh Christ do please tell me it very quickly, sir."

"The boy got ashore all right, madam," this man's diction is very missionary school. But phone-reception's rotten. First, his bass goes blurred as if behind giant choirs of crickets, then it siphons back to being coolly crisp again. "The boy we yell for him and kept him headed our guard post's way. But current, madam, very strong that part our river this time year. She got more pulled, then under, and afterwards no more, harder to see, just the head, then we—we pull the boy in. He fine, fine swimmer. They found her more toward Ton-gaville on Tuesday, is today? yes, Tuesday. The braids are like a tiny girl's. Sorry to be the one telling. Lovely child. Have her here. It must be taken care of soon the body. Even nights here, over one hundred degrees, your way measuring. Considerable the spoilage. Send her to people this address? you are being at the one-ten Milford Cul-de-Sac? Falls? You are wanting it go there?"

With the terror of an animal bleeding from its head, I am instantly awake and very clear. As he talks, I find a pen, the back of Patrick's soccer schedule, some dimestore bifocals with one lens. Finally he tells me he can either await my money-order but to use card's faster. Speed being best given the heat. Into darkness I sit quoting our American Express number aloud. I chant it aloud as I once knew by heart only the Pledge of Allegiance and 1928's *Book of Common Prayer.*

I tell where he must ship her—have you a pencil, sir? just Higgins' Mortuary, Church Street, and use the same town and zip code. "You wrote that, sir? When will she? how long does it usually take to . . . shipping-wise, is ice? are refrigerated cars involved? . . . I just don't know much about . . ."

Part of me wants to catch the next plane then escort it—her— home. Another portion is about to scream, *Bury her there. You people*

127

killed her, you and your savage rivers keep her. But I know that is insane; it is just shock, just the being concussed awake.

I somehow know I knew already.

HE IS ASKING if I have friends to whom I can turn *at this time.* He grows very gentle. Says he has two young daughters of his own. Says he cannot quite imagine but still feels for me, and apologizes, thanks me as I thank him far far more.

I hang up.

HER KID BROTHERS could sleep through a World War Three. I am not about to wake them. I will not force anyone to know one minute sooner than another soul on earth must. I slump forward in too wide a bed. (Eddie couldn't *not* buy a "king.") Here I conceived, with that pretty Boy Scout's regularized hydraulic engineering, my one Cait and two darling boys.

Slowed, I drag myself to the vertical but dare not step toward her room the way they do in movies. I wouldn't trust myself there, not with the boys bunk-bedded next door.

Putting on—for the first time—a cushy Christmas-present terry robe I've hid from her Goodwill marauding, I barefoot it downstairs. I slowly heat then stir some milk. Calming, I pour it into my favorite old mug, next sprinkle nutmeg and a dash of cinnamon on top.

Addled, leaving it—perfect and cooling on the granite counter— I return to bed and ring my former husband, her present father.

EDDIE LIVES ON a cliff near some white-sand beach in La Jolla. Three hours earlier, it's only midnight there. Edward Westfall Mulray IV was the local boy my parents sent me to finishing school

128

to snag. I got a poem into print, got Eddie, got pregnant on my honeymoon. Lucky girl, everyone said. He was the society doctor's son, lived in a neocolonial along The River Road, an early Eagle Scout, the believingest jut-jawed clear-eyed boy in town. Like his daughter, everybody's favorite, even mine.

He contributed sixty-five percent of Cait's blond-blue beauty and one hundred of her perfect PSAT math score. Fact is, I outgrew him. Vice versa, according to Ed. Every inch the civil engineer, he thinks like one, makes love like one; every Friday night: erotic-problem-solving 101, efficient, a job to do and limited time to do it in. Speed, applied force, failure not an option. Eureka. For him.

Six years back, Ed claimed he needed some adult education, a little brain stimulation. Given my 163 IQ, I felt accused. His ethics teacher proved to be a divorced girl just months past her own PhD coursework in philosophy: Spinoza, etc. Stuck on her dissertation. Her name is Tiffany Goldblatt. (Her parents played into my hands there.) I think people named after jewelry stores, even good ones, should be outlawed from teaching anything important as philosophy (even at community colleges).

But there Tif was, offering night school Plato to immigrants and restless people of middle age lost halfway through their journeys along a dim path, etc. She'd only got that far into her own career rut when she identified my Edward as her pet new Socratic dialogue.

Handsome fellow, superior mind, engineering degree from Cornell, unhappy at home with his fattening artistically-flustrated bitch-wife—plus, a guy exactly as briskly distanced as was Tif herself. (I never said she wasn't somewhat physically attractive, did I?) The first time he slept with her, I sensed it the way Caitie has X-ray eyes for any hurt crow's total health picture. Ed came home late at about this same fatal 3 a.m., tipsy. Claimed he had been out celebrating having aced an ethics exam. "But not the written part," I played my hunch. "No. The orals, right? You aced the orals on your lady-teacher.—Been quite a while since we've seen that big a push for extra credit around here, Ed."

He said, "You're scary, Jean."

I went, "You have no fuckin' earthly idea yet, honey."

I promised Eddie that. And here he had sent my prime joy and only claim to fame off far from me, unsupervised. Her semifinal summer under my roof and—from a beach chair in San Diego—he urges Cait to go single-handedly save Africa.

SO I RING him with the news. 3:28 a.m., my time. I can tell he's been asleep. I'd begged him not to sign those releases. I guess I truly am a hateful person. That's what I've been hearing for a long long time.

"Eddie, it's Jean. Listen, truly sorry to wake you. But I just got the call from Africa."

I would lie if I told you I did not actually somewhat savor this. Not the news, its impact on him. This is awful, isn't it? But I'd hated his ease in leaving me; he packed, booked his flight before explaining why. I hated how Ed had slipped Caitie a secret thousand for her Dark Continent summer pin money. Even with funding, she still hitched everywhere and went swimming around naked. Eddie had told our girl that Africa would be the making of her, certainly would beef up her conversation for a lifetime of parties. He assured Cait: Paris? Everybody your age does Paree. But being so far out into scrub jungle, teaching literacy, not bloody typical. Look great on applications, too—school, job, whatever.

*

130

"*THE* CALL FROM Africa? —Jean, for once, no tricks. Spare me competitive word games tonight. Please. I'm beat, Jean, even here it's late."

"Yes, the *call*. The one I told you and Caitlin would be coming. You both laughed, remember, Eddie? Caitlin just drowned trying to swim some damn jungle river. I had to pay to have them ship her home."

I am not proud of doing this. Nor do I think it would pass any ethics-exam vetting. But I felt stunned. People in pain yell first at those they love. It cannot just be *me*, can it? Am I alone in this, too? But yes, I let my fury at the both of them get in the way. It took over. I was weakened and it stepped right in.

I explained about the current. I knew the water must have been brown and very foamy from its undertow. The boy had got across. Was he the ambassador's son? Guards at this outpost had cheered him on to keep him focused, a strong swimmer. But Caitie had drifted into whirlpools or something. (Swimming was her single phys. ed. weakness, we both knew.) She had been found downriver a day or so later. They had her now. One decent station guard discovered her ID, traced me by phone. He said he liked her braids. The man had two daughters himself. Cait's body got retrieved and they were now sending it back home to Falls.

I HEARD THE concerned voice of his new wife very nearby. I heard Eddie tell her then cry against her and I choked on it then. "I'm sorry," I said. "Honey, I'm so sorry. It's just that I'm alone here. —I should've, I shouldn't've . . ." But it was a strong woman's voice taking over: "Jean? Tif here. Can Edward call you right back? Oh this is awful for him. And you, of course. But he thought she . . ."

I knew his wife was going to say, *Thought Caitlin hung the moon*, so I hung up first.

WHAT CAN YOU say as the mother of someone unique, eighteen, deceased? That: You keep moving because her living brothers' sandwiches must be made come morning. Because only you know that Patrick likes super-crunch peanut butter whereas Nicholas will only touch the smooth. I was like those people you hear about who've been in motorcycle accidents and get up off the tarmac and walk along the side of the road but are actually dead and still moving only out of habitual motor impulse. One step, two. Nerves take over for the offline brain. Sandwich? two pieces of bread, place contents between. Roasted chicken feet, a white body among dark ones, the water sepia from filth, and her acting Eden out again and again, but now dead. No Radcliffe-Harvard, not even finishing school, no nothing. But, no problem, I will only have to live until the twins get into college. Then I'll be done. Period, over-out. My sentence served.

I kept finding my throat dry, and why? because all that first day my mouth hung open from such constant panting. The whole morning I would come to a standstill in certain corners of our home, impasses, hallway spots-one-quarter-between-places where I'd never really stopped before but now pressed into, for the comfort of containment, their small safety. "Go stand in the corner, for talking, Jean."

Today, only voluntary punishment gave me a few seconds' concentrated ease.

THE MONDAY AFTER the Friday night we heard, I phoned the Quaker Relief Fund in Philly. They'd arranged her teaching placement. I wanted details. However gory, I needed those for recovery. Objecting as I did, I hadn't even bothered reading the fine print of her legal paperwork; her dad is supposed to be the civil engineer. Now I jotted a list of questions. In advance I wrote out a simple speech. I would not threaten a lawsuit per se, but mentioning that might get us some much-needed belated attention. I could tell: the girl who answered was another student volunteer. "Listen, please?" I started, "Caitlin Mulray, my daughter, was sent by your organization to Africa and we have reason to believe something bad has just . . ." "Yes, lots of our parents feel that way, at times. Like the other ten I have on hold right now. And, though I honestly sympathize with your concern?—you will also be answered in the order in which you—"

I don't know if my phone receiver was placed in its cradle first or if my beating dents with it into the side of our new fridge actually broke the connection.

TO COMPENSATE FOR my own lost life, how beautiful and gifted would my children have to be? Paying me back for the poet I'd just begun becoming? Offering me company equal to that of my own possible admiring readers and fellow artists?

When Plath was one of several college guest editors at *Mademoiselle*, her idol-genius Dylan Thomas appeared at the magazine office to meet with top editorial brass. And when the college temp was not invited, she protested. How? By taking a butcher knife to her own legs. Look it up: "First serious attempt." My own deferrals and disappointment I've kept far quieter. Whatever chance at brilliancy I'd given up early? Caitlin, by age three, already justified.

She launched as precisely the person bright enough, whole and poetic and famously gorgeous enough, to make me and the rest of the world know Jean had done well to bow out herself. The best of me went right into getting Cait to bloom as exactly such a non-knife-wielding somebody. And the romance of my summoning her forward, teaching her to read? That romance will be forever recalled by me alone.

The sacrifice of just one Jean? surely worth it. No countermanding petitions begged to have that stage-one rocket launcher spared. No, all agreed Cait was the actual prize and worth it. Even Jean herself concurred.

Now even *that* was lost. That "me," too . . .

FIRST I SAT blaming only myself. Finally I just threw my whole bruised being into planning Cait's service. That became everything. The second she, her body, got in, Higgins' Mortuary would phone with news of her "repatriation." (Old Man Higgins had already schooled me: that was the official term for shipping a corpse home from abroad.)

I bought an appointment book. Needed one more detailed than our fridge's big calendar listing all the twins' drum lessons, home games. On our old one I had jotted her student-charter return-flight details. Starred, the date of our lead actress's homecoming. Now I considered blacking all that out, but the boys sometimes actually checked their schedules. I knew a redacting blot might upset them even more. Too late for censorship.

Despite my having few-to-no local friends, word about her death spread quick. The twins' many buddies took their own shock home. Father Tim, our kindly if banal young rector from All Saints Episcopal, popped in unannounced then mercilessly overstayed. It's not his fault being who he is. I always see that afterwards.

Timothy is shrimp-pink and has albino eyelashes and surely

expected Princeton would make him at least look readier for the real world.

Then Father Tim sat actually saying, trying to reach for my hand, "Have you ever thought that maybe something *good* might come of this, Jean?"

"Like your finally going home?" I actually said that.

"You're tired, Jean. God bless you. I *hear* you, though. I did care deeply for Caitlin. As who did not? But I could possibly leave now if you really think that best."

"Yeah, well, do. And thank *Him* for me. For all the goodness waiting to come my way from His having drowned a girl so promising in the Malaria River. Don't you ever get *embarrassed*, Padre Tim? I mean, my own job is super-sad right now, okay. I've faced that. But Cait was just *one* person. And yet you go from death house to death house mindlessly repeating these duds they trained you boys to palm off on real adults with actual griefs? You didn't have a coat and nobody's blocking your car."

"You're tired, Jean."

"Wow, quite the voodoo mind-reader, Padre!"

Then I heard BlackMatt at the front door calling my name. Come to mourn with me. We'd have a salad, after.

I rose. Tim finally left. As Matt stepped in.

VI

REPORTERS CALLED AT once. They already knew her. I somehow talked to them all, even offered Diet Cokes. (I soon learned: journalism and motherhood are two fields jet-fueled by frequent triage caffeine blasts.) Despite everything, I managed to bake my best chocolate layer cake, ever. I saw others think me brave. I showed the press her silver-blond baby pictures. I mentioned her wizardry in sensing how to help our spaniel Cookie when once so sick. Once I observed reporters not writing this part down, I knew it was probably too nasty to fit into most family papers. I soon learned from my every gaffe about Cait. I tried keeping things "light" about the worst thing that can happen. That was all that most people could really stand to hear.

Three strong Robin Hood knocks at my front door. And here stood her school's choral director—a young married guy Cait'd said should lead the New York Philharmonic, he was so "genius-y." He'd conducted *Sweeney Todd*. Sweated out every note. Not a seat in the house.

TALL IF WILTING, Stanley Shelburne held out a CD: Caitie's two recent alto solos he'd burned without her even knowing. He spoke what he had come prepared to say: "In our school of sharps and flats, she was everyone's middle C. C for Caitlin." His voice ran deep as that chocolate dark enough to oxidize you.

This big swart half-pretty man looked wet across the eyes; he had a large jaw, a bluish five o'clock shadow. Though broad-shouldered he hunched, a hangdog appeal. I said, "Well, well, it's the famously-gifted Mr. Shelburne Cait kept praising as our nation's next Lenny Bernstein." I feared I sounded cynical; but when he slumped against me, choking, it was wonderful. His hot hand against my face, I got an almost carnal twinge. Then, recalling Father Tim's predicting something "good" coming, I felt nauseous.

Mr. Shelburne's warm tears, gushers, soon literally wet my blouse's front. I myself had not yet cried, not one polyp-neutron of real water. Everybody except me (the mailman included) seemed waterworks.

I LET MY twins stay home from school a full six days. They played their pimp-war-Afghani-ghetto video game (hideous gift from Eddie). Twins drifted into her room, listening to several of her Belle & Sebastians, sitting on Cait's futon, whatever my boys needed. They truly suffered but—whispering while in constant physical contact—they helped each other through this in a way I almost envied. My twins said nothing. They'd rest whole hours side-by-side on a couch. Boys faced our white-wreathed front door, now bolted closed, spared its former natural openness. Twins seemed to find safety only in being identical, unanimous, luckily male. But my ten-year-olds now acted eighty. Their silence I found terrifying.

Familiar.

I HAD NOT set foot inside her cleanly Amish-y bedroom. Last spring, she glazed its walls a transparent azure she said was her favorite new shade. Cait never guessed why she loved this color. And I would never tell her. It was the exact cornflower-blue of her own eyes.

I knew my simply stepping in that space, the color, might trigger everything. Once in there, all my old attempts on her behalf would look bungled, malformed. I remembered Mom enrolling me in lessons; I got a:

B– in "Solo Piano."

C+ at "Interpretive Dance": *is willing but stumbles.*

At "Adulthood"? an "Incomplete."

"Start-up Motherhood", at best a D–.

MAYBE WE JUST shouldn't even get to *have* children, narcissists like Mom and moi. Why my lifelong thing about Cait's attending Radcliffe? —Because *I'd* deserved that. Or so I thought during my two unpregnant years at Sweet Briar. I'd asked to apply to Cambridge but Mother said that'd mean too long a drive for her. I was now a forty-three-year-old dropout, unworthy, selfish, keyed-up, unsatisfied both personally and sexually. And I, being a born stage-mother, had taken all that out on Cait. Now at least I admitted it. If a bit tardily.

I laughed, I was such a total horror; I'd been dumped by my handsome Cornell husband. My own mother, Ice, had been right about me all along: "Your problem, Jean dear, is, like me, you have Madame Curie ambition but, child, your planning skills run right at *I Love Lucy* level."

AND NOW MY evil ways and sharp tongue had helped me lose my firstborn somebody. The effect this had on me was substandard, shaming: the day I heard? I admit driving straight to our town's best bakery. Parked before the shop called By Bread Alone, waxed paper and powdered sugar soon littered my lap as I fantasized about big tall goatlike Stanley Shelburne. His skin was Foreign Legion dark. He'd dampened my white cotton blouse with spots of tear-transparency. I imagined him now flooding me in tears, drowning me with his virile lower liquids. I would wade hip-deep into the headstream of Stan's jetted leavings. Me, pulling some boat, a slightly thicker Kate Hepburn, braver than any shoeless African Queen. —Horrid, eating éclairs while having sex thoughts, and NOW.

I should not, could not, cry. That, see, was a rite for the Deserving. Instead I felt some blackness banking up. A dense mass gathering in Jean's midsection. It would have to come out. 7–10 lbs. worth. One healthy baby's weight. Someday there would be such an explosion, but not yet.

ALL THE SMARTEST kids from Falls High began streaming in on us at all hours. 110 Milford Cul-de-Sac was suddenly Action Central. Didn't matter to me if they were punks, linebackers or band-geeks so long as they loved her. An older man arrived on foot, alone.

Head shaved, he moved in lurches, depending upon furniture to stand for long. Where had I seen him? Beard gone, wasn't he that bum she'd hoisted to help pee? One of the Matts told me: the loss of Caitlin had finally driven this old guy to rehab. He looked like a petrified Klondike miner, dug up then shaved by a careless undertaker; and yet his voice sounded tearful, an intelligent Irish tenor's. "May I see where she *slept?*" I heard him whisper to one twin. Patrick took a spotted old paw and pulled the bum upstairs.

Mostly the right people came. The East Indian junior who'd won the Bell Labs science award but truly needed his teeth braced. A redheaded boy so funny onstage, they did three years of comedies to cash in on his gift. (He was rumored to already have a Tootsie Roll commercial in the works.) Filled with student body officers, my home soon felt like the Hollywood Canteen.

Certain young boy-leads seemed legendary after Cait's years of dinner-hour tales to her brothers and me. Her gang had become our favorite soap opera cast. I never expected to actually *meet* certain major actors. Before Africa, at meals, I had heard my sons, usually restrained, press Cait for deeper in-crowd gossip. "Wait," Patrick shook his head. "Tracey cannot even be with Erick. Not after he left her at Tori's without a ride during that giant blizzard, are you kiddin'? Get real. Don't girls have any *pride*, Mom?"

"Have any . . . how-you-say-zees word 'pwide'? Because zat iwwe-gular French word eets *new* to me." I'd made one of my jokes. No laughs, unless six rolled eyes count. But I felt proud to simply sit here: imagine having a teenage daughter who would take time to update then fascinate her pesky kid brothers. A seventeen-year-old who'd actually tell you what daily happened at her high school! Unusual girl.

Belatedly, see, I was joining the Cult of Caitlin. It was a club I'd founded then resisted as somehow bad for her. But now that she was beyond being spoiled by her own superb reviews? I caved. She drew more praise-songs than you could quite stomach or believe. Even the Atlanta paper sent a reporter by plane. "Gave Her All: 'Love' Was Girl's Actual First Spoken Word."

SHELBURNE NOW PHONED nightly around eight, soon as his wife was "up putting down the kids." From their narrow front porch, he'd speak into his old shoe-box-sized cellular. My twins joked about this thing's being Thomas Edison's first try. To me, honestly? It looked like a huge, sad erection, all antenna, humorless, unhideable, endearing as a basset hound's gnawed-on cow-bone.

As we talked he would secretly smoke, hiding this from his mate and me (but I heard each inhale). Stan would pace, reciting small remembered facts about "our Cait." Her flute player's bee-stung mouth, the sprightly if unorthodox angle at which she held her instrument. How straight her spine, never touching chair-back. Arching.

Near our talk's end, Stanley would cough to hide tonight's con-cluding whimper. I imagined his bedraggled wife upstairs reading *Goodnight Moon* for the thousandth time to their two- and four-year-old. I soon calmed and encouraged Stan. I used terms that sounded very unlike Ice's frozen-chosen daughter: "Yes, m' gifted one. Just let it out, Stan. Our Cait, she called you 'all that,' too, friend. Just release, babe. Go on, let it flow, m' sweet boy."

I wanted him to cry all over me or worse. I would be absorbent—for him—my hips, my butt pure sponge.

MORE CARS NOW parked outside Cait's flaky mom's brick rancher than those circling the big Tudor on Lakeland, home to Tori, the slutty cheerleader. (At least that tramp, with her short denim skirt and six-inch heels, hadn't barged into our place pretending to mourn, thank God.) Tori's parking area might've featured Mercedes sports cars and one hideous gas-hogging chrome-yellow Hummer. But our drive stayed packed with battered dune-buggy Jeeps and vintage Harley-Davidsons whose drivers I forced to wear helmets. My daughter's friends were bright, often lovely-looking. Watching BlondMatt and BlackMatt together reminded me of the old Scotch ads with one white and one dark terrier. The Matts slouched near and against each other in slack arrangements all yin and yang. Though males, they were still so smooth they lived on the shy side of manly danger. They looked beautiful as certain deer. And I, con-fused, watching them, imagined the Matts as failed experiments at becoming girls. And felt almost lesbian.

Kids asked for art supplies so as to draw and write their Cait memories. Turns out, she'd been their group guidance counselor. "I can tell you she was a better mom than *my* mom," BlackMatt confessed while holding my hand. "Same here," BlondMatt added. "Oh yeah, me too. Totally," plump ceramicist Millicent flirted, unoriginal. Only a Cait could've loved her.

I baked cookies and, in one week, gained six pounds just from helping others with treats made in Caitlin's honor. A scholarship was being set up; over eleven thousand dollars already raised; that idealistic wet-eyed big-phoned Mr. Shelburne must be behind it. His nightly voice was all blackness but with highlights—like dark olives.

Stan's forearms looked ridged (so strong just from daily conduct-ing?). His biceps domed up, bald; but from the elbows downward, each arm came gift-wrapped in a black-bear's mascot fur. Stan favored short-sleeved shirts that maybe allowed for extra air across his surely-matted chest. My pitiless observant twins code-named the arms: his Shredded Wheats.

—Both my towheaded sons and their dad glowed mere vanilla-butterscotch all over. Darkness intrigued me, now especially. I felt moved when Stan jaggedly cried—a deep clicking between throat and chest, sounding part adolescent orgasm, part Elmer Fudd hiccup. His lashes blackened-separated as if caked with sudden theatre mascara. He'd begun stopping by for my fresh-baked pastries after school. He'd curl in on himself; he'd turn away from me as if ashamed to let me see his outsized emotion. If my life now felt like some war movie—a missing body at its center—Stan

142

became that film's swarthy "city guy," rendered suddenly girlish by some bumpkin buddy's death. When Shelburne got extra-teary, he just blotted eyes onto absorbent fur forearms.

"Jean?" Nights, his voice would speak into my now-busy phone. "Just me. —How're *you* holding up?"

This was as close as I came to losing it.

I swear it seemed: no one had ever asked me that before.

EN ROUTE TO band clinic, Stan started leaving notes in my porch mailbox. Once, his envelope held only a broken robin's egg (nearly the color of her eyes and room) and made me want to scream. Instead I received a lower body pain, no *hot flash* this, but one young, with a snapdragon's snapping most fierce. All this wasted tenderness burning in wait down there.

Not desire again! No, I greeted that like some voluntary root canal. But nothing spared me now. Not even sex.

WE MOVED TOWARD the date she would've returned to us. I braced for postponed feelings, a lifetime's. This would be what would've should've been the start of her senior year, as school vice president. Her older friends had mostly sped off to college; others were heading back to Friends School or Falls High, seniors at last. Those in-state university freshmen I'd assigned eulogies or solos, they promised to rush back home . . . whichever Thursday her service.

One night by phone, Shelburne asked, "What could someone as flawed as I ever *do* for her, Jean, or for you?" The answer came. For once it was literal. "Write a cantata for choir-and-orchestra then conduct it in her memory? That'd be so: you being you. But, is there even, like, time, Stan?" (I was picking up new word patterns, but where from? Off new friends, I guess.)

"You already hinted to me it should be—and I'll just quote you back to you, sir—in *C major*, right?"

"Brilliant. But you think I could, Jeannie? I mean I do still have all my composition notebooks from Curtis. But it's been so long since I even . . ."

"'If not now, when?' as Hillel tells us."

(I sounded fairly prissy-preacherly then. I sounded like a diary or some thought for the day. —No, wait, for one last time, you know what I sounded? . . . I sounded *young*!)

Via his twelve-inch cell, I heard him light another guilty cig. Feeling deep and dark myself, I spoke, "Please stub that one out, Stan. You don't *need* those now, understand? You have your talent, you have your mission, m' dear boy."

"All along you *knew* I smoked? Psychic *and* . . . attractive. —Gosh, your power is almost scary, Jean."

"You have no idea," I told him.

VII

I FINALLY ASKED Stan if he'd come play us a piano reduction of his Cantata for Caitlin in C Major: "The Monument." See, I had chosen that Elizabeth Bishop poem for him to set. I'd specified that the piece's soloist should be, like our late darling, an alto. Otherwise I left everything up to his unheralded genius. I felt that, having commissioned Stan, I ought to somehow pay him.

He confessed he was now "all but eating" his old Curtis Institute composition sketches. I hoped this spotlight might give Cait's frazzled teacher artistic credibility at last. Maybe Father Tim had been correct by accident: something good might actually squeak through here.

In our basement rec room, I keep a Chickering upright inherited from Ice. At it, a child myself, I'd once practice-practiced to get to Carnegie Hall. The thing's veneer had buckled by now; kids' juice boxes and Snapple bottles cut a hundred squares and rings across its top. (I'd sort of allowed this, hoping that such marring might let our piano fall beneath Caitlin's Goodwill attention. She favored only donations of items she crudely called "high-end-looking.")

THE DAY BEFORE our at-home Stan Shelburne world premiere, I finally welcomed a reputable piano tuner. Soon as I saw his red and white cane I volunteered to lead him down the stairs. I recalled how people robbed of one sense get instantly better at another just next door. I was counting on that, now I'd lost my sense of . . . Caitlin.

I asked if I might listen to him work and, a true indulgence, during, told him our tale—the drowned child, the commissioned piece, the Curtis grad stuck teaching band and high school chorus. (Did I not sound like Mrs. Shelburne, I mean his mom?)

The tuner said any composer deserves the best possible players, singers. He said that the Virginia Symphony Orchestra sometimes performed private gigs. "Not cheap, I don't expect," the blind piano tuner told my general direction. "But they come to a town by bus, rehearse all morning, scatter for lunch, come back, I guess, and play it that same night. If his piece is any good it's going to sound better in the hands of pros. Think of the strings, young lady."

I asked him how much. My directness sounded shocking, Ice's own. But I felt my heart rate increase at just such ruthlessness (for others, always others). Using fingers, he sat tallying. "Maybe twenty, twenty-five?"

"Thousand? Thousands, of course. They're professionals. — Funny, but my late mom did leave me a little. I'd saved it for her tuition, my daughter's. Also 'late' now, I guess . . ."

Ice had left me money. What she had willed me—after taxes, after the cost of her round-the-clock care—might come out right at nineteen to twenty-one thousand. Think what suave orchestral brass, lush strings, might do for Stan! And the community, of course.

NEXT DAY, ONCE I'd crowbarred my twins from PlayStation 2 and back to school, I made an appointment in Richmond. I overdressed and drove our rust-colored (and rusting) Volvo wagon two hours north. I explained my daughter's disappearance, the major piece being written in tribute. Ian, the young "community liaison" man, hinted how, for the amount I had, I could maybe hire a skeleton orchestra.

"Sort of appropriate . . ."

"Say what?"

"Nothing. —Grief."

But Stan must conduct: I made that my one condition.

"Who?"

"Stanley Shelburne, Curtis Institute of Music."

The boy shook his head no. I explained the composer actually also conducted for a living. I had memorized the name of Stan's most famous teacher. I tossed that out with Ice-like authority. Young Ian stared at me.

"An esteemed name, certainly. —We do have to screen, ma'am. We sometimes get *vanity calls*. A car dealer on his sixtieth birthday, say, will want to wave his arms around in front of party friends. Now I'm sensing that your booking isn't just a *vanity* one. —Still, only our next few Thursdays might be free. By then, your daughter, she'll . . . you'll surely have her . . . ready?"

Young Ian did ask if I'd mind paying maybe two-thirds up-front, a no-refund assurance, in order to hold whichever of the next three Thursdays she'd be most likely to . . . fill.

STAN COULD NOT believe it. Only after he'd arrived holding his inky score did I mention having hired the VSO (Virginia Symphony Orchestra, natch). Sweet man kept asking me to repeat. First I made him promise me, no tears.

"But this cannot be *cheap*, Jean. You sure you guys can swing it?"

"Not so pricey as you'd think. —And heck, they throw in their round-trip bus for free . . ."

"This sounds major," Stan flopped onto my piano bench. "But these musicians, they cut their teeth on *Bach* and *Brahms*. And, now, *Stan*?" Poor man laughed at himself.

Settling close, I took his haired hand in my own; by contrast mine, being so smooth, looked far younger.

"Not *Stan*," I said, low. "'Shelburne's First Symphony in C Major: the Chorale.' —Now, does *that* sound ridiculous, m' talented one? Mmmm, I think not."

"Jean, you've finally given me permission to, sort of . . . ?"

"Be yourself?"

"'Be myself,' exactly, Jeannie . . . Hey, wait one, if *you* can pay for that orchestra, I'll throw in and hire the state's best darned recording engineer. We'll just get this little treasure saved forever . . ."

"Stan!"

I called the twins downstairs for a family hearing. Wary, in white shirts, they took the root-beer-stained tweed couch. I settled beside Stan at our Chickering, newly-tuned. To celebrate, I'd had my royal-blue cardigan dry-cleaned. Even wore a little tasteful eyeliner. Subdued, you know, but there.

Stan is one of those men who gives off intense body heat. My right cheek and upper arm soon felt campfire-lit (orange). He pounded right into our cantata. I thought of Cait's trite phrase *majorly*. C-Majorly, Stan now played her anthem. I sat, meek, just to Stanley Shelburne's left. I *turned* for him. (I'd actually practiced it down here last night, using my girlhood sheet music for "Moon River.") He, rocking, sweated across ivory, punished whole octaves. Stan would nod and, my lips pursed, I'd flip that page so fast.

The piece? Boys later remarked that no tribute to Caitlin should get far without "any real tunes in it." And their desire for melody seemed reasonable and astute.

True, the piece turned out more "modern" than expected. But dynamic and, my yes, unique.

—People's characters, I know.

Music? I'm no judge.

VIII

A T LAST I "Set" the ratio of young speakers to adults. With Stan's help, I decided how to contrast the crescendo—his C major "Monument" Cantata—with a certain number of testimonials regarding Cait's activism's impact, etc.

That Ian! Our symphony's young liaison man sent me a beautiful note, my receipt, his guarantee that the next three Thursdays would be held open by the dear VSO. My one event-planning worry, it might go too long. Three hours, no. Two and change, more like it.

I could now lean toward what mattered most: the daily talk with Mr. Higgins our mortician, plus Stan's nightly musical progress report: He had hired a senior-boy computer whiz to copy orchestra parts. My phone would ring, often right at eight. It never was for Cait. Sometimes in advance, to amuse only myself, I might change clothes, apply one dot of cologne; I'd settle, waiting on a white French chaise inherited from Mother.

First thing I'd hear, "Just me, Jean. But how're *you* holding up?"

His pet name for me alluded to our both believing Stephen Foster underrated (the American Schubert?). "And how's my 'Jeannie with the Light'?"

(I've tucked that tribute away, set it on a dim cool ledge where it'll always "keep.")

SAINTS HAVE MOTHERS

*

I SHIED AWAY from accepting for myself even our program's smallest speaking role. I have always suffered terrible stage fright; my attempt to say my *Atlantic* poem aloud at a Sweet Briar convocation is one memory best-hurried-past. But BlackMatt promised: my own *clothe-ure* depended on addressing just this assembly. He'd started turning up unannounced, often at mealtimes. The twins held that against him but I told them he was desolated, that being with us meant being near Cait. "Means being near food!" Patrick laughed. But I was never sorry to warm up soup for a boy so blue-eyed soulful as BlackMatt.

The school's jazz combo had asked to play. Then a steel drum troupe auditioned (in our own driveway!). Suddenly I had to be so diplomatic (for her sake). Also volunteering, a black gospel group whose church she'd helped reshingle; first I'd heard of that.

At the urging of Shelburne and the Matts both light and dark, I finally assigned myself only one small quotation. It would be from Mother's 1928 *Book of Common Prayer*, one I had not opened in years. Though I shunned poor Father Tim, I found myself more and more respectful of the liturgy itself. I kept Ice's battered blue book beside my toilet. I would sit there muttering its round phrases till they each took on a different surface like clay or glass or beaten metal, a purity of tone and purpose that actually half-consoled.

BLACKMATT WOULD COMMENCE our service with his heraldic trumpet voluntary, the call to attention. Cait had loved Wallace Stevens, whose poems she'd once called "interplanetary bric-a-brac, Mom." (She had notebooks full of phrases this good.) So, BlondMatt would next recite a Stevens poem (after several more much-needed rehearsal-study-evenings with me).

Then three five-minute eulogies (brevity to be strictly enforced, alas). These would be offered by her aged emotional kindergarten teacher then by two friends, one Cait's age, the other a nine-year-old-girl idolater-admirer. Finally, Stanley K. Shelburne's mixed choir-and-orchestra arrangement of my favorite Bishop poem, "The Monument." That would serve as our cathartic handmade centerpiece. As specified, the Virginia Symphony's favorite alto, commuting from Newport News, had already learned Stan's leading role.

Finally, through a million butterflies, last thing, I would stand. I'd quote from memory something handpicked out of the old prayer book. Cait's father and his Tiffany, I guess, would be flying east for our service. Everything would shift into gear soon as the repatriated shipment arrived; Old Man Higgins stayed on the lookout, making various tricky international calls. As a Mason, he had three African "brothers" tracing her paperwork.

Edward phoned the house but mostly to speak to our sons. "How do you think they're *deal*ing with it?" he asked when the boys finally placed a warmed phone again into my hand.

We hit the day she would've actually been back among us. A Saturday, still starred in red on the fridge's calendar. Her student-flight info was listed, "African Queen home!" I'd overheard one twin sigh to his brother, "No spears, either." (At such a time, you are not supposed to laugh, so I just bit my lower lip.)

Patrick and Nickie, my fellow survivors, were hosting yet another sleepover. Like many divorced moms living alone, I secretly enjoy catering my kids' overnighters. An only child myself, I've stayed fascinated-consoled by the noise of a true houseful.

Now, especially.

TONIGHT A WORLD Cup finals match would come on cable. When

152

we'd learned of Cait's drowning, I asked the boys what, if anything, might soothe them. Both mentioned an extra sports-channel subscription. They recited its letters in unison. (What *would*n't ten-year-old boys do for a few more sports networks?)

As men in trouble will, my twins kept disappearing. They consoled themselves via Books of Common Sports Stats. Lately they fused with their pet text "Runs Batted In During the 1955 World Series." That constituted a new liturgy for mourning ten-year-olds. Nickie would sit holding the list on one side of our great room; Patrick, twelve feet off, eyes shut, slumped mumbling Johnny Podres's superhuman numbers. Incantation. That, I understood. Patrick's blind chant seemed some kind of praying, numerically encoded enough to work for young males. My sons, like their dad, so quickly took agony straight to statistics regarding human physical feats. And was this different from my rushing pain toward becoming music, poetry, new friendship? Numbers numbed the male ache, offered some sort of splint. They spared men the slack wet press of full female Emotion. —I've come to believe most males are afraid of most women. Truth be told, there is a reason. How soon we gals learn to hide from guys the depth of our real hopes. We might accidentally show them the Grand Canyon scope of our emotional needs, waiting below. About those we learn to hush. We just accept from men whatever piddling runs they're batting in to us.

I AWAITED ONLY repatriation. I sat on my best leather couch. If things could turn back to a time pre-African, I'd finally seize happiness with two hands. I longed to be filled or known, whichever came first. Filled not by food, however plentiful, not even by one man—a young pagan chieftain—but by some child, my whole girl-child, pressed back up in there safe.

Stan had started taking me for short rides. Once we parked beside a farm lake. The sun set, a rubbery molten pink; but I mainly watched his dashboard clock. I should really be home for the boys. They would cope, of course. But, way out here, I could just not feel any real abandon or relief. He was married. I had once been. Besides, he only wanted to talk about someone age-inappropriate, someone named Caitlin.

And, oh God, he cried again. Did it not seem strange to me? A wedded teacher of thirty-six being so soddenly in love with my child since she was freshly fifteen? No. Why? Because he needed *me* now. He had matured.

Irregular French verb of week: *Pouvoir: to be able to, "can," or "may."*

A DOZEN BOYS the twins' age kept piling in for World Cup TV soccer. Two Kips, a Christopher, several outlier Jasons. Safe as yet from puberty, they wore outsized athletic jerseys intended for mammoth adolescent linebackers.

Eager to distract my sons from their sister's un-return, I greeted each incoming waif. Kids' hair was then moussed out spiky. (Ten-year-olds believe such "product" makes them look sixteen. Their hair instead resembles infants' cowlicks crying out for blue satin hair-bows.)

These string bean hard-guys knew my house so well they'd long since ceased to knock. Sometimes, skateboarding past, one would just pop in and use my front-hall bathroom, even when the twins weren't home. "Okay if I . . . ?" The kid wouldn't even finish asking, just point toward the hall toilet with one hand, the other on his zipper. Call me derango but, being an only child and daughter, I felt honored by a bathroom door left ajar. Such careless naturalness. I

154

felt almost . . . male myself. Trusted as one boy trusts another. — Water Music.

Every boy arriving greeted me with a word or joke and, as a man's woman, I felt maybe too pleased, today especially. I would need the bustle. Kids carried soccer balls they would soon sit holding during tonight's Brazil-vs.-U.S. match. They brought boom boxes and a few dragged sleeping bags. I'd left a plate of my fresh-baked oatmeal-raisin cookies on our front-hall table. Soothed by building boy-noises upstairs, I stood making their requested dinner, "mac and cheese."

This gathering was just my latest try at helping twins slip past the shock of losing Cait. Their stillness scared me most of all. Naturally they pined for her. Hadn't she taught them each to dance to Motown hits? Her patience with them seemed, looking back, unbelievable. Cait put up with offering lessons in separate rooms on separate nights because the twins were too ashamed to let each other see how bad they really were at it.

SLEEPOVER BOYS HOOT up the stairwell. On our second-floor landing, they're already tussling. One kid keeps blowing air against his wrist to make bathroom sounds. He finds this so hilarious his giggling spoils certain explosive effects he seeks. I shake my head and, grating sharpest cheddar, stand here half-grinning. I see a new hand grab cookies. I see another backpack heave into our foyer. This one, pink canvas, looks caked with mud. "Home, everybody!"

Here stands a white girl age 13–20.

Daylight burns around her.

The girl is quail-sized. Shockingly sickeningly pretty, she steps barefoot out of nasty flip-flops. Blue light and yellow shoots beyond

her as an edging blur. Tile floor in here suddenly seems especially
flat and ballroom-huge, making me feel half-faint.

She has left our front door wide open. Why is that familiar? I
stare past her. Outside, the Blanchards' chocolate Lab trots past.
Our FedEx truck goes 25 mph. She might be any child returning
from any overnighter one block away.

I SET DOWN my grater. Beside it I place the damp hunk of orange
cheddar. I wipe one hand directly onto my new black linen slacks. Four
fingertips clutching cool granite countertop, I shift to face our visitor.

I close my eyes. I clear my throat.

I open one eye, then its mate. She still seems visible. My white
blouse's whole left front goes pounding nearly audible. Boys,
somehow sensing a shift, grow immediately louder. This vision of
one ghost-girl seems very nearly real. It could almost be she, still
with us, bursting through the usual open door she herself left ajar.

Chewing a cookie, my visitor, blinking expectant, lets all weight
pivot to her right hip. Daylight framing her seems broken to separate
colors, firing past her in short softened spikes. She's as suntanned as
our daughter was at three (when Eddie bought that first jungle gym
we couldn't pull her off of). She is more beautiful than our actual
girl, half an inch taller, six pounds lighter. The browned midsection
exposed looks ceramic-colored, its muscle tone half-knotted.

Light shows her legs slightly apart, one centimeter more bowed.
And I know, don't ask how: she is Cait, our Cait now unvirginal, no
longer "intact." No illusion, a body. Caitlin Mulray's *back*.

The hair's been hennaed a bruisey purple-black. Already its roots
show platinum. Native beaded earrings dangle mitten-sized. Talk
about blue eyes!

*

"FORGOT TO PICK me up, hunh, Ma? If I weren't so tired I would've minded less. But return jet lag's the worst. They say it's the coming back that kills. Know how I'm never tired? well, I'm *get*ting there. Our copilot was somewhat of a hottie, though over thirty. Lives out past Benson. He took pity on me waiting for you guys at baggage claim for-*eve*-er. I'll need at least ten hours' sleep. But what a growth surge this summer's been. Hey, you guys okay? Feels like ages. Sorry bout my li'l media blackout. That phone you got me was weird. Even the replacement, once you put a person on your no-call list, there was no reversing that. Thing was, by the end, I got so involved with my boys. Besides, before, whenever we talked, you kept freakin' out on me. But whoa, you look changed. What? Extra . . . focused, I'd say. Linen pants. More a career-woman-type outlook, right? Something's . . . going on for you, hunh, Mom? And a real haircut. I swear you look younger. —Mind if I catch some Z's till supper? I've never known what 'bone-tired' means, but this feels close. — The place is rearranged, too, more like a kind of . . . lobby. Study-group circles. Always thinking, hunh, Mom? —Nice touch. God, I've missed this place."

I CAN BREATHE. Not speak. Not yet. Hearing—even over soccer—a certain alto voice, sensing it the nanosecond she re-enters home, Cait's brothers stumble halfway down our stairs. Their hands are on each other.

Halted, twins gape into our kitchen. They appear dead-white, their lips half-moving. Skinny friends bunch before and behind my boys, as if to protect them from the young woman with a new inch of hips.

Pat and Nick wear matching World Cup pajamas. Their eyes shine full of tears. They keep clutching one another's upper arms.

She stares up at them. She finally acts spooked. They've refused to smile back, to move within twelve feet of her. "What? I'm back, and not one local soul's glad to *see* me?"

It is my job to tell her she is dead. Was.

"CAITLIN? CAITLIN, LISTEN." She flinches, fearful of my noise and siblings' shock. Nick hides his mouth behind one hand. I note a big tear's gloss. I shout at her as from some great distance:

"We were told you had drowned. A man called. Claimed he had your backpack. The boy swam better. I sent money to have you— shipped. I've planned the whole service. It's going to be beautiful. BlondMatt, BlackMatt, your Mr. Shelburne wrote a choral piece specially—wonderful attractive man, you were right. Such talent. We somehow interested the Virginia Symphony . . . playing next Thursday when you . . . The whole high school already held . . . candlelight vigil last Monday, and a scholarship in your name has sixty thousand . . . —Caitlin!"

I run for her so hard, I knock her backward. We're both soon almost beating each other, pressing against the wall.

Within my grip she feels so good. She smells like lanolin, airport, mud, wildflower. She's warm-to-hot mashed here against cool plaster. I kiss her neck and ear, again again. I want to kiss her so hard. I long to shake then kiss her, shake hard then kiss hard. Want to hold her safe, to press my girl right here, wedged back in safe with us forever.

Now the twins pile on. Their friends trail shy downstairs. Certain pals start freaking out: "No way. Whoooa! Do-overs."

The smartest Jason says, "Yeah, what? Is this like a—sequel?"

WE ALL LAUGH. It seems a scream. Now our pain is over. I *do* start screaming, "Hooray, alive. Boys, is this not weird, boys, er, what? Alivehoorayalivehooray!" But you see, I cannot stop. Screaming. I hop around. Then try and make a joke of not controlling it.

I can hardly cease moving. I get a coughing fit. It's that: I've had no time to grieve. So few weeks ago, came that 3 a.m. call. Think what-all I've put together since. And now, the payoff release, our saving art, cannot arrive. It is still trapped, like shrapnel ripening in its bomb.

To the pantry I run, hiding there, liking such forgiving darkness. I fall onto what must be a Costco Toilet Paper 40-Pak. Bent, I find I am gasping. The shock, I guess. The sight of my dead child, returned, unmet at airport, half-known even as she stood chewing my home-baked cookie. I squat. I throw up, but just a little, like a dog.

You were wrong; your kid's alive. Your girl might love you yet. But you yourself must now die sooner. If only from shock. And thanks to its simply being your *turn* now. You got your wish. Well, pay for it. Lord, can anybody take such stress become such joy? *Grand Opera for Dummies.* Is this a test, and might an IQ of 171 actually ace it?

In our unlit pantry, steadying myself by broom-handles, I fall more against the hassock of our future's toilet paper, go down onto my hands and knees. Next I say to the implied whiteness-blackness of our tile floor, "I will never doubt Your existence ever again, God. But *why* did You make me such a wretched person, only to give me this reward? I have failed in everything, as You know best. Nobody-whatever, I became the handmaid to a somebody by accident. Then this prize-surprise rebound. But why such bitchery? why try me so, only to reverse things? If, of course, You're even half-*there*, Player. 'Cause, hey, if You knew this had to happen, only to undo it at my expense, well, there's no excuse for You, You Tease. There's no excuse for You, Lord."

I sob. Amen. And sob.

ONCE WE'VE FINALLY settled onto furniture, we are all crying all over each other. It's wonderful. How Stan Shelburne will swoon! Twins' friends fail to even act embarrassed. Still ten, they don't know yet to be ashamed of unencrypted male emotions. Pals keep climbing over us like monkeys. All across Cait especially. A few feels get copped. Who's counting?

I HAVEN'T LAUGHED so much since our best dorm nights at St. Cecilia's. Cait's being home seems the Afterlife come early. This is giving birth once more, without the pain. I make her phone her father and, from clear across the room, I can hear Eddie, again his darling boyish self, shrilling like a girl. Then he asks if he can put Tiffany on. Tif will just die! His excited voice forces me to "tune up" all over again. But, in the excitement, Cait hangs up. She hangs up and her father never asks to speak to me. Wouldn't you think . . . ?

AMID THE RUCKUS, I head-signal Patrick nearer our staircase. "Hon, I know we said you could start moving some of *your* stuff into her room. But I need to ask you, hard as it'll be, to rush right up, clear that out real quick? Imagine *you* were getting back . . . Caitkins mustn't guess we even hoped she could be in any way re*placed* . . ."

I brace for selfishness. From someone only ten. I tell myself no one could blame him for resenting an overnight return to bunking below his brother ever-after. But, what does Patrick whisper? "You're smart to remember before she even gets upstairs, Mom."

Trotting, the kid disappears upstairs on tiptoe. Alone in our hall,

160

I gather myself, hearing little bumps as Pat evacuates his gear at top speed. Six minutes later, my son thumps back to our first floor, smiling. Patrick flashes me one shy butch thumbs-up. She never knew.

For that I will love this boy always. Imagine an identical twin, surrendering his very first chance at ever being on his own. Without a whimper, to reverse it silently. That's love, right?

—What amazing children! Three, again!

FINALLY, AFTER CHEESE-ORANGED macaroni in great amounts, she turns my way. "Can't believe they put you through this, Momma Jean. Can only feel for you. You know, I did lose my international student ID. It has a color picture and your address and phone. Must be how he came up with such specifics like the braids, which I guess is what they do. He must've counted on its being some awful hour when he knows he'll wake you. Part of their scheme to shake you down. God, what you went through. You poor thing, is all. Just thinking how we might've handled it—to save you all the grief, I mean."

I sit here silent. "Handled" it? Hmmm.

"Handled" an adored daughter's death announced via a bad phone connection by some African confidence-wizard? "Handled" arranging a fellowship in her name? "Handled" a vigil and the childhood-picture slide show? "Handled" the upcoming musical production elaborate as something Schuberty-Sondheimy? "Handled" commissioning a work of memorial art and paying out-of-pocket for enough cash-up-front skeleton musicians to come and lushly play it? Listen, baby . . . all right, I stand corrected. As usual. But half-guess what it felt like, child, losing you, of all children. And then my keeping going for your twin brothers? And with your

161

own father not budging to bother coming east to help me for even one second? And no friends here, except now . . . your friends?

I LONG TO yell, *Honey, you know who the real saints are? Not so-called candidates like you. As my college favorite Reinhold Niebuhr once explained: "True saints are the wives and parents of saints."*

Saint Somebody's mom: the old one left at home to pick up socks, screen others' calls, bake casseroles during the unbearable aftermath. Of impulsive pint-sized saints like you.

I DO NOT holler this. I simply sit here. I sit mild, rounded, sniffling, smiling at her, the Madonna content in her rotund middle age. —Cait is mine, is home, is living, is prettier than even I remember. Is all I'll ever require. But I set my fork down. Not exactly hungry now. Know what's a real good diet? Life is.

SURE I'M OUT the three thousand bucks, so what? American Express will surely forgive that bill, only fair, considering. Be great corporate publicity. Tomorrow I'll drive to Richmond fast, negotiate Ian's return of my down payment for an orchestra that was going to be merely skeletal, after all. Once that's done, I will only be "out" certain intangible emotional expenses. Cost? No more than my credibility to all of Falls. After this who will ever believe me again, when nobody did before?

My outlay? Incalculable. But an expense I'll forever keep hidden. All that matters is *she's* visible again, my own best self back whole.

(For what it's worth, the name of the firm that countersigned the *repatriation* shipping order and collected my three grand? "Isis Novelties, Ltd. Nairobi.") Avoid them.

IX

O N LEARNING OF my child's drowning, I had not, as I stated, managed to weep. Unlike my newly-sensitive ex-husband who—these days as an adopted Californian married to philosophy's own Tiffany—can grow misty-eyed over anything, including a Niçoise salad if it is tossed sufficiently beautifully. (Shelburne too, come to think of it, is a veritable Trevi Fountain. I know it's one of feminism's gains but somebody should maybe *tell* these guys, when it comes to men and sobbing?—less is more. Once, twice per male lifetime. Father's death, Mom's. One really good dog's. Otherwise, put a sock in it.)

Myself, I didn't truly cry till Cait returned. But once we got her tucked back safely home under her sky-blue comforter, I sensed I could. The very evening she arose—painful centimeter by centimeter —all six feet out of her grave, stand *back*.

The moment my living daughter walked in, I belatedly felt the lash of her father's leaving. Funny how that works. When Edward forsook me overnight six years ago, concussion, adrenaline, pride, three needy kids and watchful neighbors all kept me plodding forward. Like that robotic vacuum cleaner they advertise now, one you can leave to roam your empty house sucking up the dust and hair of others. Gorging, ramming chair legs, unable to switch itself off. Herself.

During Cait's absence, the twins and I, we worked out some-thing very dear, half-mute but quite athletic; it keeps you in shape, being so close to two fond ten-year-old males of equal strength who monkey-climb doorframes and oneself. Isometric affection my twins still offered me. Support geodesic.

Their father? cleanly gone. His theoretical Tiffany no earthly help.

THAT SELFSAME EVENING of the day Cait stunned by simply stroll-ing in alive, I took to bed early. At last, sanctioned rest. Eight p.m., alone upstairs, I let boys' eventful pajama party grow even wilder than their usual. Did I care? Full of mac and cheese, my soccer fans sounded almost happy at Brazil's early goals. Apparently the U.S. players had "choked." Booing their own nation for the first time maybe let local boys feel more international, little 007s licensed to kill abroad. It sure made them louder. "Girls! Our USA boys are playing no bettern GIRLS, man! And right out on TV where foreign people SEE 'em, man!"

Will it never end?

Three ghetto blasters all played different rappers, none any good. Boys kept thumping up and down the stairs beside my room, fridge to bike-rack to microwave. One of my customary bossy yodels down our staircase—"Hey, dweebs, keep it to a mild roar"—usually shushed them for six-minute intervals.

Tonight, trust me, childish roughhousing did not faze me. Would they like to torch the house? Matches in the top-left drawer beside the stove. Phone for pizza, strippers? Fine by Jean. She'd slip her versatile AmEx card under her bedroom door. I hope to never—even on my due date of death—feel as tired as I did that night.

All the "parenting" books tell you. What we do is self-engineered obsolescence. Once you teach your kids to (1) love, then (2) leave you, your job on earth is done.

And I thought I'd be okay with that. I'd expected to feel overlooked once my kids turn, say, fifty. But at ages ten or eighteen? No. Tonight I felt dead to them. I lacked a husband. And my own children, like their sleepover friends, seemed to recall Jean Mulray's usefulness one hour before dinnertime or whenever the next mall run was required. I could say I felt swamped, emotionally exhausted. But it was more than that. I could not collect, rejoin myself.

So, covered by the twins' room's rap droning over All-Sports TV, as part of catching up, royally sick of being the strong one, I quietly released one smallish test-sob. It caught hard. Felt extra-good. What got tough, ever reining it all back in.

I soon let myself cry. But as a diva does her scales. Strengthening. And why on earth not? Who was I NOT being sloppy for? I cried for my wretched mother, who preferred her French wallpaper and white brocaded chaise to the muddy world. I cried for my having failed Eddie. For fully-funding Shelburne while never quite interesting him. I cried for the way only Tragedy had ever made me feel comically-and-completely alive. I thought of that now-trite line: Tragedy plus Time equals Comedy. But how many geologic ages would my own joke take to hatch?

Then, as if on cue, Cait herself knocked. She slipped unasked into the room I'd once shared with her father.

"Mom? I am so sorry. Whatever crossed wires were my fault, forgive me, 'kay? I put you on the Do Not Call list once but the phone kept totally blocking without my noticing. You suddenly shut up. And that? That felt . . . mature of you. Honestly, I was relieved. Past that, now I'm here to register concern tonight. Because, I wonder, can you *hear* yourself? I know you know you're crying, okay? But by now you're sounding kind of like a beagle barking. I thought it *was* a dog. Not that 'blame' is in any way involved here. Only, maybe consider the boys and their friends, all right? I can barely imagine the strain and excitement of this, and then suddenly getting me back and all. —But, Mom, look. Cait's brought something *in*to the house for a change. Making up for all your heirloom-stuff I gave away. I feel worst about your shoes. Africa showed me: the person's only pair of footgear is so . . . I'd say, maybe, 'autobiographical'? (Whoa, *there's* an essay.) Yeah, very close-in, the shoes. You alone, Mom, get to make your charitable decisions. I see that now. That was so not right of me. Should have left you at least a couple pairs, three. It was selfish and no one is readier to admit it. —But here is what I brought you . . . Women from 'my' region? they weave these? and we all think their home-loomed products are pretty much . . . gorgeous, I mean, right? One U.S. catalogue placement could make a huuuuge difference for my village. This one cloth, Mom? I'd say is the best I ever found at any market there, ever."

She unfolds from nowhere a fabric of gold.

"CAITIE," I GO. "You're too much. You're everything they say. Me? I'm not really able to . . . not worth . . ."

"Shhh. —Market days, they sometimes wear these over their heads, a mantilla-shawl-burnoose-type deal. I owe you so much. Do. Hush now. Here, may I drape you, Mom? Omalu and her sisters, they totally taught me how to tie it perfect in back."

She hops onto my mattress. My living daughter reaches behind me. She tugs fabric across my shoulders. Up it goes till it settles, billowing around my head. Isn't it just *like* Cait? Having this on hand, she tries distracting me from bawling, does this easily as any parent diverts an infant's attention from its selfish li'l self.

166

Caitie arranges cloth, scratchy, round my hairline. My crybaby eyes must appear swollen half-shut. So much atypical emotion. I sense I look a fright. Especially when scanned from up-this-close. Next room, twins and friends chant like Comanche braves round a war-counsel fire.

I rest propped among the pillows on my bed. Cait, trying to prettify me, rises onto browned legs. She knee-walks nearer. I am lightly straddled. Her hennaed head tilts either way. She's appraising, smiling. Above me Cait seems a bazaar-saleswoman hoping to convince me I look super in her wares. I try grinning back. But I feel an amateur, uneasy responding to another's touch, to the pull of my own battered vanity. I truly have none left. I've saved back no goodwill for just myself. Goodwill! My daughter gave so much of mine away.

"More *like* it." Cait's salesgirl voice sounds insincere.

This headdress's cheap dye smells of fish, something soaked in brine. Scent hints at the unclean then suggests the contagious. Around me cloth crackles, stiff. As Cait, astride me, adjusts it, an almost-weightless box of balsa wood seems to break against my cheekbones, crush either ear. Loose metal threads poke my scalp. "You look so 'hot,' lady, know that? But you still *need* something. Guess what?" Her eyes swim huge in their blueness all before me.

I shake my head no. I'm scared of risking an answer.

Cait now curves in closer. Her gristled backside indents Mom's marshmallow tummy. She, lean, rests across the full hill-country of Momma Jean hips. No one has "been on top of me" (in or out of this bed) since her father enlisted in Ethics 101 and started matriculating under Tiffany.

Caitlin fusses with my awning burnoose. Aren't feminists the enemies of veils? This one means to make me finally pretty in the ways poor Ice had hoped. If an organdy hair ribbon won't do it, try the whole paper bag.

Boys go jumping off the top bunk. They scream over a winning soccer goal: "It's Bra-zil! Brazil's boys are Gods. USA boys are Girls. It's Gods against Girls. They're Gods, man. Gods always beat the Girls!"

"Know what *you* need, Mom? I think, see, you're getting *tired* of mothering. —And who can blame you? Here your kids are, running off everywhere. Seems to Cait, *you* might need a real mother about now. Not just some frozen fish-stick witch like yours, either . . . 'Jean.' My Africa has 'grown me.' I'm finally home and just the woman to do it. I'm here to give a little *back*."

UH-OH. ONE NUBILE female rests across me. She is trying to mask me. She cannot know how boned and boyish her hips feel sunk into my over-ample sponge-blob ones. She lifts the coarse veil to frame my face. It slips. Cait is planning some major hug or, worse, a kiss, a spirit makeover I don't need. Success-oriented as any young Ivy exec, she will not be stopped. Foil-cloth covers my one eye then both. The cloth now tastes, a toxic net.

Her words drift down through fish-stink foil, "Need . . . moth-er-ing . . . Am sensing a huge *hug-deficit*!" Strong arms hook behind me. Fabric blindfolds then gags. I head-butt toward the boyish weight.

My girl feels stronger than the twins and me combined. Africa's full-attention has enlarged her force field. Blue eyes have charmed local wildlife and half-nude tribal elders but it ain't quite working here for me! "Girls Can Do Anything," except climb up on ole Jean here.

As Caitlin Mulray, having dressed me like some village doll, a fairly big one, presses hard atop me, I recall her father newly twenty, avid as some brand-new Boy Scout knife. First I shrug to beg for air. But Cait, deranged with sudden college-essay empathy—mistakes this spasm as my next shaking sob.

Muscle-stolid, she comes in for another sloppy Liberal hug. Was her latest eco-sacrifice deodorant? She now smells not-unpleasant. But too acridly vital. My little girl's dry-honey scent seems gone for good. What smell replaces it, this close? I am near the headspring of the Mississippi-Nile. "Please, Cait . . . let me. Breath is . . . I . . . Hugging . . . hurts. —You're back a-*live*. What in hell else do you *want*?"

Itchy gilt closes my throat. Dying here. "URgh, Cai . . ." I drop back and, panicked, do shove once. With all my deranged menopausal might. I hear a pretty good *thwump*.

Boys' music pounds, Africanized, peppery, competitive, alive. Once I've beaten this golden shroud back, I regain light. And only as I tear into free air again, only then, sweat-soaked, do I note another woman, thrown seven feet across the room.

On her back, she is swearing (that Swahili?). She's been decked against a baseboard. She keeps mashing one palm to her brow, jerking it away to look for blood. Curled fetal in her corner, she now glowers. "Thanks a lot to you, too. Fucking *COW*!"

Somehow I laugh. She's made me feel so silly, nine years old and oddly free. Her insult means she lives. It means she truly is my child and mainly simply hates me. All is as before, amen.

But swelling overtakes Cait's right eye. My handiwork? I watch it grow. My girl now squints from such an aged lopsided face. Who *did* this to her? It's my face but twisted far more sideways, briefly maybe even meaner.

(Cait's friends all call her "awesome." But to somebody my age, that word can still imply "scary.")

I reach for my re-living huffing girl.

"Dearest self," I say, and climb on all fours toward her end of my bed. Instead of reaching out, she prods her bad eye's swelling. Almost socks herself to test then prove my crime. Finding no head blood, she seems to wish a great gash open.

I explain I felt trapped: she'd clamped atop me with that rag. What had she been *do*ing? I'm a classic claustrophobe, her father always said. And I never have fared well with mandatory consolation. —Nothing but sleep has happened on this mattress since her dad's last bouncy Friday night ride here. In my last six Eddie-less years, I've somehow made my peace here with the sensual Nothing of a real high thread-count.

"Sorry, honey," I call. "You meant well. But put yourself in my ... not 'shoes' but..."

We simply slump here, panting now, sweating through our clothes. Lady wrestlers, opposite corners.

I do admire her photo-ready navel.

BUT EVEN NOW I keep thinking: Her beautiful funeral will never happen, not in my lifetime. Could I have said aloud my prayer for all dead children from *The Book of Common Prayer*? Would I have finally licked the stage fright Ice called some form of epilepsy? For a sec, I wonder if we might not produce the whole show anyway? just to generally celebrate, oh, the concept of "Return"? Should Falls miss the costly world premiere of Sir Stanley Shelburne's "Caitlin Cantata"? Has it been, all along, a "vanity production"?

Still, I understand: every single citizen might love the pageant except, of course, this one, the one Repatriated, sulking in yon corner.

One last time I strain her way. But Cait is prodding her puffed eye, using an intentionally-uplifted middle finger. And only now, having just been pinned by my own girl, do I, silent, understand: Jesus Christ, know *what*? She's considered magnetic because she's as "crazy" as they say *you* are, Jean! *That's* what draws others to her. Unlike you, nobody's quite seen *through* her yet. Poor child is too much *like* you, so just go ahead and fully pity her up-front. The sec she stops being pretty—her moral knack, her smarts, those will— like yours—go overlooked from that day forward.

I call, "Shouldn't have, honey. Your weight stopped me breath-ing. I like breathing. Besides, hey, you only caught me *cry*ing. Is that such a crime, considering? Just *let* me. Couldn't you let Momma Jean haul off this first night you're alive again and—however like a hound the ole hag sounds—just let Mom *cry* for you?"

"For *YOU*, you mean!"

And this I hated. Right then, as usual: Caitlin Mulray sounded mainly right.

X

LIKE THE REST of falls, I had turned my child into someone ideal then immortal. I heard from Doc Roper's head-nurse how our darling GP had retrieved all Cait's childhood records. He then tied a black ribbon around them, keeping them in plain view out on his desk. Memorials everywhere.

Now, merely literally alive, she just needed me to do her Third World laundry. Plus, would I kindly keep her brothers' hip-hop music off while she got in some serious beauty rest, prepping for her favorite *Atlanta Journal and Constitution* reporter and his photographer due in on Thursday? "Probably dumb of me to schedule picture-taking this near so long a flight. But tell me, on a scale of one to ten, how swollen *did* you get this eye? Tell me true and I can face it. I'll either grab a bag of ice or use a whole bottle of foundation or cancel. It's totally your call, Mom."

IN SECRET I sped to Richmond the Monday after her return from African death. I'd phoned Ian to make a vague if urgent-sounding secret appointment. I asked to see my young contact alone if possible. Maybe the surprise element would finally work *for* me. Ian's door plaque still promised, Special Concert Facilitator, Virginia Symphony Liaison. I would rely on that.

He rose as I swept in wearing an old daisy-print Marimekko meant to announce a whole new emotional landscape. I saw that Ian, however, sported a black turtleneck: Proof he was hip? A mark of respect for my mourning? Or both? Or maybe some attempt to scotch my sudden need for discount, refund?

"So," his smile promised purest professional kindness. "This, our Thursday, is nearly here at last. Yes, dear Jean, everything's in readiness. We've explained your circumstance to orchestra members. Their union rep lost *his* young son in a car wreck last year. So he went on and on about our people's giving this their all, etc. The alto—who, by the by, was Third Rhine Maiden in a Met *Das Rheingold* in which Jessye was supposed to've sung years back, *her* name is Jean too, funny, has learned you-all's score coming and going, and says it's not without . . . has real merit. Called it surprisingly difficult considering it was originally being written for less experienced . . . for 'high school band.' I think you and your composer-friend will be pleased with our soloist's artistry."

"'Mixed-Band-Chorus-and-Orchestra.'"

"Of course," he said, corrected. "Holst was choirmaster at a girls' school, composed great if simplish things for them. No, our musicians are always glad to premier *new* works. Good for our grant profile, too. The *1812* and *Jupiter* do tend to come around again pretty quickly. Whereas contemporary compositions of whatever provenance give us a chance to take the pulse of—"

For emphasis, I touched his desk. "Circumstances have changed, my fine young friend. And it's deeply good news. Let me first say how easy you have made all this. Really, Ian. Myself, being someone who's published in the *Atlantic* and so forth, *I* know there are differences between amateur and professional standards. These,

173

you've eased us over so lightly. Nothing is lost on me." I pause, open my purse for the handkerchief I'd ironed especially.

"Ian? my daughter is alive. The drowning was a false report meant to only shake me down for money. A cruel plot. And did I ever fall for it! Why, her air freight alone—or the lie about their needing to ship her—set me back three thousand. On top of that, there've been other carrying costs. Which brings us to certain-other-extras. I mean my check meant to hold the orchestra for some eventual Thursday up ahead . . ."

"You aren't by chance speaking of the 'nonrefundable moneys already distributed,' Mrs. Mulray? Fifteen thousand dollars might not sound like a lot to you. —No, wait, of course it is. But we have fully sixty-nine persons on VSO payroll, not counting our cleaning crew and freelance bus drivers. Not to mention your own superbly-educated if student-loaned young Ian here.

"Let me finish, please. At times, our orchestra gets hired out to play certain big-ticket weddings. The Boston Symphony need never do this sort of work (it is considered demeaning especially by our first-chair string players). You'd be amazed how many weddings—particularly the more expensive *society* kind—get canceled at the eleventh hour, Mrs. Mulray. It usually happens when some playboy-groom just fails to turn up. The bishop is already waiting at the altar, our full orchestra has been placed in grouping all over the church and choir loft. After thirty-five minutes' playing our stalling music—usually one to four Vivaldi *Seasons* stretching across what can feel a whole year—the bride's father will tiptoe toward our busy conductor. This father, holding a cell phone, will whisper thanks while explaining that, as of this second, and the present phone-call from Miami, our services are no longer required.

"I'm asking, madam, that you put yourself in our place.

—Weddings fall through far oftener than funerals, I believe. Fact is, yours is the first such reprieve I've ever heard of. Look on the bright side. Your daughter is home and alive and, by your own account, amazing at flute-playing and all else. That's the good news of your story. One might say *she's* your refund! You created in her honor a musical work of a certain complexity and length. But, as for rebates . . ."

REPATRIATED, KEEPING HER tan *current*, Cait reserved our home's great room from two to six. She would be giving most of her interviews there. She'd begun acting like a prom queen entitled to center stage. Pointed, cool, she seemed more and more a chip off the old "Ice." I told no one of this newfound similarity to my mom. Instead I did exactly as the girl instructed, silently gagging while complying. That'd been my way of dealing with the earlier Ice's insane demands.

Cait was probably kinder than your average homecoming queen tensed up the night before her ball, but not by much. I did recall: she was a child barely eighteen. She was our "home-coming queen" okay!

The emotion of return made me feel gypped by my firstborn's hype. "'Hope,' 'hype.' Just one letter apart," so I decided at a red light. "Saying *what*?" a twin asked from my backseat. It shocked me, somehow still being *heard*.

During some breakfasts Cait quizzed me about my own operatic emotions regarding her death. On hearing of the drowning, when had I phoned whom? Dad first? Good. Had he screamed? Really? Say he had to call back? Good. Too stunned at first, probably.

Cait wondered aloud how I had found the energy to go on, to plan it all. She actually interviewed me. Should that not have pleased a mom? But it did not. Somehow I remained convinced this was just more of her vanity. She was simply gauging her present power by measuring the crater that a Caitlin-absence truly made. Looking back, I think she might have been trying to help me; but I was still too stunned to accept counseling from the likes of her. I found I almost liked her better when she was being snippy, childish. I wanted her sympathy as little as I craved another head-cloth installation. Once, when I stood washing dishes, she came up behind me, massaged my upper shoulders and asked in her huskiest voice, "And how are *we* doing, you?"

"Look," I stiffened with a tone her dad had hated. "I know I gained some weight while you were gone. But I don't yet feel qualified for my own full-out 'we.'"

"Oh. I meant the two of us, is all," she pulled away. I turned, regret, but she had barefooted off into the dining room. Via mirror ricochet, I could see her standing one room away, still being hurt by me. And then the worst thing happened. My husband had always told Caitlin she looked like Ingrid Bergman as a girl. And, at that moment, given her weight loss, while she suffered my rebuff, I saw it. She did. Her hennaed hair chopped short, she stood there: Ingrid Bergman at eighteen, a righteous beauty playing pure Saint Joan.

—Well, that certainly felt distancing.

HER STORY WAS now national news. And if the reporters she had known before were just print journalists, I now fielded phone queries from two nightly New York news shows. "A Town in Mourning Becomes a Town Overjoyed" was the general idea. One of her friends confessed he'd just sold Cait's junior yearbook for five hundred bucks to CBS. Was that bad? he asked us all. We just stood there. We had no rules. "More power to you," I had to laugh.

176

I was left feeling lopsided, coldcocked, even slightly fatter. I had made a thousand "If only . . ." bargains with a God I now considered mainly nonexistent. And yet all those feverish IOUs, they now came due.

XI

L ET'S SPEED HER tale along a bit, shall we? I have not been able to catch the rotation since. I was thrown off, is all. See, at 4:40 p.m., your daughter is dead; her orchestral mass is ready; and yet by 5:19 p.m. she has stuffed your washer with filthy skivvies, and come 8:40 p.m. she has you smothered in some gold lamé Klan head-hood.

You try on these freeze-drying extremes. It's as if something in my nervous circuitry, already split-ended, got truly finally fried. I'd first resented that she went to Africa after my urging her not to. "Over my dead body," I had said. That may well prove true.

Her being announced drowned then shipped home, her causing me to question everything, her forcing me to make my peace with missing my own favorite child forever, that was a toughie, okay? But how might I survive her simply strolling through our front door, stepping free of flip-flops, munching one of my famous oatmeal-raisin cookies? All without even a phone-call's warning? Hard. And after cadging some free ride courtesy of a married pilot thanks to her midriff made even tighter by a season's swimming with every nude tribesman this side of Botswana? I'm sorry. My daughter thinks she owns the world and now—come back to life—she truly does. Seems almost unfair how her college-entry essay concerning this very topic will nail her Princeton, Yale, maybe even Radcliffe, plus Brown, her backup school, all early admission. Early resurrection.

And where does that leave me?

Where?

Pissed is where.

At whom? Myself, as usual, I guess.

As before, my every sentiment, my each attempt, looks spastic, inappropriate. My life has been an intense training session for some event as yet unstaged, its date still unannounced. I've known there would be some test, intended just for me myself. And it was not *this* one.

—For a while, with her presumed dead, the press had written about "the surviving mother, a published poet and single parent who'd scrimped to provide her children with *Encyclopædia Britannica* and each Creative Plaything that helped stimulate them into being the stand-up citizen role models they today remain."

Cait sported the black eye a week after our wrestling match. I suspected she doctored it with eyeliner. So be it. She had chopped off her hennaed ends when that first Atlanta photographer told her it would not "read." She simply grabbed my kitchen's chicken-snipping shears and stepped toward the half-bath's mirror and, as grown men watched with a prurience I sort of shared, Cait took six swipes, dropped dark frizz into the trash basket, fluffed her crest, and stepped the Leica's way fashion-ready. No fair. A somebody.

Between interviews, I kept asking Cait if she'd yet phoned her devoted Mr. Shelburne.

"Mom? any idea the length of my Check-in Cheer-up Not-dead-yet list? Anyway, *I* didn't announce my drowning. So *you* phone whatever ones you want. But keep a list so I can then do little fol-low-ups. There's plenty in this for everyone, okay?"

*

179

THE SAME REPORTERS who'd sung eulogies to Caitlin's high school public spirit returned to chronicle a family in overjoyed shock at her return. The *Alive at Five* news team hinted I should say on-camera how Caitlin's comeback had been the single greatest moment of my whole life, right? Obviously. They wanted all my emotions laid out paint-by-number.

"The world must again look truly perfect to you, right, Jean Mulray, mother of Caitlin?"

"Yes and no, Kelli."

The cameraman's eyes rolled. I felt my cantankerousness latch back down, its metal flanges fastening extra-fierce. *I'd* become the teenage sulker who refuses a family fiction faked so easily by everybody else.

Sure, her cell got stolen, but could she not bother to borrow a friend's? And once she got a replacement, could she not have unblocked all incoming from me? —Still, we must consider *her* heroic, for forging clear back to us. I wanted to tell reporters: *If she'd simply called me or anybody local, we would've known she was alive.*

Too busy to bother.

WHAT GOT TO me the day after her return, my home phone rang back to life with a midnight jungle's full-moon vengeance. A virtual Virginia Symphony Orchestra of messaging. "Would you put in a good word for my moving up my Caitlin Mulray interview so we can wedge her comeback story on page one of our Sunday supplement? Else the boss will have my head on a platter. You've got to help me, lady. I have kids, too. This *is* the mother, right? Look, would eighty-five bucks help you offset certain scheduling expenses? No, make that a cool hundred ten, plus copies of every good picture we get of her, sent as JPEGs, Web-ready."

Hearing yet another shy knocking at my front door, I simply hung up on this paparazzo leech.

SHELBURNE LOOKED HUGE there, jammed all angled into my doorframe. Bristly, he'd seemed to have experienced some boy's final growth surge. His hair stuck out in back but the dark jaw had been shaved so thoroughly he'd nicked himself. A bit of folded toilet paper, resting in the cleft below his nose, looked to me like a tiny origami dove of peace.

Seeing him, I straightened. Today I felt overripe for his usual hug, the kindly baritone asking after me.

"Just me, Jean. —How *is* she?"

I stepped, silent, aside. He passed into her home.

"Stan, you mean that girl hasn't phoned you once during her days home, and with all my reminding and after you wrote an entire *chor*al work for . . . ?"

"Probably busy. I expect very little . . . At that age . . . they're so . . . Is she . . . *here*, Jean?"

No, I answered: my celebrated one was out being honored by her former Brownie Scout troop. But, stunned as I felt, I did not say more. I simply settled on our foyer's single wicker bench. I gestured a palm-up *help yourself* toward the waiting rooms. I even pointed Stan toward the staircase. Like that bum, older males all wanted to be led to *where she sleeps*. I told Stan that he would know Cait's room when he found it. As for Jean? She would just go on sitting on a low straw perch where nothing ever rests except overdue library books, soccer balls, zinc-oxide tubes, dry-cleaning outgoing. Now, overdue, out-rolling: here Jean waited, listening as Stan patrolled her suburban home's second floor.

He sought his beloved at every door, within each closet. The ironing board, built into its own cupboard? fell on him. A grunt. I allowed myself one laugh. Jean attended to his big (size 16) feet slapping around up there. Bongo clown-shoes crossed floors, muted by each throw rug, a grown man's pointless quest for someone literally half his age and fully indifferent to him.

I told myself I felt that same way toward *Stan* now. And after all we had been through together.

Footsteps finally halted beside the actual girl's actual futon. One married man was likely picking up stray outer- or underclothes, no doubt breathing through them. (Oh, I read a lot, I've seen films, I know how these things work in other, real lives.)

Dry-eyed, dry, with only menopause's heat to signal all her true warmth's ending, Jean simply waited near this home's front portal. He'd need to come back out this way. Back past his former "Jeannie with the Light."

Finally the man descended, quaking. "Jean? don't even *tell* her I came by. And no confronting her with any criticism on my behalf from *you*, either, hear? I'll just pretend, whenever she and I *do* meet, it's by chance. That way we'll keep it . . . clean. Don't complicate things for me, umkay? People say she's more amazing than ever . . . And you, you've been so . . . I really think your faith made all this possible, Jean. Your *will* has brought her back to me, us. Plus, you opened me up . . . to myself again. And now I can direct that on toward *her*. Bless you for knowing." Stan left. In his right back pocket, the giant walkie-talkie cell phone; in the left I saw a cusp of white, one of her socks? No, surely panties. I remembered Bongo, the abducting carny clown, seen from behind, running. I listened as Stan's old car started, on its third try.

With the last of what my mother willed me, I'd commissioned a symphony from him.

And now? Dental receptionists, behind glass, receive greater attention from most exiting patients.

I LATER INFORMED Cait: Mr. Shelburne had just extensively toured her blue room, possibly giving prayerful thanks; he had stayed up there a half an hour easy. (Not strictly true.) "So if your pillow is wet, it's from some grown man weeping for a girl too busy to return Stan's calls . . ."

"Uh, Mom? How is this you're putting me through not water-boarding abuse? —God, Mother, you *will* dramatize."

I told her, with a Caitlin around, I didn't have to.

I FELT ASHAMED everywhere I went in Falls. Had I not filed a false report? Had I not been plucked clean by phone hucksters? Had I not spent a life specializing in bungled news that made me look first alarmist then ill-informed?

But, I had just been on TV. Once-rude store managers now came out front to greet me. Even the martinet grocery manager who'd made me pay for all that grapefruit juice after the glass-breaking Bongo sadness thirteen years back. He actually took my hand, saying, "Cannot imagine. First to be tricked by some foreign terrorist, which we have to call those types. My heart would've actually stopped if *my* son stepped back in that way."

"Well, Sam," I replied, speed-reading his name tag. I was about to sound like the sad sack B-actress I'd lately become. "We feel we cannot go on, dear Sam," I paused a cheap three-beat Susan Hayward often used, two-three. "And yet . . . somehow, guy . . . we go on. We do, Sam, *don't* we?"

Then I smiled with my own brand of cheerful, uninvited-by-any-book-club woe.

*

FIRST I HAD been just one major somebody's shoe source or AA sponsor or faux-wife. I was *Mom.* Then at last I got elevated to a newer status: Saint second-rank. And for a while I found myself escalatoring toward the fully saintly. Next, that moving stairway's power failed, and with such force it knocked me down a story, a flight or two. Of course, to see her eating breakfast, to note the twins piling into her lap, of course, I rejoiced clear to the point of sunny madness. Again I ranked her beauty very high. Once more I revered how she "dealt with the press," making mental notes for my *own* next shot at it.

Saint Somebody, life-sized, waltzes in again, even further alive— surer, trimmer, more a martyr, one topic fully-tanned. I know it's not her fault.

But, really, is it mine?

XII

WAS AT OUR annual neighborhood picnic something wonderful finally happened. (To me, I mean.) Might seem a small moment for anybody else. The mothers of two girls Caitlin's age stood serving food alongside me. Plump ceramicist-Millicent's mom, plus the mother of a class "Caitlin" everybody always instead called "Winooski." We were arranging deviled eggs on platters across oilclothed card-tables.

Cait arrived late in BlondMatt's red convertible. She appeared barefoot though it was autumn already, an African folk custom she'd adopted. She acted surprised if anyone mentioned it, looking down at her own wriggle of toes. "My *what*? Oh, yes, but in many, no, *most* countries, shoes are still such a luxury, I guess we sometimes forget how . . ."

Many locals had not seen my girl since her resurrection. When Caitlin Mulray climbed into view, applause broke out. Eyes lowered, she nonetheless waved one wrist. Like royalty, sparing herself carpal-tunnel—all while militantly barefoot.

Other kids had heard she'd saved the ambassador's young son from drowning by pulling him back from the very edge of a nasty waterfall, etc. . . . Was that true? I got asked. Me? I corrected no story. "Amazing little girl," is all I've ever said. And who could argue that?

Even certain adults, the fathers of her classmates, now asked her to address civic clubs about both the state of modern Africa and any of her recent watery adventures there. Younger girls wondered if they might carry her back-from-Africa pink-gray backpack. And 96 lb. Cait—humbled to find herself considered larger than life—simply nodded, accepting child aid.

The high school glee club had chipped in and bought my daughter her own commemorative puppy. The blond cocker looked like our old Cookie. I wouldn't let Cait keep it. I'd housebroken three children and, now with my hardwood floors finally half-decent, I would just not go through that again. She used the words "monster of selfishness." Furious, she hauled off and boarded the dog at Tori's one block away. That trampy Tori, interested at last, became Cait's new close friend. Tori teetering on heels beside my barefoot child, they walked their pup together.

I now spied, following Matt's sleek convertible, a dented support car wrapped in its own blue exhaust. Mr. Shelburne got out carrying Cait's cocker. He spied me, looked away, then nodded, acting chagrined yet proud to have any role, however supporting. Gauging the crowd, so trying to be of use to Cait, Stan hoisted her pup ten inches higher. The crowd went, "Oooh." Stan had proved his—if not importance—then glum efficiency here.

I turned half-aside. The two moms flanking me tensed. They had not exactly clapped when Cait's procession arrived. Mrs. Winooski muttered so I'd have to overhear, "Oh, look. Li'l 'Mother Theresa' has turned up, late." These other women scanned my face. They'd just witnessed how Stan's role in my daughter's life had sunk to this level janitorial. The two stepped inches nearer. They must have assumed, as I once did, that Shelburne and I would likely be lovers.

186

Millicent's mom and Winooski's now swapped looks. They seemed to have prepared a little speech. "We . . . we've come to more . . . respect you, Jean. For how you planned her service . . . For all you did to help ease at least the *rest* of our Falls community through this. You didn't get stuck feeling sorry for yourself as either of *us* might. Nobody knows *how* you did it. And, even finding a man who could and would write that much music so quick, well . . . And paying out of pocket for a big-time orchestra. And now all he can find to do is . . ." Here, newer darker looks were transmitted, received. I could only nod my thanks.

"The terrible thing," Winooski went on. "Since your girl got so much of the class attention growing up, is how . . . when she . . . died, drowned, whatever, we hated ourselves. But even so, us class moms we did start hoping . . . (this not easy) . . . we admitted hoping *our* daughters might finally have their own merits seen a little better. Really great gals, ours, too. In any other class but hers? they might've been . . . And now she's *back*. Which is great of course. But we do feel at times she's . . . your Cait can be a little . . . *much*. Still, it has at least let us see YOU more clearly, Jean. With some . . . new feeling. Oh and we're sorry about going off on you about the cold spaghetti you passed off as bats' intestines. Halloween is for scaring and you sure do a job on our neighbor kids, but they line up for it, don't they? Now we just *get* you better, is all. You know, we decided over wine last night . . . *you're* the very thing she keeps trying to . . . be. So, for all that we got wrong—before she died and all—we're sorry. And, well, you just *go*, ole girl!"

How "ole"? I must be at least a year younger than these two.

Go *where*? The Outer Banks?

Still, I thanked them. Most of our picnic crowd yet milled about focused on Caitie. Having chopped off the henna, she now looked like a blond boy with dandelion fluff, creating a trend. A vogue she knew would not look good on any of her eight overnight copycats.

But what finally counted was how these moms, after leveling with me, now literally touched me. Brave girls. Had they *practiced* this, as I'd once prepped to turn Stan's pages? Each woman placed an open palm against opposing sides of my own lower back, for just two warming seconds, maybe four.

While everybody else aimed toward the most famous person in our town now, two decent ordinary women slightly older than I smiled beside me, as my guardians. Behind our pooled grins, to either side of me, they remained in touch if only for three secs, four. That was all. Just checking in.

"Bless you both," I said, quiet. "Always surprising to be noticed."

They had treated me as two loving daughters might a mom they loved. For me, it was something, was truly something.

—Of course, they probably had no idea what they'd just done.

XIII

A FTER THIS, OUR mother-daughter skirmishes, Cait's and mine, surpassed earlier dog-and-cat fights. She kept mentioning having always wished to live in California, not Falls. And I kept recalling Stan—his following Caitlin in that debased role of puppy -dog-transport. Or what irked her buying new clothes that made bare feet contrast with chosen skirts that looked like Las Vegas's idea of a French schoolgirl? Whatever started our tiffs, they came almost daily now. They concerned earlier tiffs, or even likely weather, or *Place Names for 100*. Soon as we started, twins packed up their homework and cereal bowls and left the room.

Cait: "And what're *you* staring at?"

Jean: "My eighteen-year-old daughter. Why? Along with the photographers, do I need an appointment?"

C: "Wish you had asked up-front if I was down with your blacking my eye."

J: "'Purpled,' tops. And now you're getting that nice new yellow along its edges. Hon, I was just fighting to keep breathing. I had a thing over my head, couldn't see *what* my knuckles caught. Please don't scold your mom for having grieved for you, Cait."

C: "Guess that's just one of the ways we're different. I am so not as you describe me. You, now, do take good care mainly of yourself

189

then your kids. Your concern is, I'd say, national and more for local souls. Whereas I guess I'll always be a bit more involved with . . ."

J: "'The World'? Tell me you were not going to say that. You sound like a Miss Universe Contestant. Let's see, hmmn: You're Global and I'm Falls' Broken Heart Country Club golf course. That your best shot, my dear returned Prodi-*gal*?"

C: "'Prodi-GAL'? And that's you being clever. You *think*? Mom, if you were applying somewhere with that? you would not get even *wait*-listed. I've never doubted your volume on the intellectual Richter-scale. Whatever your barometer IQ is today, nobody's ever called you stupid. People have called you scary, but . . . I'm just glad we went online and found you that Elizabeth Bishop conference. I know you'll meet lots of other people like you. I have some leftover summer spending-money I truly want to chip in for tuition, book costs. Okay, I'm a handful. But you *knew* that. You've been my life-coach fight-manager, whatever. You taught me to *read*, 'm I right? Just hope you find some peace is all. I guess until the person gets right with herself, she . . ."

(And this was a calmish day. This, while we stood preparing our separate dietetic breakfasts . . .)

FINALLY, MY OWN family considered me so cross, so critical, that Eddie and the Lady Tiffany Philosophy moved east into our house on Milford Cul-de-Sac. They promised they would "spell" me for a while. "Let me do it for you. J-E-A-N." Silence on the phone.

Muttering, I kept rememorizing my funeral poem from *The Book of Common Prayer* while attending my favorite new irregular French verb: *"Suffire: "To be enough, be sufficient."* Why isn't there one such *English* verb for saying all of that at once?

Caitlin had been phoning her dad. After our daily flare-up, I'd see her out there, all but chewing her little cell, still somehow with her. She'd be barefoot, striding back and forth, pacing inside our backyard's fence like some veldt-dwelling cat unfairly zooed. She'd wave her arm, head shaking. She wore enough African junk jewelry so she clinked like a tribal gift shop.

Cait continued nightly snitching to California, to her glamour parent: how the Warden had lost her remaining mind, such small margin as was left. Claimed I was now taking it all out on *her*. Swore I had pulverized her face on Night 1 ("like hamburger," I heard at least those words). And just when she'd needed to look her best for both Matts and print-journalism. She hinted that whenever her pals came over now, I was always in the room, referring to the good ole days . . . when she was, like, *dead*.

Cait told Edward I had begun wearing short skirts; that I kept bothering BlackMatt plus my hangdog married sob-sister Mr. Shelburne with my indispensable oatmeal-raisin cookie deliveries to home and school. Well, I'd bought one or two black crepe-y outfits as *possibles* for her big service. It shocks her to imagine that people could have really liked me, just for *me*. But in some ways, Caitlin being Caitlin, she is partly-mainly right.

It's just: Jean here had nowhere to take it, all the stuff I'd learned. I'd felt so close to others, and for going on three weeks. Together we'd constructed such a project: the Theatre of Caitlin Mulray Memory.

Around my house, I'd set out the biggest available boxes of Kleenex. Every handy ledge and coffee table was readied for grieving's leakage outbursts.

—You bring up children so they can leave you easily and well. Mission accomplished. But, what have I kept preparing *myself* for?

For those years when I'll finally be alone at home? When I can take fun college classes and at last earn the BA? Cait's pregnancy interrupted? Would there come a time when I might dust off my own poetry, maybe finally find time to make a few best friends?

Sylvia Plath has been done to death, I know. She did get her deserved Pulitzer, but posthumously. She was right at thirty. So fed up with her poor mental health, with a wandering husband however talented, with those kids keeping constant English colds. Came a day she just stuffed wet towels under the kitchen door, protecting sleeping children from the world outside and herself in here. She attached her doctor's phone number to the baby carriage's handle. Then she rammed her pretty head into the gas oven, far far back in, the reports all say. She wanted motherhood-divorce-writing over and done. Worn flat out, a mind that rare.

Well, let me say this only once: _I did not do that_.

MY DARLING DAUGHTER does look excellent on-paper and off. She photographs like a film star, no angle "bad." Tests well, too. Writes sestinas about homelessness that will make you cherish your hall thermostat. But _you_ try living with her.

Especially now she's back from Tarzan Country Day. She has delivered to favorite elderly neighbors little beaded napkin rings made by what she colonially calls "her" people. These trinkets are, in fact, so Pottery Barn. She can't see that. And of course I'll never tell her.

I know my girl is considered the greatest kid in many a local generation; her classmates even date things using her: The Summer Caitlin Mulray Didn't Know We Thought She'd Drowned.

—HOW DOES ANYONE _survive?_ And where is Caitkins now? Falls High

192

is in session. French IV, Miss Finson, room 214. Classes change in six minutes. Where does she think *I* am?

Oh she is not thinking of *me*. I've been that good a mother. Sainthood? Give me its SAT. I swear I'll ace the bugger.

XIV

I

T FEELS RIGHT, my sailing now. Somehow I am alone and at
least not seasick, bound for the tourist inn and its back-deck
seminar. Look, that must be our island dead ahead. Twisty wind-
bent trees, not one polluting car in sight. I learned about this
boardinghouse in the back of *Smithsonian*. Quite the li'l adventuress.
Others attendees will likely sit clutching their own blue Elizabeth
Bishop study binder.

I picture them at tomorrow's breakfast all wearing Abercrombie
safari outfits, sun hats, a few pith helmets. Me, dressed in green
boots, and my clothes-ure. Then I understand I've imagined heading
toward my own junior-year in Africa. Does this imply unconscious
competition with my daughter who somehow survived that continent? If so, I'm vaguely unaware of it.

Others at the table will be birder-widows, lady-librarians
similarly unattached. Gals who saw that same attractive little ad in
the magazine's classifieds, with its alluring lead word *Unique.*

Part of me hopes the owner of this Ocracoke B&B will get to
phone Eddie at any ole alarming hour, yelling how a nest of sharks
has finished me. Ed now sleeps on the king-sized bed in my own
bedroom, once also his; he rests beside his new li'l lady, his "littler"
lady. Tiffany does adore our kids. I must say that for her. She will

194

always be childless and so has wisely made a cult of his, mine. If I do become fish-food, Eddie will know I took the violent underwater death our Caitlin escaped. One thing's sure: no one will pay three thousand to FedEx *me* home.

The day I was to fly off and catch this ferry, Edward and Tiffany arrived by black limo. It's a fancy airport taxi, really, other customers along. Even so it put my rusty station-wagon to shame. Californians clamber forth all brown and lean, looking thirty-eight in matching chinos. Cait scampers out front and jumps him, legs wrapped clear around. Then the twins hoot into our front-yard. I, wearing slenderizing black, carrying a plate of my much-praised oatmeal cookies, follow.

I've hoped to stage-manage this reunion indoors, with more control of lighting. Ed shouts my way, "Well, Jean, we got our baby back, eh?" He finally turns to me and, luggage in hand, my ex says, "Whoa, this has sure put a few pounds and years on *you*."

We stand here. Tiffany studies her sandals; Caitlin, feeling vindicated, stares only at Edward. I am considering cookies' texture when I hear Nicholas tell his father: "Mom's been *brave*. And saying that was *mean*."

Group silence seems almost a victory. I fight not to cry.

"Sorry," Ed tells us. "Just concerned was all. But my timing sounds as thoughtless as Jean's always said it was. Right, folks? And here at this choice moment, too. Guess I . . . should've come sooner. To help. And Tif here told me so. —Sorry, guys, for blowing that, too. But who loves you-all?" Ed insists on high-fives all around.

"Lunch, anybody? A light Niçoise salad?" And, turning—though worried how I'll look from behind—I do still walk into my house, my right hand resting on Nicholas's blessed shoulder.

I have never felt so defended by a man.

My son just made me feel, for one long second, like Saint Somebody myself.

AS I LEFT, the twins asked why I'd need these waders. "You're going to the beach, Ma, not the jungle."

"Well, but you know how I hate getting sand into everything. And though they swear the hurricane season just ended, has anybody told the *hur*ricanes?" Nobody laughs anymore at my jokes. If they ever did. Such quips now make me sound disconnected. Even to me. The very rites of grief prove Indian-given. You think enough ten-mile beach-walks will heal me? —I wear these boots because I bore a daughter who gave away my shoes, a few pairs at a time, till I quite literally stood barefoot as Eden's First Lady.

I WORRY HOW his second wife will know that Patrick must have his super-crunch on wheat, whereas smooth on white means Nicholas. Then I realize, the boys're nearly eleven. If it matters, they will simply state their needs to good-natured Tiffany. I'll get to go back after three weeks. (Doesn't that seem cruelly long for what I did?) I will resume my station on Milford Cul-de-Sac. (Literally means *bottom of the bag*.) My sons will always love me.

Odd, I can picture all three of my children with their *own* kids. Caitlin, whatever her chosen career, will have two, minimum, so she cannot be said to have missed so seminal an experience. Soon as she's "with child" she'll know me far better. The time-bomb of it in you, the soul that is in it and therefore you, your responsibility now. But that soul owes you nothing.

At least the twins understood. We, after all, survived—as a unit—*her* surviving. The boys are still so innocent they can frontally humor and honor their workhorse mom. Twins' friends still come to pee, with me one room away, not thinking to turn on the sink or hide their sounds. Trusted music, if brief.

My children will all be great parents! I just know. Surely that says something, Jean. You yourself might be too full of crazed nuance. But, somehow, you were the only one on earth willing to stay in a house with them and do the doggone work. At least my boys still notice.

CAITLIN'S ACTED EXTRA-KIND to most everyone on earth. Even at age three, she was giving our blond cocker such care and imagination.

"Get a life, Mom," Cait has told and told me. She cannot bear to see: She *is* that. She's the only *somebody* this particular *whatever* has ever really had. I didn't choose this job slot from a list. Never asked to be divorced, left solitary as an oyster. But turns out, rearing brilliant or quasi-brilliant kids is the destiny I drew. Caitlin Mulray is my luck. And at least, through her first death, such luck still holds. (Come to think of it, only Mary the Mother of Christ and I belong to this very tiny Resurrected Children Club!)

To be fair to myself, to briefly sing or celebrate myself, I have tried to keep her coated in sunblock. Screened from the burden of knowing how, all along, she's been my Sun itself. "Get a life": Easy to snap at the very force that started yours!

For years I've nagged her about attending Radcliffe, my former dream-school. And only yesterday, as I drove her through rain toward Falls High that last time, did she bring it up.

"Actually, Mom, never wanted to correct you, specially not in front of others. But that's all called *Harvard* now. There's been no such one-sex school as Radcliffe for, like, decades. —Not to *date* you, Momma Jean."

You aren't supposed to mind your teenager shushing you. But when they die then come back, you feel its sting a wee bit more.

SINCE HER REBIRTH, I have been remembering my own first chances. I was once five, Cait's age when Bongo very nearly made off with her. As a child I often found myself left safe at home, locked into our big 1939 Colonial at the best end of The River Road. Dad would drive off to his law office; Mother had just barked downstairs that I must bring her an iced drink. Mom, argumentative on principle, could never *keep help*. Instead she'd given birth to a *live-in*.

I knew the drill. Though physically clumsy, I fought with an old-timey ice-tray. It stuck to my short hands in such horrifying sucking ways. I loosened her ice, the required three cubes. Age five, I got up onto a chair, fetched down her favorite crystal glass; I found the oval silver tray inherited. (Another later Baby-Cait-Goodwill casualty). I folded diagonally a cloth napkin, creasing so it stood up like the Pope's miter. Finally I filled Ice's glass. Coldest tap water. Let it run three minutes. Then, with full tumbler and reflecting tray held precarious before me, I approached our carpeted stairs.

I understood that if I spilled, even a drop, she would send me clear back down. I must start over. I didn't understand why, but these were her terms. I still recall the portrait-peculiarities of those twelve steps leading toward her sitting area in the bedroom's brightest bay window. Stairs number three and eleven creaked. She would be stretched there, waiting, wearing white gloves filled with cold cream, cold cold cream; she'd be arranged just so, sometimes in a white satin robe matching the very upholstery of her pale chaise. Did she hope to make furniture more her outfit or turn herself into a luxury seating destination? Though prone, she *showed* me she had been waiting.

I remember counting those steps, trying—with my limited tongue-bitten motor skills—to keep the cool tray level. I hoped I had not underfilled the glass. (That was also cause for "a send-back," as I'd pitifully titled it.) This drink was not even gin, which might have explained a lot. Just Ice water.

I picture that.

I see how different a mother I have been toward mine. A slob, you say? But at least an imaginative, passionate one. I had three children; their father left; but I stayed put. And stayed, and stayed. I offered them every scrap of my belief and much faith I couldn't even claim yet. Much of it I simply faked, of course. But I offered them all that, on a tray, a silver oval one. The very one Cait would give to the poor. Fact is, all along, it was *hers*. Hers to give.

I'VE BROUGHT A secret tucked into my new suitcase. (Look, as modern as a rocket, this model has its own built-in wheels, a feature new to a stay-at-home like me.) I've brought, along with Elizabeth Bishop's collected poems, three clean school notebooks, blank ones, secretly lifted from Caitlin's room. Maybe I should warn the *Atlantic Monthly*? I believe I feel another lyric poem coming on.

Latest irregular French verb? My newest favorite: *Fleurir—to adorn with flowers; to flourish.*

> I adorn with flowers,
> We adorn with flowers,
> *She is adorned . . .*

AS I CHAUFFEURED her to school just yesterday, both of us sat big-eyed, over-aware this trek would be the last of something.

We ran into a huge electrical storm. Street corners suddenly flooded, I pulled over, punched our emergency blinkers. Cait fell silent beside me. She hoisted that veteran pink backpack against her front, making it both her doll and breastplate. She did look young, hunched there under the silver sound of rain.

My daughter suddenly acts afraid to be alone with me. I can take anything except my kids' seeming scared of me. That's too much my *own* history. A high-pitched mosquito whine, the sound peculiar to women stuck in small spaces with other women determinedly incompatible.

At home, before Africa, when Cait, eleven, used to hear my unlight footsteps moving down the hall toward her, she'd bark into her phone, "Reek. It has hips and it's com-in!" I must've said this sort of thing about *my* mom. But this is *me*, just Jean! Cleanly if no longer stylish.

Parked along The River Road overlooking a rushing cataract. Our vehicle blinking alarmist yellow, we sit out this gale's first seven minutes. I'm nervous to even risk my own voice. Bound to irritate her, since its timbre and pleading can piss *me* off pretty good. We watch evergreen needles drop, whole branches fly. The road is picturesque with mansions and near-misses, their lampposts lit against this gale. Pine bark keeps seasoning our snapping wipers. Spruce needles coat the hood. I finally resort to our one common language, poetry. Part of an Emily Dickinson I taught her at age eight:

"I'm nobody, who are you? Are you nobody, too?"

"In your dreams," she snaps.

I assure her that I'm leaving tomorrow. "Cait, coast'll be clear. Good for us both. But I *would* like to offer you a little something, hon. Here and now. I chose the piece from Mother's old *Book of Common*—"

200

"Not my funeral prayer! —Oh no. How big of a ghoul *are* you, Jean? Whenever I think I've got to the bottom, there's always one act more. Her command-performance curtain call. Command coming from her! Mom, you're too good for this. No hard feelings, but spare me . . . ?"

"Chose it from Mother's old blue *Book of Common Prayer.* I worried that, onstage, especially after Stan's amazing music, I'd feel too grief-stricken to let out one peep. I have terrible stage fright, Cait. But, living the life I have here, I've never let you see or know that. Bake cookies enough, they'll let you dodge the podium. Yes, I found the prayer listed under *For the Death of a Child.* I condensed it then practiced at my big mirror once I got your brothers bunk-bedded for the night. With you dead, they were so terrified, they'd stay completely silent, Caitkin . . . for days. Sleeping in one bunk. Imagine them . . . still! They love you so much as do I, so much, too. Before I fetched them home from school, I would sometimes drive out to a farm lake I'd found and just park there, practicing my li'l final part aloud. Made me feel closer to you."

"Look, uh, shouldn't I have veto-power considering I am, like, alive again? For a dead child? I am not dead, nor a child. I should get a say here. Look, I understand some of what you went through, do. I never should have blocked your number. I'm totally down with that. But *I* didn't know that horrible man would trick us. And I really do honor you as the intelligent woman you are, basically. I mean, I didn't get this bright by *ac*cident. It's not *all* Dad. But, hey, it's *my* funeral . . ."

"It *was.* —Caitlin J. Mulray? this rain's now got some hail in it. See? You can either listen to my prayer for you, or maybe hike to school, young lady. I've never asked for much. It's just I want you to *know.* Want *some*body to . . ."

"Know *what*?" she clamps hands over her ears. Her voice rises over deafness self-induced: "Mother, I'm sure your prayer's a comfort, the language of it. But, what, do you want credit 'cause you still *can* memorize? Okay, cred given. You know how much fun it is not to *hear* you briefly? Admit you think I'm an overachiever. (My scores actually bear out I'm right on schedule.) But why must you almost make that mean you're *under*achieving? Look, I'm just in *high school*. Basically we're the same and stuck with it. That's what drives you mad. And, swear to God, it's not my fault. —But, honestly, Momma Jean, nobody should have to hear their own *fun*eral! *Pleeeease* don't make me hear mine! Terrible luck for the person. Anyway what do you keep *needing*? Can't we just sit here in the storm and make like two girlfriends marveling at nature 'red in tooth and claw'?"

"Tennyson!" I nail her poetry reference but hate even sounding a bit competitive. (Is it all *Double Jeopardy* with you, Jean?)

So we simply wait it out. Two females, one car, souls too local staring straight ahead, avoiding the electrocuting sight of one another. Hail, some the size of hominy, pills up past green glass. This day has turned the saturated blue of my daughter's Saint Joan eyes. I ask then, "Before I leave tomorrow, will you, could you *bless* me?" She keeps ears covered and, from the look of her, it seems, eyes shut, she's holding her breath, too. That old trick.

Sitting there, I guessed I'd chosen my public prayer not just for Caitlin Mulray. It was likely for all the bright troubled kids I forever imagine guarding. (Including that least-encouraged of my advanced placement children, the very young Jean.)

OUR ENGINES KEEP gunning. But, will you look? we're actually landing. Oh, smell that brine. New ions, fresh fish. With us closer to the Gulf Stream, seabirds do look whiter than the mainland's.

Still, this means my being banished to an island, right? Unpublished for years. No book club membership at all. But look, would you mind? Would it bore you if, while striding ashore in my new boots here, I finally do quote it? Could never make *her* hear.

Of course, now I've asked, I feel the usual stage fright. But, hey, there is no stage. This is at least my own moment, right? Who's here to even laugh? At some prayer for a dead child? And, after all, I do mean what I say. Momma Jean *always* means it.

O MERCIFUL FATHER, *whose face the angels of thy little ones do always behold in heaven. Grant us to believe that this, thy child, has been taken into the safe keeping of eternal love. Give children an abundant entrance into thy kingdom. And so conform our lives to their innocency that, at length, they shall hunger or thirst no more. The Lamb in the midst of the throne shall feed them, and God shall wipe away all tears.*

DECOY

For Paul Taylor

BOOK ONE
B.C.

Night comes down so hard around my little boat. At last one oar strikes the floating trophy. I've hunted this since dusk. It has been tangled in a nest of reeds offshore. Blind, I finally reach for it two-handed. How easily and wet it comes to me. The carving, smoothed, is cold as silver. Darkness helps me feel both sides' engraving.

With this small idol in my lap, I am free to paddle anywhere, to simply drift. Sunset's many reds have dyed themselves one black. Over water, over me, stars brighten till they each have fur. Now my boat will likely swerve beyond the shoreline's homey docks. Current soon enough should pull me out to sea. Oh, I know the odds.

But, with this onboard—hand-carved to represent me—I feel tallied. Described, I can risk everything.

I am at last a man accompanied.

OUR HOUSES STILL looked beautiful to us.

Everybody here, black and white, inherited a little something. Right away we'd reinvest.

Many bright people—born in Falls, NC—left home early. Elsewhere they do get famous faster. Still, we'd brag, "Sat behind me in third grade. Borrowed notebook paper, daily." The world press prefers such city celebrities. But, even now, I think the Lord is quickest to forgive us local souls.

We Bible believers—too punctual—were always likeliest to stay. Falls, with thirteen more churches than car dealerships, wants its citizens optimistic if stationary. Was it even our choice? Hadn't our temperaments decided? Or getting deeded land that, being highly -local, also stayed. If a person doesn't fight gravity, it wants you right where you *have* been.

Our Falls stands thirty miles from other towns. Once renowned for our tobacco auctions, we've lived to hear ourselves called "the Smoking Section." Being a farm-sized city-state, we do take good care of us. We're rarely unintentionally rude. My smart wife says to say: We still tend to worship our doctors and diagnose our preachers.

We've pledged allegiance to what my young daughter called, "one nation, under God, in the visible." Quick to smile "Prettiest morning ever!" we hide our doubts through most of each day's cock-tail hour.

And yet, till right here recently, we hadn't really known dying meant us.

AROUND HERE WE'RE kind of funny about our doctors. Since Falls lies below sea level, we like medical heroics of a towering kind. We favor extreme measures to keep us alive. The farther your hometown gets stuck off by itself, the more faith you'll put into your main medicine man. (If God's some sort of doctor, must be quite the general practitioner!)

We figure: if our physician is a man *good* enough, he'll keep our deaths at bay a couple extra years. (And if yours played college basketball, stands six-something, won fellowships to Davidson then Yale? Hell, that's worth at least a six-month bonus!)

Weekends before the trouble, people entertained. You pretty much had to. House-proud, flirtatious, leading couples took turns. We liked our martinis as dry as possible; we preferred our sex not. Sex here meant mostly married sex—but that was okay.

Party invitations? answered one day after mailing. And when your son fell off his bike three blocks from home? another adult would dash out, Band-Aid his scrape, phone you reassurance, praising Billy's coloring and manners. Heaven and Hell must share a pretty violent border. Canyon fires, screaming refugees. But here? At our river's edge? the Last Judgment seemed other people's visa problem.

Falls' 6,803 souls felt known for generations by both first-and-last names. Our homes, remodeled, looked even better to us. Not quite a heaven? but surely zoned to banish eyesore hell. And folks that left at age eighteen—even ones now well-known artists in New York—you think they're a bit happier?

Those of us who stuck by Falls, we sometimes fear we've fallen off the big-time honor-roll. And yet, our town—if on certain days a letdown—landed intact, nicely right-side-up beside the still waters. Till right here lately, we who stayed, stayed mostly cozy.

Between hot-cold extremes, you'll sometimes get this bonus. The one honeyed crease, sweet river-basin cleavage. The open sesame nuzzle-spot no newcomer ever finds.

OURS BEING A farm-town, we idolize those experts most hands-on. So when our beloved general practitioner announced he'd finally retire, neighbors threw Doc Roper forty tribute bashes. Roper? the last physician who forgot to send your annual bill. No wonder folks baked "farewell" cakes from scratch. (One was shaped like a bone-saw! That drunk, people ate it anyway.)

Ask anybody. Falls' best neighborhood? Riverside. The one guidebook calls it "most desirable." Finer homes got built along our placid waterway, the River Lithium; it somehow always cheered us, even its mists. We'd lucked out—living in earshot of water's daily moods, annual duck migrations. And Doc Roper tended our twelve square blocks and more. He was never a licensed surgeon. But lank at seventy, everybody's family physician still wielded his knife like some artist.

"New starter cyst back here, Bill. Shall we just get it *now*?" And Roper—as mild as tall behind you—described how, this Thanksgiving, his Marge would be serving duck, not turkey. Six canvasbacks he'd bagged at sunrise on the Carolina coast. "There," he touched your shoulder. "Good as new." And your surgery, afford-able, was behind you.

One neighbor, still loyal to that discredited Dr. Dennis S—, grumbled about the *Herald-Traveler*'s Roper issue. A whole insert devoted to Doc's bowing out. "Any man that admired must be holding stuff back." But *what*? The Ropers' river place stood just opposite Janet's and mine. Our teak decks plateaued at one level these forty years; any secret there must sure be sealed watertight. To date, Doc's life appeared driven, rangy, civic. That's why retirement might prove his Waterloo. We worried for him, going forward. And, incidentally, for us here, left behind.

He'd grown up local but more on Riverside's raggedy south edge. A few 1940s Colonials but mostly ugly yellow rentals. His hand-some parents paid their country club dues with the month-end strain of poor folks tithing. Even before Roper left for scholarships at Davidson before Yale Med School, classmates dubbed him *Doc*.

DECOY

(What if kids had called him *Preacher*? Would he then have come clear home to heal our spirits?) He suffered a most ladylike first name: "Marion." Seeing the boy's kindness and smarts, pals upgraded him in fifth grade. Boneless *Marion* became our useful *Doc*.

HIS WHOLE LAST duty-month got spoiled by Falls' champagne and testimonials. Hating full-frontal praise, any overpayment, Roper kept studying the silver buckle of his wristwatch-band. The emcee laughed, "Now chime in, folks. Watch him blush, today-only he's our sitting duck."

Recovered patients toasted him. A wheelchair traffic jam at Lane's End Rest Home. His Tex-Mex office-cleaning crew brought Roper home-brewed beer and a mariachi band of brothers-in-law. Doc's Sherlock diagnoses got described but only after many revolting symptoms. Folks recalled how, new to local practice, Roper had accepted barter.

In those days, he couldn't bear to turn away country people like my ailing dad and me. Back then Roper looked to be just one more serious Yalie. But his card-playing father, so rarely rich, had taught him what it meant to live on cocktail crackers. The neighbors guessed and fed the boy. Doc always talked easily with black folks who worked tobacco. So, in exchange for services, he started by accepting firewood, motorboat tune-ups for life. Tomatoes left on his new white station-wagon's roof liquefied by noon, ruining the paint job.

One thing wrong with Doc, there seemed so little "off." The man gave us admitted sinners insufficient human traction. Not one comic vice, no obsessive hobbies. Wouldn't time reverse that? Might not leisure do him in? Why stop working anyway? "If you ain't broke, don't quit *fix*ing . . . us!" one tipsy lady-partier blurted.

211

Others called his stiffing us a matter of life and death. Silent, I only nodded.

From my farm-born father, I'd inherited a punk heart and the disease as scary as its name, *familial hypercholesterolemia*. Your LDL-and HDL-count lives up in the three- and four-hundreds. No "countervailing agent" countervails. Your heart keeps trying to become a mineral. Only neighbor Roper has eased me through three, count them, full-blown attacks. "What will we do with*out* him?" people asked at church and in checkout lines. Me, I could only shrug. Didn't his sailing straight into the sunset leave my rowboat capsized just offshore? —Still, I had to wish him well.

Even so, rule one: *Make sure your favorite family doctor is at least a decade-and-a-half your* junior.

OUR NEIGHBORHOOD CURVES along one slow tea-colored tributary. The more feet of waterfront your fine home claims, the more you likely paid. Serious establishments come with narrow beaches (white sand bought by the truckload). Diving platforms float mid-Lithium. The handrails of our docks have cup-rests cut right in. Suitable to hold a dozen friends' gins and t's.

Our major fears, they've all been engineered around. Maybe that's why country people after church drove clear to town to stare across lawns of The River Road. Family money allows a margin of safety. However many inches. What scared us worst? our kids or grand-kids drowning. (Neighbors' sons—undergrads home from Vanderbilt or Sewanee—could still earn three grand a summer improving the breaststrokes of little juniors next door.)

SHOULDN'T THOSE OF us who'd stayed Falls' guardians be offered combat pay? Might not the damage done us on-duty be prorated to reflect those risks knowingly assumed? (I once sold insurance.) We stayed home to avoid danger but it had our home addresses. My wife says my four-square face should be stamped PAYS HIS PROPERTY TAXES EARLY. But maybe the harder you avoid a thing, the greater its impact incoming?

For those now-famous friends who'd abandoned Falls early, what we just survived—without them—might be the only reason we'd still interest them.

2

FOR EACH OF Doc Roper's retirement buffets, you could name the injury that inspired it: he had stitched shut the forehead of a child who somehow rammed his trike through Grandmother's patio plate-glass. And if our teen daughter (speaking generally here) suddenly found herself in the family way, our general practitioner never *took care* of her himself; but Doc was sure to know the best man in Durham—who might just know somebody helpful.

"What in hell will you *do* all day?" neighbors asked at Roper's fourth surprise barbeque. Fellows sounded interested if irked. Others, close to ending their own work-years, felt scared of being idled. Then here came Doc—self-employed, braving that, eased-out only by himself and the wife.

"Oh, boys," he smiled at deacon faces fifteen years ago, "something'll bob up. My kids gave me an Apple laptop, still in its crate somewhere. Our two in grad school sound scared I might come north, try taking classes with them. Funny, I *do* feel ready to finally become a good student! Last time, looks like I coasted on my . . . well, on my I-don't-know-what! Luck? Always have hated *sit*ting.

LOCAL SOULS

Next week Marge here has us flying to Bermuda for twenty-one whole days. —Right, my li'l Margie? Lady put her foot down. Says she's not having our usual weekend with me hooked to patients or the doggone phone. After that, we'll see . . ."

People said it was an American tragedy. He knew so much. And about us! Our septic innards, our secret chin-lifts, our actual alcohol intake in liters-per-day. Plus Doc never snitched. You could tell him anything, if you could only think something *up*!

Made you wish science would hurry. Young geniuses should mastermind a brain-transplant procedure. When his time came, imagine downloading Roper's gray matter into some strong new pink intern!

Where is it written that a sane, vigorous man of seventy has to pack it in?

Doc's yellow hair had turned all white at age thirty; that set him apart somehow, a person sanitized if not quite priestly. He'd kept himself good and trim. Swam in our river almost daily just at dawn. Still jogged, shirtless. True, while running Doc's torso was maybe more in motion than a man of forty's. But, once stopped, everything rose up near where it'd started. He was just ten years my senior, as I likely already said. On myself, I've lately noticed how soon male-tenderloin can texture toward being beef jerky. At best!

You'd often spy him at the club, fitting in a fast nine holes, if rarely played with the same duffers. He was too smart to be only perfect as you heard. It must get old, staying that observed, admired. Some days, yeah, he could act kind of testy. His jokes could have flint in them. If your accident-prone child lay bleeding on his exam table, some of Doc's quips truly cut.

"Bill?" Roper spoke (to me) over my young son's compound fracture, "Bill, can't you help your Billy boy here find any *high*er trees to

214

fall out of? Hasn't missed many in this county—now, have you, pal?" Ha *ha*. You see?

Still, he was most everybody's doctor. The competition wasn't, and his waiting room was a salad bar of classes, races. Curious, Roper's bills seemed to reach richer clients quickest and give the poorer recovery-time. Need be, he'd pass you on to specialists. Doc said he owed me a bit extra: how my own dad had perished in his care, in our company. So I've been Roper's patient-dependent for, what? going on forty years be July tenth. I've counted on our standing weekly appointment, sunup Monday mornings. Had my own in-office coffee mug, a gift from Roper's tough-talking nurses. Blanche, Sandy, and the other Sandy.

SOMETIMES ENTERING OUR town's country club I still worry I'm dressed goofy. These old tennis shoes too grass-stained? Slightly sunburned, don't I look more a rural Baptist than any chess-playing Episcopalian? But I have belonged here on a donated legacy-membership for five decades! When will I *not* feel guest-on-approval? Blame our family's slipping into Falls so late. We barely made the broad-jump from clay tobacco fields to red clay courts. And then only thanks to Dad's strange good fortune.

Riverside's tulip poplars and water-dipping willows can keep our oasis fifteen degrees cooler than bordering farmland. My poppa, though born out there in sun-glare, loved hidden Riverside nearly to the point of being pagan. By June, fields the boy plowed were sun-blasted toward ceramic. Just to carve down in and plant your seed was about like breaking plates.

Pop bragged he'd got born self-employed, lived to be indentured. Luck only came to Pop once he retired. If Doc Roper's parents stayed the best-looking fox-trotters nearest the bandstand at the club, my dad barely glimpsed membership's brick fortress, and then only over a hedge, from a public road.

"Red" Mabry was the son of a mule-driving tenant farmer from way on out in Person County. If his borrowed truck had not broken down he might never have discovered Falls' quietest neighborhood. Red had been driving since age nine. Was then he finally grew tall enough to dance while standing on his left leg, his right one operating gas or brake as he clung to the wheel.

Stranded along The River Road, awaiting some jackleg mechanic, Red wandered off into greenest luxury. (He later admitted he'd been seeking some nice quiet bush to pee on. But rich folks' bushes were all trimmed up to look like man-sized chess pieces that seemed likely to pee right back at you.) Gardening crews had come at sunrise and left by 8 a.m. Like dew itself, maintenance refreshed then disappeared. The River Road in early June was all lipstick tulips against emerald lawns.

I picture little Mabry—denim coveralls, red hair looking like his one cash crop, probably openmouthed with pleasure. He finally saw how industrial wealth, left alone amid its own upholstery, can choose to live. In 1938 no gates or guards kept anybody out.

This son of sharecropping had never glimpsed lawns acres wide. Of no silage value. Hell, you couldn't even bail stuff this short to feed your poppa's cattle. Grass here meant to be a kind of moat. It would keep your white house hid-back awninged in blue eye shadow. A row of riverside homes looked shapely yet hard to please. They were bay-windowed big-fronted as Miss Mae West. Like Mae, they posed uphill, terraced onto hips, expecting farm boy stares, their stances still jack-hammer-resistant.

Young Red noted folks' driveways flagstoned then bar-bent U-shaped. One brand-new canary-yellow LaSalle convertible sat parked out front, keys left right in it! That summer day, owing to a busted axle, Red Mabry became another teen who'd fallen hard. Got his heart set, see. Not on some hellion Zelda debutante, thank God; fixed more on a neighborhood called "highly desirable." Our hick was hooked on professional lawn care in that age of bamboo rakes before leaf-blowers; kid got fixed on having a third story set cute as a sailor-girl's cap atop your regular roof. Mabry hoped to someday spring himself (and any future kin) from sharecropper's usual, a rabbit-box of country shack.

My dad, not a little bowlegged, had been called "Red" since the midwife's first alarmed sight of him. Given his eighth-grade education, considering his poor health, the little fellow's leap to being someone "town" was probably impossible.

DR. ROPER, BEING fifty, but still looking thirty-eight, happened to be jogging past a kids' swimming party. He heard screams from the Bixby twins' sixth birthday. As neighbors, Janet and I had just popped in for cake. I became one of five men who waded out and found the little brothers' cooling bodies. We laid them face-up onshore as Doc, dropping to his knees, barked, "Align. Heads. Please." See, instead of wedging himself between them—where he must do lateral twists, wasting time—he knew to kneel up by their droopy noggins. Doc pulled both those heads onto his lap and bent across them from above. Shirtless himself, he huffed and heaved his air into our identical dead. A feeding, he pressed the Bixbys' skulls so close together Roper seemed to pant into a single mouth.

Boys had plunged under river-water hand-in-hand trying some weird twins' pact or dare. Now Doc exhaled into Timmy, then Tommy, alternating. We all stood crying, holding on to one another. Three women supported the young mother. In minutes Tim coughed a quart of the River Lithium; then Tom sat up and pointed at his brother. He accused the other of breathing first, ruining the "speriment." Roper laughed, shook his head. "What exactly was your *plan*, boys?"

All of us, shaken, went direct from tears to cackling. Kids' beautiful mother felt so grateful, so stunned at losing then regaining them, she—quiet, hysterical—knelt beside Doc and offered him . . . a kiss, openmouthed, the works. This happened in June and Katie Bixby filled out her Jantzen one-piece pretty good. All she could think to give Roper was herself. His own wife Marge had just come running, hearing shouts. Margie stood not ten feet off when Doc told Mrs. Bixby, "Thanks, dear girl, but you're in shock. Y'owe me nothing. Go take yourself a goodly snort of brandy. Then stick these daredevils in a long, hot bubble bath—well-monitored, y' hear?"

ROPER'S FATHER HAD it bad for gambling. Dapper fellow, looked like he owned Shell Oil while goading any shoeshine boy to wager: "Freddy, tell me, since you know a lot. How late *you* figure today's freight train's running?" Neighbors swore that one midnight Roper, Sr., came home naked, shoeless, wearing just a hotel blanket. Also missing, the family Chrysler. His poor wife had to go out and pay the cab. Drake Roper's 007 manner got him into those very club games he could least afford.

And Doc's mom? A true beauty forced to teach local brats piano. We'd hear her tapping out our five-eight time, seated behind the bench where we slaved over our Czerny; we'd hear Mrs. Roper toy with her pearls, turn toward the window, sigh a lot.

DOC'S OWN GROWING kids often heard from townsfolk how

fortunate they were. They'd glaze right over, snort at each other. You sensed the dad must've been pretty darn human, once finally home at seven p.m. Controlling maybe? Cold? You could only guess which usual problem was his.

Roper's son and daughter were loyal enough never to say one thing against him, at least nothing you could quote. They'd been shipped early off to Northern prep schools (as if to help them keep Dad's secrets). The daughter was now big into African-American art history; the son at Harvard, I think in the divinity-theology line. Blond lookers, both of them. We rarely saw them, even certain Thanksgivings. Sad that no new young Dr. Roper would be rushing south to try replacing him.

Though one decade older than I, Doc had a better memory. In his office, he recalled verbatim my last year's wavering blood work. At his fingertips my Dow Jones good cholesterol gone bad. Man never needed to speed-read the fat manila folder Nurse Blanche left opened for him every Monday anyway.

OUR PART OF North Carolina is so darned flat we'll do most anything to stir up some variety. Mystery, please. If not adultery, how about a hill? Oh, to have experienced some cloud-high risks. We'd even court a few pit-of-hell lows. —Results? Mostly golf courses.

The berg nearest ours named itself for a pile of mill-side stones, "Rocky Mound." Didn't that sound too bland to merit a post office? So town fathers upscaled it to: "Rocky Moun-*t*." One letter seemed to shoot the town hundreds of feet above sea-level. And us? We've always had this placid river chockablock with Ice Age stones. So, those few jagged rocks that babbled audibly? we upgraded. To a word nearly-Niagaran: "Falls"!

Tourists ask to see our waterfalls. Our what?

Residents couldn't bear to call themselves the "Fallsites." (Didn't that sound like some minor form of feldspar, like the word *falsies?*) That's when our early nineteenth century membership had several drinks and dubbed itself "the Fallen."

"How long have you been among the Fallen, or were your people born that way?"

MY DAD STUCK out eighth grade till Christmas vacation. After that, Red hammered his way to being a contractor miles from Falls. County jobs proved spotty, as rural pay was poor. Still, folks trusted him on sight. Mabry gave honest estimates, simply said what he meant. That came out surprising, funny, finally kind of rare. Inheriting the weak heart that'd killed his dad, he stayed down nearly-child-sized. He had to hire subcontractors, older, able-bodied men. And yet, he chose to marry the prettiest honor student from a one-room crossroads school. Nine months later to the day, they welcomed their towheaded baby, me. And Red Mabry—officially an invalid, exempt from soldiering in WWII—somehow supported us.

He swore our finally getting into Falls was God apologizing. For making our family tradition be terrible health. Red had strict doctors' orders to never lift a tool heavier than his clipboard and, yes, okay, its pen.

His very ears were freckled like concert tickets punch-holed. His cracked grin made you laugh at, alongside, then with it. The man pretty much radiated enthusiasm. For belief, most any belief. Faith in his own faith and others'. Love is one thing. Red's being general and village-sized, seemed less private and selfish than romance. A heart in trade. A heart like some shop sign hung right out front.

WHILE ROPER'S PARENTS played tourney bridge or spiral-peeled lemon zests for drinks, my dad and mom still rocked me on the porch of our tin-roofed farmhouse. They took turns fanning yellow jackets off baby-me as Red talked a blue streak about Falls' tree cover. "Streets like 'forest glades,' the best blocks." His county tone could swan-dive up into an Irish dreamer's. Pop got crushes on certain words. "Glade," "mitered" and "half-timbered Tudor" each held pride-of-place there for a while.

Red swore that Riverside's constant sound of flowing water would cool us off and heal us up. Red rattled on about the charm of rich people generally: how they had doctors as good as any U.S. president's; how they could make just some weekday the occasion for a party worth uncounted shrimp platters, real Chinese lanterns. Dad swore that even Falls' oldest sickest rich folks, why, they never looked near so ham-colored, sweaty, or plain-bad as his many heavy-set cousins out this way.

Dad had memorized street numbers along The River Road, near-catechism. He mapped so much about which fine family lived where since when. In my later decades spent among the Fallen, Red's start-up bloodline flowchart proved infallible. It saved me much embarrassment among cousins. Except for me, they all were. Cousins. One town girl was named Whitson Whitson and her brother bled.

If my dad had to die early, he got lots done beforehand. Our first week in Falls, Red started hunting medical help for the both of us. Pop found two town doctors far superior to a near-veterinarian who'd treated us as full-fledged members of the rural poor. Then Dad sought even better care as far away as a new college hospital over in Greenville.

Finally internist-generalist Roper returned to his hometown. There was a party in honor of that, too. He'd just finished at New

Haven. At last, with this new-minted grad just turned twenty nine, with me a shy nineteen, with Dad one feisty if twisted forty-seven, Doc accepted us as clients. Then, slower, Roper took us up as friends. He was the first to understand, then explain, what-all was wrong with us. Nobody till then could say what we *had*.

Past my condition, I never understood Roper's own. Why, with his skill and looks and Yale MD, come back to Falls? Was that not a relapse?

And why would such a one *stay*?

3

FORTY YEARS AFTER signing on as Dad's doctor and mine, after all those years of human holding and mending, Roper folded. He had given Falls a full six months' notice. Claimed his wife had made him do it. "Marge showed me the kitchen calendar and asked if I recognized one date and when I told her I'd turn seventy then she said it'd also be the day she got me back. 'Patience finally wins out over patients.' So be it. Marge has asked for so little." Still, when it hit, his disappearance felt overnight. The last appointments were completed (except last stragglers bearing cookies, photographs).

The notice Scotch-taped to his locked office door was just a piece of typing paper handwritten by Doc's head nurse:

Will no longer be seeing patients as of today, folks. Sorry. It has sure been real.

Roper sold his local practice to a recent Emory grad. That poor kid had his work cut out for him. Doc acted unsentimental. Every grocery aisle held damp-eyed wheezy well-wishers trying not to show him their new rash. How could any future avocation compete? What'd ever be alive and grimly funny as our community these last four decades?

If he took to his rocking chair, he'd surely sit there missing office hours crowded with our small-beer woes and charms. Looking back, maybe we all felt a little jealous . . . of whatever he'd take up next. His clearing out made us feel we'd been ditched. We might all be his plain steadying first spouse, the gal who slaved at catering to put her go-to guy through med school.

Though widely admired, Roper was odd in having no one best friend. Never even seemed to *miss* one. (Were there a few leading candidates? Oh, sure. His cross-the-way neighbor, yours truly, lived, watchful, among them.) Sure, I'd have "hung with him," as our grandkids said till recently. But from boyhood up, solitude appeared a part of Roper's plan. His dad had been a much-watched loner forever waiting for some CIA assignment or midnight game. And our doctor had just such stand-apart power. I respected that. Pretty much had to.

But about his golden years ahead, people predicted the worst.

"Since kindergarten, always our class *do*-er, Marion. Retired? He'd best stay busy. 'Cause soon as one of *those* sits down? In about a year you've got yourself a goner."

DOC, RETIRED, WAS back from Bermuda and had found his future! At our golf club bar, he spied old chums, made time to perch, tell us what he would be "majoring in" for his life's remainder.

Doc explained how, into that Bermuda resort, a decoy convention had just migrated. Dallas-based game hunters, sports-paraphernalia collectors. Too many Hemingway beards. Texas successes made high-octane boasts in an English teatime hotel.

Twenty-one days of beach can stretch out quite some distance. Doc said he'd already read the eight novels Marge brought, special. Those books just didn't seem real "lifelike," he groused to her. "Brands of cars in here I recognize but not what any of these crazy lazy people do all day. I'm bored *for* 'em."

International decoy dealers set up rusticated booths in an ocean-view ballroom. Midsummer, its cloakroom wasn't needed for men's camel hair, ladies' furs. So that space got commandeered by a covey of kingly silver-haired duck carvers flown in by private Lear.

Most decoys for sale were very old, priced accordingly. Roper, uninvited, wandering the great hall, soon asked dealers many smart young-man's questions. He proved one real quick study. People enjoy sitting beside a handsome doctor at a black-tie dinner; especially if such people have family heart histories and are over fifty-eight. Particularly if that doctor stands six-foot-two, is funny, and a Yalie still visibly in love with his very first wife.

Roper hadn't been stalking the ballroom long before organizers introduced themselves. They squired him toward the holders of the major antique decoys. Roper explained he was a virgin, at least to this. Gosh, there seemed a lot to know! The three rarest birds displayed had all been carved by one Josiah Hemphill, 1790–1842, Marshfield, Mass. Short lines formed to see those.

Doc soon learned Hemphill's big knack was a more "naturalistic" shaping, the bolder use of buttermilk paint. Hemphill had worked days as Latin master at a boys' academy. But post-declension, after refighting Caesar's wars one hill at a time, the glad ole bachelor was found paddling every Saturday and all summer with his blunderbuss and water spaniels. Hemphill, plump, gout-prone, sat amid a boatload of false ducks he carved, then floated. Wood ones lured the live ones into musket-range. You had to know how each duck species splashed down in its very own formation. Since live things naturally magnetize to copies of themselves that look super-pretty, you rope your fake-outs into just that pattern.

Buttermilk paint gave the Latin master's birds such high-gloss feathering. And three centuries upstream, their colors still looked as bright yet crackled as a Rembrandt landscape. (At the country club bar I listened hard to a subject not as personally interesting as congenital heart disease. Odd, though, it held me.)

Up close, the birds appeared no better than old paint-daubed wood. But if you squinted down, as Doc was taught, if you imagined yourself two hundred feet up, you sensed how Josiah's wide brushstrokes worked magic on the weary homesickness of passing cousin ducks. As they sought rest, their nightly berth seemed sweetened by that many family-resemblances horseshoed below.

Soon Doc was stepping onto one provided footstool; he squinted down on duck-backs laid across a ballroom carpet very very patterned.

"Aha," he said. "This Josiah's excellent, okay. Hell, he's so good I feel my *own* landing gear coming down."

Well, this crack drew lots of nods, off-colored yuks. Doc's quip would be quoted that whole Bermuda week among the real mover -shakers of Decoy World.

Over dinner, they told Roper how the Smithsonian owned six Hemphill curlews. Josiah's sole snow goose had just flown off the auction block into the Met Museum's American Wing. But Doc (self-knowledge always his RX specialty) confessed to feeling less a collector, more a hands-on type. "*Own*ing bores me, basically. *Do*ing . . . less." So his new collector-pals just walked him to the carvers.

One cloakroom had been lined with plastic sheeting to catch

cedar shavings already ankle-deep and fragrant. From the look of these guys' hacked-out starter-ducks, Josiah Hemphill had long-since left the building.

Doc said he met an ex–one-star general, two forced-retirement GM veeps. Their greetings sounded jolly as their politics soon proved strictly anti-immigrant. (Spoken by a man carving a duck, the word "wetback" seems a species name.)

ONE MINT-CONDITION Hemphill—A bird that floated around in Marshfield's salty bogs not many years after our nation flew the coop of English taxation—it could set you back twenty-nine to thirty-six thousand. And that was your *bar*gain Hemphill.

Whereas a regular living guy could buy himself a pine "blank," insert a couple 10mm glass eye inserts using two-step epoxy, then shape his very own mallard for under forty bucks! "Now, that's 'a deal for real.' —Hell, let *me* try that."

Home, Doc explained to the few of us still bunched at our bar called Hole Nineteen, there are still only sixty authenticated Hemphills in captivity. "No lie?" I said, sounding false and spurned, though feeling not unengaged.

4

A FIRST FATHER-SON office visit and Roper had just fed us its complicated name. I swear he recognized our exact sickness in like two minutes. Diagnosis shushed both Dad and me. And our fair-haired boy-doctor used even this pause. He actually wrote out the name of our condition on the back of a prescription pad. He passed it to Red.

DECOY

A gent, Doc guessed my dad might need to see then silently sound-out our fate one letter at a time. "Fam-il-ial hy-per-cholesterol-emia?" My father had to hold it some distance off between weathered hands. "Let's see here. That nice little opening, the 'family' part? I do get. But the next word's being this long, looks to me, sir, like a big ole coiled black snake."

"Wish I could say you'd got that wrong, Red." Dad admired how Roper gave it to us straight. Afterward we would live in treatment. Doc's good company helped. But our Mabry bodies kept hoarding both kinds of lethal fatty juices. Doc called those "lipids." There'd been a recent horror movie at the Bijou. Called *The Day of the Triffids*, it concerned future-trees that can walk around and eat the people of the future, see. Sounded like we each had one of those growing hungry inside us. And I had taken Red to see the film.

ONCE MY FATHER made this green zone my address, I sure tried blending in. Doctors' notes excused me from gym class to the school library I soon loved. Up ahead I would qualify as in-state and entitled to our fine university. At Chapel Hill I got twenty-one A's. But it's only thanks to Red that I can *pass* today. Not coursework, either. Pass as a townie. (And surely with Doc's help in learning the ropes.)

Yes, by now I get regularly mistaken—when noticed at all—as someone born to own the third-biggest half-timbered manse set along The River Road. I've actually become the fellow wearing Saturday chinos paint-stained seemingly-on-purpose, too thrifty to throw them out, too rich to care about personal appearance while seen in a house that looks this fine. Being a six-footer of a certain silvered vintage, I appear almost natural, stretched out in a Smith & Hawken chaise longue, reading my twentieth seafaring

Patrick O'Brian from our public library on this teak deck nearly seaworthy.

I greet by name our neighbors' pretty grandkids paddleboating past. I get a singsong, "Ahoy, Mister Ma-bry." Still, during one encounter in six, I expect to be challenged yet. A cringe waits half-sprung. At this age, I feel almost eager to be found out: yet another closet hick with no claim whatever to choosing hand-blocked William Morris wallpaper, upgraded to this town of nearly seven thousand!

If I still tend to hero-worship certain folks hereabouts, that habit started in my cradle. My parents spread cheesecloth over-top it, keeping off barnyard horseflies, wasps. But sometimes the white would peel away to show pure sky. Then I lay looking up at a man's auburn fringe poking out beyond his head like ropy sun rays. I kept studying a smile that couldn't help but show—in Red's own raw delight with fatherhood—his every crooked witty tooth.

GOOD THING MY folks shoehorned me into city schools early as third-grade. See, schoolmates still remember me as just one more familiar river rock, as having always lived, if hushed, among the Fallen.

Come breakfast the opening day of class, Mother asked if I really planned to wear that. See, I'd picked a favorite maroon cowboy shirt Pop had bought me at Myrtle Beach. Stitched right in were broncos, stars, plus cacti. Mom wondered aloud if I might save that back. "Maybe start out in plain black pants and your nice white church shirt? Just till we see how fancy doctors' kids dress weekdays. My way of thinking—a person can make one real loud mistake just by walking in, son. Your dad, now, he is ever a show unto himself. Short man, humongous spirits. But you and me? Though taller,

228

we're, well, till we warm-up-like—I reckon we're more hiders." I nodded, unsnapping my whole shirtfront.

Mom squired me toward a sunlit yellow classroom. I'd dressed as plain as Mother wished. From the hallway, we peeked in at other children's sporty costly clothes. Nothing looked homemade. Soon as the last bell rang she drove our Studebaker straight downtown. Mom bought me everyone else's kind of blue Keds shoes, boys' same red-striped soccer shirts.

At age eight I still fixed my hair like the country kid I was. We then called it a "ducktail." You greased it right-good all-over, then combed not just the top but both streamlined car-detailing sides. You coiled each combful inward using a tricky wrist motion I bet I could still manage, allowed sufficient time and hair. Finally you'd give the very back a flippant up-yours turn.

Mother soon asked if I shouldn't start using less Wildroot Cream Oil. Maybe try a side part. But no, till turning fourteen, I held to my own kick-ass punk-country Future Farmers of America styling. Some Riverside girls even got around to thinking it was kind of cute! I kept smoothing my blond hair back over either ear with that Edsel-like up-swerve behind. It made me feel some kind of rural hoodlum, little Elvis come to town on market day. But my secret outlaw-pride seemed lost on the golf-crazed Fallen. Here I'd been feeling s'proud, thinking my hair made me the real stand-up reb among Riverside's club kids. No one noticed.

My sixth-grade progress note I can still quote you from memory:

> *Though Bill has kept unusually silent his first few years in a town, he cannot hide being basically kind and, certain tests show, not-unintelligent.*

"But, honey, that sounds real GOOD." Mom, my fellow hider, lifted one hand to almost pat my cheek.

I already knew their discount code for me.

OF COURSE DOC was manually skilled. For a half-century the man had always been a carver. Our Caucasian backs and fronts provided him so much practice suet. Roper's hands, three octaves wide, stretched like some Russian pianist's. He had played center for Davidson. Maybe Doc's roundball-sense in the pivot helped him see things (and patients) spatially?

Our very lack of scars, from block to Riverside block, gave surest proof of Roper's subtle digits. Everyone's beautiful glass-shattering children had been returned to them unmarred. Looking down at their youngsters' beauty, they first saw their own, then—saving —his.

In Bermuda he'd got pronounced a prodigy at seventy. Veteran carvers doubted Roper could be as new to this as he swore. Doc simply scratched the back of his fine head. Doc loved playing the rube. (Jimmy Stewart was actually a Princeton trust-funder; Will Rogers prepped at military school.) Roper lowered his eyes now, joshing, "No, I swear, fellers, this one with you tonight, it's my very first-esth . . . *duck*." Laughs.

You soon heard—through our almost-too-gossipy Riverside optometrist—how Doc had already made a normative mallard. Kind of "lifelike." Correct patchy colors, mail-ordered amber eyes, orange matte feet. Roper then elevated his subject matter to wood ducks, probably the most beautiful American waterbirds. Little stunners. You've seen them in calendar photos, their markings crisp as tux shirts. Small-sized, crested, jewel-colored. (Cooked wood ducks are said to be very "tasty." But I'd as soon eat a bald eagle or my namesake grandson.)

We learned Doc had already developed a new paint. He was trying to copy the iridescent band of blue-green-black peculiar to wood duck males. A UPS truck twice daily crowded the narrow River Road. When Doc still doctored, working to improve us, his supplies all got delivered to his clinic on South Main. Today the delivery truck blocked half our drive (not that we were due anywhere). But what was he out there signing for, joking on a first-name basis with the boy in brown shorts?

BEHIND THE ROPERS' big split-level, a barn overlooked his three hundred feet of river frontage. Their son had used this as his ham-radio clubhouse; the girl later made it a dance-palace for teen sock hops. Now Doc was getting it remodeled into what he called his "studio." (Folks felt like "workshop" might've been a term a bit more masculine.)

The place now featured glass on three sides' cathedral river-views. Floor-to-ceiling windows 20 feet-tall got webbed across with narrow blond-maple shelving. Slots enough to hold a second lifetime's flock, whatever he seemed bent on making out there by his lonesome.

Wouldn't Doc miss Falls' charming talking-back *peo*ple? Did he not feel half-deaf off-duty without that attractive after-hours stethoscope bunched under his jacket collar? Who else had guessed Dad's and my obscure ailment in two minutes flat? We'd expected he would now go and volunteer in Darfur. *Doc Without Borders.* Roper and Marge flying off and healing the Third World. That'd prove a more suitable, fame-making Phase II. On her summer internship to Africa, a local high school girl—idealized as her age group's Marion—she had just drowned, upsetting every Riversider very much.

Doc often skinny-dipped in our river just past dawn. Nobody

was awake at that hour. Except restless me, of course. I'd have taken my round of morning meds. I'd often be seated on our deck, nursing my mug of decaf (Roper's orders). As he padded barefoot bare-assed to their dock, I could see the white towel just around his shoulders. He'd plunge right in, any weather. With a nerve unknown to heart patients. I'd sit here still wearing pajamas and slippers with maybe an overcoat pulled on, winter mornings. In half-light I'd enjoy the splashing of his crawl most of a mile upriver then back, his return hardly slower than the first lap. Sometimes it seemed my doctor was exercising *for* me. And, as he stood drying beside the Lithium, seeming fully unaware of me, I did know this: if my chest seized up, assuming I could somehow make myself heard, he'd jog my way so quick.

If not exactly emotionally close in any way a fellow could quantify, at least we had proximity. For a lifetime, while he went around saving lives, I at least sold those lives their life insurance. If Doc walked through most doors into rooms that rose for their beloved, I could still slide in (out) barely noticed.

I still felt myself the ducktailed farm boy come to enter his calf into state fair competition but lacking the social skills to even go find a registrar. Doc proved the Fallens' most essential unit.

Me? a longtime voter who's served as poll watcher since age twenty-two. And I accepted our different roles. There would always be the imbalance. By now I was truly fine with it.

But ducks? Wooden wood ducks? in lieu of human lives to save? Seemed to Jan and me a step down. Inventing creatures wholesale was probably nice work if you could get it. But how entertaining? I mean, where are the surprises, your birds held together with three-inch decking screws? Chopped from cedar (soft enough to carve while staying bug-resistant)?

Still, in this second career, he must appreciate how his new patients would never beg for free drug samples. Plus there'd be no waiting for payment of their outstanding bills. Bills!

5

NAKED OR NOT, you step out onto your farmhouse porch, no one gets to see you but maybe two crows and a half-blind hog. Here? in this town of 6,803? eyes everywhere, ears pressed to phones, mouths describing your simple walk to school. Every time you stepped aside to comb your hair back nice? that'd been your Broadway audition! Each restaurant offered Mabrys, via the plain act of getting food from plate to mouth, a hundred bladed mistakes waiting. Even Falls' waiters seemed tennis line judges calling our soup-eating foul or fair.

Red insisted that we go to Chez Josephine because it was right here and, people promised, French. (Well, Belgian, really.) Brave, Red ordered, "We'll take us a load of snails, fer the table."

When those sad buttered critters arrived, Dad looked sick while winking: "You first, son. They sure look . . . educational. Let me see you eat at least one."

He enjoyed daily walks past Riverside's most beautiful homes. He invented "historic names" for his six favorites. Palladian windows sure beat his boyhood's vista, the crescent moon cut into a two-holer-outhouse door. Red loved speaking with our owning-class neighbors: his concerns regarding future River Road drainage problems. "What if some freak water came surging through here, why . . ." Once home, just recounting the exchange sent him into a kind of grinning sleepiness. "Was just explaining to young Ashton, told Ashton as how . . ." This bushed look of Red's, lids half-shut, always seemed to follow his widest smiles.

My poor father's heart was so deformed, happiness cost him most.

MOST RIVERSIDE MONEY still gets siphoned from farmland surrounding us, pay dirt assumed. People admitted to fortunes made "in tobacco" but you didn't want to be caught wearing denim near a field of your stuff. If our river looks clouded brown with lithium, our land comes so packed with iron it is as red-orange as my late father's hair. Fertile crops start easterly at Falls' infamous (Fridays topless) Starlite Bar. Due west, crops edge up, then box in our Dairy Queen's parking lot. By August you eat your fast-melting ice cream out there surrounded by three green walls, beautiful shoulder-to-shoulder tobacco plants, triffids—rising silent, freakish as the National Basketball Association.

The Mabrys had forever farmed. They belonged to a dunkers' church that baptized the saved in a tributary of the sacramental Lithium itself. Yes, Red might've looked cowlicked, all but defaced by freckles. True, he appeared every inch the Hiram Hayseed. But inside there lived someone surely sleeker, paler, more refined. He'd spent his boyhood striding muddy furrows behind two mules. But his true yen always ran toward fresh-hosed sidewalks, electric-lit store windows. He praised lip-rouged marcelled town women who, as he said with some ob-gyn implications, "keep theirselves all sweet 'n nice."

Red was eager not to stay agricultural for life. He explained how persons that farm: *They are really very different from you and me.* He resented the stubborn meanness required to do battle with weevils, hookworms, floods. He explained family pride, folks being county-famous for growing one admired crop better than all others. He had competitive second cousins envied as "the Peanut Mabrys"; but he himself, as his mother never quit telling him, hailed from one uncle's branch of cousins even snobbier, "the Sweet Potato Mabrys."

6

ROPER'S BARN, NOT a barn in the sweet potato sense, started seeming a small temple-museum to whatever Doc might forge back there. We never doubted he could do something pretty doggone good. Even that miffed some on our block: it'd be hard, living within sight of a seventy-year-old model-plane-builder who suddenly constructs, say, some scale-model Cape Canaveral staging area in his own backyard. There's something Wright Brothers cranky-crazy waiting in us all. We secretly think we're always about to invent something wonderful.

But Roper's ambition was upgrading at age 70! A hormone problem? It threw into high shade even Doc's own record-71 at golf. Even I felt bitter at times, reminding myself his real name was only Marion.

And what about us? Jan and I would have enjoyed visiting, studying his modern floor-to-ceiling shelves. They were yet to be filled in like his inked Sunday crossword. Sure we respected *a man with a plan*. Isn't it odd, though? The guy was crinkled pretty old while his slick blueprints look too new.

We were over here perfecting our own off-duty slowness. Roper didn't mean to call others' bluff, of course. That would be too personal! Still, he threw into question friends' bimonthly WWII book groups, our sciatic tennis elbows, our third or maybe fourth gin(s) and tonic(s). He'd once participated. His sudden absence seemed a diagnosis.

Did he even know that my dulled hours—freed from insurance-office tedium—were partly spent flopped before any TV rerunning whatever nature show came next? What made this now seem lazy, almost simpleminded? Doc Roper's bright Phase II did.

And what, exactly, had my own Phase I been?

CAME THE DAY we could not revive my old man, long as Roper worked on that and him. Right-off Doc turned my way, promised to turn me into a Science Fair project from his days as prodigy Marion. Roper told me in advance I might expect as many as three cardiac infarctions, three spread over what time span and when. Then he told me where I'd always find him.

Doc explained just how we'd get around each one and, by God, we'd managed it so far. I say "we," and I was right there, of course. For my sake, Doc swore he would subscribe to costly cardiologic journals. He'd learn the latest blood-thinning therapies and jump-start electrode apps. Then Doc did it, he kept my chest abreast of each breakthrough in turn. And I am grateful, don't get me wrong.

But, even man-to-man, even during my final checkup in his back-office, there was still so much two fellows this full-grown just could not say. One married father of two cannot ask someone similar, *So you're taking up your artistic future, pal? Any ideas for me left couched way-back-down-in-here?*

Thank God that, early on, he'd not suggested handing me off to young Dr. Dennis S—, a too-pretty boy some called "the new Roper." Till his true criminal character poked out for all to see. Me, never trusted him. Too many eyelashes. "He's no Roper," I told one early fan. "Boy's more a stringer."

Retiring, Doc had referred me to others, though. Everybody understood that three world-class cardiologists practiced an hour and a half's drive away at Duke and UNC. Excellent technicians probably.

But, see, I didn't *know* them.

7

ON HIS RARE Saturdays-off, a certain tenant farmer's kid started hitching ten miles into Falls proper. Having discovered Riverside because one axle broke, he now went back for up-close observing. Red avoided stopping downtown. They "soaked" you, any sandwich you bought. No, for him giant houses fronting river were the real show. Red jumped out of his free ride, called thanks, simply strolled the low-cost green beauty of Riverside.

He wore what he'd worn last time: those *were* his clothes, shoes. And whose mansions were these? Owners of tobacco warehouses, furniture factories, banks, and boundless farmland, all living right along the water cheek by jowl, sailboat tied nodding to neighbor sailboats out back.

One park bench rested picturesque beside the Lithium and, seeing how it overlooked a bunch of lively funny ducks, the farm boy settled. For a good while, too. Neighbors noticed. That bench had just been placed by the Garden Club because "a seating element might look well there." It did. Red, convinced, chose to rest right here forty minutes, grinning as if about to nod or nap.

No one from Riverside ever usually actually *sat* here, really. This triangular patch of green was window dressing, first turnoff onto The River Road. It meant to say, *Gracious living starts here.* Red Mabry, thirteen, got the signal. A black Lincoln Town Car passed, then slowed to see what jewel heist this kid, rustic as a root, might be planning. Red waved.

Town planners had long ago chosen, not elms destined to die of a national disease, but durable beautiful maples. Their star-shaped leaves went from brilliant sour April-green to sweet coral-honey-yellow each fall. Even maples' bark, exposed all winter, attracted. Must resemble the smoothed sweetly-terraced backs of certain imagined Episcopal ladies hereabout.

Flanking streets, maples had managed, before World War One, to reach clear across and into one another. Now seventy feet high, they formed a continuous light-speckling tunnel.

Lunchtime! The boy Red broke out the first of two hard-boiled eggs brought as his low-cost lunch. Why pay more downtown? He knew the names of the hens that'd laid them. In his overall's bib, kept a little blue paper-tube of Morton's salt. The delicate way he sprinkled it atop his half-gnawed yolk, Poppa's pinky-up gesture, why, it would've put any snuff-pinching French nobleman to shame.

And, only after wandering around unwelcomed, after getting eyed from various mullioned windows, after being spared police questioning only because he was at least technically white, my red-haired Red hitched back to the family tenant farm.

Dairy cows stood hoofing mud, bellowing complaints. Going unmilked hurts. Evening's warm-fisted relief was back home twenty minutes late.

THE RIVER ROAD was Falls' single byway always crowned with its own "The." Smith Street was nothing but a street named Smith. But all along The River Road, owning-class folks spent weekends wandering house-to-house holding actual martini glasses. "Yoo-hoo, refills?" they called, entering without bothering to knock.

"I seen them do that with my own eyes," Red reported later with one head shake. "Is that friendly er what? They flat-*know* their favorite brand of gin is in each and ever' mansion, sure as we got fresh eggs in ours."

On our farm porch, he'd again tell us how money tends to lubricate the human mind. Three or four generations into the real deep lasting cash? Why, folks have found time to play musical instruments and to really read. Hard books, too. "Seven-hundred-pagers!" They learned-up about art; they soon bought genuine oil paintings, not just for investment, no, for simple rub-up-against life-is-good beauty! Several such pictures he had glimpsed in the front hall of this one house. And you know, each had its own electric lamp built right to the frame? that important. Like some *place* you'd stoop and see into and then pretty much *be* there. You could stay safe in it several seconds.

Yeah, Red insisted, the rich were—not so much "better" than us—nope, just "different."

If we were sturdy burlap, woven to stand up under barn temperatures?

They, having only lived indoors under mansion-conditions? why, they'd been silk since 1820.

8

AND WHERE WAS the man best qualified to keep me moving? He must be struggling to improve his wood carving. Doc now hid himself from view. If the man still jogged, he did it late at night. Must be swimming at the club pool, forsaking his river crawl come dawn. His "studio" light burned at all hours. UPS art supplies went in but nothing actually came out. About eleven months into his hobby, our local Arts Center invited Roper to "show."

Doc's being much missed, that likely inspired our will to see his woodcraft. Wasn't it a bit too early to show? But nobody had ever accused Roper of accepting favoritism; not this man who'd convinced us each that we were all *his* favorite.

Doc's office and practice had been taken over by one thin Brahmin Indian. We'd been picturing a small dark man with wire specs. Gandhi, really. Roper wore an actual blazer when he and Marge brought the recent med school grad for that inaugural Sunday brunch. Doc escorted Gita around our club table-to-table. He tried to make her seem truly one of us now. She had smooth manners and the right credentials and this *Masterpiece Theater* accent. She was obviously highborn, but not in Falls. Not along The River Road.

She looked about twenty, with her giant black eyes that seemed blotters for us blondes and redheads. She wore red lipstick with one paint-chip sample of her mouth inlaid at the center of her forehead. A popular deaf old sportsman called, "Welcome aboard, young woman. You'll be seeing lots more of me. Specially during my next colorectal, Rita."

"*Gi*-ta!" Doc laughed. —You understood she'd graduated from Atlanta's Emory, and you knew that—next checkup—she'd be thoroughly prepped from your up-to-date manila folder that Doc never needed. But I later heard two gents say that, unlike with Roper, they couldn't fancy discussing with Ms. Gita Patel, MD, any of their little recent erectile issues, etc. . . .

*

DECOY

RED GAVE HIS loved ones repeated tours of a Falls not actually his. It lay just ten miles from our farm and getting in was free . . . except for its many collection plates.

Dad admitted to a fascinated weakness for what he called "your 'town' churches." Being a contractor, he approached each sanctuary as a solemn building inspector. As the Mabrys shopped for our ideal church, bad maintenance reflected slack theology. First forays into the society of the Fallen rousted us awake many a Sabbath.

Dad's red Studebaker was always Turtle-Waxed just so. We drove to Falls to audition another neighborhood of Methodism. We were farmers entering a Protestant church that seemed barn-huge. Its pews were stocked with groomed "professionals" and our big shoes produced an echo all their own. We knew we'd never pass for visiting film stars. Sure, we understood that Falls' country club wouldn't admit us, however "country" we might look. But, not one church-usher ever body-blocked our entering even Falls' least-smiling congregation.

We surely appeared clean, our cheeks rosy from the best lye soap, our shoes spit-polished. And God knows my hair was combed! We ignored stares by doing ever more smiling. We three nodded a new-here pew-to-pew "Howdy." To make up for whatever our clothes lacked, we tried singing hymns with an extra pumping rustic spirit not always understood.

After Dad's showing us Riverside yet again, I waited for one city limits sign past the Dairy Queen. There, parents let me loosen the noose of a black tie. Most of our way home Dad offered his review of today's sanctuary and service. "Plaster around the heating intake duct in back was crumbling, see that? Deacons did a little touch-up painting but . . . And, not to nitpick, and I know it's summer vacation-time. But, I'm sorry: four people is not a choir!"

Safe again amid the quiet fields of Person County, I felt comforted. I was a Sweet Potato Mabry, native to farmland. Our ending up among the chosen frozen Fallen? I never once considered it.

I felt quite cozy enough in our tin-roofed center-hall home. A yellow school bus stopped right by the mailbox. And my dad was admired out our way. The sight of him entering any general store ("It's that 'Red' fellow, Dahlia") brought a plump wife from the storeroom, brought the yellow hounds awake.

Dad had assigned me, behind our house, a low-aerobic row of tomatoes to tend. I owned one mighty-envied cowboy shirt and, at my four-room school, I made real good grades and passed for "leader." All seemed pretty-well rooted in, nestled down. Then Red rushes through our front door, yelling. He waves around some lawyers' documents just fished from our rural box. We would get to move to Riverside. Mom and I stood holding each other. "Yes," Red said toward our silence. Yes, Mom and I, we had to come.

Colonel Paxton was, well, a Paxton. They'd been big noises around here since the sixteen hundreds. They'd donated the 1824 starter property for All Saints Episcopal plus several different golf and civic clubs, having plenty. See, the old colonel hailed from a Lord Proprietor's line. That meant his family had got its tens of thousands of acres direct off the Indians by order of some faraway English king. Worldwide chess moves broke the Paxtons' way around 1610 and pretty much ever since.

The mansion's den roof had caved from sheer stupid neglect. Paxton Hall's latest aged resident had pissed off (then stiffed) many a Falls builder. He was finally forced to start phoning contractors from outlying farm communities. Dad was barely making do, constructing housing splurges by returned GIs: an added carport, many nursery extensions. Then a revered Paxton cold-called my father.

Was Red too booked? Soon as Colonel started telling how to find his home, Red's highest-pitched voice piped, "Wait one, sir. You are *not* 2233 on The River Road! *Not* that long wavy stone wall with the grass yard lately getting so full of . . . trees?"

Dad turned up to supervise a set of botched repairs. He saw at once the roofing contractor was using poorest-grade ten-year shingles, double-charging the grizzled old man. Dad confided to the colonel he was being highway-robbed by Falls' fancy-pants builders. Red offered to bring in his own country crew at half the price. "My guys, sir, are all born Primitive Baptists, and honest as the day is long, can't *not* be." Paxton, clueless and a hermit, had forever been an easy mark. He often gave that as his reason for nonpayment.

The colonel listened from an upstairs balcony as Dad fired four roofers, then Paxton Hall's most recent plumbing outfit. This struck the miser as major excitement. A certain amount of yelling happened. Paxton's huge disintegrating place was lately visited only by restaurant deliveries, census takers, matching Mormon boys.

Red soon returned to our field-view porch with sagas of Colonel Paxton's bravery in the First War. Dad admitted as how, since then, the man had maybe grown a bit eccentric. True, he owed other repairmen a fortune. But the small checks he'd written Dad, they'd cleared just fine.

Each Paxton Hall bathroom was bigger than our rental home. Each had its own huge potted palm. Each was hung with framed photos or paintings of the present heir-owner as a young soldier then an Armistice party-giver. Back then he had been as handsome as any girl can get to be beautiful. Walls around his cut black onyx tubs were paved with pictures of wild parties held here. Several such images showed the young veteran, fully bare, in all his aroused glory.

Old Paxton had lately invited an appealing young brick-mason upstairs to see what the colonel had once looked like all over. "Now, that there's . . . something, sir. Mighty frisky you got to have been, sir. Yeah, well, better get back to work, outside and all . . ."

Paxton spent much time soaking in a faceted black tub, one located upstairs, one down. There he received carpenters and Chez Josephine takeout while, goatish, reading the New York papers. Each tub looked big enough to seat four. Hard to believe what poor care he'd taken of that God-given face and figure, not to mention his inn-sized house. But Dad swore that the old gentleman still had, hidden under all his gingery growling, an absolute heart of gold.

Neighbors complained about his lawn's weeds till those became the saplings now a tangled forest. If you didn't know that one stone Georgian house sat jammed back in there, you assumed his yard must be the start of a state park. Dad had begun bringing his newest boss man jars of Mom's famous pimento cheese. The old colonel felt amazed to have finally found an employee who'd return to the job-site weekends without charging overtime. (Underbilling could make you into a local whispered myth. True, both Roper and Dad did it. But, for me, poor as we started out, it's something I have never cottoned to.)

Paxton was glad that at least one visitor proved brave enough to risk death ascending the free-hanging spiral staircase. Creaking, it'd rocked there half-moored since Falls' wildest party ever. Dad felt honored to be received at any home along The River Road, especially one with a name famous locally since 1610. "Red, you're overdoing," Mother warned as always. See, my father had taken to performing little private repairs off-book for free at Colonel Paxton's. The blustery owner, wearing striped pajamas, would get right down on the floor beside Red, handing him the wrenches and coping saws Dad was forbidden to use.

I visited Paxton Hall just once. Dad promised I'd enjoy the old man's tales of killing certain Huns hand-to-hand. I was nearly eight and the old guy up past eighty. He looked me over and announced, "Lucky features, considering." Dad laughed. "You mean he favors *her*? Yeah, averaged out good. The Lord was merciful in that at least. And Colonel, the boy's smart as he is pretty, though he'll blush, my just saying *that* . . . See, what'd I tell you?"

I remember Paxton wore a long maroon bathrobe (silk, I guess) and two-toned golf shoes and that was all. His shins showed cuts and bruises I now connect with stumbling alcoholics forever at odds with the world but, first getting outdoors to that, battling their own furniture.

He talked about certain local ladies he had experienced, naming names, imitating sounds they made during. He edited no sex-misdeed for a child's sake and I bit my lip for shame, preventing further coloration of my whole face.

But as the colonel sat there, his robe untied and he revealed a nasty lack of underpants. This confirmed my worst suspicions about old old families, old and increasingly careless. Given wealth enough, certain tribes, like certain people, experience wholesale second childhoods. And, with the Paxtons, thirds.

In a year or so, Red had sold timber rights to the mansion's front-yard, then got it tamed enough to mow. Its U-shaped drive wore new flagstones. Pop got the house looking at least half as splendid as it had during certain hunt balls of the Calvin Coolidge years. One Saturday, almost a year into their curious friendship, Red turned up uninvited, carrying a potted geranium; he'd brought some of Mother's excellent banana pudding the colonel now swore by. Steep front doors stood open. Red soon hollered from chamber to chamber, checking bathrooms first. He found a naked Paxton floating in the upstairs tub beneath that day's sogged *New York Times*. Turned out the old penny-pincher had left my father sixty-five thousand dollars and his founders' legacy country club membership. In 1955, 65 thousand seemed to us, and others, one mighty pile of cash.

Paxton's kin lived widely scattered. Most sane people, with *that* kind of money, depart Falls first thing. They'd had no news from this family grouch in decades. Two California nephews threatened to sue. Who ever heard of a handyman inheriting so big a settlement? But, arriving at the improved mansion, finding it habitable, despite old neighbors' horror tales, Paxton's nephews piped down. In the end they let one little miracle-working contractor keep his nest egg. Hell, hadn't he earned each cent? Imagine nodding through their shell-shocked horndog uncle's latest tale of one brilliant Verdun trench maneuver leading—as if underground—to a particular bawdy postwar Charleston pool party!

Dad at once made down payment on a cottage just big enough for us but with a River Road address. It was not, he admitted, at the best end, "Still, it'll be our foot in their door." Mom and I stared at each other, purest dread.

9

JANET, NEVER ONE to wait, got my attention that first week among the Fallen. I sat enduring third-grade, feeling too new here, wearing unfamiliar Keds that pinched in back. I just occupied my desk, staring shamefaced no place. Today's topic was the Panama Canal. I felt somebody look directly at me from the left. I glanced up and over and there she sat in rubber-banded pigtails, nearest the window, staring.

My eyebrows lifted to ask, "Well, *what?*" But she simply nodded back. She did this as old farmers nod to other fellows their age— strangers met by chance downtown. Fellow sufferers. I found I could meet her gaze, could true-enough hold it. I looked away but guessed I hadn't really needed to. So I glanced again, just checking. And since that second, little has changed in her being there—wry, curious, direct—always able to respond, unblinking.

And on day one, age eight, she did something odd. She placed one index finger to her lips, forming the *Shhh* of secrecy. Next, this Riverside banker's daughter pointed my way while indicating some crook-fingered angle. She seemed hinting I should look into my lap. Foolish, I did so. Zipper fully down, pouched jockey shorts showing like opening day of the Panama Canal. I closed my eyes but did fumble, did manage to fasten things, without another soul's noticing.

When finally I found nerve to scan her way again, that girl sat focused only on a very distant Panama and our real local teacher. Hmnnn.

BEFORE THINGS CHANGED, Falls felt like a waterside retreat from foreign riots, congressional morals that'd coarsened. It was particularly sweet for those of us adults holding a certain amount (and kind) of money. After sadness hit us hard, you started hearing charges against longtime elitism.

The River Lithium's current encouraged for short stretches white kids' sailboats. It busied the bamboo fishing poles along the waterfront of "Baby Africa." That neighborhood's name lived on from just after slave days. It had been proudly picked by freed black settlers. More recently, sensitized Riverside liberals like Jan and me, we've gingerly abbreviated Baby Africa to *B.A.*—Like *L.A.*, or like shorthand for a baccalaureate degree. For decades Jan and I had daily fetched and returned from there. We were transporting our cocon-spirator, Lottie Clemens. She's the long-suffering woman who helped us rear our Jill and Billy, helped keep our home decent. B.A. also provided all the caddies and wait-staff for our Broken Heart Country Club.

—Disaster makes you doubt every decent thing that stretched back safe before it. Till then, I swear, Falls mostly kept busy amusing the *rest* of Falls. Each according to the jokes and styles of his-her own neighborhoods, naturally. Our town sat isolated amid square miles of growing tobacco. Out this far from the next village, we gave our kids piano lessons because Sunday afternoons we still wanted to hear our children really play. We *had* to entertain, inspire, and, where possible, worship one another. Who else?

And it was in this loyal spirit—only when we turned up en masse to support Doc's "art" show—that we saw how pretty good he'd started getting. Everyone was there. The Bixby twins lunged in, half-grown, hair slicked back and always looking like they'd swum in, sleek dark boys. They stayed understandable fans of Doc. Though they were named Timothy and Thomas, our town had changed this thanks to pure musical affection. "Where are *Tim*othy and *Tom*othy?" people had slipped and said from the start, and it stuck. That was how we greeted them today.

Gita waited just inside the door. Even her sunflower-yellow sari could not upstage our beloved ole bone-saw. There were just eleven wooden birds displayed. They floated in mirrored glass cases fitted with clear shelves so's you could see how, even underneath, Doc had got each one's proper little rubberized feet tucked up golden underneath.

That these blocks looked just like ducks was a given. Doc, in everything, never fell below a certain level of finish. But past that, these seemed separate spatial puzzles, perfectly solved, each completed, elegant as algebra. Is Authority something native to certain hands? Where do you either learn or—likely failing that—buy it?

Our *Herald-Traveler* (atypically accurate) mentioned in its next week's issue:

> *Doc Roper has shown another side to admire. He caught the personality of certain ducks. Here a joker, there a beautiful young mother, next "some bachelor drake on the make." Marion Roper offers his viewers more than* Field and Stream *craftsmanship. Though anatomical care is surely evidenced. Our ex-doctor's finest work gives us, you might say, duck-portraits. Who knows, folks? These could even be "featherier" versions of our much-missed GP's beloved familiar patients.*

And we, at the Falls Arts Center, buzzed on the good Napa champagne that Doc must've subsidized, stood around . . . feeling glad for him, if a little landlocked. "Familiar patients"? heck yes. —"Beloved"? Given who Roper was, that would always be harder to prove.

We were . . . not *jeal*ous of the skill exactly, just made a tad jumpy by it. (Folks untrained in art tended to call one carving "good" and the duck beside it "really super-good.") Admirers grilled Roper—had it not been hard to actually begin again? A whole new field, or stream? Must be. The start right when you turn seventy, are you kidding?

Art lovers asked Roper: How much previous experience had Doc sneaked in, carving? Hadn't our Marion cheated, getting so good so fast?

"As to my 'practicing,' before? I'll tell you, friends," Doc confided, scratching the back of his white head. "Marge always made me carve her a whole turkey . . . most Thanksgivings."

Diana de Pres, still our greatest beauty despite ugly jagged lifetime binges, cozied up against one whole side of him. Janet rolled her eyes at me as our beauty insisted, "Immortalize me. Do one of *me*, top to bottom, Doc!"

"You wanting a portrait-carving or your final physical, Diana?"

Hoots of laughter. This is the kind of cornball line that everybody loves and re-quotes in our sidelined self-amusing Falls. Pathetic what we sometimes settle for.

10

I WAS EIGHT when, the Paxton legacy deposited, Red shifted our church affiliation accordingly. He transferred membership from Second Methodist clear up to First Presbyterian. "Growth pains already," Mom said under a sigh pancake-sized. For years we'd commuted Sundays, ping-ponging between denominations. I'd once called it "stained-glass window-shopping" and Dad acted as pleased with my term as Mother found it troubling. Red immediately asked me which church window, in all of Falls, I'd like best to wake up looking at. I answered, "The rose window at First Presby. Because . . . if God was candy? that's just how He'd look."

My father slowed the car. "This boy . . . I swear, this boy will, no telling, this boy . . ." Dad bragged to our Lord and to his rearview mirror.

His standards for church music also remained very high. He felt that Second Presbyterian's able choir stopped itself just short of becoming loud or overly-melodic. Their plain white sanctuary seemed both a kind of IOU to the next world and a tasteful apology for this one. See, Red Mabry was edging us ever closer to full-blown watered-silk Episcopalianism. I think he believed that the air in All Saints' stained-glass sanctuary must be so rarefied—with its incense, 1820 German pipe organ, founder-families' names spelled out in wine-dark stained-glass—that, simply on entering, all our country noses would bleed.

But, arrived to live along The River Road, Red finally started admitting certain long-held snobberies. Against some new neighbors. Dad confessed he just didn't respect, not next-to-nothing, Riverside's tobacco bosses. Cigs were even then called "coffin nails" and got instinctively dodged by anyone with tickers weak as ours.

But furniture manufacturers? Now, those Dad rightly admired: "A chair is something you can *point* to."

And he mentioned a big Queen Anne townhome that had been fully funded by one family's brewing-distributing nonrevenue moonshine during Prohibition. "Still, it's the same type-a-money as these up-and-coming Kennedys'." Red did yield a bit. He had the absolute standards of the absolutely powerless. But how he enjoyed them.

TOO VISIBLE AMONG the Fallen he embarrassed Mom and me with his color-blindness. He stood enameling our sweet Cape Cod cottage's front door and its every shutter a tomato-red high-gloss. "I'm sorry," Dad stood back, squinting. "But, that? Now, that there is *class*." Grinning, still countrified as salt-cured ham, he'd pronounced the word, "clice."

Mom later guessed that, with people forever calling him "Red," he maybe over-favored that shade? The color looked mighty bold in a neighborhood that still considered forest green a wee bit racy.

Then Dad went and named our simple house. He awarded it a historic distinction somewhat at odds with its being a Cape Cod two-bedroom thirty years old.

"Shadowlawn" was the title he invented during one dreamy weekend spent striding around our half-furnished home in his boxer shorts. He kept muttering words that bore no relation to each other, except in his surging visions of family crests, his hope of finding one drop of blue blood among our hearty, if thinned, red.

"Glade . . . Rock . . . no, Cliff . . . Scarlett . . . Castle . . . something. 'Fern-leaf.' Nope, I reckon a Fern IS a Leaf, mainly." Mother and I tried not laughing. But he remained in a trance like some bright ten-year-old girl the day she discovers Poetry and runs around quoting reams of it at her older brothers then finally the canary.

Red next commissioned a sign. It would rest, explanatory, on our extremely unhistoric lawn. First he had woodworkers strip a pine log of its bark. Then he ordered the word Shadowlawn carved in relief big and deep. Letters' fronts were paint-rolled lipstick-red to match our cottage trim. The final product looked like something you'd see for sale at a roadside stand near the Everglades.

This item did not stay on-duty long.

WITH MOTHER'S BLESSING, with her actual bribe of a soda-shop trip for me and my new steady girl, Miss Janet Beckham, I sneaked out front after midnight. I yanked Red's sign from our newly-seeded yard. The marker had scarcely lasted halfway through its first duty-night, explaining us. Overexplaining us to a Riverside already too amused at our lottery-like arrival. Into one docile river, I heaved the non-word *Shadowlawn*. Lettering upward, cheerful as a duck, the log did not sink but happily bobbed elsewhere as if seeking finer property to describe.

DECOY

By breakfast Dad found the thing missing and, boy, was there Hell to pay! Red pressed short hands over his face going redder. "Don't let me get wound up here. You know what Doc says. They come like a thief in the night. More jealous out-of-towners! Thrill-seeking souvenir-hunters. Low. And I bet you anything, by now it's up over their damn mantel. If the poor devils even *have* one! I always do say I just hate when criminal-type-a-vandals can't help a-preying on such gentle homes as ourn. But still, you know? At least they're history-minded. Looked at one way, why, it's a *compli*-ment!"

I SAT UNDER a terrace umbrella at the club alongside Janet, my demure teen date. She wore a sort of sailor shirt, pigtails unified now in a single brown braid clear down her back. This would be one of our earliest public outings and Mom had made the reservation. Jan and I, too young to drive yet, had walked here, a shorter hike than going clear downtown. We decided, like bohemians, to have dessert for lunch. When, thrilled, I told Mom this, she said, "Go ahead. Don't guess it'll kill you."

Waiting for our treat, I found I had too little ready conversation. But with so many classmates in common, I pictured walking from desk to desk for topics. And I had just started a not-too-fascinating alphabetical roll call. "I see where Bobby Blanchard knocked his front-tooth out skating . . ." When we both overheard a high-pitched country voice from just inside. Red, not knowing we were here, had arrived at lunch to meet his afternoon foursome. Janet and I, pretending to act unparented and if possible Parisian, we just drank more from water glasses. We soon endured having to hear Dad. He got introduced to a bank manager new to Falls. "Welcome, welcome." Pop sounded like anything but a quite-recent newcomer. First, Red determined where exactly along the social-tape-measure of The River Road this fellow lived. "Aha," he said. Then, satisfied, Dad asked his usual tie-breaker.

"I guess you-all's new doctor has got to be Roper, right?" The stranger explained that, being so new here, he hadn't needed medical help quite yet; but folks did say that it quickly narrowed down to a choice between Roper and this young . . . Dennis, was it?

"Let me save you a peck of trouble, fella. You seem like a nice man. It's not no contest to it. See, my family, we've always just thought the absolute world of Roper. Why, when he takes you on he takes you on. And Doc, see—it's a long story—but he is doing . . . Well, he's flat keeping me and my precious boy alive, is all."

Silence fell at about seven tables. Ours had been hushed all along.

I myself went very still, my top lip feeling numb. Janet claimed to have been listening all this while to a woman across the terrace. Seems the gal had recently accused her ex-best-friend of being a kleptomaniac, see. Of having stolen one entire bathroom scale from this first lady's home during Bridge and then carrying it off in a huge handbag brought-special. Took it right next door where anyone could see that missing scale on display in the guest bath beside her *first* one. I faked interest but saw Janet was protecting me. She did that. I'm still not sure why. She swore she found me nice-looking and way smarter than I credited myself. Who could not be grateful?

This had been about my first try at it: taking a girl out on something planned. And it'd been going just excellent, too. Then we had to sit upwind of my old man, with Red blasting our private news to one and all. You think I wanted my girl to know how sick I was?

Though our banana splits arrived, I could not quite enter in. Before lifting the cherry off-top hers, before enjoying that at once, Jan touched the back of my hand. Said just, "Every family's embarrassing, Bill. —Now look what-all we have here. These walnuts, you think?" and lifted her long spoon.

Why had it felt so shaming? To hear poor Dad promote our Roper tie? And for some total Yankee stranger. *Why* was his testimonial this painful, Red's country overtrust? For one thing, I decided, eating, it'd sounded like some sharecropper's loyalty to his contracted landowner. That seemed not quite manly. More a slave's allegiance. Sounded kind of clingy and reminded me of something, but what? something very unpleasant.

Oh, yes, this: My father had just said out loud, before fifty people, exactly what his quiet son too often thought when safe in his own silence.

"Kept alive" by Roper? Well, no. But yes.

Still, who needs to hear that while you're out in public and with such a nice girl?

MY FAMILY'S BEING new to town, with neighbors peeking through venetian blinds, with me in need of buddies, us Mabrys mostly kept to ourselves. Farm-trained, we were used to it.

Humoring Red, Mother stayed more mindful of his heart than he could bear to be. Some nights Dad swore that all those doctors, even a wizard like Roper, had been flat-wrong. Accusing him of heart disease? Hell, that was just their way of keeping a good man down. But, even as he said so, you could hear he didn't believe it. The very tiredness making him complain was itself our diagnosis. I listened hard, already knowing that his fate was mine. Surely my folks had meant well; but I wish they'd not explained my heart disease to me my very first day of county school.

Dad had inherited this weakness from his sharecropper father. That young man, William R. Mabry the First, also worked as a tenant farmer despite his constitution's failings. While pitching hay he was known to black out, topple right over. His loving wife, always on guard for him, rushed forward to tell other hirelings, "Just leave him be. My Will, he'll get his wind back. Just do what I do. Work around him. Oh, he'll spring up." One day Will did not.

Some people receive birthright property. My chances had been fifty-fifty and I'd lost. From my warmhearted dad I had drawn a lipid-squirreling impulse that no known antidote could lower. Before we found Roper, less good doctors had spoken of our condition only by its hurtful initials. They called what we had "Coronary Artery Disease." Then they cruelly shortened even that to "C.A.D."

WE WERE SHAKY if grateful the day Doc Roper straight-out admitted our poor chances. Country doctors' summations had usually run: "You two? Got you two bad hearts, is what you got. You should *hear* yours! What to *do*? Well, sirs, slow down some. The second it gets to hurting you, I mean right when you feel 'full' across in-here, well, there's your sign to rein in that particular activity. Oh, you'll get the hang of it. Just can't do everything. It's pretty much going to be like this. —Anything else?"

Roper instantly had the name and numbers; it made me know that a grand education is one that leads you to specifics fastest. He stated how some people simply cannot "process" cholesterol, good or bad. The body holds all of it. Soon that same flawed body begins to farm its own stashed lipids out to its extremities. Lipids will soon coat the linings of basic plumbing. Then they'll clog the free-flow that living requires. "A slight genetic twitch," passed from father to son, leads to numbness in the hands and feet, to living tired then fully-winded, early endings guaranteed. Roper admitted right off: this meant that my own son, if Janet and I had one up ahead, he'd get the same fifty percent chance of being a carrier. I loved Doc's honesty but feared he told the truth. That meant, while still a relatively young man, I already lived around the crusty pump of some guy pretty-old.

There's a kind of wisdom that comes from this; but, me, I am still seeking that. I keep holding out for some factory rebate. Maybe I was destined to sell health, fire, life, property, and flood protection to Riverside's most prosperous and therefore fully fearful?

Red sat asking, "Doc sir, since you've told us what we got exactly, is there still no drug for it? What has science even been *think-ing* about?"

"No perfect solution yet, Red. If I were you two, I'd pop niacin pills about like chewing M&M's. There's a new product called MER/29 but I don't like the side effect in pigs and rabbits. Cataracts, size of grapes. Those'd spoil your developing golf game for sure. — No, your boys' ticket is regular exercise. But avoid Olympic trials, Red, got me? One study was done on folks with rheumatoid arthritis—seeing if aspirin could help their terrible pain. Didn't, but cut their incidence of stroke and heart attacks by more than half. Sounds crude, but it's cheap. There's no literature yet. So don't be telling anybody I urged an aspirin a day on you, all right? They'll think me some quack. Cigarettes? even being near others', deadly. Oh, and Red, I saw you having your way with the club's fried chicken. That's out now, hear? You'll want more greens. Since both your bodies retain superfluous lipids and won't relinquish even . . ."

Roper noted Dad's frown. An eighth-grade dropout's dread of excess vocabulary. Like magic, Doc's RX shifted, "See, Red? Is like this: Your body, when it comes to this fat? it's all Savings and no Checking. So, we've just got to work at cutting down what's being taken in. Your body can't stop chucking every bit it finds right into

Savings. Your cholesterol-account's so overloaded it's started clogging your heart. And, sad, our young Bill's here."

I felt Dad, seated beside me on our shared exam table, nod; I almost heard Red's heart-click of recognition. He'd finally understood in plainest terms our bodies' strange and killing greed. Roper saw: only his simplest explanation had eased us both.

And with us, father and son, still feeling uneasy even at being bare-chested (if only before Doc), with us each feeling scared of a curse that'd leave at least one of us alone and soon, Dad and I did allow it to happen just this once. We let my bare left shoulder touch Red's right, then stay massed there, to warm it.

I knew that Red would face his own incoming death with some forward motion of belief, acceptance. Time came, he'd rush clear out to meet it. He'd try converting it into some awaited friend.

I sat here, shivery. Sat wondering—just as we held one disease in common—might I someday match him? I mean in pure simple spirit.

Just then, to be honest, that seemed unlikely. And my fear of cowardice around our illness meant I'd earned myself a disease far worse than Dad's.

11

TURNED OUT LATER, Bobbitt's Hobby Shop downtown had been underwriting Doc's exhibits. Why? The week his first show opened, shop business (according to "Bobo" Bobbitt) jumped 39%. Doc's golfing chums lined up to learn any "art." Even a few on-sale woman-craft macramé outfits got sold in plain wrappers. One well-known former Wake Forest linebacker bought a whole "Dolly Village" to take home and paint. The huge man asked, "Bobo, can I put snow on their roofs? 'Cause I like it when there's snow piled on their little roofs."

Being only regular people, these fellows carried home ready-made "kits." Roper'd assembled his à la carte. He'd gathered the best tools, first in Bermuda then via contact with other duck-nuts on what he loved to wink was truly these guys' "World Wide Webbing."

"Doc definitely got that computer out of its crate," I told my wife.

MUST'VE BEEN AROUND then, Janet read to me from *Parade* magazine how a writer said way back, "There are no second acts in American life." (Wasn't my Red the exception? We guessed Roper hadn't heard yet, either.) Doc still talked about the upcoming joys of a man's middle-age. Imagine pretending that seventy-one was your Big Game's halftime. Life span 142 years? Sounded reasonable for him.

You started seeing his name in more newspapers than our *Falls Herald-Traveler.* Even the Raleigh one. He still looked handsome in his leathery laugh-lined way, hair a purer baby-powder-white. His smart chuckle could sound half-mean, and always that textured baritone my wife called his secret weapon. Odd, his kids now spent even their Christmases skiing Aspen or hitting the books at far-off Yankee grad schools. With Marge still looking thin and dark and pretty darned "good," the Ropers seemed to be taking Excellence to some new high-water mark. They looked . . . well, national. Something a bit disloyal there.

"Oh, face it, he's always been a little bit of a secret show-off. Admit it," Janet snapped my way one morning. I sat washing down, with decaf, all anticoagulants he'd long ago prescribed. I knew she meant well but her roundhousing on Doc just made me feel worse.

He'd done okay by me, and even by Dad at the end. Whenever a good doctor retires, his patients must feel a little jilted.

Was about then, us locals began collecting decoys. Coincidence? We all did live along a river, too. Whatever made us notice decoys, they soon became our minor craze hereabouts.

Mallards, gadwalls, pintails, redheads. Real duck names sounded so funny and like toys, you'd want one of each.

FADS REQUIRE DISCRETIONARY funds. And I guess Riverside had right deep pockets. Old farm-owning families had arrived in town to join the Fallen just after Sherman smoke-cured our county's grander homes.

By now our own friends' kids were marrying, several per weekend, another sort of biologic fad. Our lovely daughter's wedding I'd nearly paid off. She is so gifted a linguist, Middlebury tried to hire Jill her senior year there. If I start to boasting, I'll never stop. Our age group retired early. Youngish lawyers with serious golf and rogue drinking hobbies showed a growing willingness to spend weekends cohabiting under and alongside hangovers.

Certain made-up customs we enjoyed. Les Wilkins had spent much of his tobacco fortune on collecting antique cars. He'd filled an old family auction-house downtown and hired two black men to mind the fleet, keep it all tuned up. Every few months Les would drive another one up The River Road, taking kids for rides, pretending to try and pick up his friends' wives. "Judy, you could have had me in this. Instead you chose to be with Ted who is now bald? Say, Ted still got that trusty '96 Taurus, does he?"

Les was no stranger to bourbon but somehow Tennessee-Kentucky's by-products always cheered him. He owned one grand limo that'd belonged to Gloria Swanson, a giant gleaming thing, all wicker panels and silver running boards. And, right before Christmas, after sufficient eggnog, Les would throw a wreath over its hood ornament; he'd ease along slow, honking its old-fashioned trumpet horn that, for some reason, played the first eight notes of "I'm Forever Blowing Bubbles." If we got near Christmas and hadn't heard it coming down the road, we noticed, even fretted. These are the amusements of those of us who stayed. Everything becomes our own Fallen advent calendar. And in every window, one colorful local. Personalities, the clock chimes you could count on.

Televised sports showed games local fellows used to play a bit less well than they remembered. We still loved the way our houses looked. As outlying mallside suburbs filled with crude copies of Riverside Colonials from the 1920s, our originals, themselves rushed copies, looked taller, more "historical." But even our Lithium's recreational waters bring us the stray unpleasantness.

One evening Jan and I were cooking outdoors for our bunch from the club. Somebody looked off the deck and upstream past Roper's studio, and wisecracked, "Think we've got a country guest. Who invited him, Bill?" It was a dead white Brahmin bull, floating. Thing was massive, pretty swollen-up, far-gone, and its male gear on show was either huge or distended. The beast had a set of long hooked horns; the end of one had somehow got its curve jammed into the crack of one rock. Over the mossy stone, water steadily flowed, shifting the poor creature's front hooves as in some dance or seizure. Sure looked like he wanted to get loose. The bull appeared as tired of being seen as being dead.

Jan gave me a stare that said, *Take charge for once?* Though I felt willing to put on hip waders, crank up my never-fail Evinrude, prod the beast loose with one oar, I instead suggested we move our nice picnic indoors for a change, what say?

Next morning, merciful, he was gone. Then, scanning downstream, seeing no trace for a clear half-mile, I felt concern. Almost missed him.

12

YOUNG BLACK CADDIES at the club quietly instructed Red. At his invitation they kept offering Dad small hints at how he might seem more at ease here. Though Red was a legacy member, these new pals hinted he might quit using the establishment's full name. Shorthand is one perk of membership. So Red abbreviated his usual, "Shall we meet then before our one o'clock tee-off at the clubhouse in the Nineteenth Hole Bar of the Broken Heart Country Club of Falls, then?"

The Ice Age gave our club its name and odd emblem. On the cusp of one hillock rare hereabouts, nature once deposited a perfect igloo-sized stone. Seven feet tall, five wide, resting on its side, it was a giant accidental replica of the standard Valentine heart. Its twinned halves looked smoothed and rounded as buttocks at their best. Formed by chance, the thing must have busted in transit, maybe being pulled along what we now call the Lithium. Though elephant-gray outside, its inside surface showed a shiny jet-black all geode-angles. Long before Columbus, something split this thing into being a landmark the Tuscarora had navigated by. And since the 1600s, settlers had all called it the Broken Heart. You saw it inked in shorthand on our earliest English maps.

Since then, many a risk-attracted teenager, including me and Janet, had smoked around the thing, puffing, squatting. Disavowing our country club parents' hypocrisies and shallowness, we kids avoided rain by hunkering under its valved halves. We crouched for shelter near the gray sides like its own pink piglets. A broken heart so big seemed to call forth our rare tourists and the Fallen's many lonely kids. The ground around our namesake Broken Heart was mulched with generations' cigarette butts.

When Colonel Paxton's parents donated eleven hundred acres to become the course in 1901, once their family refused to let our club be named for them, this great boulder seemed the natural next-best. For locals, "the Broken Heart" referred mainly to this familiar geologic feature. Only out-of-towners ever thought the name odd for a carefree sporting institution.

My wife's sophisticated visiting college roommate Kaye sometimes ate with us there. She once asked, looking around our club's 1920s raftered stuccoed dining room, "So. Are the broken-hearted the ones turned down? or you people actually paying dues for this?"

INHERITING THE PAXTONS' founders' membership for free, Red chose to purchase used golf clubs. Why? He told Mom and me he dreaded other fellows guessing he'd never played before. "Chances are they'll *know*, sugar," Mother allowed herself the smallest of her cat smiles.

"Oh. You mean when I try and hit it and all, they'll guess?"

"Maybe you should first practice, in the backyard . . . of *Shadowlawn*?"

"Genius!" He admitted, "It's just that our move up and ever'thing, well, it's happened so danged fast. To be listed among the Fallen and then in Riverside to boot! And now, with 'club' this, 'caddy' that. Sometimes being in town full-time, I hit certain aspecks and just don't know how to 'do'!"

Mom again warned him not to strain himself. In those years everyone still walked the course. With Red become a daily club regular, I—trying to fit in at grammar school then junior high—withered, picturing him.

I'd been drafted into the ranks of the Fallen and had not volunteered. I tried keeping some of my country stillness. Jokester chatterboxes forever need new victim-listeners, right? My thoughts? Oh, they run fluent enough all day as you can hear, I hope, I hope. Only parties, just living groups of four or more, still tongue-tie me. At gatherings, me early, folks entered, smiled, called my name, nodded, speed-walked to the bar.

But Red? Red sometimes sported too-new tartan golf caps ordered from catalogues. One had *Saint Andrews* stitched across its bill. He'd never been abroad, he'd clearly never played the mythic course. Surely others, knowing this, would spare him, not asking him to reminisce. I, hushed as ever but wide awake, found my father's overstatements grueling. Right on cue for being fifteen.

Red embarrassed Mom and me only when we caught him somewhat fudging. If Dad stayed just what he was—what all Mabrys were—he was hard not to love. I just ached to see him make wishes so blamed visible. But, for him, putting them out there's what made them real. Hadn't this already brought us sixty-five thousand and a house in town? Me, I felt eager to help him learn to hide. Was I best at keeping my own dreams secret? or had I not yet fixed on one?

Red kept slinging around those overused clubs. Kept dropping Roper's name as if a school chum's. Dad loved the Broken Heart so much he even praised their so-so chicken lunches. He believed the wives of his new dentist-friends all looked like certain movie stars. "Hiya, 'Rhonda Fleming.' You do, too. Just LIKE her." He made himself pathetic, upbeat and therefore indispensable.

DECOY

Guessing he'd never be taken for a full-fledged Skull and Bones member, Dad gradually became—without quite knowing—a sort of rustic mascot. Most smooth Falls golfers had secret kinsmen hidden one or two counties away. Their uncle-farmers looked and sounded not unlike my dear clay-colored Red. So gents—by shaking hands with this new member, by accepting his very presence as the last of weird Paxton's many pranks—felt slightly better about *their* secret country kin. Executives now decided they could tithe at Broken Heart. Now their own sun-cooked uncles and forty male cousins need never set a muddied boot onto the black-white-checkered marble foyer of an actual Riverside home.

Black caddies gathered around Dad, grinning at his jokes regarding bulls and cows, town salesmen outsmarted by farm gals. Red wanted to know young caddies' plans for some eventual education, better positions in out of the rain. Certain club members could always be counted on to slip bag-carriers a few bills and the same funny remarks. They often asked about the young men's getting lucky on Saturday night, how lucky and what was her name? all that night's names? Ha. Red seemed innocent of any difference between the Paxtons and their hired repairmen bag-boys. Since before George Washington, Paxtons always had the jobs to give, right? And poorer fellows needed work. Poor boys had been honestly paid to smooth things over, mop up after each smart-mouthed Paxton since 1610. Fair exchange of services. No shame in that.

I once overheard a golfer fondly quip, "Well, you know what ole Red says . . ." I also heard Dad called "Yosemite Sam, over there." Times he made me want to either blend in fast or fade away completely. Having arrived among the Fallen without heightened

265

expectations or faked confidence, I mostly kept to myself. Poor health reinforced that. "No roughhousing ever," they'd told me on the way to first grade. So I tried to look tempered, naturalized. If a high school fad for madras pants broke out, I made sure to be among the *last* to buy my pair. Mom resembled me in this. We kept tucked-back safe.

One Sunday Dad was driving us to First Presbyterian when Mom announced she'd reaffiliated Baptist. Her chosen church looked like our old country one. We'd liked it okay before Red's craze for all things "town" landed us on Lithium's shores.

Mom found some perfectly nice women at Third Baptist of Falls. They worked as seamstresses and kindergarten teachers. And when they drove in to have tea with her, one admitted to writing down the River Road address beforehand, in case police stopped her, she could prove she'd been invited.

I made friends too, quietly priding myself on talent-scouting the best folks, not the flashiest. (Doc was the only "famous" fellow I ever really cared for.) It so happens that some of the finer people on earth are forever—arms-crossed, shrewd observers—waiting there, off to one side. Always at the jury-box edge of things, silent for a thousand reasons of their own. Mom and I found few saints strewn among the Fallen. But those pals would, like my fact-loving face-saving Janet, prove lifelong.

THOUGH RED WAS freed from farming, though he knew local stores didn't open till nine a.m., he rose early and hit the shower. He counted on its metal stall to improve and echo his Tin Pan chorale. "High as an e-le-phant's eye!" became my reveille. Mom and I stayed bathers, hiders, silent afternoon soakers, readers in the tub. Honestly, if it had been left to us, all Mabrys would yet sit fly-swatting on some hot rental porch midfield. We three would still be right out there rocking tonight, comforted by roosting chickens' late-day placement squabbling, studying someone else's tobacco acreage. Such land's main beauty was the horizon where—for our inexpensive sidelined entertainment—an entire sun set nightly.

Even groaning during Dad's wake-up serenades, I'd come to half-appreciate his nerve. I, as the town boy who borrowed a record number of public library books, soon realized how much room there is on earth for one true believer. My very gift for camouflage let me see Dad plainer. Every club and lodge and church needs at least one Red Mabry. One who'll make only positive remarks, one who always offers unfaked enthusiasm. Raw belief. In the value of believing. In what? What have you got? My father, a pure person, put forth nothing else but faith.

Dad could hardly bear to even drive us past All Saints Episcopal, 1824, slate-roofed, ivy-wrapped, Tudored with half-timbering. He knew the Black Forest town where its organ had been made, given in honor of Colonel Paxton's kinsman, killed in the Spanish-American war. Jan and I once caught Red sitting in his car nearby on a summer Friday night when their organist always practiced. Passing the place, he'd sometimes whisper, "Inside, too, it must look just-like just-like being in England."

I've never known anyone with less education and grander fantasies. It made you marvel at his potential. It made me forgive his granting me this lifetime-break called Riverside. Your ticket to the middle class is, once punched, irrevocable. If you can truly taste the difference between a four-dollar supermarket Chablis and a true reserve Malbec, then you have tasted of the apple, or the grape. No return trips. Heaven and Hell do not accept each other's currency.

Times, I wonder what sort of country Buster Keaton I'd have been, if simply left out yonder hoe-in-hand.

Times, I still feel like some well-fed wild creature mistaken for a domestic pet.

13

SOMEBODY SUBSCRIBED TO the top collector-carver magazines, then passed these along our riverside road mailbox to mailbox. We soon learned those Hemphills were called "gunning decoys," meaning the kind once built to really float. But such game-trapping had worked too well. By 1912, all that got outlawed for commercial use. Decoys had become so good at teasing migrations down into killing range, whole species were going extinct.

Only then did the craft of outdoor trickery become the art of mantel-worthy carving. Our dear America itself, such an excellent invention, first ran Westerly and wild. Then all that reversed too-soon; it galloped on back and right into the Chicago stockyards.

America, how soon you pulled shut barn-doors behind you!

Even before WWI, we'd changed over—from being a nation of hunters to growers, from outdoor do-ers to collectors of the former do-ers' nifty gear. How weirdly soon we came indoors!

One side effect of being told since childhood that your heart's diseased, you pay steady attention to breathing, to any available banister. Over much direct sun can seem a threat; you get to imagine your own death scene. It's a privilege—mapping-practice for your final voyage. (Red Mabry would get just the communal public death he wanted. Other loving men stood by in sweet attendance.) —Would mine, my death, occur on some ab-improving machine of

268

Broken Heart's weight room? In my car after activating the turn signal then pulling over, ready?

It can be an advantage, knowing. You must prepare, admit. But in most directions it's a hideous deal, getting your death sentence so rottenly-early. Age six. And yet *when*—not *if*—it comes, I'll grab whatever poetry that last free throw can give.

ROPER NEVER SEEMED to age. It wasn't only I that thought so. He'd been years ahead of me at Falls High. But our class still bobbed in his choppy wake. His dad was known to be the handsome sulker, nursing a drink at bar's end, always a silk hanky in his blazer pocket, forever the pack of new playing cards ready at hand. He proved as addicted to contract bridge as he was awful at practical finance. But, however dapper a business failure, Roper Senior had not *bought* prestige for his son. Unlike so many of these D+ jerks in presidential power lately, Doc simply made up his own credentials. He won scholarships that were, as they say now, "need-based." Everyone in Falls inherited a little something. But all Doc got from his parents was their poise, their length, their pianist's and cardsharp's tapering blond hands.

In a town so small, we rarely speak straight-out of "love." We go with "think the world of him." But didn't we share one river city's circulatory system? Small pond, one truly big duck. Big Doc.

Something in his approach felt both eager-beaver Boy-Scout-like and yet still "cool." "Doc always goes all-*out*," our conservative crowd said, with admiration and worry. We fretted how his too-public enthusiasms left the man exposed. (Not that *he* bothered noticing.) Unlike most of the Fallen—company-men with cousinly ties to R. J. Reynolds—he lived with no sponsoring endorsement. Doc didn't teach at a university hospital, too long a commute. As our general practitioner, he just generally practice, practice, practiced.

Everywhere you went in driving-distance you somehow heard of a new oddball syndrome that Doc alone had diagnosed. Once at a country store outside Castalia, the clerk asked where I was from, then told me how a man named Roper, visiting this same spot for fishing bait, had found the clerk's young niece going into a convulsion never seen before. The scared clerk guessed it must be sudden epilepsy till Doc discovered, wadded in the girl's locked fist, a wrapper from a candy bar with peanuts. "Here's our problem. Bring me—let's see here—your Dristan powders and all your pills for poison ivy."

Protective, we felt scared for Doc, or so we told ourselves. Thing was, he still expected far too much. Might not Roper pay, and big time, up ahead? Or must we?

When he bought his first white Volvo wagon, the Falls Car Dealers' Association held an emergency breakfast meeting. The GM boys admitted to the peddlers of new-here Swedish and German and Japanese imports, this was one mighty dark day for all things U.S.-made. "What's bad for GM is bad, man."

And sure enough, within a year, twelve other admired young Riverside couples defected to Scandinavia, then even switched over to our two recent enemies at world war.

The Cadillac dealer afterward admitted, "We should've kept the Ropers supplied, free. Course, he's way too proud to just accept a fully-loaded El Dorado, boys. We might shoulda rolled one into his garage, gassed, waxed and ready! —Our *de*coy, get it?"

NO FALLS COLLECTOR could yet spring for a real Josiah Hemphill. But seven homes already claimed their signature "Marions." Oddly

270

enough, he'd dropped his lifetime "Doc." Man went back to that aunt-ish ferny ole first name. He incised that moniker alone beneath the tail of every creation. That followed by a needless ©. —His nom de plume(!) contained no hint he'd ever been a Yale MD. —Now, you delete a fact like that from your CV? means that, for America and Falls, you really are already sailing in your own Phase II.

TRIAL-DRUG TESTS, early transplant lists, Doc pulled all the strings he held to keep his promise to me current. Roper hoped to get gangly me and this weak-fish heart over the fence into *my* Phase II. He always blamed himself for not reaching my own dad in time to save him. No one could have. My own final office visit with Roper, he had taken a prescription pad and jotted three names plus their switchboard phone-numbers. "Who's all this?" I asked.

"Best cardiologists at Duke and UNC. The Sultan of Brunei? he had his triple-bypass done at Duke. They say he rented the university hotel's top three stories. For his wives, kids, security and rugs. Travels with his rugs. They're his capital. He'd obviously pick the best heart guy alive. —So, Bill, what with me being at this age, I guess today means the torch is passed."

"Making me the torch, huh? Go out pretty easy, torches. —But thanks. You more than tried." And into my shirt pocket I double-folded strangers. Seemed kind of "cold" of him, but what had I expected? He couldn't stay on-duty for the sake of one. Not even for his next-door neighbor, truest pal and leading advocate-observer.

Though I was a serious case, Doc never charged me one cent more per office visit than he did certain hypochondriac ladies. They had highly seasonal complaints. Friends said with a laugh, "With spring coming on, he'll soon be seeing Julia, I bet. Julia usually gets all her 'lumps' in April. And so, poor Doc takes *his*."

(And yet he never shamed her.) "Well, Julia Abernethy, you still look great, and I think you're a perfect saint to bear all you do, dear gal!")

Looking back, how had he abided us these forty years?

14

ONLY ON ARRIVING in Falls did Red understand he was exactly as short and yam-colored as folks had always said. A "Sweet Potato Mabry" after all, he drove downtown to buy his inaugural seersucker suit. He learned at once Falls' best "good" store. All the Broken Heart golfers wore this store's seersucker, striped brown or blue, the one suit suitable for your summer church or lawn party needs. But Rosen-blooms' veteran salesmen always made you face three mirrors. You could see the whole back of your head and it felt almost sickening, a dizzying double-cross. Poor Red came home shaken, acting seasick, went straight to bed. Now he knew he'd forever live eighteen holes away from clubhouse handsome.

At supper, hair uncombed past caring, Dad said, "Praise the Lord, you don't favor *me*, son. Good you got your daddy's fixtures but your momma's features."

Mom was basically pretty. But her pale rounded looks never seemed to give her either pride or pleasure. "Everybody's got to look like *some*thing." Baptist-again, she turned aside our every compliment.

Tonight Red kept at it. "Boy, if God had to go give you my bad heart *in*side, thank God ole God at least let you be pretty as your momma in the *face*."

I blindly accepted Dad's belief in my looks. Though, like Mom, I never trusted that I appeared like much past *occupant*.

Once at the club shower room, hiding on the shy side of my opened locker door, I had to overhear some guy say, "Yeah, wife got us there so early, only people around were the caterers and Bill Mabry. Oh she apologized then!"

I OWN A coveted Evinrude outboard, mine since youth and therefore now antique. Its green metal sheathing had all gone to crumbly rust. And yet the thing turns over every time, humming stupidly forward. Doc once joked about buying it from me. "Won't quit. Like a certain nearby rusty aorta. Your ole inboard, right, pal?" It relaxed a person, having as a heart one barnacled if stubborn combustion engine.

Maybe half of healing means passing another week's false confidence to the gimp? If so, bring me even more. And I can say I loved the man for giving my own slowing life at least this image.

SOMETIMES I WANTED Falls to change and then it would, but rarely quite the way I'd hoped. When Jan and I longed aloud for "new blood" it came, but bringing traffic, people that did not know us, or even Doc!

If big money once flowed from farm shacks to riverside town houses, the circulatory system reversed. Former fields, having given up tobacco, now sprouted malls that leached residents and cash from downtown. Jan asked if I'd drive her to our one good dry cleaner on Main. Though we'd last been here a month before, everything somehow looked unpainted and old-fashioned.

Along Old Town's Summit Avenue, our founders' mansions seemed swollen, stairways dangerous for families with kids. The best such, home realtors had gussied up as new insurance firms or B&Bs. A historic marker before one rambling house explained our last Confederate soldier had died here in 1940 (attended by his funny overworked nurse-wife). The place now served as a law office. Its big front yard sign declared NO FAULT DIVORCES, CHEAP. IN AND OUT.

I remembered riding into Falls with Mom and Red for window-shopping. The sidewalks were both washed and swept. We would step solemn from store window to window. The lights were brilliant. The clothing dummies looked to be New Yorkers. And we stared in as if hoping to join their church, too!

That same downtown lately looked smudged. It looked unloved and therefore unfamiliar.

MY HEART ITSELF I hoped might just maintain. I saw no high-jump meets in my future. But my inboard's chugging did let me perk along and notice our deck's river view. I focused more on my wife's recent sighs around three p.m. I fretted over our kids' uneven early career advancements. I concentrated on keeping our house painted, always harder so near water. And on our beloved neighbors, the Ropers especially.

He told me at our mailboxes how one wooden fowl might take him one month to three to craft. That meant Doc was not the speed demon he'd always seemed. Such carving was exacting but his painting, he admitted, took far longer. My Janet marveled at his "color-sense" she called it. "Most men can't pick out more than basic red or white or blue. But these feathers he does, they're more an olive-green shading toward the weak yellow from our cockatiels' backs. I read somewhere, color-blindness mostly happens to men. Who knew he had this *in* him?" But we looked at each other and knew we'd known. He could've run the Mayo Clinic blindfolded. Compared to that, what was an excellent custom duck-coating? I heard he owned a couple brushes inset with just three camel hairs.

After his second exhibit, even our least arty guys in the younger set began to talk up decoys. What *were* these except hunks of wood with flashing cuff-link eyeballs? During drink-hour, people passed around their original heirloom Marion—hand to hand, some weird scrimmage. This pintail's surface felt sanded into soapstone, jade. To the touch, it seemed less plant matter, more some cool mineral. You almost needed a magnifying glass to appreciate the many quills he'd scratched in there; no single feather assumed. His eye on the sparrow. Each quill built, as by some architect, atop the one beneath it. "Good as new, pal," Roper used to tell our son, after suturing his eyebrow shut again.

And, where did lucky owners keep their Marions? Not in safe-deposit vaults but out atop their coffee table's magazines. Our continent's wildlife had been tamed to hold down a job now, mere paperweight. Had all our native wildness shrunk to a decorator accent securing our now-married daughters' back-issue *Vanity Fairs*? I finally admitted it to myself. I wanted one. I wanted one he'd made.

TWO NEIGHBORS NOW hunted decoys on eBay. Fellows were soon ordering any thirty-dollar hunk of speckled cork and beak. They would bag no Hemphill, no Marion that way. All of us on The River Road now knew just enough about aquatic-bird-carving to make us dangerous, snobby. (Since Doc had never let me pay him his true worth for necessary Monday office visits, I imagined I might finally off-load major cash, buying one main "art duck" dead-ahead.)

I don't want to make like the Fallens' only news came via fake birds, Jack Daniel's, and our kids' early publications. We had the usual vigorous adultery and dicey legacy-mental-health. Money woes, plentiful heart disease, overmuch ovarian and breast and prostate cancer. Usual. Locals dependent on tobacco money were sometimes driven—out of defensive product loyalty—to smoke. They'd prove the act harmless. So tobacconists and their young kids publicly stuck with it, always good for a free pack, jaunty with the cigs as FDR in profile. They stuck with it till cultivating group lung-cancers they could've surely lived without.

And one night Les Wilkins's dad's bankrupt tobacco warehouses downtown caught fire. (Luckily spared, the old auction floor where Les stashed his priceless car collection.) From our decks in Riverside, the whole downtown looked outlined in flame. Silhouetted church steeples made this seem a godly retribution.

Farm-communities were glad to feel needed by the Fallen and rushed us their every truck. The whole night yowled sirens. It felt like London's Blitz, great cascades of upward sparks hung red against stars' cold blue. But what came drifting upriver across Baby Africa then into Riverside? This smell so fine it seemed almost an idea! Tobacco-dust, all of it that'd ever sifted into floorboards or rafters since Sherman's worst, lit up the night like one fine trick cigar.

If tobacco tasted as good as it sometimes smells many more would be dead. And this seemed history's long final exhale. Jan and I soon shifted our deckchairs to face such hellish fireworks; we waved over at the Ropers, ditto out on theirs. Studying orange sky, we breathed a luxury that can only come from the very last of something. Even our superb vintage poison!

Clowning, Doc leaned at a deck-rail, himself pretending to smoke, blowing great sophisticated rings of nothing. Then, seeming to remember, he pointed over at me, tapped his wristwatch, signaled toward our house.

DECOY

Just as my Janet here had first mimed news of my raw zipper, Roper stood showing—in a gesture coded for me—I should stay out, enjoy this exquisite smoke briefly, but soon head indoors, okay? Too much of it would not be good for me. Eye to eye with him, I nodded. And all this understood between semaphoring buddies sixty feet apart!

Things had a way of circling back around among us, like our shared S-shaped river. Two couples who'd noisily divorced married opposites—"change partners," as in square-dance geometry. That and the humiliating arrest of a longtime Riverside klepto were good for about two years' talk. We'd lately dodged four hurricanes. One friend's grandson, 8, died in five weeks, of unlikely Rocky Mountain spotted fever. (People said Doc, unlike Gita, would have recognized it right away.) Two pals got hit by lightning on the Broken Heart course standing under the biggest maple just as they tell you not to. And one local scandal had state police staking out a nearby nature-park men's room. It'd become the "meeting place" for a certain type of highly-sexed lumberjack.

It shocked us when the culprits' familiar names got listed unfiltered in our *Falls Herald-Traveler*. The shop teacher with a cleft palate, our own bank-trust-officer, one beloved black choir director father of six. Firings resulted, yellow moving vans arrived and departed. A town less colorful.

The cops had used their youngest blondest cadet to be bait. *His* name went unnoted. A competition sprang up to learn if he lived among us. Shocking to hear a deaf old pal at our club say too loud, "I'll give fifty bucks to any man can tell me the name of their Decoy Dick."

BEING MYSELF THE largely self-taught son of an eighth-grade

dropout, I can now let myself feel briefly smug: about our three curly grandchildren with IQs bound to produce cute stories. "Bettern money in the bank," I know my dad would enthuse.

One five-year-old grandson (William Mabry IV) recently explained to me by phone, "Kindergarten? Boring, Grandpa Bill. Always the same. Milk, cookies, cookies, milk. But, know what? I'm breaking up my day more, see. Time goes faster when I try and teach the others fractions."

As a kid, you start off feeling different from everybody else. But as time keeps washing you along, you grow half-proud of how animal-alike we are. Whoever escapes that? Who'd want to?

Here I could, but won't, mention professional high points of my son (Haverford, Stanford) and daughter (Middlebury, Baylor). But, at my present age, the town itself seems a fraternal order I'm proudest of. Since I'd stayed here, Falls naturally stays central in me. This age, I set less store by my particular role in this madhouse beehive. We're all in it together. The law of averages throws us some geniuses, some psychos. But one stabilizing force shepherds us in-betweens, us souls born to stay local.

In the end so much comfort rises from our river. Whenever I get jangled, I just step out onto our deck. I'll inhale whatever lithium haunts the mists. I note today's water level crossing our six flat giant rocks: I listen to what today's major note is. Often a G. I swear this little river's become my nitro and my prayer.

Out here, I ask myself if Red did not die a disappointed man; moving Heaven and Hell just to get us into Falls, only to find his son an insurance peddler. But why beat myself up? I did my best with those cards palmed my way. And now? I've retired for exactly this purpose: to meditate not medicate.

We often eat lunch at this table Jan keeps draped in oilcloth. She

278

says the maple's droppings stain her better inherited linen. Sitting here I at times imagine this same musical tone after me, post-Bill. Like that rock ballad about life's "running on within me and without me." Will always be. Our standing houses still looking beautiful for our genius grandkids.

Sometimes I wonder if people's final seconds alive do bring that fabled highlight-reel. The life-flashes-before-your-eyes-type thing? Hope so.

That in itself must feel like an accomplishment.

15

IN MY EARLY twenties, I got dibs on Roper's first Monday office slot 6:45 a.m. I held it too, even skimping on vacations certain years. I'd leave Janet at the beach with Lottie and our two, after driving them to Wrightsville the Thursday before. But my Mondays were essential. Doc's nurses treated me to my own coffee mug, filling it, black; even as Roper warned again that I should skip caffeine. "Then how will I *know* I'm alive?" I said the same thing almost weekly. But by now it'd become liturgy.

"Well, Bill." He shook his head to one side. "You've got a hard choice ahead, looks like: quitting either the excitement of coffee or . . . Janet."

"One lump or two?" (My stabs at Doc's dry humor never quite made sense but we laughed anyway.) Bad health was good for at least one Monday cackle, a quick visit regarding something irrevocable. In sickness and more sickness. It ran on like this for decades, our ritual. And, between us—to me at least—it all seemed, life and death, charged up, so *per*sonal.

Before his long hands cupped the stethoscope to my front then back then front again, Roper would huff across its stainless steel (which clouded at once). His spare heat weekly took the edge off a natural chill. And soon, me seated bared to the waist, he standing fully-dressed in whites, we'd just be catching up. Between certain needed vital-signs-listening silences, Doc was quick to offer the mild neighborhood lore I loved.

Me, I never could gather much on my own. I've heard far less since he quit us.

Stated like this, our lifelong office visits sound routine. But, maybe their coming at a week's start and just past dawn, maybe that let every visit seem an extension of yesterday's All Saints eight a.m. service. A Sabbath-annex gave my week's one basic warrantee—his genius tinkering on me. He kept making little shifts in my meds. Placebos, busywork maybe. "Better, worse?" he'd start some mornings.

And what could I offer in exchange? I had little past my job-slot, insurance, group life. I had my goodwill, toward him at least. I'd gladly shared my father with him, right? For that he thanked me with my life. Doc seemed at one with all he did. With none of the levels of qualms and exemption I seemed to always bring. Roper'd just scribble out the new prescription, more as subject matter than any real cause for hope. Then he'd pat me on the bare back, also a sign for me to get dressed; he'd send me forth: "Steady and holding, pal. I'm liking the sound of the ole Evinrude inboard this week."

I mean, it meant something, you know?

THE ARTICLE IN our latest AARP bulletin was titled "At Last Unmortgaged, Second-Chance Lives Newly Afloat." Big as life, there Doc and Margie were on record, page 96, photographed in his retrofitted Riverside studio. White interior walls surrounded his workstation, a world mostly glass. The Swedish-modern shelves showed—in curly-tailed profile—his past four years of daily work. Quote:

> "I do try keeping my best ones held back for myself," a lean Roper admitted. "I find I like being around them daily. My quorum. As with family, you hope to learn from living close-by your finest early mistakes!"

Bet that made his absentee kids real happy.

STILL, YOU WERE mainly glad for him as yet. Maybe it was one use for his intuition. But, if your hands contain the power of life, wouldn't it seem a demotion, to have all that wasted on wood? Sure, wood lasts. But to what end?

And yet, I figured, even now, with him retired, even with his taxi meter set to "off-duty," if worse came to worst, my Janet could always run find him. And if she had to interrupt close-focus bird-carving? I wouldn't mind.

Magazines spoke of his being belatedly "discovered." But hadn't we known Roper all these decades now? Even so, must be wonderful for him. I'd chanced to see his studio light burning, lately past three a.m. Of course Doc's art must've been some true form of *work*. But somehow, to me, it felt like slacking. Roper, as usual, seemed to have gotten away with everything.

Invited to exhibit new birds at the British Decoy and Wildfowl Carving Championships, he and Marge got flown to London. Only during his third local show did I see how much he'd grown. Imagine, older than I and still getting daily better at something! A display

case off to one side was labeled MY LITTLE EXPERIMENTS.
—Pretentious?

This material seemed far more private than his finished projects.
You felt you got to scan some Nobel scientist's lab notebooks. Onto
wooden wings and tail feathers, Roper kept trying to shape believ-
able water beads, see.

If you borrowed Janet's 3.0 bifocals and bent close, you'd note
convincing pearls of water. He had coaxed these up from the same
hardwood that'd formed the feathers damp beneath them. Doc
then saturated the droplet with a glowing sheeny gray-blue. We
heard he'd figured out this paint formula in his see-through studio
no home-towner ever got to visit. Parked across its lot now, we
now noticed high-end Lexuses (turquoise) with New Mexico tags.
You saw the yellow Hummers of photographers from big-
time magazines.

Folks made corny local jokes about how "people living in glass
houses shouldn't stow loons." There he kept the best of his best and
we learned he'd had a killer burglar-alarm installed. You knew
why—once you stooped before this glass case, once you studied
Roper's carved water. You almost wanted to break through glass
yourself. You'd risk the cuts. If only you could touch the outfanned
wing and its spray of river water.

Wet would probably come off between your thumb and forefin-
ger. Odd, but this liquid seemed legally our community's. Didn't it
truly hail from our local river? And, though you knew the big
droplet was just wood, gesso, silver metallic paint, it'd surely feel
oily with Doc's essence, some luxury hard-earned, it'd come off slick
between your fingers, pure native DNA.

16

SINCE GRADE SCHOOL I carried in my back jean pocket (1) the all-important comb, and (2) a doctor's excuse: "Bill here must take Study Hall not Phys. Ed." True, the note bought me many happy library hours. It also forced a kid to imagine the circumstances of his death. All before he's quite plotted out his life. True for Dad, too.

But he'd long ago adjusted. Even as an honorary town person he rose before first light. Showering with off-key show tunes, he was like the rooster who thinks his rusty song alone orders the sun into place. Though Dad no longer needed to work hard, he kept taking odd jobs. "For fun," Red shrugged. He admitted with a droopy half smile, it was also one way of getting into those giant homes where we'd not otherwise be welcomed.

To repair such piles, he hired the few Falls plumber-electricians he'd judged trustworthy. Dad stayed loyal to his country crew but their trucks seldom seemed operational; that made their even getting to town strangely hard. Red guessed the Primitive Baptists felt uneasy among the fourteen-inch crown moldings and orgy photos of the Fallen.

Dad had helped Doc Roper build his own home dock. Dad could walk from our place to this split-level Frank Lloyd Wright knockoff being remodeled. Marge Roper said, "We were told it's based on Fallingwater." But the Lithium ran outside their house not through it.

Doc and Red had taken to each other at once. Roper was just then opening his practice here. He and Marge had bought the big river place. It was a financial stretch for young marrieds but I guess that, like Jan, Marge had some old-family money. Rumors varied quite how much. Starting out in practice then, Doc still traded his services for others'. He'd accepted one man's lifetime house-painting in exchange for family office visits. I wonder now if my father didn't do Doc's jobber-overseeing as a swap for more frequent family cardiac checkups.

Red's specific case (and mine) seemed to at once engage our young GP as a scientist. This disease, passed from father to son, was just beginning to get some of the research Dad and I felt sure it deserved. Not long after I moved back home as a graduate of Chapel Hill, Roper invited Dad and me in for our joint monthly consultation.

Only then did I finally ask Roper how he'd been so quick to recognize our obscure condition. He pointed to Red's eyelids. Flecked skin under either brow had always been slightly alligatored. Doc explained these pocket-bumps were stored cholesterol. The body couldn't deploy its horded lipids fast enough. So the organism stashed such gunk at outer edges only. Mabry bodies were laboring to keep at least hearts' arteries clear.

"In worst cases, you'll see a circle of cholesterol rising up from within the eyeball itself, a perfect ridge around the iris. But on that count? you both look free and clear. Eyes good as new."

After a final pressing of his warmed stethoscope to our fronts-backs, Doc stood directly before my shirtless father, "Say your own dad died young, Red? Remind me, what age exactly?"

"Well, sir, let me see here. He'd of been right at thirty-six, yeah. Sure was."

"And, just beforehand? had he been particularly stressed? I mean, what was your dad *do*ing when he died?"

"*Stressed?* Daddy was plowing. It was '34."

"Aha. Makes sense. —Well, I don't want either of you going any-where near a mule, hear? Even if a nice one keeps bringing its bit and harness up to you. That clear, guys?"

Dressing, shy, we thanked Roper. He'd given our problem complete attention. I searched his face and manner for just how dire it was, our disease. Did he admire us less now? Still, we Mabrys sure felt singled out. Later, I'd worry that Doc treated everyone this way. Of course I knew that was a merit. Should be. Even so . . .

"OUR" DOCTOR, ROPER forever put my dad at ease in ways Red rarely guessed were planned. Roper combined the strangest quality of being both an ordinary-sounding guy and our truest local aristocrat. Some saving coolness always pressed right up against his warmed front surface. Some short-term joke hid his long-range plan for you.

Maybe old Paxton had enjoyed the actual pedigree stretching back before this wilderness got itself up as a republic. And Colonel Paxton might've finally become a true philanthropist by rewarding my father's innocent faith in beauty and a good address. But, it was Roper's calm that eased our country tribe into feeling half-secure with its strange new life. Doc's own gambling father, his mother musical with sighs, they'd at least taught him the sort of manners that never seem just manners. He let the Mabrys' being healthy appear someday possible. Roper made even our sudden club membership feel, if sudden, somewhat natural. Was this just part of his doctoring? Or did he truly mean it? Or was it maybe likely some of both?

I WAS FRESH home from our excellent state university (nation's oldest, chartered 1789). Red had wanted me to join some fraternity or at least get into a fine new dorm. I found myself happiest renting in the small mill village beyond the university train tracks. There I noted a FOR RENT sign hand-lettered on a worker's whitewashed cottage. It seemed brother to the one Paxton had sprung us from.

Janet attended the Women's College in Greensboro and some weekends I'd hitchhike the fifty miles to her campus. She was studying art history and her student art show painting (of the Lithium) won Honorable Mention. It was not abstract but I thought it was the best. Thumb out, headed toward her, I always felt a little wild, and closer to my dad.

UNC professors knew nothing of The River Road. Its codes and demands would sound laughable to such Harvard, Princeton men. "Parochial" was their own fond word for this beautiful state that underpaid them.

I worked hard there, wonderfully anonymous by choice. Teachers soon seemed to respect my mind, even some of my writing. I got to study Homer, a bit of Latin, European history alongside advanced math. I came home to find myself both over- and underqualified. Finally I turned up a temp job at Riverside's best insurance agency. The boss needed a salesman Boy Friday with a club membership, someone from our water's-edge neighborhood. I guess I was the only Riverside college grad adrift enough to consider taking such a position. Sure I belonged to Broken Heart, but I stood to inherit little more than my father's name and house.

The insurance mogul was a golfing bachelor and, after six months of my being punctual and somber and concerned, he told me he sure liked my clear blank style. "But I have to say you give new meaning, Bill, to the words 'silent partner.' Still, I prob'ly talk enough for four, and your sales're solid. People trust you. Widows especially. Some guys just have that. Can't be bought." Two years later he said he'd someday pass the firm along to me. If, that is, I didn't find such work too painfully dull. He'd long ago confessed: His well-paid secretary ran all the triplicate paperwork. Adjustors working for our national firm assessed the actual damage. I would sell people on protecting their lives and property. How hard could it be?

The boss managed to stay out most days glad-handing new clients on the links of Broken Heart. He was obliged to drink with others after hitting around a few balls, all a write-off and a lark.

At his office Roper explained to Dad and me how, given our disease, insurance would prove a great choice for my talents. It'd prolong my life. "If dealing with people's crazy made-up claims doesn't leave you barking-mad. But deskwork, that's the ticket, Bill. Let people come to you. You have a face they'll like then start to count on. Just don't go climbing rooflines like your mountain-goat poppa here. Oh, I saw you up checking slates on the Blanchards' roof. —But Red, I'm like you, hate sitting. Far as that, here's my latest advice for you: Quit your playing all eighteen holes. Nine's plenty. And, for now, just once a week, hear? Clock more time on that putting green. You need it almost as bad as me. Oh, I've seen those big swings of yours windmilling up and down the fairway. With that much upper-body work, Arnold Palmer, you might be taking risks."

"I do put ever'thing into it, Doc, sir."

"Yeah, I see that. And there's your trouble, pal. You heard of 'heart trouble'? Well, steer clear of giving *your* grade of slippage a bit more trouble than what it's got. So let me slip you one last tip, Mabry Senior . . . Hell-for-leather as you're working those links, don't hire any of our young hotshot caddies. They're in such an almighty rush to wedge in one more round a day. Just make you anxious, their advice. No, you'll want to ask for old Maitland Miller. You've seen him, tall, white-haired fellow, keeps to himself? Tell Mait I sent you. He's been out there since that course was still fine Paxton tobacco. Mait, now, he's older than you by 'round twenty years. He's not going to rush you. Be good medicine, letting him pace you. But, even better, Red, I'm told there's great sport in contract bridge, one mighty fun game . . ." And you could see Doc bank a smile. He knew he'd set Dad off and now leaned back to enjoy it.

17

JANET AND I had known Doc and Marge since forever. But despite my feeling free to see Doc at his office pretty much anytime, invitations to the Marion Ropers' home became less forthcoming. We had all been young marrieds together. Then we'd enjoyed two full seasons of their direct social grace. Who knows why they'd taken us up, then set us down again?

Was it something I said? Did I agree with Doc too soon? Or stare at him too long as he stood showing how he made his potent unbruised James Bond martinis? Maybe I forgot to thank Marge as I was leaving once?

"We were too close already, living right here," Janet shrugged. "Those two can't turn over in bed without our hearing." I gave her a look. "Well, you know what I mean."

But it felt painful. With them so busy and so near us on the river. It's not like they threw massive parties and cut us out. But we couldn't help noting which three couples the Ropers preferred this year (ones way younger than us, of course). And every five to seven weeks, here those beauties all came, carrying champagne and flowers, hollering indoors ridiculous new nicknames. We ourselves felt equally "attractive," "up-to-date." Jan and I read certain articles in the library's *New York Review*; we'd forever subscribed to *two* newsweeklies. But I reckon old friends like us are often the last to know. Was it my sickness? Was it our son's being Haverford and his at Harvard? He could have told me. I would've accepted it.

And yet we still loyally waved to him reading on his brand-new redwood deck. "It's too red," Janet said (to please me).

"Oh, honey, it'll fade soon enough," I called, as if taking Doc's part, only not.

Then Roper would be out there shirtless, strapped into bandolier binoculars; he'd become a crazed birder.

Not two years ago, this guy had been considered one crack duck hunter. His office watercolors had shown dawn-silhouetted boaters, guns aimed at chevrons of doomed incoming geese. Now, he acted grateful only for those bagged birds pals brought from the coast. These were handed over for Doc to study. Roper had gone passive-pacifist thanks to retirement and to art. He now stored his specimen-waterfowl in a huge Kenmore freezer bought just to keep these fresh. We heard how Doc had given away his excellent inherited Browning (to their help's rambunctious teenage sons!). People said he lived almost as a vegetarian, so reverent had he become after daily meditating on his flying-swimming creatures.

He stopped making certain pointed jokes. He then stopped "getting" them. When a beloved cutup shoe clerk saw Doc step into his store, the owner called, for all to hear, "Please waddle into our web-footed section, Donald Doc." Roper gave him one scalding look, veered out. It'd been a stupid thing to say but was meant as tribute. To survive in Falls, you have to take a joke. Or pretend to.

Neighbors judged our Roper had floated a bit above his raising. True, his bridge-obsessed dad had "class" if rarely a spare twenty. — And now Doc was letting any cut-rate airline's magazine come

photograph that precious studio, while never admitting his closest
Falls admirers.

Still, I owed him.

It was at his third show I saw it. And chose to buy his all-time
greatest work of art.

18

NOT TO BOAST but, from twelve feet's distance, I spied Doc's masterpiece. Roper's *portraits* of wood ducks were, I'd admitted from the
start, unbelievable.

In the wild, wood ducks are, of course, the prettiest things you'll
see dressing up any American creek. White specks, red beak, eyes
almost lime-green, really God's own Woolworth paintbox. A
chestnut-colored breast spread with white dots the size of daily
aspirin. And this one had a jaunty crest that looked back-combed
just so. A little Elvis, not yet drugged unhappy, but already a tad
aware of his own damp swiveling beauty.

I bent eye to eye with this plucky bird. I met myself, age fourteen. Even the bird's swept-back "Mohawk" somehow spoke to me.
Now, how to *adopt*—meaning *buy*—this punk of a duck. The thing,
first glance, just had such *heart*.

Prices were not posted. I saw none of the usual rash of red stick-
ers meaning *sold*. I felt embarrassed offering a close friend many
thousands for something of no use, except your looking at it. Which
is a use, I guess I know.

Even so, really really wanting it, asking for and getting Janet's
own nod, I finally cornered my pal. "You signed the bottom of this
bird, Doc. Now let me show you I can carve my name at least across

the bottom of this check. Jan and I will give our little guy a nice dry home. I'll take him."

Such a smile Doc gave me. "Bill? Gosh, I'm honored. Truly. Fact is, seems the way this world of decoy collecting is set up, I'm expected to park this particular baby with a top Manhattan collector. That way, they tell me, Woody here will be seen by certain museum folks. Don't ask *me*. Seems that's how ye ole art world flowchart works. But there'll be others ahead for you and Janet, promise. You've got quite an eye. Wood ducks give me the biggest headaches. So they're always the most fun, like my best patients, you regulars, m' best patients. I hate that a New Yorker's already called dibs on this little dandy. But nowadays I'm putting all my new things in the agent's lap first-thing. Easier, finally. —But I sure appreciate that interest, Bill."

"Aha," I said. I stood here. The checkbook in my hand truly felt like my dick hanging out for all to see.

I stood remembering his cruel joke about my son's clumsiness, even as our boy lay there gray-green with a bone-jutting fracture. "Well, Doc, thanks for even con*sid*ering our offer." Politeness kills the fastest. "*Real*-ly. Just to even be considered in the running . . ."

He sure heard my edge. He knew my heart. He'd once described it as likely someday "to flutter then, quite honestly, implode." Doc now stepped a full foot closer. He even clamped a hand around my bicep. I tensed it quick into a bulk more manly. Roper hinted under his breath how not even HE could pay retail for his own darned carvings lately!

That too hurt my feelings . . . I guess I can afford what I usually set my heart on, thank you very much.

Fact is, not to talk ugly about him, but Roper was becoming kind of "artistic." I don't enjoy stating this. But it's sure what others were saying. Suede elbow patches appeared overnight on the old blond tweed jacket locals had seen on him since Davidson. He and Marge had bought a young pair of Josiah Hemphill–like springer spaniels, though everybody knew he'd given away his dad's one beautiful unhocked bird gun. Janet predicted worse, "When we see him smoking a Sherlock Holmes pipe, we won't be too shocked, now, will we, Bill?" How could I even tell Jan about his turning down my offer like this? Still smarts.

(In North Carolina, we've always put a premium on modesty. Mom advised I was already a lifelong "hider." Still, it's wrong to let others guess you have real money. Best underdress. No cowboy shirts inside the city limits. Understate to the power of five. That's code here. But even so, I would have paid him twenty-five thousand for the damn thing is all I'm saying. Thirty. No, I'd go clear to . . . sixty-five. —I mean what is friendship for, man?)

OF COURSE, IN modern life, decoys no longer *mean* to draw south-bound fowl down toward your waiting gun. I know that. But, robbed of that cocky junior wood duck meant as mine, I got grouchy about folk art generally. Started wondering:

When does "Americana" become that?

Carved ducks, once meant to help you feed your family, aren't they now just national good-luck charms? Find them on U.S. stamps or speckling wallpaper at inns. Only when decoys were outlawed after tricking too many birds to death did we find them fully "lovable" at last. (Regarding our handsome nation's future in the hungry world, is there not a *hint* here?)

Yes, I was pissed at losing my drake. Loyalty goes unrewarded when you're seen as one who'll stay no matter what. My leverage, if any? Canceling the Ropers' home owners' policy?

DECOY

Miffed, silent, I decided it was really kind of odd anyway, trying to exactly imitate another living thing. Who'd *do* that? I mean, imagine if, say, all life-sized bronze figure sculpture got painted to look exactly like human beings. What if art museums left out beautiful half-naked lady-statues to try and lure living breathing young men indoors? And why? to trick, trap, kill and eat them? See my point?

I hurried home from the show, champagne-high in a way that made me feel, even walking, not quite balanced. Jan was kind enough not to ask if I'd got the one I'd set my heart on. As she settled before our usual nightly news, I told her I sensed one of my sinking spells coming, just needed a quick nap. Twenty minutes, tops. I went right down into a kind of suicidal sleep. Had this windy, saturated dream in color:

Imagine you are flying south, migrating, actually. You lead your air-group and—with raw sun sinking quick—you keep scouting, seeking any inlet where your kind might settle, feed, rest.

Some memory of gunfire elsewhere keeps you circling the blue cove below. Others—behind and beside you—await your signal-dive. Only that will prove how all this under you is safe. You're tired and so are other flyers. But the inlet down there looks too ideal. True, some of your own sort already float there. Still, this might be a trick. But then you notice another one such as you. A more splendid example of your species, your sex. This male's already bobbing at his ease to one side, guarding his own thirty. Even from on high you note the drake's bold coloring, his bearing unflappable. And so, descending, bringing in your group to aim for water's surface nearest him, you imagine greeting such a one. A fellow leader, his size notable, his markings almost . . . gunshots. Sharp pops, feathery explosions left and right. Three fall, now four, as you ascend.

Beating upward, panicked, you sense at once: your group's undoing is your own too-trusting need for another worthy's company. That's what got four good ones killed back there. Your visible authority is really just your own male loneliness kept perfectly hidden. That other leader? likely wood. Unflappable, all right.

You, shaken, betrayed by your own kind, wing on. No loyalty. Not like you, he cannot have been quite real. Resemblance itself can be stolen. Attraction? Lethal. Turns so quick against you. Can kill you and all of yours.

19

THE BIXBY TWINS, barely teenaged, had grown amazing-looking, already built like anything. Their child faces were now carried around atop these panther limbs. Boys knocked at our door, announcing they'd be showing off their matched diving at the club, July Fourth. Could we come? They were walking all over Riverside inviting old friends. Sweet when kids that young still want to sit and talk to silver oldsters like Jan and me. They asked by name about Jill and Billy, though our kids had been years ahead of them in school.

Of course, we felt closer to the twins for having seen them go underwater and drown powder-blue. I'd not forget pulling these newts from our Lithium so someone else could fill them with his air. You'd think the boys might ever-after find our river terrifying; but no—absolute water babies.

At the club, twins greeted everyone. Barely fifteen, tanned completely dark, each wore a Band-Aid-sized black Speedo, a short haircut exactly matching his brother's. Rumor had it they'd just "been with" a handsome married lady of forty. Both with her at once, fore and aft, it was said then immediately believed. Her husband spent months away at tobacco market in Georgia. Turns out, most married ladies her age can keep secrets far better than identical newbies, fifteen.

Riversiders' disapproval was offset by some awe at imagining the sight. The Fallen imagined this woman corrupting our Tomothy-Timothy concurrently; folks felt a hushed respect for her gall, her sheer twofer enterprise. She had hired the boys for a fix-it job, "Come help me clean my gutters?" Afterward, passing this put-together lady at the mall, nobody quite issued her the "cut-direct." Instead, freighted humid looks got offered. Especially by other women of a certain age. Looks said, *How?* The *why* was understood. People all do crazy things when it's their last-chance-ever. I told you, Riverside is rarely unintentionally rude.

Presiding at Broken Heart's pool, Kate Bixby, the twins' glad mother, played hostess and was gracious and dear despite all that weight she's put on. (Why so unhappy, you think?) Luckily, the forty-year-old seductress in question had the Protestant good sense to stay away.

Tomothy and Timothy's mirror-image dives made us all feel proud then stronger. People said they had a clear shot at the upcoming Atlanta Olympic trials. You could tell already: fond as we were of them, Bixbys seemed destined to be among the Fallen who did not stay.

Greetings at their diving demonstration made me feel a solid part of Riverside. It was in the clubhouse bathroom afterward I got another bulletin concerning me. It arrived in the usual way I seem to learn: myself viewed via outside diagnosis, more than any deep personal reflection, hard as I try.

Shy, I'd chosen the farthest row of urinals. From there I

overheard one of my favorite tennis partners at the sinks telling his chum, "Yeah, we caught Bill Mabry with Mom, at home. Having tea. And trying to sell her *flood* insurance! A hundred and fifty miles from the ocean. And her always claiming she can't even afford new dentures. Hers do whistle. And here he is sitting looking out at the ducks with her, and pushing that. Brochures out, the works. Given Bill's history, people feel for him. Don't think he doesn't use that pity in his business, too. But, trying and pile coverage onto someone Mother's age? My sisters and I think he's overstepping."

NOW I HAD been shunned as a Marion collector eager to pay retail, I can hardly overstate how shamed I felt. He had no idea what-all he meant to me, but then did *I*? Losing that mere object, it left me truly shaken, silently enraged, convinced I should possibly go rogue. Bill, the Indie! I mean, how hard could it be? To take a hunk of wood and make it be or go . . . duck-shaped? Just out of spite, I'd maybe start with a wood duck. Where is it written that an able man retires to no lifeline stronger than his cable news?

I avoided Bobbitt's Hobby Shop where the Roper fan club gathered. I made a trip to Raleigh I sort of hid even from Jan. There I bought superlative German gear. "State-of-the-art everything," the guy promised. Tomorrow I'd try my first one as an experiment. I'd do it all in my tool shop where we keep grandkids' life jackets and temperamental weed-eaters. Safe back there, even if I found myself a slow starter, all thumbs, not even the wife need know.

As I might have said, the week our boy finished Haverford (with high honors), Janet went out and bought herself a pair of cockatiels, noisy seed-scatterers. She embarrassed me even more by naming them for our now-absent son and daughter. But, today, for raw inspiration, I did step into our kitchen, did stare into their cage. "Hi, Jill. Hi, Billy." Real birds, after all, if unfit to ever model as matching American wood ducks.

I retired to my shop-studio feeling pumped up, almost wicked, granted a second and more sexual life. I'd once overheard my son tell a pal how some choir girl lighting candles at All Saints made him "get wood during service." That term, new to me, I found funny.

But now to business. Using my twelve hundred dollars of Kraut engineering and tempered Sheffield steel, I would mold and make it, major wood. I set the virgin cedar block into my bench vise, secured it. *That's* not going anywhere. "Step One, Phase II. Completed, Houston."

TURNS OUT EVERYTHING my father possessed in anti-golfing talent, I'd inherited at anything artistic. It's not just about intelligence, is it? Within ten minutes I discovered an even deeper secret—lack of even any actual motor skill. (In your head, you can see a thing so clearly . . .) It remained my news alone; right till Jan had to drive me to the ER. Just eighteen stitches, really. Told Janet I'd been fixing the lawn mower. She grunted, *"That'd* be a first."

Next day, one hand mittened in gauze, I sneaked down to our river. I took that red-stained block and chucked it. Tossed my wood-handled Sheffield blades into our crooked little river. I recalled downloading Red's handmade if subcontracted Shadowlawn sign. I enjoyed watching every darned item bobble off toward the Atlantic far far away.

We all have our gifts. —Don't we?

At Doc's exhibit I'd bent at the knees, I'd stared so hard into his glass case. I had felt pride that slid at once into longing. Shelves had mirrors behind them; cruel, that. You saw your own blocky stubbled face edging streamlined wildlife. "Sad" can sometime seem a default setting for our whole flock of the Fallen over sixty.

I kept replaying how he'd turned down my blank-check. My good-faith-offer for that little "me" bird, half-angel, half-juvenile delinquent. Grabbed by some poacher, it'd likely been shipped off to the City. Ransomed north, needing only my wad of cash to keep it here in Falls, a fellow stay-at-home. Doc's pip of a masterpiece, exiled to New York's East Side, institutionalized far from here and me. Atop some white Formica pedestal.

—Hoping for what? a museum or open water.

20

I'D FELT SO healthy being twenty-two, home with the framed Chapel Hill "bachelor of science." Beside it, in my insurance office, I hung the laminated "antiqued" certificate proving me also a licensed CPA. Jan and I were just back from our honeymoon (Washington, D.C., for some reason). Partly educated, fully married and employed, I first claimed, then fought to hold, Doc's first Monday slot. If some hospital emergency took him elsewhere, I'd sometimes bob in anyway, joke around with his nurses. Hefty efficient Blanche and both funny Sandys. Same names, unrelated, they'd started saying they were sisters as a joke. Now they admitted sharing the same Clairol "Ash Blond" and it made them, in crisp white with folded caps, seem even cuter, almost-twins. I felt they counted on my turning up to get their week launched with a joke, good one, an old favorite.

Everyday sameness? At least it made life feel potentially longer. Right hand on the steering wheel, left on your emergency brake. By the standards of Eden, Falls' routes and habits might've seemed poky. But things flowed along as shallow yet easeful as our busy-work Lithium itself. Insurance soon became clockwork, regularized and well-paying if in steady dribs and drabs. (I've always been a faster study than anybody else around here mostly cared to know.) By trade I was a cheerful seller of insurance. And I ensured I'd daily sell myself as a cheerful version of that. Call me a decoy 9–5. From my Fidelity notepad I summoned our national adjusters to sites of grease fires, fender benders. But Riverside somehow seemed exempt from maiming tractor-accidents, barn burnings, country gore.

EARLY SEPTEMBER IS my favorite time for outdoor exercise. Maples have started rusting that first mellow tint. Air along our river holds a crisp sort of start-of-school Granny Smith promise. So find me pounding away at the backboard of the Broken Heart tennis courts.

Even as a country boy of eight I preferred tennis to golf. The sight of my first court seemed like a perfect memory of order. Like those faint blue lines on school paper. Given my cardiac picture, I'd never be Wimbledon material. On my doctor's advice I tend to favor doubles but still love the game. Odd, I associate its pleasures with enjoying flossing my teeth. Nets? Strings? Always the constant cleanly sounds of tennis leave me feeling purified. Bit clearer in the head.

Dad admitted disappointment. My failing to take up golf hurt him, he admitted. Tennis seemed a gelded game to this ex-farmer, "You're practically indoors. Might as well play bridge." But, belief in Golf? it's like God—either you've always accepted it or, on sight, you find the very idea ridiculous. Those pompomed caps? men's pastel pants and shiny white shoes, the rickety length of the clubs and the sneaky size of that ball! From the start, all of it struck me as some visual joke designed by a real mean gay *New Yorker* cartoonist.

Red begged me to at least caddy for him. "I mean, we're lifetime legacy members and you are m' only begotten son, son." But Roper, noting our recent shortness of breath, had politicked us toward half-rounds. Doc knew how long it took poor Dad to chop across the course.

Red was running out of even unpopular partners. The oldest had found his game too slow, ragged, yet peppery. City veneer fell away as he cursed the pro's poor preparation of Red himself. By now Dad played through mostly alone. At golf, Red's usual workmanlike focus got outfoxed only by his comic lack of talent. "Address the ball," he'd say aloud, stepping toward it, as if trying to make a small if obstinate new friend.

This was a few years before our club required carts. They meant to keep foursomes moving at a new industrial pace. (Here lately, the Broken Heart Admissions Committee's been throwing open the gates to more and more retired New Jerseyites. Remaining dot-com money, certain loudish Johnny-come-latelies. A shame, really.)

Red had taken our doctor's advice years back. He now worked around the schedule of that revered senior caddy, Maitland "Mait" Miller. A skinny handsome blue-black man, Mait had very white hair. It grew in pleasing mossy coins set around his skull like some type of crown or cap. Red once joked: Mait had been "thinking the game" so long his hair had become all cotton golf balls.

As Doc promised, Mait's caddying gave the suave impression of someone never hurried. "Ball went in the drink? That do happen. Nothing worry 'bout. I got us another two dozen, dry, right here. Which one these looks luckiest?"

Maitland Miller served as deacon in his church, had a daughter at Reed. As old as he was, lank and nonchalant, he might've caddied for each justice who'd sat on the Supreme Court since William Howard Taft. Nowadays he might be a college president. Back then he helped white fellows whittle points off their "mental game" for life. Though they'd never seen him play, never once invited that, they trusted his every grunted hint and nod.

Doc Roper turned up at Broken Heart this same sunny day midweek. From my backboard, I could see him yonder on our putting green, perfecting shot after shot with his usual directed patience. Roper's hair stood out up spiky white against clubhouse bricks. Like me and many players here today, Doc seemed constantly scolding himself with how-to's. "There you go at the elbow again, you." Had to laugh, imagining Doc making any public goof-up he couldn't at once correct.

I wondered if he'd glimpsed me over here punishing the backboard. (I always seemed more aware of where he stood than he of me.) Hoped Roper'd spy me exercising; that way I'd get points in his office early Monday. Always did try preparing some starter topic as I am told folks do for their weekly head-shrinkers.

It being a Wednesday noon, few other members were around; mainly waitresses in white watering petunias on our terrace, gossiping about some big upcoming Moose Lodge dance. You had a sort of peaceful backstage feeling. Nothing counted today. No one was looking. My vital signs felt vital and I was just twenty-two. How glad I was for my skinny candid Janet and our beautiful house full of her family antiques.

My essential players were all nearby: Doc, alone with his putting, giving at the knees as charts all show. Pop out somewhere, getting shaken-head sympathy from Mait at each bad shot. And here I was, pounding lethal serves against defenseless green plywood. I pictured Red chopping away but due back at one for our lunch buffet. He still swore by Broken Heart's oily fried chicken but seemed proud he'd cut down thanks to medical advice: just two drumsticks, one breast. "That's *it*," a Christian martyr, Red would shove back from the table. I stood wondering if I might ask Doc to join us (hating to impose). I had turned his way when seeing something living rush across the greens.

What I first took for a deer turned into a man, a black man, then someone familiar. Mait Miller, minus any golf bag, advanced at whatever speed you could make in such long limps. He held something up above his head. A red bandanna. Spying him from this distance, knowing him to be over seventy-five, I wondered at his hurry, worried for his heart. Then I noticed he kept waving his hankie as some signal, running, stopping, waving, running, bending, winded. I noted Mait aim his flag always at Doc.

I screamed Roper's name while pointing. He scanned, saw, dropped his putter, took a running leap onto the club manager's cart, key in its ignition. I piled on behind. We were soon to Maitland at a sand trap's edge. He'd bent, hands to knees. The old guy stood huffing toward the grass.

"Is Mr. Red. He down on sixteen. He out. Made him one giant swing. I heard something turn. Break aloose. Not soft, wet. More like the handle popping off a china cup. Swear I heard something inside he chest just *go*."

We were there in two minutes. Red lay on his back staring up into a yellowed maple. He still clutched the aluminum club. His fists stayed fused around his iron's leather grip, pinkies linked as friends'd all tried teaching him.

Dirt on his forehead showed he'd first pitched facedown; Maitland had likely rolled him into a more restful position half against some maple roots. I squatted and touched Red's cheek. The day's temperature was right at fifty-five, and so was his. Eyes open wide, such a look lay starched across my father's face. Determination mixed with some incoming glory expected any minute. ("How was *that?*") I tried pressing shut his eyes but lids stayed fixed, amazed—from the inside out.

Doc, unceremonious, shoved me aside, checked Dad's airways, tore open his shirt. The butt of Roper's right hand went slamming to work on him. Blows sounded harder than I liked but Doc knew best. I remembered Red's saying that here, in town, he did not always know how to behave, to "do." Me too, me now. Something would soon be called for, some emotion or efficiency. I studied how Doc pounded a human torso, punishing one organ to recall its duty and main habit. I, Bill, watched as if I were some camp kid in first-aid class, doubting I could ever do all that. (What real *use* was I to others?)

Maitland Miller wandered off, he acted the most upset. Kept mumbling, not quite to me, "Didn't mean nothing by it. Hates this part the job. Lost Mr. Alston, Judge Draper, then Mr. Blanchard Sharp went. They quit they jobs. Got plenty money left. But be out here every morning, still hurrying. I told Mr. Red, say, 'Go easy.' Then I run. But Mait ain't fast as Mait been being."

I broke the spell. Dared touch his arm. Promised Maitland he was the hero of the hour. Told him Dad had already outlived his own pop's span by twenty-odd years. I said that Mom and I would want Mait at Dad's funeral, please. I would talk to the manager. Maitland Miller had caddied for Red all these good last years. Dad gave famous tips because he finally could. That at least seemed fair.

Mait, shaking his head, walked off mumbling, red hankie to mop his brow. He settled on the far side of that maple, one live man and one dead. I saw cars start slowing out at the corner of Club and River. Given Red's hair color and bantam size, from there they'd know the fallen.

Somebody had phoned the rescue squad but our groundskeeper wouldn't let their ambulance ruin his greens. So here medics came, running their gurney around a sand trap, guys all in white showed up stark against this bright green world. I must've been stunned. Everything looked painted. Everything visible played a part in making this be one huge September show-day. No hiding place in it. Straight sunlight came at you, yellow as yolk, and warmed you; but blue shade on the back of your head pulled you off toward coolness. Left split, I turned around.

Our afternoon had just enough wind in it to make these old trees sound huge. Overhead sweeps and creakings of high limbs left me feeling boy-sized stuck down here among adults' odd chest-pounding ritual. Everything grand and serious. Me, extra, misplaced, in town.

I squatted nearer Doc still pumping. Beside my father's head I noted what first appeared a single mushroom growing in the grass. Bright and red and white, it rested amid fresh-chopped divots. Thing proved to be Pop's wooden tee and, atop it, the new white ball right where it'd started.

Doc Roper kept hunched over Red, delivering well-paced blows to a chest narrow and yielding. Dad's face, neck, hands had been forever sun-baked. Brown-red, they seemed carved from a mineral different than his body's. This chest looked decades younger, flour-white as any child's. Face-up he appeared trusting, awaiting some verdict, frail past even being dead. I noticed odd red patches crossing him—collarbones to ribs, a raw mass, overlapping starfished shapes. Some old scars? bad new tattooing? Slow, I

304

understood these hundred savage tender marks were Roper's handprints.

Astride Red, Doc still slammed so. I can yet hear that sound, ribs giving like nautical rope under stress. Bent now beside our doctor, I warned myself not to betray one childish emotion here, much less girlish ones. Hated disappointing Roper. We had dreaded this so long, and here, as he predicted, it was happening. Had happened.

I could see Doc's jaw set, profile neutral if distorted asymmetrical from his fighting back tears. The EMS boys had long ago strapped an oxygen mask onto Red. Now they stood back and aside. They'd recognized Roper at a hundred yards. Their waiting acknowledged he outranked them. But, twenty minutes in, they started giving each other looks, phoning bulletins to one irked supervisor. Someone else, alive, needed help now. It was clear my dad was dead. Seeing Doc's pace slow some, one young medic finally helped Roper rise. He'd worked with such force he appeared briefly weak, even tipsy, arms flung out for balance. Doc lurched off to one side, his back turned, avoiding a short form being lifted to its stretcher.

Doc leaned against one tree as I moved to comfort or thank him or maybe report how this shock was registering with *my* ticker! But Roper turned on me as if outraged. Under damp white hair I saw those strange blue eyes fried open.

"Nothing. Could do nothing. And Red, he'd just asked me to play-through with him. Maybe I could've slowed him some, Bill? But, no, I had to be working on my stupid putting which will never be worth shit anyway. Bill? how hard would it've been? My tagging along no matter how much *time* it took? —Well, we're not going to let this happen to *you*. Advances made every day. You're twenty-two. I swear I'll keep right up. And you there with me, son. I hate this for you. Everybody despised Paxton. He snitched on every woman he ever had. Man robbed anybody ever tried fixing up that barn of his. But, you know? his choosing Red to make an heir? that was the coolest thing he ever did. Red! Pleasure just being around some-body finally wringing the real *fun* out of stuff, you know? Sure you do. But, know this, you're *my* guy now. Umkay? I hate his going. But, swear to God, I've *got* you now."

Doc gripped my right hand; I returned his exact caliber of male force till we sort of stood here Indian-wrestling. Soon we actually on-purpose hurt each other, part of our pact to make this stick. Being Red's two all-time favorite young men, being out here under the maples on sixteen, we finally seemed more than brothers. The man swore he'd keep me going years longer than he'd managed with our Red. And, till today at least, my partner Roper, he's honored his promise, hasn't he?

BEFORE I EVEN phoned my bride at our new home, I drove straight to Mom's. I later realized, by the time she heard my car out front, not his, she knew. No, earlier. See, somehow she'd already changed into her best black Sunday dress. Matching black shoes. Hair pulled back then pinned. No brooch. Nothing but a wedding ring. In town, she knew to keep it simple, solid colors. Otherwise they might know. So, always understate. Today especially.

As I lunged in, she rose. Just the sight of me still in sweaty tennis whites made her lean against the doorjamb and ask it: "Where?"

"On sixteen."

"Ooh and after he promised me he'd quit at nine. But you're not *with* him. You let him go. Son, where have they *got* Red?"

"Downtown, wherever ambulances wind up. We'll find him, I'll

306

take you there. But, look, sweetheart, Doc was right with him. Tried heart-massage, just tried and tried. So Dad had the best last chance."

"Well, there it is." She sat again then turned away from me. I felt she was cross that he had died with me, not her.

"First, Bill, you'll run home. Change out of those shorts. Tell Janet and don't even say you came told me first. She's your wife now. Go to her. And, son, I reckon we'd best start. Been so long coming, hasn't it? There's certain things'll now need doing."

I stepped closer to stop her, to explain how all this other could wait. But she held up one palm. I saw she needed to say out her little speech. *Let her*, I told myself but the sound of the voice in me saying that seemed exactly Red's.

Her fine white skin showed against everything black. Right then she was such a beautiful woman, my mother. I stood here appreciating her with a licensed force that shocked me. I felt my strength had somehow doubled. Inheritance. With Red and his dear noise stopped, she came across as someone so poised and clear, kind. At seventeen, she'd married him knowing exactly what waited. Today I finally saw her just as he did and it offered such a wild pure charge.

"I'll want this place sold, Bill. My sister she's been after me to move back out to her farm in and with her, time comes. Time's here, I reckon. Yeah, be moving in with Ida. She's always had that spare room, ground floor, two nice windows. So I'll be there mainly. Look, from here on out, son, you might find me less in a town mood. Never really took to Falls. Except for Third Baptist, can't seem to feel relaxed here. It was Red's little side-trip, with us all trying and fit in and act like the Fallen. But it sure did suit my men. With me? Didn't like to say a word again' it, not back then. Not after he kind of *won* Falls like a prize. But I never left off being 'country.' And it's not one thing wrong with that. Look what I've got myself wearing here! They choose clothes like they upholster their couches. Black. Got me where I'm looking like a nun. But once I'm out with Ida, hiding with just us, why, I'll want to wear any ole floral-print house-dress. Bagged-out, missing buttons? Should I care? Shoes run-down in back. That used to be luxury for me and m' folks. So, you go get your wife and carry her back over here once you've changed. White shirt'd be nice, jacket, no tie. See? here I am . . . him dead, worried how we'll look downtown at their offices."

She rose again and called me over, nearer her face, as if to whisper some new secret. I leaned in, finally put one arm around her. Against my cheek she whispered, "Oh, Bill, what are we going to do without our wonderful friend?!"

I shook my head. No answer.

But a new thought of hers now seemed to cheer Mom. "Well, there's one thing's sure. You and me we'll go right-today, we'll find him a mighty nice plot. —A 'town' grave. Right, son?"

I HOPED TO wangle for Red a spot in All Saints Episcopal's moss-green churchyard. One ancient magnolia canopies its marbled lambs and man-sized angels. Buried there are presidential candidates and Secretaries of the Navy. Of course, this being Falls, oldest families monopolize its real estate, too.

Red, he'd never dared set foot into this famous church itself; it meant too much to him. I knew as how graveyard slots here ran real scarce and pricey. You could not just be One Who Stayed, however noble your local existence. But, since Janet's family had belonged to All Saints since Millard Fillmore's day, I thought Red might get grandfathered in yet again. I hated the beggar's role but sat down, took deep breaths, forced myself to phone.

Rector Tim's secretary was an English war bride with one posh and pearly accent. "Yes, All Saints. How might I help you?" Her formal voice slowed me some. The words "All Saints" seemed kind of exclusive, in fact, pure dare. I hate name-droppers. And here I was about to beg for something impossible, just to say I'd tried. "No, you can't," I answered, hanging up.

I'd lacked the brass to become a diplomatic climber even in my grief. Still too pending a person, I couldn't even *fake* Dad's natural push. Even to get him safely under hallowed ground.

So Mom and I, grave-wise, we just went with First Presbyterian. True, their flat memorial park allows "no aboveground flowers." Yeah, it's located more out toward the Dairy Queen. It lacks antique magnolia cover and is too new but still, pretty enough, maintained. Besides, Red had tithed Presbyterian, so they were fine having us.

I SAT UP that night of the day he died. Sat trying to write a grave-stone-text sufficiently poetic. Funny, Jan had wanted to stay up with me and I appreciated that, her level head for confronting trouble straight-on. But I told my wife I had to do this part alone.

A beautiful antique writing desk overlooks the river in our great room, a bird's-eye maple thing with carved feet and from Jan's family plantation. But it seemed too fancy for my chore. Describing other people is a big responsibility, especially at the end. I moved around our place, holding open the blank back pages of my insurance premium book. The pad that usually only notes others' car wrecks, trees fallen into friends' homes. I wandered my own house, some overawed visitor among my wife's grand things. And the one workspace that felt easiest proved Lottie Clemens's cubbyhole off our utility room.

My task needed a place carved out for taking work-hour breaks.

When Lottie Clemens cleaned for us and looked after things, she had her own backstage changing room between the washer-dryer and the pantry. Lottie daily arrived in civvies and shifted in and out of her uniform here before we drove her home. I noted her headquarters had a narrow daybed, an armoire, one massive iron hat rack that she'd hung with folding umbrellas and clear rain bonnets to protect her expensive braided hairdos. Thumbtacked before the card table, school photos of her four sons, the eldest grinning under highschool mortarboards. Lottie called it her office and it was a simple functional room and the only place in our fine split-level river-view house I felt somehow close to Red. Tonight it looked like a room at a farm.

Here I'd face the simplifying work of trying to see him whole. Here, for the first time, I felt like an only child. He had always seemed, in his forward-leaning belief, someone roughly my age. First I made a sort of poem filling two pages of insurance premium ledger; it went long and stayed bad. Bad country Baptist sentiment. I knew that, but still settled right into it, rolled around there, like a dog in the carcass of dead wildlife. Then I tore all that up and hid it in one sweater pocket.

Finally, feeling plainer in this staging area where our good help weekly prepared herself to help us, I went more country-sensible. I grew more manly, recalling the sheer city-expense of carving too many letters into marble. Finally I got it somewhat shortened. By dawn, in Lottie's office, I sensed I had it.

William Rooney Mabry II
1924–1975
Citizen

DECOY

21

DAD'S FUNERAL WAS right well-attended. Leading families who couldn't come sent idled older cousins or those servant-helpers who'd dealt with Red most directly. Marge and Doc rode with us. Ten dark cars arrived in a divided convoy, his redheaded relations quick to stand far far apart. Separate glaring groups, Hatfields and McCoys. Had to be the "Peanut" Mabrys vs. the "Sweet Potato" ones. They looked cousinly as Israelis and Palestinians, that likely being half the trouble.

Red, alone among Mabrys, failed to be counted among those that stayed. Somehow he'd found the nerve to light out for town. And by gosh, Red had plowed out a place for himself and his blood, right here among the mightiest Fallen, verily even along The River Road. So, two clans' arriving "en masse" while still warring, gave best proof of this burial's being (strictly locally, of course) a state occasion.

Maitland Miller and his heavyset wife turned up by cab. They kindly refused to sit with Mom and Jan and Doc and Marge and me but seemed to appreciate the thought. Along with Mait and his Mrs., four of our younger caddies appeared up, edgy, scanning with stage fright this big a white church. They were quick to find me and Doc, to shake our hands, praising Red. "He been one the only *real* ones out there."

All dressed today in black suits and white shirts, their rich skin sleek as if oiled, they didn't seem the nicknamed youngsters from our clubhouse. Not in their flashy shirts, freed from lugging old white men's bags, today, on a rear pew picked by them, lined up to honor Red, their wariness gave them a strictness and reserve. They could've been the young Oxford-educated presidents of emerging African nations.

311

*

I'D PHONED RIVERSIDE'S best lady-realtor about selling Mother's Cape Cod. Mom stood listening in. The agent, as if expecting me, snapped, "Fine, but I could not even think of showing you-all's little place with its existing-colored doors and shutters."

So, one week after the funeral, I gave myself the chore. Knowing it would prove winding, I'd have to pace myself. Couldn't bear to hire another man for such a private duty.

Mom, already become the total hider, knew my chore. She dodged both that and daylight, deep indoors.

I took thick, plain enamel to his brighter choice.

"Red," I said as I drowned it all in white.

THE MONDAY AFTER Friday's burial my usual checkup was slated and I kept it and Roper breathed as usual to warm his stethoscope's steel and listened to me dutiful front-and-back and finally patted my shoulder but neither of us said one word the whole time, not daring to. It would be very hard if any or all of the emotion got out. I didn't trust myself. As usual, I chose to wait. *When till, Bill? Wait for what? Dignity, Revelation, Legacy? Love? To wait for Later: that seemed my major inborn task.*

I simply sat there on an exam table that had seemed both Dad's and mine, sat here singly.

I knew that the twenty-seven thousand dollars' profit we'd made selling his house would please Red very much. Three days after the funeral Mom already lived out in the country with her widowed sister. They themselves had wallpapered "her" room, giggling at every difficulty of gooped paste and paper's rolling corners. Its pattern proved both sprigged and striped, featuring giant purple lilac blooms. It was certainly a print no Riversider would ever have used, even in some "for the fun of it" chauffeur's garage-apartment's half-bath. I knew that Mom was in on this joke, to some extent. Of course I didn't press it. Clear, she'd never again live in any room painted just one tasteful color.

I stayed on in Falls, of course. But as a former farm kid, I never could feel town-born. I was never a soul fully local anywhere but halfway, about where the tobacco field around our Dairy Queen stands. Brilliant? No. And not gifted with any one particular skill past trying out a million silent decencies. I found most of those had gone sort of unnoted. That left me what? Whom? Where? Left me here.

"Having stayed" became a Purple Heart, for meritorious immobility. And likely I would stay on here where too little happened but the usual subtraction. Now "stay" meant being grounded by my father's grave. The Presbyterians kept it trimmed with Presbyterian efficiency, leaving me little to do but stand there and look down at it.

But, however uneasy I am about my achievements in life, if only in secret, I do give myself this: In the privacy of my heart, telling no one ever, some evenings looking back on my own better sort of days, I'll tell myself, fully meaning it: I admit that my father found me noble, gifted, a naturalized Riversider almost royal. And so, if only in his eyes, I do stay that: the sole surviving son and heir to the happy Earl of Shadowlawn.

22

BY NOW, IF, vacationing, you mentioned your hometown, the name of a certain craftsman might buoy up. His hand-hewn second-career had got so much press, even strangers asked if you'd seen, possibly even *met*, him? The retired doctor was now richly established as "Marion, carved by his hand ©."

Though also getting along in years, Doc looked little different from when he retired. He changed so slowly and that made him freakish, if also more a sort of good-luck tribal totem-pole. Only Marge had aged, maybe lacking a passion on the order of Roper's. You cannot get that by decoy-proxy.

I should know.

You can tell I'm heading toward the trouble. Not that we have not had bumps already. But no good story is a story only everyday. All of us only get away with just so much and then only for so long. Even in a moneyed river town, even someplace whose water is part amber lithium, part clear nicotine, life can retract its promise overnight. Can become a vale of tears breaking over you its sudden lashing. We had named ourselves "Falls," copying Niagara (no truth in advertising there!). Maybe we were about to pay for stealing the Big-Time's thunder?

These were our end-days, looking back. The time Before. And Roper might or might not turn up at others' cocktail parties. That depended on how "tacky" the paint felt on his "maybe all-time breakthrough coot." Doc overexplained the merits of everybody's Internet. You'd think he had invented it, boasting he could blow up any colored bird-image, could magnify then graph it to many times actual size. Did we actually *care*?

Sometimes at the club or downtown, you still caught sight of him. The guy no longer wore his reassuring after-hours witch-doctor's pendant, the stethoscope. Lately a jewelers' loupe shone, clipped to his tortoiseshell reading specs. He did pretty detailed work and, after all, the guy was now up over eighty.

314

Times, I longed to take him aside and sit and reminisce about our Red. As you'd get to swap tales only with a favorite sibling. To do that while on a camping trip, off canoeing up the Lithium, would be great. Just starting every sentence, "Remember that time Red . . . ? and that crazy time our dad, he . . . ?"

IT WAS IMPOSSIBLE not to respect Doc, so long-established here; but then, our witch-doctor, he held out—silent—for even more. Didn't withhold anything, exactly. But you feared he might. So you yourself made up the difference. For him, you produced a certain unreciprocated low-grade feeling; you forced it into something stronger, more bulked-up, yet your effort was still unimpressive. It finally felt humiliating, the strange suspense he exacted from the likes of ordinary me. Did he flirt with anyone? And, if not, why did everyone believe themselves the first?

How many women in his office had—like Kate Bixby that day her boys drowned then lived—offered more, all? But Doc never seemed to take free samples. And this just drew more offers. Roper seemed to barely notice us while off-duty; and yet, he always assumed our full infirm attention anywhere he went. Still, something kept a person coming back.

ESPECIALLY AFTER RED died in our company, it seemed Doc's company alone met some basic medical need of mine. "First, do no harm." That in itself is a mouthful. Roper's river-swim each dawn across from my place had simply seemed what any good doctor would do for his nearest patient. That Australian crawl left me still sitting nice and dry on my deck and yet feeling half-flooded with borrowed pheromones. I cannot explain it. Nobody was alone in feeling this, I swear. The list of locals that Doc had saved soon seemed the roster of home owners under eighty-five. We all still had these immense riverside houses, echoing louder since our kids had somehow grown and gladly moved; but the houses, for all their costs and repairs, still looked beautiful to us. Monuments, but honoring what? Still, as much else failed, ownership gave us its own time-release back-channel consolation.

Doc had forever known that facts about his other patients would fascinate us. Doc stayed rightly stingy with those. But a hunk of log carved so its "head" tucks under its "wing"? Could that ever rival news of whether polio would let the Collier girl ever walk again? Doc failed to note that life outranks art every time.

His poor Margie was left joking: "The man eats, sleeps, drinks ducks. I'm not a golf widow. I married a doctor, got a quack." *He'd* probably made that up, but she retailed it as her apology for him. People laughed at such a joke only because we'd always loved her. Good sport, Marge. Incredible rangy soccer player during her Randolph-Macon years. And once, when Doc was away at a Miami wood-tool convention, a Cambodian girl from the old mall's new nail place turned up at the Roper house seeking him, her waters just broken. Marge got the girl down in a porch lounge chair and delivered the baby herself. "All in a day's . . ." she said with that tough half-masculine tone of hers. Soccer captain, even at eighty. I'd noted that, as Roper and I got spindlier, somewhat artistic (spiritually in my case), our wives sort of toughened up, division of labor; Jan and Marge doubled down as stronger, more the bosses. To me they each looked a notch or two more bowlegged like poor Red. The pink razors along the bathtub's ledge? seemed there less for removing feminine leg stubble than possible new growth on their handsome chinny-chin-chins. But maybe this is sour grapes from a failing male whose actuarial life had never been long.

We sensed that, like us, Marge felt left a bit high and dry.

Roper'd never had an excess of the office-hour small talk we all craved like niacin, B-complex. Now? Any stray encounter in Sears' power-tool department started and quit with one of his mute nods. Retired, he seemed to have departed the office hours of language.

People had seen his canoe ashore and far upriver, his little brown tent pitched for some overnighter. Him alone, selfishly alone. Binoculars, a camou-parka and one fierce glance from Doc must mean: my trusty rusted Evinrude was disturbing some import-ant-species-nesting-habitat he alone could guard.

Roper no longer seemed just absentminded. That'd been scariest when our village's weakening ventricles preoccupied the guy. Now he looked clear past your head, as if startled by your hair? no, he was squinting beyond, at what? oh, that red exit sign.

He would rather be sculpting. Even his rare jokes now seemed a pocketful of carving tools that might cut you mid-hug.

Was around this time that I, having washed out as a carver myself (healing nicely, if with certain scarring Doc would not have left), considered paying retail for a real Josiah Hemphill. The Christie's catalogue had one coming up. But I soon understood this was just my way to get Doc over to our place. A Hemphill, he'd come see. Pretty crude, I decided. One jerky decoy of a chess move. I was simply trying to pay for a last live visit from my real old friend, if he'd ever truly been one.

—How come I could send to a Manhattan gallery and acquire some Federal-period Hemphill but not get one brand-new across-the-road "Marion"? During my ever-shorter daily walks, I wondered this. (Sometimes to the point of muttering aloud.) The route of my daily constitutional? Past whatever home now lacked dogs that barked at me. Little slights, even from store clerks, preoccupied me.

I kept casting back for reassurance. Found myself remembering, when I'd hitchhiked home from college, I once sat reading a translation of *The Odyssey* near our pool at Broken Heart. Doc, already 31, tanned dark as oiled teak, had gone off the high-dive, jackknifing midair. Amazing swimmer.

My own body gave signs it itself wanted to retire. From any strenuous further use. I could still drive a car anywhere. And I was a much safer driver than Jan liked to complain. Her jokes had always cast herself as Sensible and me as Her Dreamer. Like my true-believer dad, I guess. But artist at what? Which dreams exactly? Fame? Sex? Love? Elsewhere? After several enough drinks, Janet now did party-stand-up about my myopic U-turns and increasing inability to think in Reverse. But once I'd got us into the mall lot, once there, my even getting *out* of the car was something you might not want to watch too closely. I had seen my dad do this slow dance with himself at fifty-one. Made me think of a bug on its back, six legs scrambling, grabbing for doorframe, anything to gain the traction needed to get this creature pulled to the vertical. Then, having risen, for your trouble, another visa problem awaited, finding yourself at the next barricade, short of usable air. I sent my Janet on ahead, told her to go into Restoration Hardware and wait by their lamps. Jan was always drawn to their antique-y look but never bought one. She complained, "They *still* look too new." I told her, "Oh, I can do that. Can 'antique' it in my wood shop." "How, may I ask?" She sounded exhausted with knowledge of me.

"By *touching* it," I said. Which made her blanch then cackle. "I love you, you are so *sick*, Bill." By now, that had become her compliment! Let my Janet laugh.

I can handle anything but pity.

*

DECOY

MY WIFE'S COLLEGE roommate came to visit every other year for "Kaye's beauty rest." She'd come fresh from divorce court again, her newest face-lift mended upward unevenly.

Kaye is smart in ways our little town cannot let itself be: she is witty and unforgiving *out loud*. Jan and I enjoy her company more than she knows, maybe more than she quite deserves. Kaye is old tobacco money and has what some people call style and others call edge. Kaye inherited enough, then married even more, three times running; so she always says exactly what she thinks in real-time. That, it seems, is no strict guarantor of happiness.

After weekend drinks enough, Kaye even gets *us* sounding like her. She would be leaving tomorrow for Barcelona because somebody she knew was free to have a luncheon there late Thursday. Jan and I marveled. But we, un-jet-lagged, felt blessed at this age to count ourselves among those that stayed aground. —No local guessed what-all terrible we'd just been confiding to Kaye. And God knows, that many gins in, *she* wouldn't remember.

I stood gladly preparing a second pitcher of dry dry Bombay Sapphire martinis. I'd swing these libations out onto the deck to heighten viewing tonight's already-terrific sunset.

Couldn't help overhearing our sophisticated guest quiz my wife, "Gosh, Jan? Who is that looking at a heron through binoculars and with no shirt? And here I thought Randolph Scott was extinct. Handsomest thing breathing. What is he, about fifty-eight? Looks to be on safari. Just my type and I never even knew that *was* a type. Seeing how I'm finally free of my fat dear oilman Roy, that'd be perfect for me. Who *is* the man?"

"That's not a man, dear, that's 'Doc.'" Janet coughed a laugh, one slightly bitterer than I ever liked others to hear. "And he'll turn eighty-two come June. There are parties already planned. Sad to say for you and others, there is a *Mrs.* Safari. The two're so happily married—they've upset many of us with daily comparisons. Doc there used to be our doctor, did wonders for Bill's heart. Miracles, in fact. But that eventually bored Doc. (Me, I think the ole alpha-bird lost his power when he lost his patients but he doesn't know that yet.) Now he's becoming a famous artist of sorts. Craftsman, anyway. So, you see, dear, he's not *just* a man. He sort of pokes up in the middle of us, kind of a weather vane. People tend to read the wind by *him.* I really think there's something wrong with him. Women want to save him so they can later be saved by him. And even men, otherwise intelligent men, they . . . well, I don't know *what* they want from him. But I've certainly shuddered picturing it. Roper over there makes everybody think things are better than they are. He promised Bill's sweet dad that he was tending the poor guy's subpar heart, no problem, good as new. But guess who dropped dead, practically in front of our medicine man? (*But where is my Bill with another several of these?*) In the end, Doc never seems to make any of it stick. Not exactly leading people on, more like writing prescription IOUs. But everything he promises is, it's . . . undeliverable. You know how they call certain guys confidence artists? Well, he does look good on paper, but . . . underneath there's something very puritan, starved-out. He's like a good copy of something that was, God knows, probably lots better coming out of the gate. — Meaning just the sort of guy all local women fall in love with . . . and I mean all! Plus about half our weaker men."

Amused, then surprised, I had started out, holding our best silver tray, its crystal pitcher full.

I saw we needed extra olives.

I turned back.

BOOK TWO
A.D.

A PERSON'S PARENTS LABOR mightily to place that person on top-drawer waterfront land in the neighborhood where, if you cannot crawl home from tonight's cocktail party, you might just dog-paddle. What happens next will seem to surge from nowhere. That's just how it swept in on us house-to-house.

Person lives in a neighborhood called Riverside since age eight. Person assumes that the muddy inching little trickle rich with lithium will stay put like that store-bought background noise meant to help uneasy sleepers finally doze.

Yonder river should provide contrasting color for your Bermuda grass against its slow brown bend. It should not "say nothin' and just keep rollin' along." It is meant to offer a few annual edible grandkid-caught sunfish and shad. The shared neighborhood water feature seems dug to help you teach your kids sportsmanship in boating.

First came a hurricane named Gretel. Fierce winds had been predicted. Never gusted much past 50. It ain't even a hurricane if it drops to 74. Since *H* follows *G*, jokes ran we should fear brother *Hansel* next. As usual, we felt we'd got off pretty easy, at least in this more desirable part of town. All of Riverside went to bed after one more than our standard several drinks. We slept soundly, having ducked another biggie.

But, though we slept so well, we soon would wake to trouble, friend, right here in River City.

THE FIRST JAN and I recognized something was off we heard our birds Billy and Jill going berserk downstairs. That would have been about three a.m. The cockatiels Jan had foolishly bought then named for our absent kids to offset "empty nest" feelings? they squawked like the devil. Janet sits up saying, "What's got into them? Storm was a fizzle. I'll just go check, Billy. Remember how that one mouse spooked them so?"

Pitch-black-dark, and Jan climbs off the edge of our four-poster, opens the door into the hall. She wanders to our staircase and is halfway down before I hear her turning my way. Janet's usual calm governs every word. "Billy. Billy? There's . . . Our birds might just be *drowning*."

Well, *that* got me up.

YOU ACCEPT AS how things will change but never overnight. You expect the mercy of a little slowness. I put on bedroom slippers and a silk robe as if it were Christmas morning and I'm just going down to photograph the kids opening their Santa loot. But tonight, to wander downstairs and to be suddenly wading. To slush, arms lifted, into your dark dining room. To "ford" your dining room. Then you hit something smelling like a badly-kept kennel and strangers' motor oil making one wrong mix. And all arrived here, silent, since you went to sleep among your fellow Fallen. That the water in your house feels river-cold seemed logical enough; far creepier, these

DECOY

stripes of warm. God knows what's fomenting in this chemical slop.
It seems a Hell rehearsal, with water being fire. Its lithium does not
cut our shock tonight. You descend into a house become aquarium.
It offers further practice at your getting good at saying goodbye.
Bye-bye to property, so long responsibility, and finally, maybe, solid
earthen matter itself. "Dust to dust" is at least tidier than "Dust
to mud."

Heroic, I waded into our kitchen and, idiotic, turned on each
non-working light-switch. Lucky for us there was most of a moon,
and it made everything go silver, mercury. Caged birds still kept
going crazy and then I saw it. Something swimming near them,
circling our marble-topped "island." I blindly found a broom and
prodded toward what seemed a black beaver-otter paddling hard.
One hissing yowl proved this must be the Blanchards' Siamese cat.
How it had washed into our home, I couldn't guess. I saw why Jan's
birds were freaking out. But, eating something feathered seemed
the last thing a cat this wet might crave.

"Jan, honey? We've got the Blanchards' *Tang* or *Chang* in here
swimming laps." "*Ming*," she corrected. Then we had the comedy of
my trying to save a drowning pet so irritated it would kill you for
getting it above the waterline. Finally I found Jan's thickest oven
mitts and, holding this thrashing oil-blackened creature far from
me head-outermost, I heaved it up on top of the fridge. It did not
sound real grateful there.

No, we counted ourselves among the lucky ones, really. Because
of a river hillside, our home stands three stories, not Riverside's
usual two. We soon sat on our roof beside caged cockatiels wet and
noisy. We sat between two dresser drawers stacked with family
photos, stock coupons; Janet's laptop (couldn't find its case). It contained the all-important will. Brilliant, I was about to leave all my

heart meds lined neat along our bedside table. Quite a night then day ahead. Of course, first thing, I checked across the street.

Doc and Marge's place showed no flashlight glare, no sign of life. They'd likely already made a James Bond motorboat escape, somehow without asking us along. I had the bass boat but Janet worried that wrestling with that and even getting my reliable Evinrude cranked would overtax me. At first I defied her. Got down into it finally, worried if the short rope still securing it to our underwater dock would hold. The Evinrude called "Old Reliable" for years would not turn over. No way. It was dead and I had my omen. And Jan had her first of several thousand *I told you so's*.

If our dear neighbor Mitch (my friendly insurance competitor) hadn't motored past right then in his aluminum outboard, I think we might still be perched up there at the roofline like birds ourselves. Our cockatiels, even on a good dry day, are ill-tempered, very irritating pets. They *do* nothing. Janet bought them without consulting me, right when our second kid went off to school. "They were on sale, two for the price of one. They're married, the clerk said." "Well, in that case." Next Jan made both of us seem even more conventional: by naming the male for Bill, Jr., and the girl for our brilliant linguist daughter, Jill. And I never once complained. Too much to even say.

When you lose everything overnight you gain at least surprising information. After that first gulping "Uh-oh," there can come a start-up giddiness. It registers almost as relief. Maybe only a man as old as I would think: *No more hiring teenagers to overpay for grassmowing.* I'd come to hate our enslaving acre and a half! And to think how much my dad had valued a green yard of no farm-animal food value. If Red grew up fantasizing about town, my dreams had lately run toward a silent farmhouse, Presbyterian-plain, zero-maintenance

—it would hold me, seated cross-legged alone on the plank porch, a Zen monk hayseed whose only crops would be invisible hanging garden meditations.

Washed out, I imagined myself if Dad had not inherited. What if we'd been forced to apply for club membership using only my own looks and cash? If I lived in the country, would it be this wet? But I learned at once to try and hide any such idle speculation from my wife.

Most of our antiques downstairs had come from "Barton," Janet's mother's family's Edenton plantation. Me, being a tenant farmer's son, I'd inherited no object of importance. The Mabrys' everything had been provisional as next month's rent. The importance of Barton's 1799 sideboards and wing chairs to Jan would prove far greater than I'd ever even guessed.

Sounds absurd to say my wife mistook such farm furniture for the missing plantation itself. Might seem silly to admit how the loss of one slave-made cypress breakfront would give my unsentimental darling a nervous breakdown. But that is really sort of just what was about to happen.

2

WE (AND SIX hundred others) spent that first night in a National Guard armory. If its gym made for an unsightly B&B, at least the price was right. No friends could take us in, being flooded out as we. Many humans endure Some One Night When Everything Changes. Somehow, we, the Fallens' 6,803, all drew September 15th.

The richest people in Falls occupied Riverside's twelve square blocks surrounding us, ours. Falls' poorest folks live at sixes-and-sevens down near the closed cotton mill in B.A., Baby Africa. Its stretch of silt land has always been considered so worthless, freed slaves were given it for free. So, into this overlighted army multipurpose room, all us river rats crawled, finally together.

Whatever our class or race, we lugged the selfsame items: family Bibles, deeds, love letters, photos of dead parents, of living children and grandkids. We held our damp pets shivering inside bath mats, pillowcases. For once, we did not just nod howdy; we looked each other square in the eyes. Mait said, "Now, ain't this a bitch, Mr. Bill?" Here he stood, Dad's calming caddy. Miller's hair looked even whiter, with good reason. Almost before I knew quite who he was, Mait, greeted this evening, seemed a dear old friend. Think of all we'd been through together.

I asked, "You-all swamped, too?"

"Pretty much it got everything. And right when I had worked my yard up to where I could just about *look* at it." He studied the floor.

WE NONE OF us appeared our tip-top best, I promise you. In this gym crisscrossed by cots, echoing yapping dogs and crying kids, you heard a jumpy madcap energy short-circuited. You heard an intentional costume party's loudness. Everybody talked too loud and all our info came through eavesdropping, but at least we were alive. Half the children underfoot kept "acting out" unsupervised; the rest, in corners, stayed bent in thumb-sucking, fetal positions.

We bunched here imagining how it'd happened, to be attacked from the rear, our placeholder waterway gushing suddenly with Mississippi ambitions.

The "Why?" we'd leave to helpless half-drowned rectors to explain. The "How?"—our government should've known and warned us.

DECOY

We sat on our provided cots, Vietnam surplus, stating common knowledge: the weather'd lately changed; hurricanes more frequent and far meaner. These days officials had to name so many storms a year they used up every English letter clear to X. Then they reverted to a second alphabet, the Greek one. (That in itself sounded a bit un-American.) Meanwhile the right-wingers in D.C. still ask each other, "Is there *really* global warming? Surely we need another blue-ribbon study." Republicans must not watch as much Weather Channel as Jan and I do in our rooted waning years.

The wife and I found, among other milling refugees, Lottie Clemens, our retired longtime child-care friend and cleaner. In her housecoat pocket, I saw a zip-lock bag full of costume jewelry. We seemed to be meeting on some train speeding toward the same internment camp. "The house! How the *house?*" She yelled for news of a place she'd weekly vacuumed forty years. Janet and I glanced at each other, then simplified our answer. We spared everyone's dignity by skipping details. We just shook our heads no.

"Don't be telling me that now. Unh-unh. Not the *house* . . ."

"But, Lottie, your boys?"

"Oh, they safe. Youngest two running round here somewhere. Both that age where they all-the-time playing they don't know me. Even while sitting there facing they own momma in the same *boat!*"

Then we kissed each other. I sort of cried all over Lottie—pillow breasts and wiry arms—she fell against and between us. With our last formality and feeble manners shot, we re-understood. Our lives, our childbearing years and these longer hot-flashing ones, our whole life spans had been spent together in one shuttling station-wagon and those same few rooms. Rooms now ruined. Including, I belatedly noted, Lottie's useful office.

—I vowed then, if we ever got through this I'd enlarge her

pension. She is a decent funny woman with four sons, twelve grand-kids, all somehow boys. (And I did live to boost her retirement. I'm not bragging. My truly stepping up to actually financing her old age, it was already overdue about four years.)

THE SMALLER THE town, the bigger the event looms. Or so I told myself. But the scale of both seemed huge tonight. The Department of Interior raffles off the wetlands meant to absorb our runoff rain. With Wal-Mart parking-lots paved hard, no sponginess is left. Water's got to go *some*where, so it came picking our locks. We all sat discussing this as someone said, "If I told you you were about to see Diana de Pres without makeup, would you believe me? Miracles and wonders." We turned, and the men, tired and old as we felt, somehow, helping each other, stood. If only saluting the memory of first seeing her enter a club dance eons back.

RIVERSIDE'S GREATEST CAUCASIAN beauty of our age, the witty bourbon-loving Diana de Pres, dragged our way, chuckling. "Well, this is what's left of the goods, boys," and she did a runway turn, witty in ruin. It still registered as sexy. Force of habit from all sides.

She stood blinking in not-good light wearing only a tarp and donated hip boots, nothing much underneath. Since childhood, not even her *hus*bands had ever seen her bare-faced. Our gorgeous hard-drinking Diana—compared for life to that poorer local farm-gal, the unbeatable good sport Ava Gardner—our same Diana now stood, sans jewelry, minus a dot or dash of lipstick and eye paint, erased nearly unrecognizable. Poor thing looked like one wet cockatiel. We made room for her on the cot and passed her a spare blanket. "It is not yet bourbon time? Mitch found me in a tree," she

328

kept trying to sound chipper but mixed up her next: "Was up the paddle without a creek."

Then she looked at us. Di saw we knew what she meant and she need not give a do-over. We were all the same age. Diana fell to sleep almost at once. And my dear Janet, who loathes all divas, was too in shock to even properly gloat.

ENCOUNTERING YOUR NEIGHBORS in this overlit gym felt like a class reunion convened in some lesser circle of prison Hell. Even the National Guard's hanging lamps had all been caged like convicts.

You hugged your most casual friends, and why? because they'd also survived. (Some of us had not. Two pals we'd known for life had been electrocuted by a falling power line; one beloved married pair drowned inside their own new sports car during a botched dash north that washed them straight off Mill Road's dam.)

Now greeting chums, finding them unhurt, you need not say a word. You knew that their "good stuff" must be, like your heir-looms, so much soggy pulp. —Jan and I slouched here with the crowd we usually saw only at the club near month's end when you needed to eat a little of the food you'll pay for anyway.

ALL THAT MATTERED was our knowing others and being recognized by them. Broke, fresh out of shelter, we had so little else to recommend us. We *were* our aging faces. Credit lines? Our former looks. Others' memory of which beautiful house had been our own. But tonight made for a wonderful once-in-a-lifetime bond. Revival meeting. It felt either like the end of something, or a radical fresh start.

Sat feeling glad that poor Red Mabry had not heard certain flood sounds: the way many of our six hundred paired River Road maples, once robbed of supporting soil, fell into and against each other. The sound? If bowling pins were big as dinosaurs. Trees then pressed by current toward the first farm, the next town.

JUST ONE STRETCH of this armory's baseboard heat *re*ally worked; I counted twenty wide-open family Bibles spread there on gym flooring, toasting some. Damp Good Books were attended by people waiting for those to slowly dry. As if stirring little campfires, seated folks would idly reach down and flip from the crisper Old to a wetter New Testament. I heard certain guardians muttering to themselves. I slowly understood these sounds were not just shocked complaints but stubborn busted prayers.

Bibles seemed more valuable for their crocheted cross-shaped bookmarks, browned Palm Sunday fronds. Some showed handwritten names and birth dates, marriages then death dates. Books, black and white, attended by people white and black, being dried face-up wide-open as if meant to breathe.

Hard to describe why that first evening should seem one of the most joyful of my life. Or maybe "memorable," which is joy at its most attention-getting. Had I, as a house-proud man with a retired insurance-office income, been secretly waiting for higher-octane trouble? For some outside woe past my being built around a heart this bad?

The second night would prove the killer.

And don't even mention Night #3.

Those of us who'd stayed in Falls now had no place TO stay.

Jan's first impulse was borrowing a cell phone, calling our far-flung kids to reassure, "You didn't even *know*? It's not on the national news yet? Well, but we're okay, thanks. The house? likely a dead-loss but your dad and I aren't. What? Oh, honey, I will. Your dad's waving his love as usual. Just didn't want you worried sick—and here you had no idea!"

Emotion never behaves. Like mercury, that particular material is seriously hard to grasp. Its mass keeps turning into beads, then vice versa. (Example: The day my son graduated from Haverford, I should have felt ecstatic. "With special distinction," the dean announced. But traces of my dad's (and *his* dad's) cardiac condition had long since been found in our Bill #IV, passed on to him via me. Meds were part of his life, too. Why did three sick generations' sadness find me that one dressed-up day? Fact is, I felt so guilty for having passed my boy such a plug heart, I honestly considered suicide. A rifle in the garage seemed the least "botheration" to Janet's antiques and rugs. So why was this flood night unlike any other? This night of the day when I lost our house and cars and her great-great-grandfolks' only oil portraits, why should an unaccountable elation now come to call?

Maybe because, being like everybody else, I felt briefly washed of guilt. I could claim God's love or be another hard luck case or both, whichever suited me. I need no longer actually succeed. Not like those that fled Falls early to strain for stardom elsewhere. I was Bill Mabry, formerly of The River Road, which was presently The River.

Maybe I had suddenly floated into my own fated Phase *II*?

Somebody announced our dinner tonight would be hot dogs, meant for the grammar school now closed, either with or without buns.

SINCE EVEN NOW our part of the world is still farmed, most of us keep big deep freezers. Janet and I had shucked, then "put up" this past summer's exceptional Silver Queen corn grown on her family's last country holding. Like Doc's duck specimen freezer, other neighbors' were stocked with game, but theirs proved edible. Everybody specializes in a different delicacy.

The Blanchards have a summer place in Maine and so they always fly home south with August's lobsters onboard. Everybody stashes shrimp we peeled ourselves, quail we've plucked, and all of it was suddenly left unrefrigerated. We knew we'd have no electricity hereabouts for weeks, at least. Easily a million bucks' worth of our neighbors' best possible food was now going going gone.

Timothy and Tomothy Bixby got suddenly inspired. Being teens they were insisting on being called "Thomas" and "Timothy." But nobody could give up that other, it was such fun to say. They'd become famous when Doc Roper breathed them both back to life. (Later rumors claimed that all along they'd been secretly Roper's sons! Not true.) Twins were slated for full-ride swim team scholarships at the University of Miami.

We heard how, as the Bixbys' pool emptied into their sodden house, boys had already wrestled their mom's butane gas grill up into their red pickup's bed. Boys set all good stuff from their own family-freezer over a slow flame—venison, homemade sausage, lump-crab picked by many a loud Bixby watching UNC basketball on Riverside's first giant screen.

While one twin kept the grill lit in the truck's bed, the other (practically-amphibious for life) launched their outboard. He sped off to fetch the best from others' room-temp freezers. We River Roaders all knew, as by internal pirate map, where the finest of everything edible must be thawing. We also guessed if that house stood on red clay high enough to not yet be submerged.

Approached by a Bixby, folks were delighted to see their perishables used. Being largely Scotch-Irish, we do hate waste. (Fact is, the richer the Scots, the more the squandering of leftovers is hated, the more Scots salt away to become their future generations' sometimes-wasteful wealth.) Twins made this food bank seem a game. Didn't much matter *who* was eating your cache, so long as it got utilized, maybe enjoyed.

The Bixbys, though famously, almost identically, handsome, were hardly chefs. But tonight's ingredients proved of such high quality, something extra happened. All that okra and halibut. Tuna steaks. Pheasant breasts, white sea scallops tender as baby bottoms, mahimahi caught from charter-boats way way out. By the time twins pulled their truck through armory's double doors, you could already smell their brew on glorious slow boil. Dogs were trying to get in. The scent, it traveled like a song. It was the smell of B.C.

Boys stood hand-casting spices into one huge bubbling pot: bay leaves, cayenne. I'd call their game-muddle pure *Male* food. No parsley sprigs, no candlelit "presentation," as Jan's lately been calling it. No, you've got your one pooled substance, available tonight only. Into this one load, a man puts everything he means and is. How good did it taste? You had to have been there.

Since regular utensils were mostly underwater, kids stirred their brew with one aluminum canoe-oar. We were already lined up, about to eat the dry hot dogs provided. We'd felt glad enough for those! Now here came Timothy-Tomothy, brown as Seminoles, wearing flip-flops, cut-off jeans. Beautiful hellions from birth, they appeared a platoon about six-strong, not just two kids on some frat-house lark. I watched food-serving twins move as one unit and marveled how that must feel. To still be sleek with health, with hearts the size of such torsos, shoulders. Imagine having a man-friend so close, this efficient and forever within reach.

There was a certain married white lady who, a few years back, had baptized Tomothy-Timothy into sexual practice. She looked significantly older now while the twins looked somehow even younger. She was here tonight and hungry as the rest of us. Her traveling husband, now queued behind her, was among the few Riversiders present unaware of her history. She came tentatively forward, for food. Both Bixbys grinned down at her. Tomothy said, "For you and your man, a double portion, ma'am. Mighty good neighbors you've been." All she said back was, "No problem." Her husband, an explainer, then explained to her and everyone nearby, "Outstanding youngsters, these. Enterprising."

All of us, the poor and the loaded, wearing every nasty kind of housedress or running-outfit, we sure lined up quick beside the Bixbys' red Dodge truck. We stood obedient as orphans, holding our paper plates. Odd, I kept thinking of my dad's "town" grave, underwater, a shock for him.

I noticed certain Republicans, one I'd heard rail for years against any person who'd ever take a single handout. I saw how they kept edging themselves and each other toward the line's front. I seemed to see the comedy of things with fresh eyes. I seemed to have forgotten something that dulled me, held me back.

We soon retreated to our cots. We sat there eating. Best stuff you ever put into your mouth. Sitting in a room this big, it tasted far better for being absolutely everybody's. If this was a leveling, it had a fine collective flavor. I'd taken no meds in six hours but felt so avid, clear.

That first long night, we talked. We went back for Bixby seconds, thirds. We just ate and cried and ate.

3

I'D EXITED MY sixties, feeling over-aware of Dad's dying mid-swing at age fifty-one. I had come to despise the worries of keeping up a big old riverside house. It'd been Red's great wish for himself, meaning me.

Its water's-edge window screens kept rusting lacy, kept making you appear a failure. I'd been warned against any further heavy lifting. Hence the pointless expense of hiring high-school kids who might show up and mow and edge your acre and a half even twice a month at any price.

Yes, our stone house at river's edge was kind of a museum to scenes of former family good times. Lately it'd served mainly as the ideal setting for her heirloom furniture. Country-made Chippendale, first threatened by Sherman's torches; now global-warming's wet! No fair!

And yet, with this much standing water, no longer would I have to micromanage some place our kids required three days each Christmas. I'd never again slice myself while fixing the danged lawn mower. (See, I believed my own lies about home owner's hardship.) Sitting on an army cot, I had at last become a "portable unit" after a lifetime hooked to one thick black extension cord. I was no longer a risk-averse insurance salesman to whom nothing had ever happened. True, now I more or less *had* nothing. Except of course some money in the bank. But tonight that eventual unknown amount seemed quite abstract, dry ice. I imagined I had nothing past the not-uninteresting story of losing it all! Surely there was a lesson floating in here somewhere: I again felt poor as that kid in a Myrtle Beach cowboy shirt, proud of his ducktail, the mullet of its day.

With our exceptional armory meal now eaten, somebody produced his old college sterling flask. Jack Daniel's is some invention. Slow burn, it topped off that stew just right. Slumped back on "our" cots, we lounged here, passing its proofing around. Though inwardly hysterical, post-traumatic whatever-ed, we flask-passing husbands and wives somehow briefly felt like smart teenagers during their first long unchaperoned night as camp counselors.

Was only then a tennis partner said, "Bill, is it true what they're saying about poor Roper?"

I FIGURED DOC'S had been washed out like everybody along The River Road. (Fact is I'd forgotten Roper these past few hours, kind of an unusual and secret freshening relief.) Our friend told how Doc and Marge had lost their house and everything, naturally, like the rest. But, maybe worse than forfeiting home and cars, Doc's wide bay windows overlooking the river?—those 20-foot studio windows honeycombed with shelving to display his decade and more of Marion masterpieces?—well, they'd busted out early. Popping loose, those lifted free, then sort of rafted off a ways. The glass had been found intact out past the Halseys' diving raft. But all his masterful ducks?

It seemed that even before the Ropers' ground floor got soaked, Doc's waterside studio, river-view on three sides, had been crushed, gutted. Once Doc and Marge were roused by the young spaniels' barking, Roper dived off their second-story roof, swam out there wearing pajama bottoms. Apart from a newly-started decoy still clamped fast in his worktable vise, all two hundred of his finest saved-back waterbirds, they'd floated free.

Doc's life's work—Phase *Two* of it, I mean—cleanly gone missing. But wouldn't the corps of his work turn up once the all-clear signal sounded? Wouldn't scattered ducks form a flotilla and someway swim home to Doc? To dock!

His freezer full of dead creatures had also been bounced around by wild currents, wrestled to one side, then busted open like a coffin. Now even Roper's frozen specimen birds were swimming free again.

"WHAT A SHAME," I finally said, sounding insincere even to myself. "But let's us try and keep it in perspective? Before, we heard how the Blanchards' granddaughter wandered into their half-basement looking for their cat (which is likely still on top of our fridge) and somehow fell, then almost drowned down there before they heard her. The Eddie McCombs made a run for high ground in their new T-bird, got swept off Mill Road's bridge. I guess Hackney and Betty Eatman were found in their bed still wearing their eye masks and earplugs. And everybody we know has become 'a Homeless' in two hours. And yet, even so, like me, you're all still hung up on how Roper's lost some wood painted to seem . . . to be . . . uh? ducks? Why do we always put him first? Ya'll notice that? Even tonight. Will we ever get over his stitching us up? That was his *job*. I may be tipsy from Tad's flask, but sometimes (and I think Janet'll back me up in this) I believe . . . *Doc* is a decoy! He *looks* like us other ducks. But his paint's a bit bright. Man hasn't moved around much lately, has he? Why's he always s'perfect? Why will we forgive him anything?"

Janet said, "Bill."

But I finished, "And yet, too, I am, I'm basically so *sad* for him. Complicated, I guess. Sorry. Amazing person, of course. Everybody loves him to pieces. Me, too, so much, God knows. But with all this other happening, it's . . . it's just . . ."

Others swapped looks but most gave immediate nods. Sure, I'd overstated. Sure, somehow my own self-pity always included Doc. But my other thoughts could not be news to anybody present. Janet flashed me her familiar *You've really gone too far again* look. And I felt that, sure.

—Look, is it possible we truly secretly hate the best our flock can offer? Why was I so daily interested then pissed at him? Because of Roper's underrating me? Hadn't he kept me alive? Did I resent his ceasing to "treat" me just as my left side's numbing got worse? Did I blame Doc's losing faith in my own boyish "potential" as I shot past seventy?

And what did I expect he'd think I might someday *do*? Why had I, the man best seen from afar if at all, chosen as my closest friend the best-loved man in town? The very guy who'd need buddyhood least! Some secret wish to live in permanent checkmate? Why'd he refuse to let me own his best carved beauty? I half-imagined it, under my arm, essential flood-luggage tonight. Funny, but just then I decided that the two of us, Doc and I, are a lot alike, especially when alone! Twins, nearly. But, as soon as anybody's solitude is interrupted, see . . . ? I'd never solve that data-collecting quality-control problem. But tonight, one mystery resolved itself. I'd always wondered why Doc, sixth in his Yale class, chose to come on back to Falls and stay. Now I understood: It'd been his one best way to be alone. Here he was a "doc" for us before med school, already a given. He could leave us with that most attractive replica. It let Roper live as solitary as I felt. Still, any bird's-eye view of his rounds would've shown you a man mobbed.

So, why had I been waking all these years to have my coffee on our deck, just to sort of note where all the Roper cars had parked last night before I could even feel *awake*? Why did I hope he'd make one last dawn river-swim? *Why?* I always felt that I was missing something. Who'd tell me?

STRANGE, BUT, HEARING about his losses, first thing that came was sadness Roper'd never invited me back into his precious inner sanctum. Ruined now. He might've shown me everything he made, even before he did the others. Second, I felt some odd relief at the end of "Marion's" art. A menacing emotion, one I'm not real proud of. Recovering some scrap of my dignity, I did finally tell our half-drunk crowd, "At least the carvings he sold *out* of town will still show all he could do. And, hey, come to think of it, if Doc had let me buy that wood duck (his best single work, though he never seemed to know) and if I had just put that in the showcase on our *third* floor . . ."

"It'd be Gone with the Wind *like the rest of everything us Riversiders ever owned, fool!*" So one tennis partner snapped.

I laughed, "Yeah, well. Point taken . . ."

OF COURSE, WE still had Janet's empty-nesters' cockatiels, birds that irritated me so much I was ready to make stuffed ducks of *them.*

At ten p.m. that first public night of many, officials had doused our armory's overhead lamps. Some people switched on hoarded little flashlights. The only other brightness came from near the bathrooms or out in the ugly khaki foyer. Not five minutes in, one small dog yelped, I could tell, crying in its sleep. Some omen: Yorkies having nightmares on Night #1. Water still rising, and personnel seeing things.

I fought to doze in that giant room full of snoring men. (How had their wives not long ago *shot* them, us?) Between our cots, near the birds' covered cage and her laptop, I held Janet's hand. She'd conked out at once, though Jan ("Didn't catch a wink") would deny it all tomorrow.

To ease toward any drifting scrap of sleep, I found myself mentally collecting poor Roper's scattered birds. It became a mission that only some close friend might undertake. Like colored rosary beads—two hundred or more of our pal's very best were out now, unparoled; released down forks of ditches, they kept somehow spreading into rivers that eventually crosshatched deltas become one raw ocean. Till last night, each bird had been worth thousands. I imagined them already exiting our state on whirlpooled currents, some sucked down into gasping sewers. While I kept trying to sleep, a map assembled above my cot. Like those old manhunt charts you see in police movies, grease-penciled within narrowing circles, sectors, "where suspect last seen."

MY BLOOD THINNERS, various meds, had last been spied at home, set neatly along one raftlike bedside table. Pill bottles now riding this same duck-water.

"That's mighty rough," I'd said to friends. "Roper had so much *work* in those. But, hey, he can make others. The sec this is over, we'll all start again. And so will 'Marion,' unsinkable . . ."

But, lying here beneath an itchy army blanket, one hand in my wife's hand, the other curled behind my head, I knew better: I was already somehow aging up pretty good myself. Doc had stumbled headlong up into his eighties, right? Even at my age, given my condition, I knew true resiliency requires serious health, pretty solid ground to stand on.

Pretending I would sleep, I guessed I'd really only rest. Kept recalling news of Roper's achievements throughout school, even with me trailing ten years behind him. Every club you joined he

340

had either founded or presided over. Some groups never even bothered with an election his year. Cincinnatus. Others forced the man to lead. There was some quality. Not just his looks or style, whatever. Did I *want* it? Was *that* it? Or maybe I hoped to grow more *like* him, even now? He meant so much to me, I just didn't yet know why.

He might find energy to rebuild their house. Might even design a new place for Marge and him on slightly higher ground. But to recreate that unexpected bonus round he'd carved from his last decade? that was going to be a long shot. Restarting Phase II a second time, at eighty-two? Tough for anybody.

Even for a Doc.

AROUND ME, WHISPERERS still catalogued who'd been saved, who not. Which veterinary hospital had gone under, killing our beloved pets hidden exactly there for safety's sake. And which geniuses among us actually owned flood insurance? Three households! One, Mitch's, the other Riverside insurance agent of choice; the second Janet's and mine. A third, one river-edge pennywise widow-dowager-client of mine who'd signed up over objections. All of us, we would keep quiet about the embarrassment of having stayed put while also keeping ourselves "covered."

I felt myself struggling to relax while on the brink of some finding: I'd been recognized by neighbors with embraces I could feel were truly meant. That finally convinced me. All along, I'd been a major part of Riverside. Safe in that at last. But *why*?

Because it was all gone now.

Somehow, tired unto death, I muttered that: "It's gone now, it's gone now, it's . . ." and slept like some dim if trusting child.

Gosh, I missed my father.

4

I WOKE DECIDING we were having an adventure. Mr. Safari had come for us. Our kids once made me re-re-read *Peter Pan in Kensington Gardens* aloud to them night after night. We loved the flying part but I made them stay grounded in beds at least till reading ended. That darn Peter had been a genius; he knew to stop growing on the non-shaving side of puberty. He could look over into adulthood's promised land but he preferred not to take that bait. And this morning I recalled the flying boy's simple line, "Dying would be an awfully big adventure."

A thanks-and-recovery service was announced for noon that day at All Saints Episcopal. *Thanks* seemed misplaced, *recovery* impossible, but we went. The one FEMA woman said she couldn't let us stay in the armory all morning, said they'd need to sweep up, empty our trash cans.

The old brick sanctuary Dad had loved still stood downtown, on fairly high ground. The donors, 1820s Paxtons, must've seen to this before our town maples obscured Falls' highs and lows. I'd heard that First Presbyterian and its graveyard were submerged knee-deep. There was a borrowed cabin cruiser tied to a handy basketball goal. Old friends, minus the Ropers, all piled in. Somebody said this beautiful boat had once belonged to Doc Dennis S——.

As a boy, I used to dream of flying. With your hometown drowned, you move over it, as if both underwater and at angel's height. The smells come as surprises, too. We passed the chimney of our best African-American beauty salon; adjoining water wore a bubble roof of shampoo. Air grew sweet with all that coconutty lost cologne. I wanted to swing back for a second sniff but our friend's inboard soon chewed into an ill-placed treetop. We just clambered out onto a loading dock then waded-walked the rest of the way.

Somehow we three couples went from moaning to giggling over nothing, like kids, not a worry in the world. The full sun was out as if to show us more perfectly everything lost. Our deck shoes kept making comical Little Rascals squishy sounds. I felt stunned to where, if any of my male tennis partners had taken my free hand (like how kindergarten boys wander around), I would have enjoyed that. All rules gone. Most. A good-sized catfish made a U-turn at the corner of Church Street and Main. With that there came this streaming sense of a new chance. Another life, elsewhere. But walking in water proves harder than that same action in air. I had to slow down, stop at intervals . . . catching . . . breath. Others indulged me, circling back, then trudging but at my pace.

Marge Roper stood in our church's forecourt, already running interference. She explained that everything was fine, though Doc was not himself quite yet. Everybody guessed his loss must feel particularly bitter. You can buy new TVs, etc., but your own art hand-carved . . . ? Odd, today I remembered wondering why this man had not—given his amazing skill—carved small people, instead. They surely outrank everything. Me, now, if I could sculpt or write, as a subject, only people would interest me. Why they do stuff! There'd be so much to know! But, making decoys, hadn't he just been doing further xerox copies of known imitations of what started as pure waterbirds? With human portraits, no two can ever look alike. Hell, if I could have ever been a great artist, I bet I could've been a *great* artist.

I SOON NOTED Roper standing by himself off in back. Everyone had heard, his coveted works were inhaled by deluge. And we'd turned up just as somebody brought one of his lost decoys back to him. The gal had found it, floating, head forward, right-side up.

She hand-delivered it straight to this service, guessing Doc might be here. The young woman served cocktails out at the Starlite and maybe on Fridays "danced." After her mother's cancer, the family was said to still owe Roper huge back-bills. Delighted, she turned up in her full barmaid war paint. Hadn't the young doc once swapped service? Well, she'd fished this relic from a ditch near her trailer seven miles from Riverside. Had it wrapped up special in a Hardee's burger bag! Gal must've felt in an amazing position to now barter down those thousands overdue. She did not ask aloud how much this art was worth to him; but you saw that question buckling her tender made-up face. "Bless you," Marge said, simple. As if human thanks were all the payment needed. The poor girl blinked. But, even if disappointed herself, she lingered, expecting it would cheer *him*.

This cedar teal had drifted through some spilled barn-red enamel. One whole wing's paint flapped free like burned human skin. Contact with water had already ruined its side, though the ably-carved neck and head remained unwarped. The finder, meaning well, now handed this duck to Roper right here before the church for all to see. Unpaid, she'd still waited for the smile, his recovery. If Marge wondered how exactly to stop this happening, she maybe felt too drained to intervene.

DOC SIMPLY HELD the thing. He looked down at it resting in both his hands. Roper's blue-white eyes were fixed right on it. And yet Doc acted as if he'd never seen a duck before, much less a carved one, much less the odd concept of a "decoy" meant to fake out a real one as one of its own kind.

Made a fairly sorry sight. Seeing Roper at a loss, Julia Abernethy and several other former lady-patients "tuned up" pretty good. I stared at the awkward way he clutched the object. Later, during service, I'd note how Doc absently gripped it as some child might— by the head—fist around its neck. You sensed he was anywhere but in our shared present tense. I watched him so. One word came to me: "adrift."

Doc stared ahead as if awaiting some signal or alarm from right in back of him. Not much paint was really left on the recovered carving. That let me know. Floodwater must be highly acidic, petro-chemicaled, so much hog waste. It would prove terribly toxic to us all. Just twelve hours in water had burned paint off his carving, the equivalent of an hour's belt-sanding.

Already, I think, we knew. It wasn't just the water's doings that seemed bad. Water itself was.

STRANGE THING ABOUT people old as us. Some get visibly rickety for a while, then they'll briefly heal right up on you. Others look youthful forever till, after catching one cold, after your not seeing them for three weeks, they turn up at Les Wilkins's pool party. And you must ask your host, "Who is that shaky *old* one on the end?"

"Why, that's Emmie, silly. You-all were in Miss Thorp's third grade together. Your *eyes* are failing."

"Something round here's falling apart, boy-o. —Ain't just my eyes."

Was like that now with Roper.

During service, as the German organ's Bach processional sounded particularly sad because especially perfect, Roper leaned forward, spine clear off the pew. He stared, fixed, ahead. Doc seemed to have forgotten the liturgy he'd had by heart since age three. (Selfish, I couldn't help hope he'd remember a long-range plan he'd mapped out once to keep my sad-sack heart at click.)

When others, exiting, spoke his way, Doc did try, did nod. Did fight to *seem* polite. But that in itself looked unlike him, his acting just dutiful. Roper squinted as at strangers. He still cradled that peeling bird the way some college running back will nurse the pigskin in the crook of his right arm. Odd, but behind Doc, a stained-glass Madonna held her bandaged babe in the same darn cradling pose.

I could tell that Roper hadn't wanted to come. Probably dreaded facing sympathy, a crowd. But Marge, usually fairly agreeable-acting, had likely forced him. Hoping his being near familiars might jolt Doc back toward normal. He must've begged to keep away from church, while hiding where? They had no above-water home or car. The guy suddenly looked like someone scared to be left alone.

This past master at teasing people, at remembering our exact lipid-triffid totals—today failed to start or hold one conversation. I briefly tried. "Got to be mighty upsetting . . ." was my own brilliant start. But Marge cut me one sad look, no-go. Doc blinked. I knew she was right. I shut up but it hurt me that I, of all folks, had just failed to make true contact. Given what I had to mean to him, this stupid blurt of mine would just slay me later.

After service, in the crowd, he attempted answering others but only if Marge forced him: "They're *talk*ing to you, honey. You see Whit and Cora here."

"Cora," he nodded. "Cora, how's your bad athlete's foot?"

Cora, slowed, said, "Better," but looked away. Never before had Doc revealed one office secret aloud. Cora here had just lost her house, family photos, bull terrier and cars. Itchy feet—the least of her problems.

DECOY

We all noted how Margie stared at Doc—now an ancient-looking white man stuck vulnerable out in midday glare. He as yet stood carrying one wooden duck by its neck; the thing hung at his side with no more care than a commuter offers the usual battered briefcase.

Not him! people said. Of all our unlikeliest strong ones, don't let it be our Doc unravels all at once.

Sure he'd just lost his handiwork. But what else personal had drifted off with Marion's copyrighted aquatic birds? Hadn't Doc carved those things *to* float? Hadn't he weighted their chests with molten lead he then painted over? Surely he'd intended their superb balance, sailboat poise. Doc's cedar exemplars had proved so stream-lined they hadn't simply sunk in his backyard, had they? There he might've retrieved them, saved the paint. But, no, his proved far too lifelike. Doc's birds, painted bold as little flags, rode sudden currents perfectly; become real emblems of American freedom. Born indoors, they'd gone off in search of true wilderness. They *took* to it. Like, well . . . like what they were. Or at least so perfectly resembled.

Their very excellence scattered Doc's the fastest!

WE'D ALREADY HEARD how at dawn yesterday he paid big money, hiring a speedboat from one of Tomothy's friends. We guessed this vessel should've been out saving people, right? But Roper'd commandeered it. The Bixby kids did owe him a favor, big time. Doc had ordered wide sweeps to track his waterfowl. No luck. Disobedient creations, creatures! To risk sounding biblical a sec: having tasted of the water of the knowledge of good and evil, they left home and Roper fast.

I could already fancy them, spread out like some little floating Chaplin-tramps bobbing on stray trenches along farm roads,

347

working their way at twenty-feet-an-hour up woodland creeks. A few by now must probably be a hundred miles of standing-water away, rocking clear out on the chill Atlantic.

EASY TO SAY his were only "fakes," hacked from wood then enameled. Being all thumbs myself (including the one with stitch marks in it), I knew his task's great difficulty. I sensed how rare was the quiet talent for making what appeared literally wild. (His birds never looked farm-raised; instead Roper's were visibly little scrappers, criminal renegades living by their strengths in the unfair open.)

You might say: people who love something too much, live at greater risk. And yet, that's bound to be the one sane way forward. Surely our determination to never lose what we've made to love, that, in itself, means an early sort of decoy death.

I'd seen our house go under. Naturally, I missed it. All afternoon, while wandering the reopened armory, I kept patting my pockets for keys (now underwater). I hated how our kids couldn't now come home and stay upstairs in rooms full of their Little League trophies and the complete Nancy Drew. They'd never rewalk literal ground where they first crawled then stepped then struggled upward to battle one another. I found I even missed their little squabbles. An only child myself, I always loved the role of referee.

I mostly fancied sunset light in the northwest corner of our foyer, thrown against old willow-bough wallpaper through bubbled glass at six o'clock on winter afternoons. That picture hit me with a daily pang like lost love. It was, I guess.

And yet, unlike Doc with all his powers to forfeit, I was left feeling, if admittedly poorer, about a decade younger. Now I got a clearer picture of my first house, before Paxton's oddball legacy to Red. It had been set up on four unsteady-looking piles of bricks, the simple white of a country box. Our lawn grew tobacco. We had, not a river stealing around behind, but one whole honest horizon that stayed put.

Having lost our place on The River Road, I felt shaken simpler. I did feel lighter-weight. Poor, I felt adventurous.

5

SIX MONTHS AFTER the flood a few locals still believed it: believed they could simply dry out their old homes, soon move back in. Seemed as logical as most painful delusions.

Already four pulmonary deaths among our crowd: all the heaviest smokers went that quick. Especially those two-packers-a-day who'd insisted on then going home to dig up their better inherited peony bushes. Peonies can live over sixty years. Our coughing diggers breathed in all that fresh shovel-loosened filth. And, after the pain of home-delivered oxygen tanks, four amiable locals died that first half-year A.D. —After Deluge.

The minute we'd seen maple-syrup-brown liquid burglarize our homes, most of us had known. No going back. Hadn't we decoded the ruined paint on Doc's first recovered decoy? Old folks now, we, like him, lived symptomatically. He had been the first to send a dove across the flood, a test case to see if, finding no land, it might not return safe. It came back okay but immediately blistered. It had not made him hopeful that his bird looked soaked in kerosene, then red paint, with a final wash of hog-piss battery acid.

Receded water left a scummy chalk, pink-brown across our every twig and doorknob. It was a dangerous-looking color, right out of our 1950s science fiction films.

There's a Bible line about rendering unto Caesar what is Caesar's, and unto God, God's. Riverside's new variation ran, "When in doubt, side with the River. Render unto River whatever's River's."

Which *was?*

Everything except our wits.

Everything except our dry ole dry-martini lives, thank God!

WE COULD ALL list our treasures lost. We agreed about what had been most valuable moneywise: Les Wilkins's two-million-dollar antique car collection, stored in the lately-Chapter-Elevened Wilkins Tobacco Auction Warehouse.

Poor Les had sunk many an inherited penny into his two 1937 Cord Phaeton convertibles, a squadron of early Bentleys and Jags, plus, best, the 1928 Hispano-Suiza touring car elaborate as its maker's name. It had been all beaten silver and lacquered burgundy, commissioned by Gloria Swanson. Streamlined, fitted inside with blond-wood carving, it'd always seemed more a ship than any auto. Its silver horn played a song about blowing bubbles. All submerged in four minutes. Asked how he felt, Les answered for months after, "Flat tire, flat tire."

His wife finally admitted she'd had to keep Les restrained those first ten days. She'd locked him in their borrowed home's attic sewing room. Poor guy kept wanting to swim underwater in order to simply sit behind the wheel of Swanson's sunken Hispano-Suisa and sound its silver trumpets and end his life down there, in style.

Also gone to mud: Julia Abernethy's real Degas drawing, a beautiful racehorse one. Raleigh's art museum had been after it for decades but you know how close-fisted most Abernethys are.

Still, we all concurred about the loss that stirred us most. Unlike

Les's Hollywood town cars or Julia's French pastel, this was the one lost masterwork made *here*. Carved by someone who'd stayed, and likewise meant his creations to. He'd chosen birds he knew as peculiar to our region. —A fleet now scattered to the Seven Seas.

At our Recovery Talent Show, everybody's favorite gossipy ophthalmologist brought down the house playing a borrowed banjo as he hound-dogged:

> *I left a million five and change,*
> *Down by the river-side,*
> *Down by . . .*

Four full-tilt divorces had been well and nastily in progress. Then water rose many feet. And, once these bickering folks, the parents of assorted pretty semi-disappointing children, spent hours pulling each other through a million gallons of sewage, by the time they were found high up the Blanchards' water oak, they appeared to be French-kissing. They proved so wet if fused, it was hard to get the lovebirds separately saved!

They'd never split now. They would only fight like beasts of burden for the right to carry one another forward; out of this world into whatever if any adventure's coming next. A childhood sweetheart rededicated herself to her first husband, after having committed five children and one half-century to another, some Yankee. "And you, my lifelong friends, whyn't you *tell* me? —Tony never friggin *got* Falls."

Certain other marriages, from their wedding days forth, had been called "disasters waiting to happen." Now one had. Would it make these shipwreck unions seem better or worse? We'd best wait and see. What *else* had we to do?

Our gang lived uneasily reestablished in an over-new development. "Hilltop" is no more a hill than Falls is a waterfall. But this clay tract rises a scant two feet above-sea-level, much higher than dear sunken Riverside. Cotton grew here and so our newly planted grass still shows plowings' crenellations.

Our homes up here they're all smaller-blander than the grand half-timbered barns we once filled with kids and junk. Prestige? a goner. Disaster claimed our antiquities and made us finally efficient! We sacrificed elbow-room but spared ourselves five daily huffing ascents toward a second story, only to forget why we climbed. Our crowd was sixty to ninety now; the river had done editorial home-downsizing *for* us.

Finally, we all now lived "maintenance included." No need for hiring daily maids, weekly yardmen. Free at last! I will never touch another lawn mower.

Age has its privileges.

6

THE MARION ROPERS bought into Hilltop last. They took that smallish skylighted unit at our block's far end. Post-flood, us refugee Riversiders tended to party hardier. Frantic weeknight dance things. We played Benny Goodman, James Brown, Sarah Vaughan, the Beatles. Anything. No, anything but rap. Somebody's kid had given them discs. "No rap!" Diana de Pres cried. "After what we've been through?" Our crowd certainly drank more, or maybe just more openly. "Like fish," was one flood joke now out of favor, overused.

"How you feeling? You look washed-out." That was another line we'd long since bored of. Every English phrase and pun suddenly seemed liquid-based. Each brimmed with refreshed permission to sip bourbon. By now, why the hell *not*?

What was the bank going to do, come confiscate your Chippendale highboy, your things, your *house*? Would they punish us seniors with sledgehammers, forcing ladies to go make little rocks out of rocks big as the Broken Heart? Might they stick us into nice dry jail cells, serve us three meals a day? If so, right now might be good.

Our long cocktail blasts featured finger foods scarcely underwriting-offsetting vodka and gin. Our parties grew feverish again and endless. We felt moneyed the way four-year-olds at birthday parties feel, cake and candles all the proof of luck we'd need.

Today was today and we would gobble it. Shrinks from Raleigh commuted, overbooked. IRAs, "wealth management," we had just enough put aside not to think constantly of that. Of course, there was always a worry of outlasting nest-eggs, depending on our kids, becoming bores, then nuisances. Foreign travel seemed a threat now. Venice? Water for streets? Been there, swum those. As for cruises!

I used to say things like, "So much of life comes down to our river." Well, it could all come up on you overnight like food poisoning.

Old neighbors now live within easy hearty-partying distance. — Given yards so small—true drinkers can literally crawl home. Poor Les Wilkins sometimes does. Down on all fours like a basset hound. He misses specific cars so much, he'll tell you how he got ahold of each. Like Casanova, ancient, recounting servant girls seduced. Les still lives in mourning for sixty antique autos. Odd, the fates waiting each of us. My own? To mythologize the farm-boy past of a dad who wanted all that "country" sheared off him like bad wool. To die in sight of the one off-duty doctor who might've saved you.

We seem to be returning to our old dance-card days, reliving certain engagement party blowouts of our crazed youths. Last night,

Diana de Pres got sick from Brandy Alexanders and the outcome looked even less pretty than it had on her, all over her, at age sixteen.

MARGE ROPER WOULD turn up alone at a few cocktail hours but never did stay long. The few times she brought Doc he'd hover in the foyer. He would answer only direct questions, eyes averted. That brilliant gift for diagnosis—wasted scanning floor tiles, an umbrella stand.

Doc kept mainly to himself. Nothing new in that. But now he was seen taking walks. People claimed his therapist had suggested hikes might be good for him. Might give Doc something "focused" to do, mornings-evenings. Roper'd dropped a lot of weight. People said he now looked "ropy," an accurate word that contained both his curious name and new unknotting appearance.

Roper had taken to patrolling while using one tall stick he'd found. No carving on it, alas. We all wanted him to start again, even simplest whittling. Only that might be Doc's ticket to his grand delayed Phase III.

Marge said he now called such long strolls "looking" or "going out looking." Margie told my Jan that, many nights at dinner, Doc made perfect sense. For up to twenty minutes he seemed to know exactly what had happened, to be up to date. On one subject alone did he stay crazed: his life's scattered hand-work. He just knew he wanted it back. Did he see his decoys as patients wandered off, needing Doc alone? No. I wish. He wanted wood simply for being the very carved material made valuable by his once having valued it.

MY HEART, ABOUT like Dad's, had been not-good for decades, then got worse all at once. Flood-inspired adrenaline had fooled me into feeling resurrected for whole weeks. My heart's tire-patch inner-tube analogy had, for me, been overdone. Soon nothing's left *but* balloon, caulking and the stints, seals.

Dr. Gita asked me why I had not been to see her for the checkups lately. Why had I never stayed in touch with certain Duke-UNC specialists? Hadn't Roper referred me the day I quit my Monday checkups? She told me Doc had made her vow she'd give me special care. The manila-bound notes he'd left were rubber-banded, novel-thick. And poor Gita herself, hadn't she mailed me a handwritten note, reminding me, remember? But I'd been avoiding her, had I not?

I scratched my head, imitating a former internist. "Well, ma'am, once Doc retired, guess I sort of forgot."

"Yes. I am hearing a great deal of that, William. Never have met so many thought he worked for them alone. You've at least let me keep your prescriptions going. But I'm afraid that, by putting off all appointments this year and a half since the flood—I must be very clear here—you've lost a good bit more function. You're understanding me? At least nod, please." So I did, nod.

FOUND I DIDN'T much care either way. Found the flood had sucked back every bit of quickening that'd first rafted me through it. That energy got reneged plus a surcharge for its use. Found I couldn't do all that many "activities" per day anymore. One, tops.

Janet begged me not to drive. But without a car I'd be one dead duck truly finished. I told her, if I felt Doc's predicted "flutter before implosion" I'd hit the blinkers, pull over pretty darn quick. She always swore I was being selfish. Said I was bound to kill "some fine young family." Jan feared I'd take out a worthy attractive couple and their several kids. I knew she was only remembering us. Our Volvo station-wagon (not unlike the Ropers') had once been a mess of car seats, bottle-warmers plugged into our dashboard lighter, pink kitty toys spongy underfoot. Jan had made me, an old man, into the enemy of Family Promise. Or maybe Time had.

Post-flood, remembering my own father's end, I gave up even hanging near the links. The club bar has always been called Hole Nineteen. That phrase took on a grave-side clifflike edge for me. Hell, I'd lately been forced to finally give up even morning decaf! My quality of life? Of *what*?

I moped around these new-built eleven hundred square feet.

I realized that, for my last four years in the old place B.C., I had been taking daily naps, in Jill's . . . in my daughter's girlhood room. Every frilly hand-drawn thing in there I noted, kept just in its place. I wrote notes and paid bills in Lottie's office. Small spaces I liked best. Less chance of misplacing things with all pertinent objects at hand, in view.

Now I wished for a stellar late-life hobby, *very* late. I kept mainly watching our animal shows on PBS, rereading WWII, trying not to drive my poor patient Janet mad by my driving too often. But if she visited neighbors or got a long-enough phone-call, I would snitch the car keys. Couldn't help it. After the flood she'd refused to buy me a replacement car. Claimed she could better monitor the one. Escaped, I often drove downhill into our old neighborhood, roads cracked but familiar. Most toxic houses had been razed per health department orders.

ABOUT THEN, MAYBE a year and a half post-flood, you'd sometimes see Doc walking far off the interstate. Raleigh now sent its traffic and four-lanes clear out Falls' way. Farm lanes from my boyhood muscled up with off-ramps.

Roper might be near the concrete drainage-trench under some

busy cloverleaf. Down there, alongside roadkill beagles, cement's graffiti, bent grocery carts, you'd spy his windblown head. It'd once been the preferred hood ornament of Davidson, then Yale, that headful of local life-saving was lost to use, to us. To me. His best friend.

He'd be striding along depending on his guide-stick. You'd see Roper poking through piles of drifted leaves. He'd move along, overturning garbage, always alone, prodding, on the stalk for something. My Janet had spotted him wandered way out past Red Oak Grange. Doc was poling himself along a roadside gully, his tennis-shoes resembling cinder blocks of mud. She told how he dragged forward, head-down, scanning the way certain poorer folks hereabouts once hunted Coke bottles for selling back to stores.

Surely he was seeking one of his Manhattan-worthy artworks. Or was he looking for one real live duck, to be a new model, to inspire him? The sight of Roper's quest felt so sad it grew half-sickening. He'd never been one to sit still.

You reach an age when you open your morning newspapers not to Sports, the Funnies, but Obits. At our age, Jan and I knew dozens who had "preceded us," as morticians must say. Such acquaintances became your own silent majority of friends. But it wasn't that. That in itself is strangely not so tough on people of our given vintage. It's not the lost; it's the lingerers that slay you! You don't usually have to see the deceased up and out *walk*ing.

With him in motion, Doc's white hair now looked rat-nest flyaway as Einstein's. White eyebrows, once sleek as otter fur, now coiled with stray white hairs overshooting everywhichaway. Try as Marge might to tidy them, Roper's clothes looked bunched as burlap, ditch-colored, flecked with sticky seeds.

Doc had been the last one you'd expect to go like this, with all his skills and couth and looks. His dad a cardsharp, his mom a pianist, his superb digits a birthright. A dead loss now. Had we ever been fair to him? Had he volunteered to save those of us who stayed? or had we drafted him the second schoolkids made Marion go "Doc"? Roper's hands had left on us his best sort of signature: no trace of scar. All those binding little surgeries, ending with his Swiss-watch stitches, they'd long since gone invisible. For forty years, no need to put a © on any of his living creatures. Doc had tied the black catgut knot as he said: "No mark likely. You'll see. Good as new in no time, pal."

These few words still felt sure, short, as sunk clear into us as his sutures!

OF COURSE MARGE tried to get him carving again. Everybody did: "With all this water, bet you're *inspired*, huh?" Margie even risked the humiliation of buying him a Bobbitt's Hobby Shop napkin-ring kit. Maybe something simple would make him remember? But now only his own *fin*ished products drew him. Decoys. They were lures, okay.

Till the flood, simply *owning* had bored him. He'd told those big-spender Texans in Bermuda he cared nothing for buying; only *making* held him. Now he'd lost his talent for that, Doc Roper turned miser. He was a man fixed solely on gathering the work of one boy-wonder *Marion*! He'd become no better than any other of our country club's decoy-buyers. No better than me, than *I*, the poor bugger!

After forty years, Doc had left his job of saving us. All that huffing to warm a stethoscope, his personal-courtesy heat. That'd been Monday morning's first best medicine, lost. He'd left the healing task with no seeming regret. Even with all the forty-odd thank-you parties in his honor, Roper had never given what you'd call a farewell-speech. We did it all for him. He hadn't felt pressured to prepare a different "Goodbye, I love you guys, too" for each big barbeque.

I would've. I probably might've written it out on three-by-fives then memorized it so I could sound more . . . you know, more grandly offhand . . . more, well, like *him*.

But, hey, Doc didn't *need* to endear. Man already had us all curled right there in his hands. Talent! At base, its uneven distribution is so unfair in a democracy.

(Me? when *I* retired, my staff of five gave me one potted chrysanthemum, a bottle of drugstore champagne, the giant greeting card signed by our entire secretarial-and-paralegal team. Plus, "Hey, Bill, can I help you tote that box of your desk stuff to your car? You sure? Well, don't strain yourself right here at the end, guy. I mean 'at the starting-line.' Life's just getting cranked for you, you ole frat-boy party-animal. Get out the hip flask and a list of 900 numbers." (What *were* 900 numbers? I laughed, pretending to know.) Basically, over and out. From an agency long ago renamed for me! No particular praise. Certainly no formal speech *about* me and, God knows, none requested *from* me. Till now. Is *this* my own self-administered funeral oration? Who else is left to give or hear it?

DOC HAD GONE on to reclaim, even dignify, his unfair handle "Marion." Strapped with a liability, he made it famous. That's the idea. That's American revenge!

Thanks to his old-school pull in medical circles years back, I'd finally worked my way to the top of the list for a transplant. But by now, see, I was too old to really qualify. I didn't "have the heart" to claim an interchangeable human part, not when ruddy kids the Bixbys' age lay waiting!

I could think to say that, sure, I'd loved Doc. I could say I had wanted to *be* the man. But had I also wanted to, what? massage or maybe "touch" or "ease" the fellow in some other way? Had I turned *that* way? Had I, without knowing, become one of *those*—wearing their matching vest, tie and pocket hankie of the same priss-pot plaid? Was I another bachelor at another party gushing instead of speaking, making too much drama out of his dietetic childless life? Cute stories of his Yorkie's antics? Had I been miscast as husband-dad or maybe just faked it? Had I got myself rolled into Falls' city gates like the Trojan horse? himself a kind of decoy maybe. A wooden horse stuffed full of waiting warriors, male. Close quarters, beards, smells, a most macho silence.

I held on to the memory of a young doctor's clutching my hand so hard just after Dad died. Roper, tears in eyes already scarily blue, he'd squeezed my right paw while swearing that, having just let his patient slip off on the fairway, I would live forever-after in his care and hands. "I've *got* you, Bill!"

Who, except Doc, had ever promised that?

MAYBE I WANTED more. Had I wanted to "do it" with him or whatever? This is painful. There, I said it. But, really, where intimate contact with another male's concerned, I swear I wouldn't know how to go *about* it. Where would a fellow even start? A kiss? To kiss a mouth with stubble all around it? Nahh.

But even so, at my age, I'll admit to wanting *any*thing that might've once been true. (Whether I later re*mem*ber such a wish is quite another matter!) I know: I did hope for a bit more than I got. That is all I can now think to say.

With Doc finally downgraded into looking like some ole leather door hinge, I can maybe finally speak. But no longer actually *to* him,

360

see? That chance appears lost. Odd but, for me, he doesn't even seem quite "old" yet. I still consider him all ages at once, since I myself seem to daily hopscotch across most of those same surplus annex decades.

But I confess that it was excellent—every year and day of our overlapping life spans—living just across the road from one another.

7

ONCE, A.D., I talked Jan into going for a country drive. Secretly I hoped to find a little property near some lake. A cabin maybe? Zero upkeep. Just let wildflowers grow. Nice porch.

But unlike Falls, devastation out there stayed uncleared. We passed flooded fields littered with Falls' refrigerators, house roofs, brand-new swing sets. The idea of enduring a deluge alone, no neighbor to fetch you off your roof, that sent us right back to our blank new place contented. Our condo still smells of drywall. So much the better.

Jan hates even going near our old neighborhood. "Nothing's down there but the river, a false friend." But I missed what I called "our lot in life": the mold-growing brick foundation where a mighty fortress stood for sixty years.

To even get near the place I must sneak the car keys now. Either my driving is getting worse or Jan's more critical or both.

THE FORMER PRETTIEST ride in eastern North Carolina now means ignoring the health department bulletins.

CONDEMNED OFF-LIMITS STRUCTURES, TRESPASSERS

Considered Looters. Rat Bait Poison, Danger To Unleashed Dogs.

Oh it's a barrel of laughs down there these days. That badland border between Heaven and Hell must be riddled with just such vermin, smoke and signage.

Turning onto The River Road, I still feel a sort of quickening. Poor Janet can't even bear to see snapshots of our old place. But even the newish station-wagon parks itself right where it should, the horse knows the way. Somehow, being here doesn't make me only sad.

I sit in our driveway and overlook the underpinnings of a house no longer here. Location, location, location, all that's left. Do you believe they still charge me property taxes? if at valuations greatly reduced. How fast Virginia creeper has claimed the north chimney, poison ivy's scaled the south.

At my wheel, arms crossed, I pose as Security. Some cocky boy-guard Colonel Paxton might've hired. But the kid's now minding the Old Mabry place. Like Doc, these days I feel my mission here is simply "looking."

Alone, I can admit that I have always been secretly insanely ambitious. But, for what? Shouldn't I know by now? Waiting, staring idled downriver, looking clear through what was Roper redwood deck, I spy a stretch of sandbank once public park. Its evergreen planting got swept away by current that first night. New saplings have taken root there. Mostly weed trees—sumacs and hackwoods. The river knits and braids along, all innocence. *Who, me?* after its rampage.

And I, here in my starter position as father-husband-neighbor, I do hope the police will come with questions. I'm spoiling for a

challenge from far younger men. That way I can show my license—
1526 River Road still written on it bold. Parked here, with no
pressing business appointments, I try recovering whatever Riverside
I liked best. This is a luxury peculiar to my age. The living and the
dead make up your quorum and are all on call.

So I go back, before marriage, pre-ownership, to my much-
missed Red, his introductory-offer. We're a family, back before
Paxton gave us our free pass.

Dad's tour of the stars' homes commenced as soon as Sunday
service ended. I would claim the Studebaker's flannel backseat. We
had just worshipped at Second Methodist, while guiltily considering buying up toward First Presbyterian. Red pulled past First to
check out how many new cars it had. And for Episcopalianism?
That might only be achieved in our next generation.

At preachers' last Amen, town believers scattered, starved.
Bound for delicious-smelling home roasts; to reservations at Chez
Josephine or Sanitary Seafood. But Dad, unswerving, aimed the
waxed red Studebaker riverward. Our lunch budget might prove
limited. (Chicken salad sandwiches today featuring a hen past
steady laying.) Even so, a grand tour awaited.

Studebaker whitewalls? Dad had Cloroxed those as clean as
Astaire's spats. Strangers, we took The River Road's first S-curve.
Leaving much of summer's heat behind, we soon banked, cooling
and downhill, past yonder little vest-pocket park.

There, Red (the boy) had made a French picnic from two hard-
boiled eggs. And now, with the doxology fresh behind us, he called
to order truest worship. "Will you lookeee at all this back up in
here?" Red asked us and the world generally. *Enter into His gates with
thanksgiving, His courts with praise.*

Their houses already looked beautiful to us. Lawns stretched too wide to be anything but show-off meadows. Beyond those, vertical homes, caulked with fresh face-paint, lined like beauties about to be confirmed. Striped awnings trapped coolness back of second-story windows. Homes soon appeared almost a single sawtoothed stage-set, painted just so. For luring humbler folk right down into this river shade.

That Sunday mid-July, home-places of the rich all seemed only made of shady porches, steep foyers. Once you stepped over welcome mats, would there even be a place to sit or sleep? Such beautiful Victorian valentines, homes might prove depthless as birdhouses.

But us? we'd not get far enough indoors to check. We'd just enjoy the sight of carpet yards. We could enjoy our safety, being hicks out on a public road. From here, such places looked lovely as all promises well-kept.

Why had riverfront-living so spoken to the bowlegged contractor driving us? Red wanted it for us. That Sabbath, he chugged along at twelve mph. Dad pointed out heart-shaped goldfish ponds, the engineering of a Queen Anne turret. And I, in his backseat, slouched ever-lower.

None of my country classmates would see us ogling here. But our car already drew smirks from neighbor girls on bikes. They were beauties wearing shorts. They had hair so blond, it wasn't even yellow like our best farm girls'. Here, it shone toward a silver that no store-bought home-slopped dye could fake.

I saw girls as pretty as girls should ever legally get to be this side of intentional international torture of such farm boys as Dad and me! But why were they wearing short-shorts on the Lord's Day? And why outdoors, goofing around at this post-church Sabbath-dinner-hour? Their smiling at our poker-faced tourism made me wince like someone burned. I felt a mixture: pity for myself, desire for them, and one huge secret wish not unlike Dad's. Did I want to live among them or punish them from afar for their vanity and luck and legs?

But he was hollering into his rearview mirror, "Set up straight, son. Show 'em that posture. Gals your age're out here grinning a big River Road greetings. Gals sure get 'developed' fast in town. And you? scrunched-down a-hiding! Sit *up*. You're a good-looking whippersnap. You covering your face!? Why, if I'd of had your looks . . . I might could have got somewheres with our life. —See yonder? Since last week the Eatman Battles have had a whole new flagstone terrace laid. Leading to their dock. Probably fine Dovetail Construction work. It just appreciates their property value. Like I always say, 'Why not en*joy* your money?' Imagine, son. Your bike would be parked alongside our own house. Your Sunfish boat, the sails up, docked out back! How'd you like them apples, hunh, Billy?"

"Yessir," I droned. Glad there was no hope. Of Pop ever getting what he swore we all deserved. Meanwhile, behind us, six cars, two of them Packards, pressed closer trying to finally pass. Good taste alone kept them from honking us off the road.

And only now, from this far riverbank, only while recalling Dad's tour of all he wanted for us, do I see why Riverside summers stayed so cool. It had more than just the shading lid of maples, more than just the mild river itself.

Earlier we'd driven through hot farmland, flat and glaring. We were now headed down, down a slow grade into the only river chasm hereabouts. No wonder wetness kept things here a bright currency-green. This road along a river was incised below sea-level. This wide avenue eased us right down into moisture, a beautiful gash or trench. Fill this with water? you're done for. All your property's in the Panama Canal. And the Mabrys' life wish?

To be allowed to settle exactly here.
They put out the bait. It brought us.

8

SIX MORE DAMAGED "Marions" had been retrieved. One they found washed as far as Greenville, thirty-four miles, carried over all that flooded farmland. It was a mallard, cleaved down the exact center; but still it floated, bobbing weirdly sunny-side up. Its swamp-soaked bill, back-curved, made the bird appear to smile. Had it gone smug (or crazed) with everything it'd seen?

—Myself, I am an optimist, about nothing.

Because Doc engraved his Internet-registered name into his creations' bottoms, others would get returned that whole next year. (One from South Carolina's Great Pee Dee River but folks traced its carver here to Falls.)

Marge kept him nested in, secreted away right down our street. Riding past, Jan and I, we'd sometimes catch sight of her cutting his hair on their side patio. Doc's head bent so far forward he looked about to fall as he sat wrapped in a checked tablecloth. The old man seemed irked at suffering such grooming, her free hand held his noggin still.

Margie's gaunt now but ever more vigilant and butch. Odd, she looks more bowlegged. Her hair's chopped short any old way. (Being so on-guard for two, she finds no beauty-parlor time. "A shame," Jan says. "Time-off would do her a world of good, hearing others' little troubles.") Still, Marge's always been so basically fine-looking, she's never needed much sissy-tending.

The Ropers' back-door Hilltop neighbors, the Blanchards, who had lost their cat and almost their granddaughter, swear that Doc often sleeps alone in his old tobacco-colored pup tent pitched far up under their back deck, for further privacy.

SOMETIMES SHE'LL DRIVE him clear out of town where they're sure to meet no concerned friends. She parks while he basically "looks," as the Ropers both agree to call it. Marge keeps him in sight but all while simply settled at the wheel, reading that day's Raleigh paper, flossing, talking to her kids by phone, listening to oldies or Public Radio.

She said that when a couple of his carvings started returning by mail as if via their own will, the sight of ruined ones went harder on Doc. Simpler to believe his waterbirds were somehow "gone." Migratory, off to seek their fortunes, looking flag-perfect as his decoys did when starting out.

I found it sad but enviable, Marge's daily carpooling him some-place new. I offered to be her driver stand-in. She thanked me with the saddest smile. "By now, he trusts nobody but me. Not even you, Bill. And we both know, that's saying a lot."

"Appreciate that, Marge." I lowered my eyes, too grateful.

He needed motion, daily hunting. Instead of dawn river-swims, he took to this striding. She'd drive him out still farther and farther. Had he ever told her what he hoped to find? Did his wife dare ask? Theirs proved such a marriage, "in sickness and in health." A thing now grown unto itself. Beautiful how patient, how simply she lived inside the damage done to him. *Now, that's a love story*, I thought, not bothering Janet by my saying it aloud. Somehow that'd sound critical of *her.* —Roper-marriage comparisons, even now!

If Margie got home ten minutes late from grocery shopping, she confessed to sometimes finding he'd stolen off "to go look." This proved pretty dangerous. See, Doc's route stayed fixed along our county's old waterways. Thanks to city planners and prosperity, many tributaries have been trained through exurban infrastructure, pipes and aqueducts. Lithium, it's been sent grave-deep, giving us no surface balm. Clear springs where a decoy or some live bird could splash? all imprisoned underground. Streams might bubble up across some unzoned field only to plunge blind, back under the interstate.

But Doc, following the old brook with a dowser's nose, barely noticed. He mostly stared down. The man seemed unaware of new highways' barricading wetlands' way. Being a former Boy Scout (Eagle!) —how literally he mapped a stream! The man and his stick walked right through (then out of) any brook-straddling dress shop at a sudden tony mall, startling security.

THE RISKS ROPER trailed everywhere, he alone never saw. The man never actually looked back: as Doc's former patients kept pulling their cars over, wanting to help. No time for signaling, folks just veered off-road to offer, what? cash? Starbucks? rides home? He had taught us how to breathe wet kids alive while out for his jog. He had heart-massaged a dead man twenty bonus-minutes extra just in case. His rescuer's impulse came back and schooled us all. We each longed for the right and privilege of finding him horizontal so we might just once work on *him*. However badly.

But even if some former patient hollered, sprung out of his car, blocked the old guy's path, Doc would shake his head no. Cornered, he'd fight you. His wooden staff laid quite a dent into the hood of co-Olympic-gold-medalist Tomothy Bixby's new red Miata. Finally, the unscarred folks that Doc had left "as good as new" were forced to give up sparing *him*. Safer for us all, just leaving him endangered. He seemed everywhere, replicas.

Out driving myself, I had the mixed luck of spotting him. Wanting to help I cringed instead. Then risked a few wild U-turns to hurry anyplace else. He had looked . . . feral. What would I even *say*? I felt a traitor to my early starstruck sense of him. Roper'd promised to keep me alive and, till this sec at least, hadn't he? But seeing him so publicly addled seemed a gentling hint to let myself go now. Permission. A hall pass.

Part of me longed to join my mentor in his roadside quest. Hike beside him, pointing, "Great to be out looking with you. But, uh-oh, bud, we missed a ditch." And yet, this short of breath, I couldn't have kept up with his long blue-heron strides. Even if he'd ever finally invited me.

Janet begged that I stop taking out the car alone. She made me get one of those emergency beepers. You wear it around your neck 24–7. Cowbell. This way I could summon 911 without even needing the digital skill to dial three numbers. "Having fallen, simply press red button," instructions state. But *why*?

Jan suddenly claimed she loved riding shotgun with me, even if I was headed off to buy spare lightbulbs. Monitoring, pure and simple. I knew she kept nitroglycerin ampules in her handbag. And the cell phone? given my state, she now carried hers from room to room. Subtle. I just needed one hour alone per day. Too much to ask at my age? I recalled first being stared at by Jan with me sitting unzipped, grade three. And, for better or worse, my unsentimental friend had never stopped, never looked at anyone else.

She feared my next "episode" might crash me into other cars. Every nearby vehicle seemed to contain her ideal young family, ourselves forty years ago. My bad driving and worse heart had become the enemy of precisely us.

"*Episodes.*" Getting closer together. Contractions, hints. Dilations of egress by centimeters, signs that some canal way out of the world was finally clearing. Last month at a mall shoe store, after buying nice new fleece slippers, I dropped my receipt. As I bent to grab it, their white carpet started looking so good, contrasting with the cold air up at usual six-foot adult male level, I went down to be more toward flooring's weave.

Perfect bed, placed exactly where Daddy presently needed one. Janet insisted I had fallen. I later vowed to her: It had not been an actual fall. More that I simply eased lower, by degree, toward floor covering of increasing interest. Once achieved, the horizontal there felt very valuable indeed.

Young clerks refused to let me enjoy it long. First I heard them above me barking at each other, "You check. Touch his neck or wherever they do, and see. No, you. You've got seniority." I had to laugh at this. Relieved, they jumped, then swore. "Oh . . . ma . . . God. Well, good. The paperwork alone! And already it's been such a week!"

Despite my explanations of what a great floor surface they had going here, the kids would just not let me keep admiring it up close. The prettiest girl drove me home. She then led me across the deck, into our house. I don't know why the sight of Janet's stricken face made me cackle so. Did Jan imagine I was finally bringing home the reason for my live-in absence all these years, my mistress-nurse age 22? That gave me a momentary giggling power surge. Till, weirdly strong, the two of them lifted me right onto the bed.

ON DAYS I feel very clear and able, I still try and sneak her car keys. Sounds like some juvenile delinquent with his greaser's ducktail. Making the big bank-heist getaway in a two-year-old Volvo wagon! But look, these days I go barely twelve mph. Like Dad as self-appointed docent to Riverside's top mansions. People honk at me, I go so slow, which is good. Keeps me more alert. Jan'll be standing at our community mailboxes or talking by phone to Marge (in lowered tones about lessening expectations for their men), and me? I'm just then rolling downhill in neutral. Sly, my Steve McQueen exit strategy! Go un-noisy into that dark night . . . I've grown into one cunning pioneering "Red" old man.

I tend to drive along the ragged marsh edges of Mall World. That coincidentally is where Doc mostly hikes now. I tell myself I am somehow using my aloneness to protect him and his. I plan guarding him with whatever's least likely to bother Doc as he is now.

Marge tried restricting him to the strip mall nearest our development. But even old men are hard to contain. I just want to see him. Whatever he keeps seeking, I sense he's now pursuing that for me. Or is it me he's half-forgotten and now absently seeks? Even in ditches, minor sinkhole graves.

It's counterproductive, living in a town so small. Limits your escaping unobserved. More new charismatic churches, while car dealerships keep closing, and no Harley-Davidson outlet for the Fallen. So small a place when one has hopes so Roper-huge. And, what did I *want* for him and myself? That . . . that's on the tip of my tongue. It's just, to me, the two of us always seemed secretly made of finer stuff. Alike in being different. But what chance did we have, in a zone so rural, strict and married?

It's hard to spot my dearest wanderer-friend outdoors and in such public need. What's tougher still? Not seeing him at all!

Anybody hereabouts can tell you—and for years—why I'd have done just anything for Roper.

9

DRIVING CALMS ME. Hands around the wheel, I briefly forget my own factory-second arteries. For miles I ignore even Doc's splintery mind. I like the Swedish clicking of my turn signal. He'll sometimes suddenly appear. Along roadside, you'll see him scare certain schoolkids holding signs for their booster-club car wash.

Last month I spied him way off in the distance. He kept prodding the bank of some irrigation pond. Doc, following his stick, came wading its shoreline silhouetted. He looked like both a ragged crane and some homeless Audubon, hunting all that he'd so slowly painted, then too quickly lost.

A few locals freely talk of getting up a petition. They've urged Marge to ship our shaman-friend off somewhere. "For help." Light-dosage shock-therapy is back in fashion: a flash of lightning might offset his head full of goose down and black water.

They claim Roper is now "sending the wrong signal to Falls' newcomers." Among drinkers at Hole Nineteen, I actually heard our Republican mayor, one of Doc's former patients, explain how the man has become "both a traffic nuisance and eyesore."

Everybody says that life is short and yet it's highly possible to overstay.

Take me. Please! Surely our "best if used by" dates, Doc's and mine, have themselves by now retired to Bermuda! Maybe he and I are twinned, even in this. On principle I favor elective mercy-killing if the patient's clear and perfectly ready. Surely a human right.

—Still I keep waiting for some sleep-inducing hypo warmed by breath, some pink-slip prescription: "Please excuse Bill permanently from Phys. Ed. and, far as that goes, from Phys. Send him instead to Library Study Hall forever." Meanwhile, Doc searches.

DECOY

*

AFTER YEARS SPENT succeeding far from home, Roper's children have started coming back. Jan and I, we'll lately notice the daughter or sometimes the boy out walking their dad.

And I, being around more due to certain congestive setbacks not worth recording here, chanced to stand watching the street from our new sunporch. Magazines now bore me. True, we keep the Raleigh *News & Observer* going, but we've unsubscribed from *Time*. At our age, everything piles up so.

I called to Janet one room away and quizzed her. If *all* our neighbors' kids return for regular visits, why do the Roper kids' delayed trips stand out? Oldsters on our block speak of Doc's kids as extra-saintly, flying south so much here lately. We even saw the rangy theologian, up a tall ladder, installing his parents' storm windows. He kept having to wave at the parade of interested older cars.

Janet, her hands coated in Christmas baking flour, said, "What?" then, chin on my shoulder, leaned half against me. We studied Doc and Marge's daughter. Arms crossed, this pale young woman simply waited. Eyes half-shut in sunlight, she stood at the curb. I pointed, "What, she's going more platinum?"

"Get your eyes rechecked. It's white. She's nearly fifty, Billy. The children all are. My rule of thumb, add twenty years to everyone, that usually comes out about right."

"White!" I said.

Doc's daughter let him explore. Bushes and curbs, at his own pace. She just minded our general practitioner, his sitter today.

"Maybe we notice," Janet guessed, "because she's finally coming home to doctor *him*? Could be that's why his kids fight to take their turns now. Coast clear. Doc's forgot to show he's too independent to need anybody's help. —His girl looks easy enough doing it, doesn't

373

she? Like she has all the time in the world. It was the last thing her old man forgot. But he's finally stopped saying no."

Listening, nodding, without any reason, I wanted to cry. Had Jan meant to make me? —Cheap emotions seem unlike us. Me.

Looking out, I did manage, "Patient child. —Still quite pretty. She got his eyes."

10

THIS IS THE end, come all of a sudden at last. You will be almost as glad for it as I. Oh, and thank you for sticking with me through this hell and high water. Between paradise and the tar pit there must be quite a violent border ahead, passport-issues.

During my whole life I've never said so much at once as in this thinking-dreaming-recall-chant, last thing. Being one who's stayed, I'm trying to find the balance needed now for traveling. Like that liquid metal Doc funneled last thing into his carvings' undersides. To keep birds upright on their shelf or steadied in black water.

Finally what I've most wanted and feared finds me like an honor. Why bother trying to prepare for our own good deaths? We'll each know how. At least, well enough to finally get 'er done. And, if we "choke"? Well, all the better.

—I was driving, see, to buy skim milk, plus cuttlebones for those immortal cockatiels. I'd just invented this chore. Told myself it mattered, might produce a small adventure. Help justify my stealing dear Jan's car keys one more time.

You know that juncture near the new mall where beggars haunt our medians? They'll try and clean your car window. Red-haired, smoking cigs, big beer guts, they wear khaki, pretending they're retired military. CONFUSED BUSH SAND-WAR VET WILL STILL WORK. But they leave smudges so you have to pay to get *those* cleared. They try to snag folding money from older fellows like me. (Democrat though I am, these guys really burn me up.) I spied one up ahead hiking fast a full yard into my lane. I let myself honk. Felt good to. His overcoat was army surplus, the stride rolled forward, lanky, deliberate. Rearview alone showed his shepherd's staff.

I pull right over, no time for signaling. Dead ahead of Doc, I angle, waiting. Last-thing I'll try and trap him. Straight ahead, the sunset's quite a blaze. Red taillights lead that way and irritate it. Sinking sun shows a sky like golden sand piled with ruby mountains halfway through some mad spin cycle. My windshield's smeared with undeserved pastels. Janet has been vigilant all day keeping me "grounded." I thought she'd never nod off, needlepointing her OLD AGE AIN'T FOR SISSIES pillow slip. (Poor ole sissies must age, too.)

He hurtles along this dangerous commercial stretch. He staffs along his wild clear energy. Traffic shoots around him; cars keep honking, going sixty-easy in a zone marked forty-five.

I've parked poorly, too near an open ditch. My left arm curves around the steering wheel; I throw the right along seat-back. Where *is* he? A flashing ambulance veers wide of him. The driver's screaming, "Fool!"

Feeling breathless, waiting, I've buzzed our passenger window down. Ready for the coot, I'm hunched forward to stop my friend. But I keep hearing the car engine or maybe some tire acting up, stray whumping knocks. Only now do I study my chest. The ole ticker's just a-pounding. My white shirtfront literally shifts forward-back. Not real good of a personal sign, I guess. Seeing a passing stick, I shout, "Doc! Yer ole Bill here. Need a lift?" No answer. I start screaming, "Help me, *help* me, sir!"

The figure halts. I see a body bend, look in. I note how creased the face. Moon-cracked, it fills my window. The head cocks. I see an expression half-known. If I'd only somehow stayed this man's familiar.

"*Bill* here, Doc. No sweat. Crawl in. Boy, have I missed you. Remember when we were like brothers? Remember Dad's dying, trusting us like that? Just me here, your Bill, sir. Needin' help for sure. See, nobody knows the trouble or what to *do* with me these days. —Ideas, pal?"

I POINT AT my own pounding chest. He looks. Doc really looks. Then my right hand shoots his way, "Put her *there*, pardner!" Stupid thing to try. Trick him into touching me once more.

He swings back, skull hitting window-frame. I'd just been hoping for a final borrowed spark.

Traffic passes. Where are they all *go*ing? My paw feels cold, exposed in air between us. Sunset keeps candy-tinting everything. He gapes at my extended hand.

Then I see him notice: recent dark lesions biting into its back. He appears, if not concerned, at least still scientific.

"Well, *look* at you." A dry old voice husks Roper's deeper wetter first one. His hands have both lost weight: now spindles, needles, sinew. He says directly to my hand, "Bill's liver spots . . . more sunken now."

Doc bows through open car window, the stick propped outside. My beloved helper touches me. In that touch I swear I feel a father's card-sense, the Mom's Chopin, and Yale. He turns my wrist his way. He scans whatever one hand's backside shows. From his palm's heat I get the smallest splash.

My doctor, best on earth, is reading me alive again! Imagine. He studies newer dents. He's judging how blue veins now weave to the surface. In golden light Doc shifts the old mitt, reaches down along its wrist. Fingertips seeking my pulse. Tickles. I cannot explain the relief. Just to have been touched. Interest is healing.

Doc's lips move. He's counting beats, my vital signs. His eyes slide west where they can linger, tally, private. Traffic whizzes wide of us. Wind keeps moving his crazed hair. Eyes narrow their pouches. He gazes my way, but as if across some vast marsh. Roper's eyes, always a strong blue, appear electrocuted several shades brighter. Leery. Senile only? Maybe burned clear back to his startled bartering youth.

"This ole Bill I'm seeing? Is, right? Bit confused here. That still you, son?"

"Yes, sir."

"But where'd you go, 'Mondays, six forty-five a.m.'? Started out our weeks right, 'member? But, there was a flood, you know. Is this really Red's Billy? Looks like time's messed you up pretty good, huh? Tough deal all-round. As for your having pulse, son . . . ?"

I simply nod, eyebrows up as invitation.

"Well, hell, Bill, boy. Nobody's been taking *care* of you. Probably said *I* would. But, being up this age, I keep tellin' 'em—just can't *do* it all anymore."

"But you, Doc, *you're* still moving!"

"Hopping, more like. Frog legs in the skillet. No. For all practical purposes, professionally-speaking, son? the two of us we're *dead*! Hate to be the one telling you. No, maybe best it's me. Fact is you got no vital signs to mention. Reflexes're all that's left us. Surprised she even let you have the car. Goners, the both of us."

"Well, thank you. See, nobody would *tell* me. You know, all along I felt we . . . I always wished we could've . . . But, didn't we have *fun*?"

"Had the *what?*" His hearing's shot. Doc releases my hand, all but throws it back at me. Everything cools further. The man ducks out backward. He's already upright, moving, his staff fast-forwarding along more ditch, crackling weeds ahead. Again he has forgotten me. No backward-sideways glance. But that's okay.

Now I can lower my right hand, right? Can simply press it to my slamming rib cage. I finally know. I've heard it from the best. If I breathe now it is to count the few breaths he predicted. Very big adventure slated incoming, sir.

Car ignition purrs as I direct my front-tires a foot more off tarmac but overshoot. With one thudding metal shriek-thud, my whole front seat topples right.

Car's tipped pretty good into the drainage-ditch. Sun keeps sinking over our second-best mall. Sunset's going nowhere fast. Looks like skyline there wants only to go back toward perfect wilderness again. Before golf, pre-farms, prior to people, even Tuscarora ones, when creatures lived here unmonitored and whole. That's what I want and where I seek. Any minute now. The rest.

I note my blinkers going. Cocked off-road here, help's unlikely. Falls? all new people. Gone those days when any kid falling off his bike brought Band-Aid strangers out of beautiful homes. Half now from Mexico City, the rest pure Jersey City, nice-enough total-strangers. Among the Fallen who chose to stay, few my age have managed staying put. Nobody to recognize my car. No one to know my fluky heart, my true friend, my Red, my country club connection, my loves, love . . .

Still, we did just talk. Among our best conversations, at least our most efficient. And he was telling me . . . ? oh yes, that "we must remember to be dead now." *Houston? Phase III achieved at last.* Note to self: High-time you hightail it, Ducktail.

DECOY

Once he swore, "I've *got* you, Bill." Now, not. Catch-and-release. We're all wildlife. Basically, it's all catch-and-release.

JAN WILL WAKE over her needlework, phone the cops. "He's out again, boys." Still, that gives me time aplenty to take care of business, leave the building. I've got this ugly plastic dog tag at my throat. Aren't necklaces effeminate? Punch its red button, they'll swarm in on me. But no, at last I have the needed information. From the only one on earth who'd know then tell. So few such men. To be recognized, diagnosed, dismissed, and nearly-blessed. Who'd dare ask more?

That single young male wood duck is still Doc's finest. Something about its cockiness, crest. My wished last mission: collecting that. Doc and I, we never needed to say much. Between buddies, a whole whole lot went understood.

—Pleased to now go drifting. Safe from any sternum-busting code-blue. Didn't crash her car into a perfect young family. Promised Janet that, at least. We're up-to-date, God bless her long patience with me. Shouldn't have monopolized someone so good. Could've run any multinational, that one.

Hammocked here behind safety belt, I will want to go and hunt the boy-one naturally. Woody the Wood Duck, son of Red. A flotation device I myself could not have carved. His masterpiece, a sort of portrait of me, know it or not. He always saw so much in me. Too much?

("Hardly a pulse," he said. You know, I *thought* there was a problem.)

I TRUST SEATBELT to hold me half up. Nodding, I hear his sensible order, "Align. Head. Please." Obeying, I feel clarity return. Soon

I'm finding a horizon I've kept aiming for since farm life. Car's not even needed now (some larval stage abandoned). Now my old gray space opens to more liquid time. I seem on-water, am Tomothy Timothy Bixby—amphibious. Alone and somehow setting out by rowboat, so . . . gunwales creak, two battered oars. Ocean current's basically in charge. Evening alone on the water. Fine by me, though chill. Should've brought my windbreaker. Out here somewhere, just offshore, my simple stand-in bobs. Daring me to find him, teasing.

His carver knew me pretty well. I want art's findings now and have come to collect. This was my own long ago, and how can that be wrong? I somehow sense my trophy just ahead. So much dark water, little ruddering's now possible. Day is giving way. Passing the little docks, I see lamps switching on in beachfront family homes. Sunset wicks up all the blues into one red soon turned thorough black. Shadows keeping mashing down on darkness even blacker. And over water, over me, stars brighten till they each have fur. Male, most stars. The search is long and I have lost one oar but, among yet another brace of reeds, touch alone tells me I am near it.

Here, now, this. Finally my very own one, actually my first. For keeps, too. How easily and wet it comes to me. Un-shy if silver-cold to touch. Darkness helps me feel its sides' engraving, every feather's cut as strict as Bible braille. Not one mistake, no faking. It bulks here in my hands. Made just for me, made almost *as* me. Since I've lacked my own fuller version, I'll trust his one of me just that much more.

Tonight its weight feels excellent, exact as the mystery of being male. It rests safe here in my lap. Air's turned colder, salted. But thanks to this loss returned, I swear I feel sum-totaled. Fear no evil in me, ever. Oh I know this is just a carving. Not an actual life.

(But, did I even half-deserve another person, a whole splendid extra one of those and just for me?)

BOY, BUT NIGHT comes down so hard around our little boat.

I cling to this object, man-made. Still, I knew the man made it. Seems, what? Confused. There's just one thing I've forgot to do. What? But wasn't that the agreement? I was either meant to *be* or *love* him . . . Cannot for the life of me remember which. At least he kindly sent me out with this. Sure seemed to think the world of me. And yet, I . . . what? I go.

A man accompanied. A man one certain other worthy man described.

> *See, that is why I value this.*
> *See, that is why I've waited.*

ACKNOWLEDGMENTS

WRITERS NEED READERS while the inkjet letterings still warm. I am honored to thank my own responsive, candid friends: Jane Holding, Elizabeth Spencer, Diana Ricketts, Paul Taylor, Joanne Meschery, Cecil Wooten, Danny Kaiser, Erica Eisdorfer, David Deming, Shirley Drechsel, Chuck Adams, Charles Millard, Alan Shapiro, Mona Simpson, Sam Stephenson, Will Menaker, Katie Adams, Dave Cole, Ret. District Court Judge Patricia Devine, therapist Bob Vaillancourt, computer therapist Paul Rosenberg, Nancy Demorest and Bruce Gurganus. Dr. Jess Peter, cardiac advisor to certain of my characters, helped me diagnose the imaginary.

My agent, Amanda Urban, has shown both loving discernment and rare patience with my perfectionism or whatever it is.

I am especially happy to acknowledge my new editor, Robert Weil. His affectionate respect for my work first brought me to Liveright. May this be the first of many books to emerge under Bob Weil's scrupulous, imaginative care.

Time is the greatest gift. For that, I stand indebted to the John Simon Guggenheim Foundation. The Lannan Foundation and the Corporation of Yaddo each took me in, offering a block of clear time. This book is the byproduct of gratitude.

Thank you, friends. And thank you, readers.

A Visit From the Goon Squad

Jennifer Egan

ISBN: 978-1-78033-096-9 (paperback)
ISBN: 978-1-78033-116-4 (ebook)
Price: £8.99

Winner of the Pulitzer Prize for Fiction

'A must read. Irresistible. Fiction of the highest quality.'
Sunday Times

From Africa to Naples, New York to San Francisco, record producers to genocidal generals, Jennifer Egan tears through her characters' lives with verve and guile. From the 1970s to our not-too-distant future, we follow the fortunes of Bennie Salazar, an ageing music mogul, and Sasha, his young PA, in Egan's latest spellbinding novel that captures their lives' ebb and flow; sometimes popular and affluent, sometimes not.

With elegant prose and often heart-wrenching simplicity, Egan depicts the sad consequences of those who couldn't fake it during their wild youth – madness, suicide or prison – in her wryly humorous story of temptation and loss.

A Thousand Pardons

Jonathan Dee

ISBN: 978-1-47210-833-3 (paperback)
ISBN: 978-1-47210-738-1 (ebook)
Price: £7.99

'*A Thousand Pardons* is that rare thing: a genuine literary thriller. Eerily suspenseful and packed with dramatic event, it also offers a trenchant, hilarious portrait of our collective longing for authenticity in these over-mediated times.' Jennifer Egan

Ben and Helen Armistead have reached breaking point. Once a privileged and loving couple, it takes just a single act of recklessness for Ben to deal their marriage a final blow, spectacularly demolishing everything they built together.

Separated from Ben, Helen and her teenage daughter, Sara, move to Manhattan. Thrust back into the working world, Helen takes a job in PR and discovers she has a rare gift, indispensable in the realm of image control: she can convince arrogant men to admit their mistakes, spinning crises into second chances. Yet redemption is more easily granted in her professional life than her personal one.

The Privileges

Jonathan Dee

ISBN: 978-1-84901-593-6 (paperback)
ISBN: 978-1-84901-424-3 (ebook)
Price: £8.99

'Beautifully written and artfully plotted.'
Observer

Smart, socially gifted, and chronically impatient, Adam and Cynthia Morey are so perfect for each other that united they become a kind of fortress against the world. In their hurry to start a new life, they marry young and have two children before Cynthia reaches the age of twenty-five. Adam is a rising star in the world of private equity and becomes his boss's protégé. With a beautiful home in the upper-class precincts of Manhattan, gorgeous children, and plenty of money, they are, by any reasonable standard, successful.

But the Moreys' standard is not the same as other people's. As Cynthia, at home with the kids day after identical day, begins to drift, Adam is confronted with a decision that tests how much he is willing to risk to ensure his family's happiness and to recapture the sense that, for him and his wife, the only acceptable life is one of infinite possibility.

'Elegant and entertaining.'
Sunday Times

'A deliciously sophisticated engine of literary darkness.'
Guardian

Reservation Road

John Burnham Schwartz

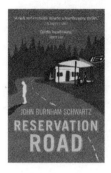

ISBN: 978-1-78033-458-5 (paperback)
ISBN: 978-1-78033-518-6 (ebook)
Price: £7.99

'A dark and irresistible miracle: a heartbreaking thriller.'
Los Angeles Times

At the close of a beautiful summer day near the quiet Connecticut town where they live, the Learner family – Ethan and Grace, their children, Josh and Emma – stop at a gas station on their way home from a concert. Josh Learner, lost in a ten-year-old's private world, is standing at the edge of the road when a car comes racing around the bend. He is hit and instantly killed. The car speeds away.

In a gripping narrative woven from the voices of those at the heart of the tragedy, *Reservation Road* tells the story of two ordinary families facing an extraordinary crisis – a book that reads like a thriller but opens up a world rich with psychological nuance and emotional wisdom. *Reservation Road* explores the terrain of grief even as it astonishes with unexpected redemption.

'Haunting . . . A powerful and affecting novel.'
The New York Times

'A poignant thriller . . . the novel's resolution is quietly breathtaking.'
Vanity Fair